Praise for Margaret Miles's brilliant debut
A WICKED WAY TO BURN

"A BEWITCHING ADVENTURE . . . THIS NEW ENGLAND
MYSTERY OF 1763 SHOULD CERTAINLY ROUND OUT THE
HISTORICAL MYSTERY SCENE NICELY."

—*Mystery Lovers Bookshop News*

"THE FIRST-TIME AUTHOR BRILLIANTLY PAINTS THE
PROSPEROUS NEW ENGLAND LIFESTYLE. . . . AN
INTRIGUING CASE OF HABEAS CORPUS IN THE
CAPABLE HANDS OF ECCENTRIC PROTAGONISTS. EVEN
THE VICTIM SHINES AS A CRAFTY CODGER AND HELPS
TURN A STRONG STORY IDEA."

—*Booknews* from the Poisoned Pen

"AN ENTERTAINING READ."

—*Tales from a Red Herring*

"A COLONIAL SCULLY AND MULDER . . . KEEPS THE
READER SAILING THROUGH THE PAGES."

—*The Drood Review of Mystery*

"OUGHT TO APPEAL TO FANS OF MARGARET LAW-
RENCE'S POST–REVOLUTIONARY WAR SERIES."

—*The Purloined Letter*

Also by Margaret Miles

A WICKED WAY TO BURN

Too Soon
for Flowers

Margaret
Miles

🐓 Bantam Books

New York   Toronto   London
Sydney   Auckland

Yet shall thy grave with rising flow'rs be drest,
And the green turf lie lightly on thy breast.

— ALEXANDER POPE, "Elegy to
the Memory of an Unfortunate Lady"

Too Soon for Flowers

Chapter 1

THE YEAR 1764 opened with a grim portent, when fire destroyed much of Harvard College during a blizzard one January eve—an event like none other since the creation of that great institution well over a century before.

No one was quite sure how the blaze started; some put the blame on logs burning high into a chimney, others on a stealthy burrowing beneath a hearth. Fortunately, few scholars were endangered, for most of them had gone home for a month of rest. But the College did house temporary lodgers. And so, Governor Francis Bernard, members of the Massachusetts General Court, and notable alumnus John Hancock joined in the fight against the conflagration. (As Fate would have it, at least one would be well compensated for his losses that snowy night: before the year was out, the sudden death of his merchant uncle would make young Hancock the second wealthiest soul in all the colonies.)

Yet a far greater threat stalked the province, which was the reason these men, representing towns across its breadth, had been driven over the Charles River to gather in Cambridge. For a dreaded and ancient plague had once again begun to rage. A dozen victims of smallpox had been discovered in Boston before Christmas; of these, all but two had died. Then more, and still more cases were dutifully reported, until the Neck was awash with a tide of people hurrying away, leaving flagged houses, feverish souls, and grieving families behind.

Massachusetts was indeed unprotected, for most had been born after the last great epidemic of '21, when one in twelve in Boston had died. Fewer had been taken during the smaller outbreaks in '52 and '60. But the town was aware of its continuing danger and inoculation was again debated, as it had been for over forty years.

At first, afraid that a general application of the procedure might encourage the pestilence, the authorities refused to condone it. Later, when faced with an epidemic, they recanted. Now, sweet May breezes carried rising hopes that an end to the outbreak was in sight, and it was frequently agreed that Science, and Reason, had finally triumphed.

There was no doubt that among thousands quickly inoculated only a few score had died, making death far less likely for the treated than for those who took the disease the old way. As the new cases were usually lighter, so, too, were complications and pocking. Yet in spite of inoculation's obvious benefits, some stubborn individuals continued to reject the relatively safe and simple practice—as Richard Longfellow complained to Edmund Montagu one spring morning, while both rode along the Boston-Worcester road.

"Arguing with Diana is much like trying to convince a cat," said Longfellow as the two men traveled abreast on impatient stallions. Behind them, a black and white mare pulled an open chaise carrying two women. "Reason doesn't have a great deal of effect," he went on, "and one is eventually forced to offer rewards. In my sister's case, she gave way only when I promised her a sea voyage *and* a large sum for her dressmakers. Now, Diana will be protected, in spite of her fear of scarring. I think you will find a useful lesson there," he concluded.

"Without a doubt," mused the Englishman beside him. Captain Edward Montagu kept to himself his own suspicions of what lessons Diana Longfellow might have learned, and just how long ago. The captain glanced over the gilded epaulet on his right shoulder to catch the young lady's eye. Odd, how Longfellow refused to see that his half-sister had grown into something more than a spoiled child. Today she was beautifully clad in pale yellow brocade patterned with raised roses, while her auburn hair was artfully arranged in a deceptively simple style. Diana was even more lovely than usual, Captain Montagu decided with a sigh.

Unhappily, they had seen little of each other lately. Certainly, nothing had occurred to inflame him quite like last October's meeting in Bracebridge, when he had found himself alone in her brother's kitchen with the young temptress. He had come dangerously close to yielding to his passions; and perhaps he had lost his heart that evening, after all. Yet he wondered—how many others had Diana encouraged, before? Or even since?

Captain Montagu touched his cocked hat and received a flirtatious answer from bright green eyes and loquacious lashes, as Miss Longfellow turned her head away. "He'll always believe it was his doing," she went on to the plainly dressed woman beside her who held the reins. "Which is all the better for me! Richard has increased my dress money without argument. Beyond that, I've extracted his promise to take me to view the Dutchmen in New York! Some weeks ago—I did tell you, Charlotte, that I visited in Newport for two weeks? Well, while I was there, I had a letter from Dr. Warren answering one I had sent to *him*, asking for his advice. After I considered his reasons, I decided to take the inoculation—not wanting, of course, to be the last one in town. They say nearly five thousand have lately submitted, while only a very few have succumbed . . ." As Diana's anxious voice trailed away, Charlotte Willett gently turned the conversation.

"Is Dr. Warren still on Castle Island?"

"Yes, he is, inoculating the poor at the town's expense. But rich men are also there, and I would imagine they pay him quite well—they'll surely be a boon to his practice later. He's been quarantined in the harbor for weeks now, and it's said he will soon know the town from top to bottom, which will be a great waste of his time, in my opinion . . . though I have also heard Dr. Warren finds this amusing, heaven knows why! The best news, however, is that he's to be married when all of this is over. Oh, yes! He'll get a large fortune with Elizabeth Hooton, and she has a pretty face, too. Still, she's only eighteen, and it seems to me that a wiser woman would wait a little longer, to see what might develop . . . but Elizabeth has already vowed to everyone that she's in love with him, so I suppose she might as well. It's a practical move for the doctor, certainly, though it saddens many ladies in Boston . . . and perhaps one or two out of it?"

Diana bent for a glimpse of her friend's face, hidden beneath a straw brim. But Charlotte ignored the look, though her eyes did soften. She could easily recall what it was to be just twenty, as Diana was, however different her own life had been five years before. Now, while the chaise took her closer to home, she thought back to the previous autumn.

Last October, Dr. Joseph Warren had made his first visit to the village of Bracebridge, a place midway between Boston and the town of Worcester, at the invitation of

Richard Longfellow. As a village selectman, Longfellow had asked Warren to examine the remains of a man rumored to have been murdered. Charlotte had soon decided the young physician would make a pleasant and useful acquaintance, and perhaps even a superior husband—though not for her. Four years had passed, yet her feelings for Aaron Willett were still strong, and his presence continued to make itself felt in ways that were difficult to ignore. She, too, had married young, when just eighteen. And she, too, had married for love.

Feeling a familiar pain in her breast, Mrs. Willett silently wished Dr. Warren long life and happiness with his bride, while Diana twirled her parasol and relayed additional news of Boston society—such as it was these days, with most of it camping out somewhere else. Meanwhile, the wind caressed, the bright clouds flew, birds called to one another in the arrangement of their own affairs, and the trio of horses clopped along.

Charlotte next noticed Longfellow's enthusiasm in his discourse with Captain Montagu. The captain had often been in attendance during the past week at the home of Diana and her mother—once Longfellow's home, as well. Though one day it would be Richard Longfellow's again, the residence was today occupied solely by women, a fact that seemed to feed his tendency toward melancholy. Happily, exchanging barbs with Captain Montagu caused Longfellow's hazel eyes to snap with electric sparks, and held off his darker moods. Edmund, too, seemed to be enjoying himself. The captain was certainly more affable than when they had all come together for the first time on this same road, little more than six months before. His natural reserve was less obvious, and his cold, aristocratic manner of speaking had softened. Though Diana seemed less inclined to pursue him as if he were a mouse and she a cat, Charlotte suspected her friend might increasingly be thinking of retaining this gentleman as a live prize. As for his own ideas—well, no one could ever be sure what Edmund Montagu really thought. Of course, an officer and agent of the Crown had duties and obligations not commonly understood—though she had also learned that in the case of this particular officer, much was kept hidden by design.

It was probably for the best, thought Charlotte with lingering regret, that Edmund would soon leave them at the junction with the post road, to spend a few weeks in New Hampshire as one of a summer party, on an estate along the Merrimack. With tomorrow's inoculation, Diana would surely be unlikely to appreciate visitors for some time.

"What are those little things?" the young lady now demanded, pointing to the edge of the road.

"Which?" asked Mrs. Willett. She squinted to see more clearly.

"The yellow flowers, there in the grass. I believe I'll soon have a bouquet. I wonder if they have a scent?"

The captain coaxed his horse ahead, and dismounted. With a flourish, he removed his triangular hat and deposited it safely beneath one arm, causing his white tie-wig to glow in the sun. While the others watched, he bent to pinch several blooms from a clump of fragrant primroses at the highway's edge; soon, he straightened with a handful. He then approached the chaise, which Mrs. Willett had brought to a halt.

"May I suggest a brief walk, to say farewell?" Captain Montagu murmured, offering the bright bouquet to Miss Longfellow. He was rewarded with the young lady's hand as she climbed down. He kept it while he guided her away from the road toward another wave of flowers. Moments later, he had captured an entire arm under his own.

"I would like you to know," he began haltingly, "that I . . . I have asked your brother for the favor of being called, in the event—if the unexpected should occur." He finished stiffly, unsatisfied with his choice of words. Would he ever be able to speak plainly and simply to this woman? Or would their every meeting end with his feeling as if a loaded pistol were pointed at his head?

"Called at my demise, do you mean? Or before?" she answered vaguely. The captain disengaged his arm.

"In the event that you might want to see me. One last time," he concluded, pleased at the feeling the cruel words gave him.

"Well, I *could* wish to see you then, I suppose," Diana replied. She leaned forward carefully, for her busk and stays restrained the movement of her slender waist. Then she picked a flower for herself and added it to those the captain had already given her. Though the act was somewhat difficult, its effect was graceful.

"What," she asked abruptly, "if I do not die, Edmund— but instead become disfigured? Then, what would your feelings be?"

Both had seen women who had been ravaged by the disease. Though most of these unfortunate creatures chose to remain entombed at home forever, a few, usually poor and aged, freely exposed their twisted hands and scarred faces, frightening children and sometimes even their elders. After this epidemic, there would surely be more.

Montagu was the first to shake off the disturbing vision. He patted puffs of dust from the arms of his new blue coat, whose wide military lapels were held back with many brass buttons set off by gold piping.

"If you were to be seriously afflicted," he replied, "then I would, of course, come to compliment your bravery— and to see if seclusion had made you any better at the whist table, where you still lack something as a partner."

"I *knew* you hated me because I would not help you win your fortune last winter, poor man! So, you must continue to survive on your meager pay, in spite of the family title."

"Very true," he answered with a wry smile. This pretty thing could be cruel, as well, when she chose to be. It was common knowledge that Miss Longfellow's dowry would be a large one. She would obviously expect, and deserve, to marry a man of wealth—wealth he himself did not possess.

"It is possible, you know," Diana continued airily, "that I only play poorly in order to spare my neighbors . . . and to keep their money from flowing back to London one day, with you! For do you not urge us to hold on to all the coin we can get?"

"I did not realize economy was an interest of yours, Miss Longfellow," he said politely, to irritate her further. When he'd achieved some success the captain went on in a practical vein, appealing to the lady's intellect. It was a tactic that had been known to flatter (sometimes even to astonish) a female, especially an attractive one who was generally given only insipid conversation.

"I would still encourage you to hold on to your reserves of both gold and silver, especially considering the upheaval in trade the coast has lately suffered," he said seriously. "But what do you plan to give your dressmaker for your imported satins and silks? Potatoes? When I see the women of Boston wearing homespun wools and linens, I'll know they have learned good sense and become true converts to sound economic policy. Though the Lord knows, the city's *politicians* have been talking enough of self-sufficiency lately—largely, I suspect, for the satisfaction of obstructing British interests! But I have no wish to argue with you today, Miss Longfellow."

"Well, go and argue with someone who will listen in New Hampshire, then," Diana replied, holding her head high as she affected a sulk. "I'm sure the ladies there will be no happier than I to hear you suggest we drape ourselves in sackcloth."

"Yet none in New Hampshire could appear more

charming than one Boston lady I know, were she to wear brocade or burlap."

Diana tossed a curl away from her lovely face, dimpling with pleasure though the very thought of sackcloth made her want to scratch.

The captain was moved by this show of spirit, and by the lady's rare ability to scoff at the future. It was something she did far better, and far more often, than he. Listening to her musical laugh, he noticed abruptly that the flowers in her hand had already begun to wilt and fade.

He looked up, and took careful note of Diana Longfellow's faultless complexion. Then, Edmund Montagu took her soft hand in his own once more, while he heard a trill of foreboding play upon his hopeful heart.

AFTER THE CAPTAIN had made his final farewells and disappeared on the road leading north, under a blue stretch of increasing pressure that must have reached clear to Canada (as Longfellow, who had a new barometer, remarked to himself), the lone rider dropped back and bent to speak.

"Carlotta," he asked Mrs. Willett as they entered a wood full of scolding jays, "speaking of love, as I presume you were doing, have you spoken with Diana about the girl?"

"Oh—Phoebe!" Charlotte exclaimed. In fact, she hadn't, for while they were in Boston she had decided to keep Diana's thoughts away from the procedure scheduled for tomorrow. Now, she turned her azure eyes to a sky of similar hue, trying to think of how to start.

"Phoebe? Can the family of one of your rustics be familiar with the classics?" Diana returned, displaying her usual lack of respect for the countryside and its inhabitants.

"Phoebe is a Concord rustic—not a Bracebridge one,"

Charlotte responded evenly. This clarified the situation somewhat, for everyone knew that the residents of Concord showed a certain lack of common sense. "In a few months, she's to wed Will Sloan. One of Hannah's sons."

"Hannah Sloan!" Diana laughed haughtily. "A candidate to join the Harpies, if ever I saw one."

Charlotte drew a breath, then tried once more. "Recently, Will's father and the boys added a new section to the house; then, Phoebe came to visit, bringing some of her own furnishings—but her father insists she be inoculated, and last week he ordered her back to Concord. Phoebe told Hannah she'd rather face the procedure here, and we thought you might appreciate her company while you're recovering . . . so now, if you agree, she will be inoculated here in Bracebridge."

"You could be right," Miss Longfellow replied guardedly. "For while it was considerate of you to throw young Wainwright into the bargain, Charlotte, I don't imagine your cowherd will make much of a confidant. This girl Phoebe—is she clever? Is she presentable?"

"She sketches well . . ."

"An artist? How fortunate! I have several admirers who are always after me for a portrait, or a lock of hair, or goodness knows what. All right, then, there shall be three of us—Lem, Phoebe, and myself—not counting your old kitchen cat, of course. Only imagine having a mother-in-law with such a face! I doubt if I could survive it, but I also doubt any of the Sloan boys will ever ask me to . . ."

Her brother's laugh echoed among the trees, and a marked scurrying among the leaves caused his sister to look upward in alarm.

"I'm sure you'll find Phoebe pleasant company," Charlotte said soothingly, "for the two or three weeks you're together."

"But what if I should change my mind?"

"I've already explained," Longfellow warned, leaning

farther toward the carriage, "that with the risk of contagion, all of you must stay in the house until the quarantine is over."

"But what if they become *tiresome?*" Diana asked peevishly, realizing that three weeks might well seem a lifetime.

"Then you may spend your time by yourself, reading or writing, studying your French, or looking through the window. I only hope nothing has delayed Dr. Tucker. I asked him to come ahead this morning. Carlotta, you'll meet him when you and I dine this afternoon at the inn. My sister, I fear, must sup tragically on gruel this evening."

"I think not," the patient-to-be replied flatly. "The idea of fasting, Richard, let alone purging, is not only repulsive but ridiculous! One needs a strong constitution to fight a fever. So I've heard, and so I shall instruct Dr. Tucker when I meet him. I will continue to eat heartily for as long as I can. And tomorrow is quite soon enough to dine with Hannah Sloan."

"Then we shall be four, after all, for a Last Supper," her brother relented. He stretched in the saddle to remove the kinks from his long frame. "By the way, did I mention I've planned an experiment?"

"Thank Heaven *this* time I won't be in your house to be discomfited."

"No . . . you'll be in Mrs. Willett's. But Tucker and I have discussed an inoculation for you, Diana, that is somewhat unusual. As a scientific study, the results promise to be quite interesting. I may even write them up myself."

"What!" cried Diana, causing the animal ahead of her to lurch as it missed a step.

"Nothing too unpleasant, I assure you," her brother returned, sensing that the time was not, perhaps, quite ripe for this particular discussion. "But we'll talk it over later. Plenty of time before tomorrow."

At that he urged his horse into a trot, anticipating

his dinner, while behind him the chaise carrying the two women—one of whom was now openly seething—rattled on toward the village of Bracebridge.

AN HOUR LATER Mrs. Willett stood holding back the muslin curtain at her bedroom window, looking over the vegetables and herbs laid out below.

It had been a relief to find things running smoothly at home. Convinced that Lem Wainwright, at fifteen, could handle both dairy and barn, she'd left Hannah to look after only the house. Will Sloan, too, had helped—good practice, for during the quarantine he would take over several of Lem's duties. Charlotte knew Will could be awfully foolish, and still had a tendency to frolic like a colt. Just two days before, she had heard, he'd raced the cart down the road and over a rock, breaking a wheel. Lem had then arranged for Nathan to fix it in the inn's forge across the road. So, everything was again in good order.

Though Lem and Hannah were obviously pleased to have her home, the sweetest salute had come from her old dog, whose joyous dance around her feet ended with an ecstatic roll in the grass, after which he herded her from the road to her door with a gale of howls. Once, when the farm held sheep, Orpheus had learned cunning, patience, and a disdain for that woolly species' limited intelligence—all of which Charlotte suspected he also applied to most humans. But it was clear that he was glad to have his mistress back by his side.

She turned, letting the curtain drop. For the next few weeks, this familiar, low-beamed bedchamber would be Diana's. Here the young woman would suffer the aches, the fever, the pocks everyone prayed would be mercifully mild. Charlotte suddenly felt a prickling of tears.

In the next room, four years before, Richard Longfellow had watched his fiancée die. And with Eleanor

Howard's passing, Charlotte suffered the loss of her only sister. Then, in the same week, in this very room—in this bed—her own strong and healthy husband lay down, succumbing within hours to the same high fever and terrible choking. It was hardly Charlotte's first encounter with death, for her mother had borne and lost two infants while she herself was a child. Her parents, too, had been taken a year before Eleanor and Aaron, during a summer that saw cholera in Bracebridge. Now, they all rested in a small family plot at the top of the orchard hill behind the farmhouse.

Young Mrs. Willett ran a hand over her quilted wedding coverlet as her thoughts shifted again to the bed's next inhabitant. For Diana, the prospect of dying was hardly real. Deprived of her father when she had been too young to understand, Diana still enjoyed the rest of her family, including Richard, her mother, and her aunts. She'd lately spoken of inoculation as if it would be a test of wits, and wills—something to add to her list of social conquests. In short, Diana Longfellow had been introduced to Death, but she had not, as yet, lived with him on intimate terms. Despite her Boston airs, Richard's worldly sister continued to exhibit an innocent bravado. For the moment, it was part of her charm.

Mrs. Willett now remembered that her neighbor was not a patient man, and most especially he was not patient when he was hungry. She quickly disrobed and put away the salt-and-pepper petticoat she'd worn. Standing in shift and stays, she decided to leave the pliant whalebone on for the afternoon. Bending over a painted china basin, she swiftly washed the road dust from her face and arms, then stepped into a skirt of light green linen, whose flax fibers had once grown nearby. She pulled on a low, elbow-frilled bodice of yellow cambric, recalling the day she'd dipped it into a kettle of boiled chamomile. Finally, after crossing and tucking a gossamer scarf thrown over her shoulders, she buckled on shoes of red morocco leather (one of many gifts brought back from Longfellow's travels) and hurried down the stairs.

A glance at the long, thin glass by the front door made her laugh aloud, for her colorful appearance suggested the squash patch that would soon begin to bloom and bear in her garden. Had she not begun to feel a renewed flowering herself? Or had her trip to Boston caused her to yearn, like Diana, for a fashionable effect?

It was something, Charlotte decided, to think about later, when she had more time.

Chapter 2

A QUARTER OF an hour later, a party was escorted into the taproom of the Bracebridge Inn by proprietor Jonathan Pratt, who led them to a table already occupied.

Setting down his glass of rum punch, Dr. Benjamin Tucker rose with a beaming face. He was introduced to Mrs. Willett; then, he bent to kiss the hand of Miss Longfellow, clearly admiring the supple flesh at the upper edge of a tight silk gown of a brilliant blue.

The physician was a distinguished looking man, Charlotte soon concluded. His girth was greater than average, but his height and broad shoulders gave him an appearance of strength, rather than corpulence. He was a little stooped with age, yet perhaps this also came from lowering a bewigged head to listen to his patients. The wig itself—well, it must have seen better days. And of course his cheeks were somewhat sunken from the loss of several teeth, but that was to be expected in a man of his years, which she estimated to be a little more than fifty.

The ladies sat lightly on the embroidered seats of two cushioned chairs. Once they were settled, Jonathan gave the gentlemen handwritten cards. These bore a list soon to be translated into succulent dishes, which would then be served in the smaller of two upstairs dining rooms overlooking the road.

"I've called for wine," Longfellow told Dr. Tucker, "but perhaps you would prefer another punch?"

"Thank you, no. I must keep a clear head for tomorrow," the physician replied seriously. Meanwhile, Charlotte made a note of his blue-veined, red-tipped nose, and wondered a little. The taproom was quite warm. Leaf-tinted rays of sunlight came through tall windows that framed maples coming into full green. Charlotte began to wield her fan while she waited for Longfellow to hand her the bill of fare. Then she, too, looked it over, and smiled her approval to their rotund host.

"The venison loin is fresh, rather than hung," Jonathan Pratt explained, "and will be well cooked, at Mr. Longfellow's request. Though I'm sure you're already aware of your host's peculiar tastes," he went on, his brows raised, his eyes settling on the linen trousers Longfellow wore—a garb that allowed him to trade tradition for comfort, while suggesting something of the air of a sailor, or an admirer of peasants (which in truth he was). The fact that, like other farmers, he wore no wig only added to the impression, though it could also have been argued he favored the current style of London's poets, and her new romantics. In any case, his was a fine head of dark hair only beginning to hint at hidden veins of silver.

"What about the pudding?" he asked, stretching and crossing his long legs beneath the table. "Jonathan, did you try the fresh figs I brought from town? They just came up the coast with a load of Carolina rice."

"I did," replied Pratt, "and I thank you. The several I sampled were delicious! I promise you an exceptionally figgy pudding, as well as some delectable spring spinach and river cress."

"Oh, by the way, allow me to present Dr. Benjamin Tucker. He'll be performing the inoculations in the morning. You've probably already guessed as much. You might also have concluded from his courtly bearing that he is a Virginian."

"I am deeply honored, sir," said the doctor, rising. Both men bowed, and Dr. Tucker sat down again.

"You're very welcome, Doctor, I'm sure." Jonathan Pratt eyed the other's well-constructed russet coat, lime-colored small clothes, snowy neck cloth, and deeply ruffled sleeves. In his experience, not all physicians were as clean, or as well mannered. "Now, sirs and ladies, if you will pardon me, I will just see to your dinner."

As soon as the landlord departed, Diana Longfellow began to look about to see who might be admiring her, and who might be worthy of her own attention. Meanwhile, her brother stared blankly at a dark oil painting on the wall, listening to his stomach. It was left to Mrs. Willett to lead the conversation.

"Do you find the practice of medicine different in Massachusetts from what you have seen in Virginia, Dr. Tucker?"

"It is somewhat different, madam, but not from geography, I think—for most of us have our training directly or indirectly from across the sea—at least, those who rely on something beyond superstitions, nostrums, and spells! No, I believe the larger difference involves a variance of time. When I first practiced, in Williamsburg—so many years ago that it surprises me to think of it—few there had real medical training. Planters and clergymen took care of most folk, while surgeons might pull a tooth, or occasionally lop something off. There was a general reliance on old

wives' tales, and herbal recipes learned at home. You yourself, madam, must often have heard and rejected the sort
of thing I refer to."

Charlotte's own opinion of the value of plants and the
worth of observation was higher than Dr. Tucker's. But for
the moment she kept this to herself.

"Today," the doctor continued, "there are far more
physicians who have gone abroad to learn useful theory.
I myself was apprenticed to a physician in London for
two years. Such learning now gives us a greater range of
remedies . . ."

"And a greater price you usually charge, too," Longfellow interjected, drumming his fingers on the table.

"True," replied Dr. Tucker with a sad smile. "In New
England, particularly, that often seems to be the sore point
in treatment."

"But what brought you here to Massachusetts, Dr.
Tucker?" Diana asked. She had finished surveying the
room and found it dull, as usual. "I believe," she went on
wistfully, "that society in Williamsburg is very refined, and
lacks little."

"That is quite true, Miss Longfellow. Quite true! But,
the material comforts its inhabitants enjoy, and their love
of informing others of what is ancient and correct, tend to
keep them from liking change. They judge news ideas
harshly, cruelly even, given any provocation at all. Boston, I believe, is the best place for curious men in the
colonies. Having lived there for three years, I still find
it fascinating—really almost cosmopolitan—almost like
London herself! Do you not find this so, Miss Longfellow?"

"Certainly. I suppose that's why I long to be back in
Sudbury Street the minute I arrive here . . . but while we
are in the country, Doctor, we must make the best of it—at
least, that is what my brother tells me. I can be thankful, at
any rate, that few of my acquaintance will have the pain of
watching me suffer. . . ."

"I'm sure your own pain will be minimal, Miss Longfellow! And when you relate this experience to your friends at home, when we have returned to our fair metropolis, I hope you'll be able to commend your physician for providing you with a relatively pleasant fortnight of rest and relaxation."

Suddenly, Diana recalled the morning's conversation, and began to formulate a strategy to make the best of her enforced withdrawal from the world. "You do, of course, play whist, Dr. Tucker?" she inquired. As the two went on to praise the great game, Longfellow and Mrs. Willett began their own quiet conversation.

"He seems resigned to a life far from his former home, where I imagine he must still have relations," Charlotte said softly.

"Proving, as I often say, that men of Science can make themselves comfortable anywhere, as long as they have leisure to observe the world."

"And yet, he didn't exactly answer—"

Her objection was interrupted by the arrival of a servant bearing glasses and decanters of wine. Before long, there was a toast to the party, followed by another to the success of the next day's endeavor—which allowed Diana, thought her brother, to assume the pose of a suffering but beauteous Saint Sebastian, happily without the arrows.

It was at this point, when Charlotte glanced back to Benjamin Tucker, that she saw the doctor's face stiffen suddenly, while he stared over her shoulder. In another moment he had abruptly drained his wineglass, apparently in an attempt to steady nerves offended by something, or someone. Seconds later, a bright voice was heard above the taproom's buzz.

"Why, Dr. Tucker, of all people!"

Charlotte turned in her chair to observe a dashing gentleman of fair complexion and blushing cheeks, though these were marked by a few pocks, one or two not quite faded. His powdered hair was held back by a crimson ribbon, while he wore a shining, silver-threaded waistcoat under a close-cut coat of light blue. "Mr. Pelham!" she heard the doctor rasp.

"Forgive me if I intrude." The beautifully attired young man apologized, yet at the same time, his engaging smile (and perhaps his opulent air) willed Benjamin Tucker to rise.

"No, I believe, er . . . Mr. Richard Longfellow, do you know David Pelham? Mr. Pelham is from Boston, where his family was once—"

The doctor stopped, uncertain.

"I am the tail end . . . of a noble lion," said Mr. Pelham. Then he gave a chuckle of guilty pleasure, before assuming a more solemn air. "Many of my family do, indeed, keep company at the Common's edge with our most revered elders—though few of them go out walking socially, of an evening. Or so we hope, for a churchyard is the place where they all sleep! How do you do, sir?" he concluded as Longfellow at last made his way to his feet with an amused smile of his own.

"Sir, my neighbor, Mrs. Willett—my sister, Miss Longfellow."

David Pelham bowed deeply to both ladies, but he seemed especially drawn to Diana, Charlotte noted. And was there a hint of life's sorrows, as well as its joys, in the depths of his dark eyes?

"Happily, I have had the great pleasure of meeting Miss Longfellow. In the proper company of most sensible friends," he added, in answer to her brother's quick reappraisal.

Charlotte saw that Diana studied Mr. Pelham with sudden intensity, once he had turned his face away. She herself imagined this clever, even cocky, soul displayed a cheerful façade only to cover some deeper emotion. She reconsidered his pun . . . *the tail end of a long line.* Had Mr.

Pelham recently been in mourning? Pain, she knew, was often the underpinning of wit—in the same way that self-effacement, in surprising turnabout, might indicate strong character.

"Sensible friends?" Longfellow replied. "As one might expect, I find *sense* to be somewhat unusual in my sister's acquaintances, but I will give yours, Mr. Pelham, the benefit of doubt, and hope for the best. Do you stay here at the inn?"

The younger man tilted his head, as if deciding. "I came yesterday, and plan to remain until something draws me away again. It is a pleasant place to rest, and far more healthy than the town at the moment."

"Quite. That is why my sister has come to take the inoculation."

"Please accept my good wishes, Miss Longfellow," said her admirer, "and you must not worry. I was 'done' in March, and found it no more than amusing. If I might be of any assistance—"

"Ah—we are about to have our dinner," Longfellow informed them, for he had seen Jonathan Pratt reenter the room and gesture toward the stairs.

"Then I will go." Mr. Pelham gave a brief bow to them all. "Though I had hoped, Dr. Tucker, that I might beg a word or two, perhaps later this evening? Do you suppose you could come up and share a glass with me, after you dine?"

Coming out of a reverie, Benjamin Tucker hastened to reply. "I would be greatly honored, sir."

Charlotte sensed this politeness to be a stretching of the truth, for the doctor's voice seemed curiously unsteady. But what reason might he have to be unsettled by this fellow Bostonian, who appeared to be eager only to please?

David Pelham again allowed his eyes to rest on Diana Longfellow. Then he turned, and withdrew.

More might have been said about the provocative Mr.

Pelham, if Jonathan Pratt had not bustled the diners upstairs. In the course of enjoying several extremely adequate dishes, and talking of themselves (while avoiding the subject of the morrow's business), no one questioned the doctor about his handsome friend. And Dr. Tucker made no further explanation of his own.

WITH DINNER CONCLUDED, Richard Longfellow walked with both ladies through air that had again the bite of New England spring, across the road to his home; there, Diana was settled in for one evening. Then he escorted Mrs. Willett back to her own fireside.

Meanwhile, Dr. Benjamin Tucker climbed the broad stairs that led to several sleeping chambers situated along an upper corridor of the Bracebridge Inn. He stopped at the third door along the left passage. Hat in hand, he paused and observed the highly polished floorboards for half a minute. He then rapped softly. Hearing a voice call from inside, the doctor slowly turned the knob, and entered.

"Ah, Ben!" said David Pelham, who sat coatless in a cushioned chair. He genially indicated another drawn close to the fire. The doctor saw that its glow made Pelham's features seem more finely chiseled, his several pocks more noticeable. "I am glad you could spare me some of your evening," Pelham continued. "You have dined well?"

Dr. Tucker hiccuped in reply.

"Then it would be *de trop* to offer you more. Too much wine," Pelham said carefully, "can play the devil with a man's constitution . . . and his skills . . . as I'm sure you'll agree. Coffee, then? No? You're probably right. With such marvelous country air I believe we all must look forward to our sleep. I may stay here for some time, if only for the quiet country evenings—" He broke off to enjoy a yawn.

Against his will, Dr. Tucker followed suit. "Bracebridge does seem a healthful place," the physician admitted. "Certainly more so than Boston, at the moment. And I will enjoy . . . the change from my regular duties."

"I suspect your stay here in Bracebridge might have benefits beyond improving your own health, and that of your lovely charge. I can even imagine that your patient, Doctor, will prove quite a plum to you—as well as being a peach to look at! Though it's surely uncouth of me to compare a young lady to any fruit, even out of her hearing," he added, his grin growing into an infectious smile. "For that, sir, I beg your forgiveness. But you see, Diana Longfellow is someone . . . someone I have admired for a long while, though necessarily from a distance. Once, of course, she was far beyond my hopes, as I had very little to offer such a lady. Now, though, there may be a chance. And a woman does become ripe for marriage, does she not? Oh—I beg your pardon, once more. I am afraid seeing her again has made me almost giddy! I will be truthful in more than this. You see, Doctor, I became aware of your plan to inoculate and watch over Miss Longfellow several days ago. That is why I was hardly surprised to see you, though you obviously were amazed to see me!"

"But, how—?" Dr. Tucker attempted.

"I realize that our paths haven't crossed lately. Of course, there was my wedding voyage to the Continent, for Alicia's health, and our brief return; you may have heard I renewed my travels after her tragic death, trying to forget what I could. But I have returned this last time in a far happier frame of mind."

"Indeed?" Dr. Tucker responded wearily. He was distracted by a small shiver that passed through his midsection, and wondered if he sickened of a late bout of the spring ague. He would need, he thought, to watch his bowels.

"As most of Boston knows, I have gone from having only a little to having quite a lot, lately. Now I warm to the idea of capturing a loving heart, to share my good fortune! It does seem this particular young lady is reluctant to be caught—yet for me, her spirit is one of the most exciting of her many charms. Glorious, ethereal Diana! Perhaps not *quite* a goddess," he smiled, "but I think it no wonder Miss Longfellow is surrounded by admirers . . . rather like frogs, leaping about a perfect swan!"

Again, Pelham's aspect became clouded, as he seemed to reflect. "You know, a man without wealth is often encouraged to marry for money. But when he has done so, a lady may look askance at his new designs—perhaps with good reason. This has been my excuse for keeping my hopes quiet for some time . . . until I could find a way to prove my worth to Miss Longfellow."

"I still fail to understand what you could want with me," said the doctor finally.

"As my own life has improved, Ben, I've learned yours has become barely tolerable, after certain ill-founded rumors began to fly about the town. I was saddened to discover your decline, but it soon occurred to me that I may now be in a position to do you a good turn. Is it *really* three years since we first met, in Boston? It seems such a very long time ago."

Dr. Tucker gave another hiccup, then lowered his eyes to consider his roiled thoughts.

"I would like to reclaim our friendship, Doctor . . . in spite of our current difference in social standing. Some, of course, think that sort of thing is of little import, while others . . . Miss Longfellow, for instance . . . yet I do feel I owe you something. If I had not presented you to certain men of affairs, and had you not invested in that land company—Though you never know—Young George and the Board of Trade may soon change their collective mind and revoke the King's new Proclamation, if they can be said to have a mind, other than that fool Townshend! Some day, they will be forced to reopen the West to settlement, for I hear a great many are going around the mountains to settle there, anyway. But I fear from your expression that none of this is helping you to digest your dinner."

"It doesn't seem to be helping me in any way at all," Tucker replied, repressing a sigh. He looked down at Pelham's bright silver buckles studded with ruby-tipped Scottish thistles, and then to his own of plain, tarnished brass.

"It is because I was once in your shoes," David Pelham said kindly, looking down as well, "after the severe reverses suffered by my own family, that I know how those shoes can pinch and pain. If one is not careful, you know, they may warp the foot forever. Poverty is no pretty thing! Yet I have also learned that even among the wealthy, life has its difficulties. So, perhaps we should forgive one another for trespasses we have suffered—even sins that may have been committed—and move on. Life is sad for all, and much too soon, there will be an end to it. Let us see if we can counter your fall from grace, Doctor, and you might throw a good turn for me into the bargain; in the end, this may make many of us far happier! For my part, I will do what I can to recommend you to Boston, and help you to expand your practice. We must keep in closer touch, sir, you and I. Who knows, you might even find in *me* a patient, once again," David Pelham finished, his lips twisting wryly at this affront to Fate.

Tucker pulled a linen handkerchief from his inner pocket, then wiped his brow, which was beginning to perspire freely.

"Although you will be glad to know that the old trouble you treated has not recurred. A fine job—yes, indeed, I will recommend you personally to my friends—and you must use your influence to bring me to Miss Longfellow's side. There it is. As her physician, if you would encourage beneficial visits while she is in quarantine, I will attempt to amuse Miss Longfellow with my own recent experiences, and try to win her with a display of my character, such as it is. At the same time, *I will be able to keep an eye on you.*"

The last was flung out with a sudden hint of warning. Dr. Tucker shifted, under a pair of eyes that seemed suddenly to pierce his own. "You will be most careful, will you not, Doctor? This affair will require none of your metallic preparations, I presume?"

"Such things will not be necessary, I am sure. However . . . what if Miss Longfellow should object?" Tucker queried uneasily.

"Object? Oh, I see! I assure you there are no conditions to my offer, nor will you suffer if my cause should fail. I will still endeavor to assist you."

"And the old story—?"

"What you told me that evening in the Bunch of Grapes, three years ago? It was a confidence between gentlemen in their cups, was it not? Unhappily, I know the loss of an infant is to be expected in marriage—or even out of it. Though in Virginia some suspect your chemical concoctions, I, personally, am in no position to malign them. As for the more recent Boston affair, with the other young woman—"

Again their eyes locked, until Tucker tore his own away.

"We both know a physician depends on the confidence of society," the doctor retorted, "but I have found such confidence difficult to maintain—especially when I am made the victim of lies I myself only hear the half of, told behind my back—told, I presume, by those who would have me gone . . . rumors spread even by those of my own profession, I suppose, as in Virginia! And because I am free to say little to the world regarding my patients, as you well realize, it is difficult to defend myself—or even to maintain my honor! And then, and *then*, when I am cast aside by one such as yourself, the appearance must go against me—"

"But what else could I have done, with Alicia begging me to consult with her own physician? Women *will* listen to gossip, even though it is unfounded, and must have their favorites. Could I argue with a loving young wife— especially one already so ill? Someone I knew to be dying? *Would your honor be so fed, sir?*"

Again, pain veiled David Pelham's eyes, but he soon became its master. "I will do what I can to help you, and I hope you will allow me to visit Miss Longfellow, so that I might earn her respect, and affection. But I see that you are fatigued by your day. And I know you have a great deal to do tomorrow, so I bid you good night."

Dr. Tucker rose to his feet, swaying slightly.

"You are too kind, sir," he replied, though he now seemed to hear a keening note in his own voice, which he found disturbing. But David Pelham was oblivious, for he had already settled back in an effort to collect himself.

His eyes were still closed when Benjamin Tucker softly shut the door.

THROUGH A NARROW window beside the inn's main entrance, Jonathan Pratt watched Benjamin Tucker move down the stone walk into the lilac and green of the crisp evening. The landlord prayed it wasn't something his guest had eaten that had lowered his spirits so noticeably. Then he shrugged, imagining that contemplation of the coming day's duties had most certainly snatched the joy from the fellow's manner. A moment later, Lydia Pratt rustled out of a dark corner, and Jonathan soon found that his wife, too, had Dr. Tucker on her mind.

"You do know the Reverend Rowe is extremely concerned about that man's presence in Bracebridge," she
began with obvious displeasure. "He's upset the entire village, coming here bearing the seeds of pestilence! The
whole idea of inoculation goes against the will of God!
That is what Reverend Rowe says."

Jonathan nodded gravely. It filled him with wonder to
think that he had once been drawn by something in this
perpetually affronted woman. What could it have been?
How easily he had forgiven the previous autumn's dal-
liance with a guest, which was suspected by all of Bracebridge, for it had brought him little discomfort—far less,
in fact, than her new alliance with Reverend Rowe, who
practiced seduction in his own strange way. Lydia now let
the clergyman direct her suspicions, as well as her impressive font of malice, in support of his search for evil among
his flock. The reverend had other helpers, of course, but
Lydia had become one of his most devoted disciples.

Yet the truth was, he needed someone other than
servants to help run the inn that bustled around him.
That, too, was something at which Lydia excelled. It was a
dilemma with which Jonathan Pratt had learned to live, by
sometimes resorting to subterfuge, and always cultivating
a deaf ear.

"You treat this Tucker as if you enjoy having him suck
up our wine and hospitality, while he threatens to kill us
one and all," his spouse went on, fixing her husband with a
glare.

"But, Lydia, I couldn't turn him away, after he was invited here by one of our selectmen. He seems presentable
enough . . . and besides, I have hopes that he may improve
while he's here."

"Indeed?" Lydia arched her long, dark eyebrow.

"If only you will lead him, my dear, by your many kind-
nesses and your good example, along a better path. I believe the reverend would tell you this is one of a woman's

many duties. Though of course she is also to follow, and obey her husband in all things."

Lydia did not answer. But the look of boundless annoyance that flitted across her thin face was enough to make Jonathan Pratt smile as he returned his own gaze to the gathering dusk.

Chapter 3

—○ *Tuesday*

THERE WAS SOMETHING glorious, the Reverend Christian Rowe decided as he stood at the edge of the placid millpond, in the dawn breaking on the dark trees above him, over the straight saplings as on the mossy limbs of their elders, twisted with age. For all were gilded, as they were touched by the virgin day. It reminded him, somehow, of the biblical patriarchs. King Solomon, sick with longing, had sung of young love in the morning.

"Until the day break . . ."

A passionate man, certainly. His father, King David, had also satisfied a remarkable lust, taking the woman Bathsheba after glimpsing her washing, then seeing to it that her husband was slain. As the father, so grows the son. His own father, thought the preacher, had found ways to satisfy himself with forbidden fruit, although possessed of a meek and submissive wife.

Reverend Rowe took a deep breath of moist, fragrant

air. Then he clasped his hands tightly together behind his dark coat as he scanned the pond's rim. What else did the Song say? *"Who is she that looketh forth as the morning, fair as the moon, clear as the sun, and terrible as an army with banners?"* Whoever *she* was, she was only one of many, for in Solomon's house it was also said, *"there are threescore queens, and fourscore concubines, and virgins without number."* It must have been a most lively establishment, Rowe thought with rising emotion.

The trouble with women was, they all had a terrible facility for falling into sin. You could not entirely blame them, of course. It was a natural condition, put into them by the Lord, well explained in His Scripture. It was up to Man to transport them through life, and for most men, one woman was enough of a burden to carry. But . . . might it not also be God's wish that *leaders* of men, ones with marked strength of will, should take more than one woman, as had the patriarchs? The Lord only knew what might happen if all of one's flock were to try the same thing—but a leader and a scholar might do well to emulate the wise men of old, by allowing himself an occasional, rejuvenating foray.

The reverend looked down, observing the sun's blinding light on the surface of the still, dark pond. Once again, he wondered at his turn of mind this morning; again, he attributed it to a single cause. Phoebe Morris—a fragrant, pristine lily—was to be contaminated this very day.

Last week he had spoken at some length to Phoebe, and to her young man, William Sloan. He had counseled them not only as a pre-nuptial service to the boy's family, but as a testing of the girl, for she might one day apply for membership in his church. The minister knew little of this child of Concord, but he intended to find out a great deal more. He suspected she had certain tendencies. She surely held power over men, whether she knew it or not. And that was not good.

The reverend had explained to the two young people that they would soon be joined in spirit and in body, in an honorable estate. And they would multiply. Taking the boy aside, he had asked if Will knew of the need for a man to satisfy a woman, to ensure that conception would take place. Then, seeing the boy seemed to grasp this duty, the reverend had also warned him. . . .

The mill's wooden wheel rolled softly above the gently flowing water, ready to turn the stone within whenever the miller should desire to engage it. Another bit of verse, this time from Isaiah, crept into Christian Rowe's mind to further confound him.

> *O virgin daughter of Babylon . . . take the millstones,*
> *and grind meal: uncover thy locks, make bare the leg,*
> *uncover the thigh, pass over the rivers . . . thy naked-*
> *ness shall be uncovered, yea, thy shame shall be seen:*
> *I will take vengeance. . . .*

Rowe shivered, and quickly blamed the damp air. Had not Phoebe Morris passed over the Musketaquid, a bit of which eddied quietly here before him, on her way from Concord? Yet why had she come? Will Sloan was more mule than boy. But at least he had a temper, which he would need for keeping this young wife to himself, once she truly discovered her passion. Phoebe, like others nearby, was too alluring for her own safety. Rather like Mrs. Willett, up the hill. Was this one stubborn as well? Or would she listen to reason . . . to talk of duty . . . to cajoling? He would see.

But today, Miss Morris would submit to a thing shockingly like a pagan ceremony—along with the far less tractable Miss Longfellow. Despite his curiosity, Reverend Rowe vowed again to keep away, for he knew the thing to be wrong. He did envy the misguided physician from Boston, though. Such interesting feelings it must give one to lay the pustulant thread, after cutting into a slender arm. Occasionally, it might be advisable, after all, for youth to engage in something unclean, if they could then be saved from greater peril. But it could hardly be so with the smallpox! No, interfering directly with the Lord's will was deadly folly.

The sun was swiftly becoming hotter, and Reverend Rowe wished to remove his coat to cool himself. But first he intended to make his way back to his stone parsonage where he would find other duties to think about, thus allowing his over-exercised passions to sink back into the cooler depths of Reason. At least, that was his hope, as he walked quickly from the ever brightening pond.

"I DO HOPE a simple bed is good enough for Miss Longfellow." Hannah Sloan held on to the small of her back, digging in with fingers that were rough and red from lye soap and hard scrubbing.

Charlotte had helped the older woman lift a new summer mattress of sweet straw onto the slats of a bed frame, in one of Mrs. Willett's two upstairs chambers. After they added the coverings, she moved toward the window and stood in the late morning sun, where she thought through the arrangements still to be made before the trials of Lem, Phoebe, and Diana began.

"Lem and Will brought Mr. Longfellow's small bed over for Phoebe earlier," continued Hannah. "It's down in your study. That should save me trips up and down those stairs, for which I'm thankful, and I'm as happy to sleep up here as in the kitchen. But I can't see why Will has to see her every single day, as if he's under some kind of a spell! I know the doctor says he may, if he stays a proper distance, but can't they keep to themselves for a few weeks? I'll be away from my own home until it's over, though they say a body who's had it won't carry it—not that I believe everything that's told to me by physicians—yet Mr. Sloan is not complaining about *my* absence. Will is such a stubborn boy," she charged, not for the first time. "Always wanting his own way."

"True," said Charlotte. "But, Hannah, who does not? Though I wonder . . . were you and Mr. Sloan never eager to be close?" Considering the seven children the couple had produced, Mrs. Willett supposed she knew the answer.

"Fffffttt," was all that Hannah replied. Yet judging by the look on her round face, the question had raised a memory.

"It won't be easy, only to talk across the windowsill," Charlotte concluded, trying not to smile. "But I suppose they will survive."

"You might pray that I'm as fortunate, for it tires me just to think of the fetching and hauling I'll have to do, to look after those three in their beds. It's a good thing I've brought my chest of simples for my own aches and pains, which I'm sure I'll soon have more of! You won't find me relying on this clever Dr. Tucker." Hannah tossed this over her shoulder as she shuffled down the narrow hall and into the stairway. "Still, I'm being paid well enough for my trouble, thanks to Mr. Longfellow's goodness, though others call it something else again. You know, quite a few claim this inoculation's a terrible danger to themselves. Some even say it goes against God's laws."

"So I hear," Mrs. Willett answered mildly, wondering for a moment whether the many interpreters of God's laws, or the legions who argued the colony's, posed the greater threat to health and happiness in New England.

In the kitchen they found Phoebe just returned. After removing her outdoor bonnet, the girl tied a smaller cap over a pile of hair as soft and tawny as doeskin.

"Did the meeting go well?" asked Charlotte. She hung the kettle, then tossed a stick of pine into the fire. She and

Hannah both knew that Phoebe had come from a visit to the Longfellow house down the hill. Now, her lithe and supple figure gave a happy twirl, suggesting a seed of milkweed revolving on the wind. She truly was lovely.

"Miss Longfellow *was* very kind, as you said! And I think—I hope—she will approve of me as a companion," came the pleased reply. This morning Phoebe's face was rouged by activity, while an expression of real joy played about her features. What a relief, thought Charlotte, to see her so happy. When an unknown Miss Morris first visited the village at the end of winter, she had frequently seemed pensive, even to the point of distraction. Some had supposed this more than a little odd in a child who had every reason to look toward marriage with hope and pleasure. But Phoebe was not a child; in fact, she was very nearly Diana Longfellow's age. And many, even among the young, were hurt by life, which was not always what one wished. There was nothing terribly surprising in their occasional melancholy. But somehow, Will Sloan had made Phoebe increasingly comfortable as she looked forward to their life together. And if she did suffer from something in her past, she no longer showed it.

"It is such a beautiful house," the girl went on, sitting down lightly on the arm of a settle. "I should love to sketch the rooms I saw, and send the drawings back to Concord, so that my sister Betsy could admire them, too!"

"Now that you've met the fine lady," said Hannah, "see that you don't get on her cross side. Boston folk can be peculiar."

At this, Phoebe suddenly lost her animation, as well as her confidence.

"But I know she'll be happy to have you make a likeness or two," Charlotte quickly interposed, bringing curiosity, at least, back to the girl's face. "Diana often speaks of her fondness for the arts." It would have been closer to the truth to say that Diana was fond of artists, but Charlotte decided to let Phoebe make that discovery for herself.

"Then I'm glad I've brought all of my sketchbooks with me, so that she can see them. Miss Longfellow told me she plans to go to New York soon, and will visit the theaters! Oh, how I should love to see a play! Though I have read them, of course, sometimes even aloud with others, to once see Shakespeare played upon a *real stage* would be so like a beautiful dream—"

"Fine nonsense, and a sure road to the Devil," Hannah snorted. "It's a good thing they won't allow such goings-on in Boston's public places. Now, help me wash these pots. Then you can go and say good-bye to Will. The doctor and Miss Longfellow are to be here at noon."

Phoebe rose dutifully to do as she was told. She picked up a dishcloth, while Hannah poured hot water from the hearth kettle into a large basin.

After a moment's thought, Charlotte hurried upstairs to pack a bag to carry across to Longfellow's house—for it was there she would take her meals, and sleep, until the quarantine was pronounced over.

IN MRS. WILLETT's dairy, behind the northeast corner of the house, Lem Wainwright and Will Sloan rinsed out the last of the milk buckets and set them out to dry in the sun.

"Make sure you give them the same amount through the length of the trough, or there'll be trouble," Lem insisted as he walked back inside.

"Do you suppose I haven't seen a cow before?" Will asked crossly. "Though I suppose I may not know them as well as *you*, since you once spent your nights with these fine ladies, until Mrs. Willett hauled you into the house."

"I've slept with worse," Lem replied, remembering his four brothers still at home, kicking in a crowded bed. "But you'll see each animal's different, Will. Delilah over there—"

Will Sloan was not listening. "Before long, I expect to sleep with far better," he muttered, nudging red hair from his freckled face.

At a loss for a reply, Lem shook his head. Will might be a year older, he thought, but he would doubtless never grow much wiser.

Although Lem, too, came from a succession of poor farmers, he planned to go to Harvard College. It wasn't something he'd thought of himself; he'd been encouraged by Richard Longfellow, who'd promised to be his sponsor. But now, it seemed to most in the village that Lem's expectations had risen so high there was doubt he was still one of their own. It was a dilemma—one of many on the way to becoming a man.

"Just try to keep them all happy," he urged, his thoughts returning to the welfare of the cows. "And I wouldn't let Phoebe know you're talking about her that way, unless you want to get your ears clouted."

Will laughed out loud at the thought, but made no other comment.

"While we're talking about nocturnal arrangements—"

"In plain English, please, Mister Wainwright."

"Are you really planning to sleep out in the garden until they let us out?"

"I'm setting up a lean-to tonight," Will answered. "It's not so cold, and I'll be able to hear if Phoebe should call. Or scream," he added ominously.

"Or your mother might want you," Lem countered. He watched Will spit exuberantly into the straw with a look of having tasted milk gone bad. "And how you must be looking forward to talking with your fiancée at arm's length, through a window."

"Unless she'll let me help her out of it," Will returned

with an unpleasant stare. "Wouldn't that make my mother stew, if she found out?"

"If Phoebe would go along with you . . . which she won't."

"She might, if I asked her to. She's gone along with me before, on one thing and another. . . ."

"If my aunt were a goose, she might lay eggs," Lem threw back. Yet he felt uneasy, seeing a new irritation on his companion's darkening face.

"You think she doesn't want to?" Will Sloan challenged.

"I don't think Phoebe will let herself be talked into anything. After all, she's got far and away more sense than you, Will."

"We'll see about that. But what if I do catch the small-pox? They say she'll have it mild, and that means so will I. Maybe I'll walk in and see her tonight!"

"And when you leave, if you've caught it, you just might carry the sickness out of Mrs. Willett's house and into your own. Have you thought of that? My mother wasn't pleased when she heard this doctor was coming, since my brothers and sisters haven't had the smallpox, either—though there's not much she can say about it to Mr. Longfellow. But what if it *does* get out? I'd hate to be in your shoes when my mother, or yours, hears you've managed to catch the pox on your own!"

"Then *damme* if I don't!" Will shouted back. He barely avoided injury as a bovine leg swept out, nearly clipping his thigh with a sharp reproof. The boy jibbed and swore at the near miss, before adding, "Nothing in life's for sure, son, except that women will tie you up in knots, and bring you a world of trouble! But sometimes a man's got to take a chance. You'll learn that once you get to Harvard, I suppose, when they pass you your first bucket of rum and ale. They tell me some of those fellows get so drunk on flip— Look out, there's the doctor! I'd better go and find Phoebe, before they lock her away!"

With that Will rushed off, anxious to throw himself into the arms of his betrothed, leaving his friend to finish with only Mrs. Willett's herd for company. As he continued to work Lem solemnly considered the risk he was about to take with his own life. But before long, he found himself instead pondering a familiar paradox.

What on earth could a warm and beautiful woman like Phoebe Morris see in a randy, ill-tempered lout like Will Sloan?

BEFORE THE EYES of six others around a pine table in Charlotte Willett's kitchen, Benjamin Tucker raised his scalpel over the golden hairs on Lem Wainwright's forearm. Then he brought the blade down swiftly, making a shallow wound in soft skin, along the inside of the surprisingly muscular limb. Quickly, the doctor took tiny split-wood tweezers from a clean cloth spread on the kitchen table, inserted them into a vial, and pulled out a thin, moist thread, which he then laid gently into the inch-long incision. That accomplished, he set down his tools carefully, and moved his spectacles back into position.

"There," the doctor breathed. Again he noticed that the lips of one of his patients, reddened from nervous chewing, were quivering, while her face remained deathly pale.

Across the table, it seemed to Mrs. Willett that Phoebe was hardly more moved by their encounter than was her physician. She looked to Richard Longfellow to see if he, too, had been alerted by the earlier exchange of startled expressions, but her neighbor apparently had more scientific concerns this morning.

Minutes before, the physician had opened his leather bag to take out a cork-stoppered glass tube wrapped in flannel. Inside was a small square of linen, made damp (he had earlier explained to Longfellow) by pus from under the drying scabs of a lightly affected patient in the city, obtained two days previously. The matter had been kept contained and warm so that, like bread yeast, it would remain potent. Because the initial case had been light, others resulting from inoculation promised to be mercifully uneventful, too. At least, that was the theory, and it often held up in practice—though not always. Some physicians tried to lengthen the odds against serious illness by prescribing rolled pills of powdered metals, plant materials, even sugar, while withholding meat, butter, and bread. Results were mixed. It was uncertain whether diet, beyond the adoption of a plain one naturally favored by those who were ill, made any difference. At Diana's urging, Dr. Tucker had agreed not to restrict any particular food. He only promised to watch the course of the disease carefully, in case complications were to develop. (Though he had to admit to himself, at least, that however the disease took one, there was not much to do beyond waiting for the illness to end, one way or another.)

"Well done, my boy," said Dr. Tucker, laying down a patch of clean linen on Lem's wound, then applying a gauze wrapping. "We'll take a look tomorrow, to see what progress you've made. Now, Miss Longfellow . . ."

With a move she'd practiced before a mirror more than once, Diana held out her arm, pulling a ruffled sleeve away from the skin above her elbow.

"Miss Longfellow?" the doctor asked with some surprise. "Have you forgotten? Or have you decided against our plan?"

Diana colored in confusion. In the excitement of the moment, she had, indeed, forgotten she was to be saved from the knife by a more unusual method of inoculation. At her brother's urging, both she and Phoebe were to inhale a powder through straws, to see if they might avoid even the mild symptoms that Lem, following the usual procedure, had been promised. Exactly what this strange powder was made of, or where it came from, Diana had been careful not to ask.

Sections of hollow straw were given to each of the young women. The doctor poured the contents from another stoppered vial onto two pieces of writing paper. Diana went first, holding the turban she wore, pretending as she inhaled that it was snuff—though she had already found that practice not to her liking.

"Try not to sneeze," Dr. Tucker cautioned.

Miss Longfellow did as she was told. Her expression brought a sympathetic chortle, disguised as a cough, from Mrs. Willett, who only now realized how tautly her own nerves were stretched.

It was Phoebe's turn. As if inhaling a blossom's scent, Phoebe sniffed twice, until all the powder was gone. Closing her eyes, she set the straw down and folded her hands in the lap of her homespun apron; meanwhile, Diana continued to make minor adjustments to her own voluminous robe of parti-colored satin.

"And that," Longfellow said emphatically, "is that."

Hannah Sloan let out her breath. "It makes me glad I was taken in the normal way a long while ago," she grumbled, going back to her pots by the fire. "And I'm not in a hurry to try such a thing on my *own* children. Going out of your way to court trouble! Paying for the privilege—and then praying for the best!"

"That is about the sum of it," said Dr. Tucker modestly, following her to the fire. He threw in the vials and the flannel. The tweezers, straws, and paper soon followed as Hannah stood gaping.

"*Those pots hold my good dinner!*" she cried out to him in horror.

"Nothing to worry about, Mrs. Sloan. Fire destroys the matter and kills the contagion in it. Anything that comes into contact with the patients' pustules should also be so destroyed, or washed thoroughly. In the case of letters, I'll leave you sulphur powder for fumigation. Remember, it is most important that the smallpox should not spread! I've written out instructions, which I'll leave for you to consult when I'm gone. They'll answer most queries about the course of the disease."

"But tell us now, Doctor, what we may look forward to," said Diana Longfellow, who was forced to admire her own calm. She also asked herself if the beads of moisture she felt at the back of her neck could be seen by the others. If this was to be part of the thing, she thought, she would need to consult a mirror frequently, and keep her powder handy.

"I would be glad to explain, Miss Longfellow," Dr. Tucker replied. "You will see nothing at all for a few days, or even longer—though not as long as if you had been exposed naturally. Depending on each patient, a mild fever will arise. This will last for a few days more, possibly with various aches and pains. You might then notice the appearance of small bumps, like grains of rice, under the skin; these eventually become blisters, and are most often found on the face and upper body, as well as on the hands. We sometimes refer to this as the 'flowering' of the disease . . . though unfortunately the pustules are rather less than sweet. That is where much putrid matter resides, and where scarring may occur. But these pustules will soon break, and then crust over. The scabs that form should fall away within a week. After this, all risk of contagion is gone, and you are safe from the disease for the rest of your days."

"A fair trade, it seems to me," Longfellow said to Diana. "And it's likely you and Phoebe will have few symptoms. In a warm house, with plenty of clean linen and whatever else you require, you might even enjoy the rest. Though when I was inoculated in England, many years ago, I had quite a time. I'll long remember several friendships swiftly forged—"

"They all survived?" Diana asked, keeping her voice low so that it might not quiver.

"The friendships? Hardly. Oh, you mean the patients! Certainly—in fact, we soon began squabbling over the golf sticks brought in by a Stuart. I believe we each had them out on the lawn for a try before a week was out."

"I see." Diana was encouraged, if somewhat skeptical. "Then you may send for a Scotsman to lighten my mood, Richard, but as croquet would be more regal, perhaps you can find instead a member of the French nobility."

"It is just possible that Montagu can come up with one. Shall we send him a note?"

"At the moment, I would rather you went home, so I can look over my new pattern books. Come along with me, Miss Morris. We will be better off alone. Charlotte, I hope to see you every day. You needn't bring my brother with you." With that, the newly inoculated young ladies made their way upstairs, one resembling a harem consort on holiday, the other a chastened waif.

Lem also retired, going into his small room off the kitchen. Dr. Tucker washed his hands in the kitchen basin, then carefully dried the lace at his sleeves.

"I'm not certain you'll have an easy road, Hannah," Longfellow sympathized as they eventually took their leave.

"I only pray I'm *alive* in two weeks' time," the ample woman returned grimly while she followed them out into the soft air. "Yet if I do survive, I won't know whether to bless the Lord or blame the Other—for after this, I don't see how I can ever hope to be the same again!"

Chapter 4

THAT EVENING, AFTER a light supper and a stroll through the nearer grounds of Longfellow's estate, Mrs. Willett took sherry with her neighbor and Dr. Benjamin Tucker.

"Now, we wait," Longfellow said from a winged armchair in his study.

"It's often said anticipation is worse than the actual thing," replied Dr. Tucker. Despite his encouragement, Charlotte had already sensed the doctor was less confident than on the previous evening. But after all, he had shouldered responsibility this morning for three lives.

"One might also say that a dog's bark is worse than its bite," retorted Longfellow, "until one is actually bitten! Still, I suppose we can hold every hope of the thing passing easily." He pulled a piece of string from his pocket and held it above the head of a brindled cat who had come to investigate the party around the fire.

"Here, Tabby!"

The lanky animal, little more than a kitten, came to Longfellow, stared at his string, reached up a paw to bat it, and sat down.

"Good fellow!" Longfellow praised, breaking off a piece of butter biscuit. Tabby sniffed, turned on his long paw, and left the room. Longfellow swallowed the piece of biscuit himself as he turned back to the others.

"I've only begun to experiment with commands, but already there is a *rapprochement* between us, as he learns who is master. Last evening he brought a deer mouse into my bedchamber and laid it at my feet."

"How thoughtful," Dr. Tucker commented, while Charlotte smiled into her sherry.

"It makes one wonder at what is often called *Christian* charity," Longfellow returned. "At first, in adopting a pair of felines, I planned to observe the differences between our two species. Instead, I'm amazed to see we have a great deal in common."

"For instance?" Charlotte asked, interested as always in Longfellow's observations.

"It would seem that Tabby and Tiger are as keen on gardening as I am. At least, they greatly enjoy my glass house, and I've concluded they practice several of horticulture's first principles."

"How do you mean?" asked Tucker, accepting a second glass.

"They take a natural interest in digging, which lightens the soil. They see the value of enriching the ground broadly, for they never contribute to the same spot twice. And, they kill the birds that are after fruits and berries I go to a great deal of trouble to cultivate. Each, you see, plays a part in maintaining the Grand Balance of Nature."

The doctor considered before he answered. "I believe I would prefer a dog," he finally decided.

"Not in a glass house," Longfellow retorted darkly. "I chased a mongrel last month who destroyed more in a minute than the cats have harmed in three months' time. Dogs may take an interest in one's life, Tucker, but they are hardly what you'd call thoughtful animals. Now, Orpheus, of course, is an unusual dog," Longfellow admitted with a look to Mrs. Willett, "for he always behaves as a gentleman should—better, really, than many I've encountered."

"I'll tell him you appreciate his breeding," Charlotte replied, "though I am less sure of it myself. We can all be glad he shares your good opinion of the cats. But, Richard, will you enlighten me about something else?"

"With great pleasure, Carlotta."

"The powder Dr. Tucker gave to Diana and Phoebe, through the straws. What was it, exactly?"

"I didn't want to say this in front of Diana, but we decided to try the scab from a recent smallpox patient, which Tucker dried and ground." Warming to his subject, Longfellow stood and began to walk about. "As you know, it's now quite common to place a bit of scab, or the matter from beneath one, into an incision. But inhaling the powder appears to be a much older idea originating with the Chinese, which one of my Venetian correspondents passed on to me several years ago. He swore the technique promised less fever and scarring. And I know Diana abhors the idea of so much as a mosquito's bite marring her complexion; that is why I decided we might try something new— at least, to the Western world."

Dr. Tucker, too, looked pleased. "One day we may be spoken of as innovators, like the Lady Mary Wortley Montagu!"

"Tucker tells me," Longfellow confided to Mrs. Willett, "that she lost great beauty to the pox and never recovered her eyelashes, all of which dropped off at the time of her infection."

"They do say that her pocks were very full. But she remained a woman of great wit and spirit," the doctor assured them. "No doubt that's why she took it upon herself, after first seeing the practice of inoculation in Constantinople, to do all she could to convince others to attempt it."

"Her Ladyship's own child, I believe, was the first to be inoculated in Britain, during the epidemic of '21," said Longfellow. "This was shortly before the Princess of Wales tried the practice on her own small daughters."

"Much to *her* credit," said the doctor.

"You may not have heard, Tucker, that when Dr. Boylston introduced it here in Boston the same year, his life was threatened by a mob—even after Cotton Mather himself urged inoculation. In fact, old Cotton had a bomb thrown through his window, to dissuade him."

"I had supposed the old Boston clergy were against it, as I'm told your own cleric is still," Dr. Tucker answered slowly.

"Most were. Although that's all changed now. Except, of course, for a few fanatics. Actually, we may have a good many left, but don't forget, Mather was not only a preacher—he was also a graduate of Harvard College, and a member of the Royal Society. So he knew something about Science. Extremely fortunate for Boston, as he made many others see the light."

It was also fortunate, thought Charlotte, that few clergymen now believed, as Mather had, that witches walk among us and might be removed from society in unpleasant ways. But no man, obviously, was perfect—even though he had graduated from Harvard College.

The doctor shook his head. "It's difficult for me to comprehend how anyone could doubt the procedure to be worthwhile. Why, the figures alone are convincing! Only one or two percent of the inoculated will die, while we can expect a full fifteen percent to succumb, who take it from contagion."

"Only a fool would refuse its benefits," Longfellow agreed, scrutinizing his own slightly pock-marked features in the hanging Venetian mirror. "A century or two in the future, I suppose they will scorn those who today shun a risk to life of merely one percent, out of blind fear. Of course, by then a cure will surely have been found for the disease itself." For a while, both men silently considered the boundless hopes of Science, born to strive against the monumental ignorance of mankind.*

"I know inoculation is a wonderful advancement," Charlotte said eventually. "Still, I feel fortunate to have received my own immunity with no risk at all, to anyone."

"How was this, Mrs. Willett?" the doctor asked in a puzzled tone.

"When I was younger, I took the cowpox in the dairy."

"But that is no proof against infection!" Dr. Tucker responded sharply, alarmed that the woman before him might soon be taken, as well.

"Mrs. Willett has been near infected patients before this, and assures me she felt no ill effects," Longfellow told the physician, turning from his own reflection.

"But without scientific certainty," Tucker argued, "you *must* agree that she should be more careful!"

"It is obvious, Tucker, that you have had limited experience with milkmaids. Among humble people—and as a farmer, I include myself in this group—I've often heard it said that one cannot contract smallpox after having cowpox. Hannah Sloan tells me the Irish have held the same view for generations."

"Please, sir, go on," begged the physician, setting down his sherry glass.

"It's often the case that where there's a horse with what we in the country call grease-heels, with oozing

---

*Though smallpox is currently said to exist only in laboratories, a cure for it has yet to be found.

fetlocks, you might also find a cow with udder ulcers, and soon after, a milkmaid with the cowpox."

"Is this a serious disease?"

"Not at all."

"But, if that is true, then we should all *encourage* the cowpox," Dr. Tucker reasoned. "Which, I believe, you do not."

"That has occurred to me. But think. Until a princess, or at least a duchess, can be induced to try her hand at milking an infected beast, the fawning part of humanity will never go along—even at the risk of a mere pock or two on the hand. But then, most would not jump out of a frying pan, having found their feet on fire. I refer here with equal disdain to the garden variety of man, as well as to more regal specimens."

"Yes . . ."

"And you know how even physicians resist innovation."

"I do, yes!"

"But you give me an idea "

"Eh?"

"Yes. The next time I see a cow with pustules on its udders, I will see if I can shift some of the matter from there—"

"Richard?"

"Carlotta?"

"Perhaps, as Dr. Tucker will be with us for a while, you might talk with him about this another day?"

"Mmmm, yes. I can see . . . Well." He paused, but found the subject irresistible. "Of course, if one were to take the infectious matter from such a pustule on a person, rather than a cow! That might be considered more seemly. Actually, it's quite unfortunate Diana's already been done . . . but if we could convince another of our local—"

"Richard! A question?"

"Certainly, Mrs. Willett."

"Do you suppose that none of the men who favored burning Dr. Boylston walk the streets of Boston today?"

"Well, I suspect there could still be a few . . ."

"I suspect some very much like them live even closer than that."

Rubbing his chin, Longfellow considered. "Though I have my doubts our fellow townsmen would destroy one of their own elected officials, I suppose this might *not* be the best time to advance new medical theory, Tucker. And you, Mrs. Willett, know I am the first to stoop, if that is what it takes, in order to spare the feelings of the good villagers."

Charlotte thought it best to leave that statement alone.

"Speaking of neighbors," she said, "I wonder, Dr. Tucker, if you spoke with your friend Mr. Pelham last night?"

"I did, madam," Tucker replied after a moment, during which he tasted his sherry once more.

"I wonder—does he have other acquaintances in the area?"

"I believe not."

"And yet he chooses this place to visit, for a rest . . ."

"You might like to invite him here to dine, Tucker," Longfellow suggested. "We might all enjoy the distraction of fresh conversation during the next weeks. Pelham seemed to me a fellow of at least some intelligence."

"Well, Mr. Pelham did mention to me," the doctor began cautiously, "that he would enjoy meeting Miss Longfellow again. He has even asked—if I might see if it could be arranged. Of course, her quarantine makes a dinner somewhat difficult, so I doubt . . ."

"He might prefer to dine at the inn at that, and give Lydia Pratt his company, if his eye is only for the ladies," Longfellow answered with a look of irritation. "However! I forget that we can offer Mrs. Willett as an ornament to our table, Doctor! Forgive me, Carlotta."

Dr. Tucker appeared to be reorganizing his thoughts, until he found an acceptable one. "We're not closely acquainted socially, you see, Mr. Pelham and I. Our past was little more than a handful of tavern dinners, between poor physician and patient. Now, there is, of course, a great difference in our wealth, and in our standing in the town."

"I see. Then I must make him the offer myself. Well, I believe my own name has some cachet in Boston, though I've lived away from it for a few years. He can refuse if he will—which would scarcely be a loss to us! But I'm surprised I haven't heard more of Mr. Pelham in town," Longfellow mused.

Dr. Tucker sent a hand to his yellowed wig, where it fingered a bleached side curl. At the same time, he couldn't keep himself from eyeing the decanter of sherry with longing. "I believe," the physician finally responded, "that Mr. Pelham traveled to Europe after the death of his wife, many months ago. He lived there for quite a while before, as well."

"Excellent! A traveler with interesting stories, one hopes. More wine, Tucker? But here's Cicero. Pour Tucker some sherry, will you? I suppose you're on your way to the inn for your evening's entertainment?"

The venerable African, dressed more carefully than the average inhabitant of Bracebridge, nodded. He bent slowly, picked up the bottle with both hands, and performed his task with precision.

"Trouble with your spine?" Longfellow asked with a squint. Cicero gave a bow, then took a step backward.

"While I do appreciate the performance—is it meant to be Iago? Or possibly Cleopatra's asp-bearer. At any rate, I don't believe you will fool the good doctor for long. Our thespian," Longfellow went on, "was once the highly valued major-domo of our household until my father's death freed him from bondage, and the wish to excel. Cicero now works for excessive wages, and his duties are largely doing whatever he chooses—rather like an aging governess."

The former property of the Longfellows of Boston exhibited the ghost of a smile.

"He may feel," warned Longfellow, "that a Virginian will enjoy a bit of servility; but it is probably only a plot to soften you for a later savaging at the backgammon board—when he sees you have become thoroughly bored with the country. At any rate, Tucker, if you want something done for you about the place, you had better ask me first," Longfellow concluded. "But go and learn the news, Yorick, so we'll have someone to pick apart at breakfast. Oh—and when Pratt brings your Madeira, you might ask him to invite Mr. Pelham to visit us tomorrow morning."

With a sphinx-like smile Cicero left them, dropping a soft leave-taking to Charlotte on his way to the door.

"As you were talking of your neighbors, Mrs. Willett," the physician then tried cautiously, "I will admit to being curious about one of them. I refer to Miss Morris."

"Phoebe Morris is from Concord, Dr. Tucker," Mrs. Willett replied, "which is where most of her family can be found, I think. Do you know them?"

"I am afraid not . . . yet I believe I did treat Miss Morris in Boston, briefly. Three years ago. She was barely sixteen—" Tucker broke off to sip from his replenished glass, before he continued. "You know little of her history, then?"

"Very little, for she only came here recently."

"And yet she's to be married, you say?"

This time, Longfellow offered the answer. "The Sloans frequently trade goods with Concord farmers, several of them cousins, and the boy has probably visited that place quite often."

"He is a young man?"

"Quite young. Now sixteen, I think?"

Mrs. Willett nodded.

"There could be certain advantages," said Dr. Tucker, almost to himself.

"In keeping a boy from worse? Quite possibly," his host allowed, "especially when one has a habit of getting into trouble—though I believe the kind he's headed for now will be new to Will Sloan."

"At least, Miss Morris will gain a protector from a dangerous world."

"Do you consider this place so?" Charlotte asked the doctor in surprise.

"Beauty," replied Tucker, "is ever under siege, I fear. As you must know yourself, madam," he added gallantly.

"Yet Aphrodite often finds means for having her own way," Longfellow decided.

"Not all of them pleasant," muttered the physician. Then he shifted uncomfortably. There was a silence, but soon, Longfellow began to hum. He went to the pianoforte, and in a moment began to sing out in a light baritone, while his fingers moved over the keys to produce a martial air.

> "Love sounds the alarm,
> And fear is a flying!
> When beauty's the prize,
> What mortal fears dying?"

While the singer shuffled and repeated Gay's lines, as Handel's somewhat newer tune required, Charlotte smiled toward Dr. Tucker, noticing as she did so that he seemed to take the song seriously.

To sadder notes, Richard Longfellow went on with nicely calculated pathos.

> "In defense of my treasure,
> I'd bleed at each vein—
> Without her no pleasure,

For life is a pain.
Without her no pleasure,
Without her no pleasure,
For life is a pain . . .
For life is a pain."

The physician's face showed something like pain of its own, which was hardly merited by the performance, thought Charlotte. Longfellow, too, examined the physician with curiosity, once he had finished.

"I see love disagrees with you tonight, Tucker!" his host declared. "Perhaps later, we might have a try at Bach. There is a great deal of mathematical interest in Bach, but very little passion."

Nodding, the physician reached for his glass once more.

"I only thought," Longfellow continued, "that you might enjoy the reference to blood-letting, as I believe you often work in that area—"

In the middle of a sip, the doctor inhaled when he should have swallowed. Longfellow and Mrs. Willett watched him pitch forward convulsively, thrusting a handkerchief against his face as he suffered a fit of coughing.

Longfellow hurried to his guest, and pounded him on the back until the other weakly raised a hand for his host to cease his ministrations.

"It's all right," came his muffled cry through the linen. "I think it will be best if I walk it away! I'll return in a while."

Charlotte and Longfellow settled back as they listened to Benjamin Tucker's footsteps cross the hall and ascend the stairs.

"It's not often one has the pleasure of expecting to see his physician expire," Longfellow commented. But Charlotte only stared at the brightly colored molding along the high ceiling.

In a moment, Tabby wandered back to investigate the cause of the physician's hasty retreat. The cat's trainer immediately produced the piece of string, and bent forward as Mrs. Willett asked, "How did you come to choose Dr. Tucker, Richard?"

"Tucker? He recently inoculated the boys attached to a bookshop on King Street. He spends a great deal of time there, as I do when I'm in town. Tucker, too, has a particular interest in scientific theory, and he seemed an honorable Virginia gentleman, if a little down-at-heels. He told me he'd welcome a rest, and gladly quit his rooms in Boston, for a generous fee."

"I see," answered Charlotte, wondering all the more.

AT THE END of the day's final milking, Mrs. Willett left an unusually quiet Will Sloan to finish cleaning up on his own, as she walked from the dairy to the sun-touched side of the farmhouse. Phoebe was away from the closed study window, but Charlotte spoke briefly to Diana, who leaned out of her own room above. Before long, Mrs. Willett turned to walk through the pasture toward the Musketaquid's marshes, with Orpheus loping happily by her side.

The pink air of the evening was cool; but with a countrywoman's intuition she knew that when the sun was reborn it would produce an even warmer day, with a southerly wind to force the last reluctant buds. Already, she noticed, the meadow grew thick around frost-thrown stones, which made walking somewhat perilous.

She had to be careful, but Orpheus took no such trouble. Under Charlotte's admiring eye, the dog bounded from boulder to bog, sniffing and prodding his territory like a proud and wary farmer. It pleased them both to know the long winter was finally over, and summer about to begin. To Charlotte, this meant freedom to walk farther into the countryside, to observe new life, and to cultivate and harvest from her gardens, orchard, and hay fields. To Orpheus, apparently, the season meant frogs, new nests in hedgerows, and suspicious holes in rock walls. Each soul, Charlotte thought again, had its own pursuits, its own happiness, its own way of defining home.

That idea turned her thoughts again to Benjamin Tucker. No one had ever gotten around to asking, at dinner, about Tucker's family. But perhaps he, too, had suffered sad losses; maybe that was what had driven him to resettle in an unfamiliar place. By his speech and manner, she suspected he'd been brought up in proper, even prosperous, circumstances. Yet his lace cuffs were poorly mended, the ribbons on the garters at his knees did not quite match, and one of his stockings had begun to unravel at the back of his calf. These things could indicate a careless character—or they could as easily show only a need for a good wife . . . or at least an efficient housekeeper. Or, she thought, one could suppose Dr. Tucker suffered from financial difficulties. Whatever the cause of his untidiness, she was not about to embarrass him by asking, and knew of no one else who might be able to satisfy her curiosity. So she decided she would have to accept the physician for what he was in Bracebridge, no matter what he was, or had been, elsewhere.

Even so, he was a curious soul! For instance, why had he shown such an aversion to Richard's song? Had love once been a thorn in Dr. Tucker's side? Was it still? And could that explain his displacement from Williamsburg? There was also his interest in Phoebe Morris, whom he'd treated before. A curious coincidence, surely, to meet her again after three years, here in Bracebridge! Yet he had said little about it—in fact, he'd seemed reassured when she herself admitted none of them knew the girl well. But again, whatever was between the two had apparently taken place some time ago. While Phoebe had seemed less than pleased to see the doctor, she *had* placed herself in his care. Really, thought Mrs. Willett reasonably, though it tweaked her imagination, it was none of her business, after all.

She turned at the crest of a hummock and looked back to see her house reddened by the setting sun. There in the garden, opposite what was now Phoebe's bedchamber, stood something new—a contrivance made of poles and canvas: Will Sloan's new shelter. Charlotte recalled her own early attempts at setting up just such a temporary camp on nearly the same spot, when she and her brother Jeremy were small. Turning away, she continued toward the river, seeing Jem's face with her mind's eye.

By his own reports, her brother was learning more of the physical sciences in Edinburgh, while she took care of the farm that had been left to him. Charlotte had received a letter only the week before, but that would mean the news was now at least six weeks old. From time to time, she wished she had wings, so that she might know what Jem did the very day she thought of him, across the great green pond (as their father had called the broad Atlantic). This evening, however, she was content to remain where she was. Recently, she'd seen the teeming coffee houses and taverns, the rich shops and stores of Boston. She had also seen people sorely affected by the spectre of smallpox, and by the lack of employment after the departure of military business, now that the Great War was over. She had returned home to a familiar place where one might always profit from daily chores, and where simple pleasures were the only ones expected, as the seasons changed.

Charlotte suddenly felt in need of a strong cup of tea. Starting back toward Longfellow's house, she watched a loose window wink at the last of the setting sun. Frogs began a chorus in answer to the rising wind, hidden beneath wild flag scattered around the meadow grass like fallen stars. The flowers reminded her of something else. Earlier, she had seen long, greenish fingers—pointing omens from the earth—rising along the southern dairy wall. Tomorrow, before they became too tough, she would snap some off and make an asparagus pie. The thought helped to keep her feet firmly on the ground as she made her way across a darkening field, toward the beckoning house, and bed.

IN HER BORROWED chamber just up the hill, Diana Longfellow continued to read on top of her quilt until the light had fallen off to nearly nothing, and the candle she had brought up from below had need of trimming. This accomplished, she rose to light a second. The moon, past full, would not be up for a good while, and the night would become far darker before it got any brighter.

This conclusion was a reflection not only of Diana's celestial knowledge (which would have surprised more than a few of her acquaintances) but also of her gloomy mood. Tossing down a collection of Shakespeare's tragedies, she then decided to pace the room for a while. That felt better, especially as a shift of soft Indian cotton played against her legs to soothe her. When she finally tired of that, she sat in her chair.

Struck by a new idea, Diana took paper, ink, and pen from her traveling bureau, and began a letter to Miss Lucinda Devens of Boston.

Tuesday evening, Bracebridge
from Mrs. Willett's house

Dear Lucy—

I have Promised to relate to you Everything of interest about my Inoculation and Quarantine, but I must start by saying how I truly Loathe the countryside! There is so little here to Sustain one's Soul! Yesterday, Richard arranged a large dinner, during which we were given overdone Deer to eat; yet I suppose I should look for Squirrel Stew from our housekeeper's pot, before long!

The Inoculation itself was painless. I was able to avoid the Fearful Blade by inhaling a powder which promises to give small trouble for the desired Effect. My Brother has *finally* done something to benefit someone, and made the thing far easier than I had imagined. Let us Pray I will have no great story to tell, when I see you! But a boy called Lem, who lives with Mrs. Willett, had the Thread in the usual way, so perhaps I will see something Exciting, after all.

We have now added a Third Guest to our little party—Phoebe Morris, who will marry a local swain before the Summer is through. The girl comes from Concord and so she can hardly be Stylish, but she is an admirable Sketcher, and has a quiet humility I find refreshing. Phoebe has shown me some of her Work done in Crayon; this is remarkably Good. She plans to begin in Watercolors soon, and I may act as her guide. (You'll recall I have had informal lessons from one or two Gentlemen.) While we are here, Phoebe will attempt several Portraits, and I, of course, shall be her Subject. I am sure they will be well received when I return; so you see, you need not Worry that I have nothing of importance to do. Miss Morris is hardly John Copley—but since that young man is now too Occupied even to stop and drink Tea (while I as yet have no Fortune with which to tempt him to paint me), Miss Morris will have to do!

Here is a Peculiar Thing. You know David

Pelham, of course, who wed Alicia Farnsworth, and then went to England or somewhere, after she died? Well, Lucy, he is Here! Yesterday, he approached our Table before we dined to beg a Word. Pelham is the Last person I expected to see in a backwater place like Bracebridge. Naturally, he seemed very Pleased to see me, but, since I do not believe I will be Allowed to see anyone other than my fellow sufferers, and Richard and Charlotte, until this is over, I don't suppose Anything will come of it. A pity, since he seems more Cheerful than he once was, and of course he is far more Wealthy, which probably explains it! I have noticed him Admiring me in town once or twice since his return. Mr. Pelham, it appears, also knows my Physician. This is an old Virginian named Tucker, found by my Brother Lord knows where—at least, I have never heard of him, though he Claims to have lived in Boston these three years! It all makes for a situation I find rather Strange. Still, Dr. Tucker is not an Ill-Spoken man—and his acquaintance with Mr. Pelham gives one some Hope for him, I expect, Socially.

But oh, this place makes me feel Cross, for there is so little to Do! Nothing happens at night; there are few Carriages, no Bells to speak of, not even a Hawker out in the street, for there *is* no street, only a Dusty Road. I wonder how I shall Sleep. What I would not give for a Twilight Walk about the Common, arm in arm with a Gentleman (or even you, Lucy), on our way to a Distinguished house, and a flippant Evening of Cards.

Enough, for Tonight. I hear Phoebe's Romeo (or perhaps Titania's ass) come to the Window below, which opens on Miss Morris's chamber. I will quickly shut my own to keep *these* delicate ears from Burning in the Rising Flames of Young Love! And so,

Adieu—
Diana

After she lowered the window, Diana folded and sealed the page, and added an address to the outside. Then she resumed her place in bed, this time between soft sheets. While enjoying the clean scent of lavender, she picked up her book, considered her own life for another moment, and finally abandoned herself to the Bard's immortal words.

Some in Bracebridge that night went to bed to sleep, praying they would not dream. But Diana longed for dreams to come, dreams of someone she knew not. Anything, as Miss Longfellow so often sighed, for variety.

Chapter 5

The NEXT MORNING, Longfellow and Cicero stood in the glass house built onto the side of a towering stone barn, discussing the odd habits displayed by plants and humanity. Between them were long wooden planks covered with seedlings.

"Well, *something's* eating them," Longfellow concluded. He picked up a clay pot, then held it over his head to look beneath the leaves of a young cabbage.

"There's a white fly in here," said Cicero, staring up toward sunlight that filtered through fronds of a tall palm.

"I search for the green worm, which should be— Hah!" Longfellow reached up to pluck the offending cabbage worm from the plant, then let the grub fall to the dirt floor, where he made a smear of it under his booted toe. "I'd say it needs another application of tobacco—which I will make stronger." Reaching to a shelf below the table, he brought up a wooden box. The old man looked on with the distress of someone who might enjoy putting the objects it held to a different use, while Longfellow tore and crumbled a dry leaf section into a glazed jar already half full of a foul-smelling liquid.

"They say the smoke may keep away the plague," Cicero offered. But he had no real hope of changing his employer's mind. This painful discussion was not new— it had simply been reborn in a new form a few weeks earlier, when the box of cigars (an ill-conceived gift from Mrs. Willett's brother-in-law, Captain Noah Willett) had arrived.

"I'm well aware of what its supporters say, as another excuse for poisoning themselves," Longfellow rejoined. "Though even these nefarious articles may have some place in a well-ordered world, if one finds a scientific use for them . . . as we have. By mixing the ash with ink, I'm told one might obtain a remedy for fungus of the skin. I have even heard of a man who recommends working a cigar into a horse's bowel, to treat a severe case of colic; but I have yet to see anyone of good sense insert one into his mouth and light it. . . ."

Longfellow next strained off a few ounces of the tobacco decoction into a stoppered bottle, its top pierced with holes. Adding some wetted soap, he shook the bottle vigorously, then began the task of sprinkling as he paid close attention to each small cabbage. "Worms," he muttered, "worms at the very core of hope . . . worms that produce such lovely white moths. Which reminds me—I wonder how Diana is feeling today."

"Mrs. Willett reports they are all well—although your sister fidgets."

"When does she not?"

Cicero sensed danger in Longfellow's less than charitable mood; still, he ventured a further observation.

"It is too hot in here."

"Is it? If you say it, then it must be so. Individuals of

your age usually find a bread oven too cool to support life. Well, then, what do you suggest we do?"

"First, we might get rid of the white fly."

"There is no white fly, as I've told you *twice*! Only seed fluff, from opening some of last year's pods. It would seem your vision is failing. Any day, I expect to see you and Mrs. Willett leading one another about the village, stumbling over small children." Once again, Longfellow squinted his own eyes to better appraise the cabbage in his hand.

"We might have the top windows whitewashed. I've already opened the side glass this morning, and it's not enough."

Longfellow paused to gauge for himself the temperature of his surroundings. "Go ahead. It may well ease your joints to do a little climbing. Be careful of the ladder."

Cicero sighed, for he was not fond of heights, but soon the old man saw something that gave him a moment of pure joy. He pointed it out to Richard Longfellow, who turned to observe one of the cats clawing madly at the trunk of a large and graceful tree fern—a prized specimen brought with great care from the Caribbean.

"Sainted apostles! *Out, you monster!*" the cat's master cried, hurrying down the length of the aisle while Tabby prudently withdrew into a pile of empty pots. Man and feline performed a singular dance until, cornered by Longfellow and Cicero, the sleek animal leaped effortlessly to land behind both pursuers, then streaked toward the door.

The roundly cursed cat might have been following his ears as well as his instincts, for in another moment the door opened, and Tabby shot out.

"Have I come at a good time, or bad?" David Pelham inquired, once he had recovered from his surprise.

"One is much like another here. Come in, Pelham. I suppose you're interested in horticulture," said Longfellow.

"I enjoy exotic collections as much as the next man,

but I always leave the business of helping them survive to others. I hardly think I have the talent for it, myself."

Longfellow, who had heard this kind of nonsense before, had only scorn for those who refused to pay attention to the workings on which all life depended. However, considering his position as host to an invited guest, he manfully held back his feelings.

"Cicero, this is Mr. David Pelham. Cicero and I, too, were Bostonians, Pelham, before we were drawn here."

"A freedman . . . ?" Mr. Pelham asked, looking from one to the other. Meanwhile, Cicero made his own appraisal of the cinnamon-colored costume before him, completed by an aroma of orange flower pomade at the head, and large buckles of gold on the feet below.

"Free in the legal sense, if not the metaphysical," said Longfellow. "Cicero may leave whenever he chooses. But he stays—largely, I believe, because he must torment me. Yet he pays for the privilege! At the moment, he is about to mount an expedition to the roof, for which I do not recommend an audience." He then led Mr. Pelham out of the glass house, across the backyard, and around to the front of the house, where they entered. The visitor was thus allowed to avoid the kitchen, admire the broad entry hall, and catch a glimpse into the great formal room to its right, before approaching the west-facing study. There they greeted Charlotte and Benjamin Tucker, who were sipping mid-morning cups of tea. Longfellow pulled two straight-backed chairs away from the wall, and lowered himself next to the physician.

"I'll be back in a moment with a new pot and a cake," said Charlotte as she rose, causing Mr. Pelham to bob up again. "Have you no house servants?" he asked his host when he finally sat down.

"Two or three women, daughters of a neighbor, who come weekly to remove the dust and replace the linen. Beyond that, I'm well able to take care of myself."

"But—your kitchen! With no servants, what do you do for your dinner?"

"Sustenance can always be found at the inn; occasionally, Mrs. Willett takes pity on us and extends an invitation. But we often make do with what we can concoct. You might see for yourself, if you would care to join us one day. This Sunday, perhaps? When I'm in the mood, I enjoy culinary experiments: goat in a curry, served with fermented milk curds, for an example. I wonder goat's not eaten more. The idea came to me from a correspondent who is in the India trade—at least he was, though I hear he has recently succumbed to a stomach complaint."

Dr. Tucker cleared his throat, but made no comment.

Attracted by Longfellow's pianoforte, David Pelham rose with a smile and made his way to the instrument, where he ran his fingers over the ivory keys, picking out a simple tune until Charlotte returned with a tray. He then took a seat beside her, accepting cup and saucer and a slice of cake, though he immediately set both down on a small table nearby.

"I had hoped," he began, "to have the pleasure of seeing Miss Longfellow today."

"Diana won't be allowed to leave Mrs. Willett's house for another two weeks, at least," her brother informed him.

"Then—might I be allowed to visit her there? I may be of some use, if Miss Longfellow wants cheerful conversation, or perhaps someone to read to her. It would be my great pleasure, I assure you."

Longfellow chewed his cake thoughtfully before he answered. "You will have to consult her physician on the wisdom of having another visitor in the house," he eventually replied, "though I can see no real harm . . ."

"Sir?" asked Mr. Pelham.

Dr. Tucker, too, appeared to consider. Then he lowered his gaze, and blinked full into Mrs. Willett's face. For a moment, Charlotte had an odd feeling she could not account for.

"Mr. Pelham may certainly visit from time to time," Dr. Tucker decided.

"Thank you, Doctor! I am delighted!"

"In fact," said Longfellow, "you might as easily lift the spirits of *two* young ladies."

"Oh, yes?" David Pelham asked politely.

"Another is there—Phoebe Morris by name—a girl already known to Dr. Tucker, it seems."

Mrs. Willett noticed David Pelham's hand, reflected in the Venetian mirror, tighten suddenly into a fist. When he turned to stare at Tucker, the physician gave a sickly smile.

"She's soon to wed a local lad," said Benjamin Tucker, while his face contorted strangely.

"Then I wish her happiness." David Pelham abandoned his refreshment for an exploratory trip around the room, during which he examined several objects. "What a superior study. A room of good proportions, impressive windows for a country place, and interesting decoration. I would be happy to spend a great deal of time here myself, I believe."

He lifted the lid of a rosewood box resting on a bookshelf to one side of the mantel. Inside were two matched pistols. "These are splendid!" he gasped with admiration.

"I bought them on the Continent," said Longfellow, "from a Corsican. The man was sorry to sell them, but desperate for funds. I suspect the Europeans are fonder of small arms than we. Perhaps that's because they have more to fear from their neighbors."

"Yet I myself practice with a set obtained when I began to fear going unprotected at night—yes, even in Boston! But you never fire them?" asked Pelham, as he studied the weapons more closely.

"Rarely. When I feel an urge to practice with a weapon, I generally choose the longbow. Far better exercise."

"A fine part of English tradition," Pelham conceded.

"As well as that of America," Longfellow pointed out, smiling at the contrast between the traditional archers of the two continents.

"An interesting point. However, bow and quiver might be odd things to carry, on a walk down Cornhill."

"Colorful, at least. What is your opinion, Doctor?"

"I would like to see all firearms discouraged," Tucker replied curtly. "I've seen what they can do to a body, and too many young men develop a fascination with them. They also make a highwayman's business far easier than it might be, when they go armed among peaceful citizens such as myself, who carry no weapons."

"Would you then take our military muskets and fowling pieces from us, too?" asked Longfellow, hoping to encourage vigorous conversation.

"I doubt such a choice would ever be left to me! Though I hardly find muskets or fowling pieces necessary these days, when I go out to procure a piece of beefsteak or a sausage." The doctor hoisted himself from his comfortable chair. "But now, I must go across the garden to my patients."

Charlotte had been sitting quietly, thinking it inadvisable to comment on a subject most men believed women ill prepared to discuss. (Still, Aaron had often asked her to lead him over the fields on his arrival in Bracebridge—had even taught her to load and fire his rifle, which still hung over the kitchen hearth, though she now had not the heart to use it.)

"May I join you?" she abruptly asked the departing physician.

"Of course, madam, of course! I would greatly welcome an assistant."

"They do have a curious decoration," Longfellow went on to David Pelham, as his admiring guest continued to stroke the silver, wood, and steel of the finely crafted firearm in his hands.

HIS GLASSES PERCHED on top of his head, Benjamin Tucker bent as close as he dared to Diana Longfellow's chest. He watched it rise and fall for a moment, straightened, then sat back on his chair at the side of her bed.

"Nothing yet there; nor anything on the neck, face, or hands. In fact, I don't believe there's even a fever. How do you feel, Miss Longfellow?"

"Like taking a long walk across the meadows. Alone."

"That, I'm afraid, you may not do," replied the doctor.

Diana gave him a swift look of displeasure, but soon returned to her previous ennui.

"There's no need for you to stay in bed," Charlotte suggested gently. "You might try a walk around the house; it has the advantage of not soiling the slippers."

"Oh, I've tried that. I tried to talk with Phoebe this morning, but she said so little, and besides, I can't sit still for her today. I have even visited with Lem, but he seems to prefer his Latin to me! Since I paid scant attention when Richard's ancient tutor was in the house, I'm no help there. I have even," she said, lifting her eyes toward the ceiling, "spoken with Hannah. You can imagine what pleasure either of us derived from that."

"What did you discuss?"

"How one goes about cleaning brass. I found it not very interesting."

"Perhaps you may soon be able to shine in a different way."

"How, Charlotte?" Diana asked eagerly.

"Mr. Pelham has asked to be allowed to visit you, for

what he suggests might be cheerful conversation," Mrs. Willett returned with a smile.

"He hasn't!" Diana cried, looking down at her house costume.

"I'm afraid I gave my approval," said her physician, as he took her wrist to feel her pulse. "Was that unwise?"

"Well . . . I do have some idea Mr. Pelham will forgive something less than elegance in dress—after all, he *was* married. The tattle, Charlotte, is that when he was quite poor—though his family was once quite proud—he took a rich wife for her fortune and little else, apparently. I always found Alicia Farnsworth to be a dry, retiring sort of person. And sickly, of course. But he may have loved her for some reason, if that matters. Unfortunately, she soon died. It's the opinion of several ladies I know that Mr. Pelham was sure she would—but they also say that he should not hesitate to wed again—if only he asked *them*!"

"There are," said Charlotte, "many reasons for marriage. Was Miss Farnsworth interested in learning? Sometimes, when one lacks health—"

"I'm afraid I can't say, Charlotte. Though when I think of it, I have noticed Mr. Pelham actually listening at the town's evening lectures, so perhaps *he* is able to talk of something besides one's appearance, or the state of the weather—unlike many others. In fact, he *must* be a man of many experiences, having traveled, and been married . . . so I suppose a visit is perfectly fine, Dr. Tucker."

"I can assure you, Miss Longfellow, that Mr. Pelham admires you greatly—something he has made very plain to me," her physician replied with a crack in his voice.

"Really? In that case, let me do something about my hair. He can't expect too much, under the circumstances. If only Patty were here! Charlotte, where is my mirror?"

Soon after the mirror had been located, and when Diana had found a comb, a choice of caps, and a handful of ribbons, her visitors left the wonderfully revived young woman to her task.

ONCE HE AND Mrs. Willett had gone down the stairs and across the kitchen, Dr. Tucker knocked on the door to the small side room. The shelved chamber had once held stores, and sometimes sheltered itinerant craftsmen who showed up to mend shoes, repair clocks, or add heads to their ready-made portraits. More recently, the room had become Lem's sleeping chamber, although in winter he had to share it with bushels of potatoes and apples.

Fully dressed and lying atop a striped blanket, the boy turned from his book with an inquiring look.

"Don't get up," said Dr. Tucker. "For once, you're allowed to stay there all day, if you like." Tucker brushed the hair from the boy's forehead, and found only smooth skin. "No aches, no pains at all? No weariness?"

"A small headache. It's not bad."

"The countryside breeds superior young men," Dr. Tucker noted to Charlotte, who nodded her assent and wondered if Lem might be hungry, as usual. Before she could ask, the doctor uncoiled the bandage on the boy's arm, looked at the suppurating wound closely, wrinkled his nose, and covered the area back up again. He signaled that he'd concluded his examination.

"We'll leave you to your studies," said Dr. Tucker in parting. "By the way, what do you conclude, on reading the great Caesar's adventures?"

"That they are the reason my head aches."

"An interesting theory," the physician said with a dry chuckle. "I seem to recall observing the same phenomenon, a very long time ago."

Leaving his second patient to fend with history on his

own, Dr. Tucker led Mrs. Willett through a kitchen portal and into the main room of the house. Eventually, they passed through the open door of her study.

Phoebe was the only one of the inoculated who seemed feverish. At least, her face was more flushed than usual, Charlotte noted when they entered the room.

"Do you feel ill, Miss Morris?" the physician asked at once.

"No." Phoebe's reply came in a low voice. Her eyes moved from Dr. Tucker to Mrs. Willett.

"Then, do you wish you were home?" Charlotte guessed, worrying that the girl should have been sent back to Concord after all.

"I once looked forward to seeing more of the world," Phoebe replied vaguely. She lay back as Dr. Tucker reached for one of her hands.

"Your new life here will be exciting," Charlotte assured her. "But you might find time to travel, too, in the next twenty or thirty years."

"Have you seen Will this morning?" Phoebe asked her suddenly.

"He's well, but a little pensive."

"That is unlike Will, isn't it?" Finally a smile skipped across her face. But it swiftly faded. "Have . . . have you seen him as well, Doctor?"

"No, indeed. You have a good pulse," he told the girl. "However, I advise you to stay in bed. Eat lightly, sip small beer or cider when you can. That should calm you. It occurs to me, Miss Morris, that we've not spoken of your medical history."

"No," Phoebe answered, "but perhaps—could we talk of it now?" This time, her own hand reached out for the doctor's, while her steadfast eyes attempted a message her lips seemed unwilling to convey.

Charlotte had supposed another woman in the room would make Phoebe feel easier. Now, she saw that Miss

Morris wished to speak to the physician without her. She watched as Tucker covered Phoebe's fingers gently, while to his face came a look that seemed to combine sharp sensations of pleasure and pain.

She rose to leave, then waited a moment longer; still, she heard no objection. Then she went out of the room somewhat uneasily, leaving Phoebe and Dr. Tucker alone.

MUCH LATER IN the day, Mrs. Willett sat on a milking stool, while nearby, Will Sloan pulled with slow regularity at a soft bag. In the dairy's doorway, mosquitoes, an occasional long-tailed mayfly, and swarms of gilded gnats gave movement and sound to the evening air. Charlotte wore a thin veil to keep the worst at a distance. Encountering Will's weathered neck and face, the biters found they had even less chance of success.

"You'll see Phoebe again tonight, won't you?" she asked over a cow's twitching back.

"I expect so," Will called dreamily from another flank.

"Would you give her a message?"

"If you want."

"I have forgotten to tell her I brought back a length of fabric, as she requested, from Boston. It's for a skirt to wear at the wedding, with the short jacket she's already made."

"Do you expect me to gossip like a girl, about *clothes*?" Will demanded, suddenly suspicious.

"A married man should know about them. How else can he keep an eye on what his wife needs—and explain to her how well she looks?"

"I won't need to look at what she has on to tell her that!"

"But like it or not, she'll expect it. So—the cloth is white linen, with a pattern of light green sprigs. And it has tiny apple-red knots. I think she'll be pleased."

"More than I'll be to tell her," Will muttered.

"How long have you known the soon-to-be Mrs. Sloan?" Charlotte soon went on, to pass the time.

"Almost a year."

"Has she told you much about what her life has been like in Concord?"

"Didn't need to. I've been there a dozen times, so I saw for myself."

"Do you like it there?"

"It's all right. When we stay the night, her family gives my brother and me a room that looks out over the river. If I'd only had a fowler last time, I could have shot ducks for dinner, without even getting out of bed."

"Has Phoebe ever spoken of visiting Boston, Will?"

"No. But her younger sister Betsy said she was there once, and ate lobsters. And I think it was with Phoebe, so Phoebe must have gone there, I suppose."

Not for the first time, Charlotte marveled at the workings of love—for what other reason could these two have to marry? They seemed an unlikely match, and probably knew very little of each other. Surely, Phoebe had a keen curiosity in things Will had little use for. Perhaps a trip together would open his eyes, the way a month's visit had spread the world before a grateful Mrs. Willett, who had traveled with her new husband to Philadelphia for the month of their honeymoon.

"She might enjoy spending a week or two in Boston, if you'd take her there," Charlotte suggested. "For your wedding trip. It would be a good chance to get to know one another, without brothers and sisters there to tease you. And you could eat all the lobster and oysters and fresh scrod you'd ever want. I think Phoebe would like to go. Especially to be sharing something new with you."

"I *know* she would," Will began. But he never finished, for soon he'd drifted off into a trance again.

Charlotte smiled and let him go.

• • •

AN HOUR AND a half later, Will Sloan stood whistling softly outside the west window of Phoebe's new bedchamber. The sun had already gone down, ending the long day, and a freshening breeze made the boy glad he'd put on a second shirt over the first. In another moment he saw his fiancée appear, carrying a candle. Setting the light down on the sill, Phoebe raised the lower sash as far as she could.

"Throw on a shawl—it's cold out here," Will told her, unsure if he had given advice or an order. Whichever it was, he was pleased to see the girl draw a wrap from a chair and adjust it over her shoulders before she leaned out.

"Will—I've waited so long!"

"My mother sent me off earlier. You do look beautiful tonight . . . sweetheart." At this moment, in the twilight, with her hair loose and long, she reminded him of a princess in disguise, waiting to be discovered by a wandering shepherd—or, as it happened, by an errand boy and milker of cows. Once again, Will Sloan told himself he was a very fortunate young man.

"And I think . . . I'm sure that gown's becoming. Especially with those little pieces you put in, shining back at the candle."

Phoebe looked down to her green shift, whose cambric sleeves she'd worked into a pattern of vines with silver thread. As she gazed back up, tears brimmed in her eyes. This soon had the effect of dissolving Will's gallantry into a fount of passion—though a small part of his mind was able to note that Mrs. Willett had given him sound advice.

Abandoning all thought, Will moved forward impulsively. But his betrothed swiftly backed away from the sill.

"Stay there! Will, you promised!"

"I only promised not to come inside—if you would sleep down here where I could see you. But I wish you would come and sleep with me tonight, Phoebe." He whispered now, so that no one else would hear. "You could, if you wanted to! Nobody would know, if you slipped out, later . . ."

"Will, you promised you'd do as I say."

Will Sloan thought of another evening a few weeks before, when he'd had his own way. "But Phoebe, you know I need you!"

"I know, Will," she answered softly.

"Are you sure you miss me, too? As much, I mean? Do you miss . . . ?"

"Yes," she said simply.

"I don't know why you had to do this, Phoebe." The boy was unable to keep his frustration from his rising voice. "You didn't have to go in there! If you'd only *told* your father—"

"You know I had to do what he thinks best."

"But after we marry, I'll take his place in that!"

Phoebe smiled briefly, then seemed again about to break into tears.

"Phoebe, what is it?" Will asked tenderly.

"I was only thinking . . ."

"What?"

"Of Boston."

"Boston!" Will shook his brick-red hair in amazement. "Sometimes I think Mrs. Willett just might be a witch, like some around here say . . ."

"What?" asked Phoebe, startled out of her own thoughts.

"She just told me to ask you about Boston! Do you think we should go there, Phoebe, for a marriage trip? I have family we could stay with. You'd probably like to visit yours again, too. Did you enjoy it when you went before? Oh, and about your skirt, for the wedding—"

"Will—I won't marry you! Not now, not ever!"

"What do you mean, saying something terrible like that!"

Her eyes sought the heavens, where the stars flickered back. "Listen, Will," Phoebe began again, her voice trembling, "my father sent me to Boston three years ago, to stay with my Aunt Mary. He told me I would see drawings and paintings—he said I might paint portraits, too, of people in Concord. And he hoped I might meet others who were interested in such things. Perhaps even suitors . . ."

Will frowned, reconsidering his previous regard for Phoebe's father.

"But when I got to Boston, it didn't happen the way . . . the way I'd imagined. Then I was ill, and a physician came. For a rash . . ."

"I've had plenty of those myself, but it was usually just nettles," Will interrupted.

"But something else happened, too, Will. And then, today—oh! I hoped you'd never suspect, since you never saw, when we . . . that I—I was not . . ."

"What do you mean?" demanded her young lover.

"Oh, Will! I'm afraid!"

"Afraid! Of what? You've no reason—"

"I *can't* marry you, Will," she answered fiercely. "Nor anyone else!"

Will Sloan thought it over, and then he felt his pulse begin to pound like thunder. In another moment, the ground under his feet seemed to rise and fall as he suspected swells might, beneath a dory on a great sea.

"Why?" he whispered hoarsely.

"Please, Will, please!"

"*Why*, Phoebe—?"

"I don't mean to hurt you—but there's nothing else I can do!" the unfortunate girl hurried on. "More, I won't tell you. I *can't*, Will!"

"Oh, no?" he growled, moving closer to the window.

• • •

THE EARTH CONTINUED to turn, as the faint stars grew brighter. The moon appeared in the east, its pocked face rising to reign until the break of day. That night, the cold brilliance of the Huntress was slightly diminished; still, she soon lit up the sleeping countryside with a pearly sheen, like that which is often seen through tears.

Into that pale light, a dark figure tumbled awkwardly out of the window of Charlotte Willett's study. After it had gone away, all was again quiet . . . except for occasional sobs, or so they seemed, somewhere in the night.

Chapter 6

—◦ Thursday

NEARLY DONE WITH the early milking, Charlotte Willett asked herself the question once more: Where on earth was Will Sloan?

Had the boy overslept? She supposed he might have lingered well into the evening, talking with his bride. Courtship, after all, could be an exhausting business! And Will wouldn't be the only one to have lost sleep for pleasure, on a spring night like the one just over. She had looked from her own window for a while, after the climbing moon awakened her with its brightness. She'd watched an owl flit like a pale ghost from treetop to field, to return with a lifeless, long-tailed trophy in its claws. It had been a fine night for many of God's creatures—though less so for others, she knew with equal certainty.

When she had finished milking, she walked with Orpheus through wet grass to the opposite side of the house. Will was not in his lean-to. Perhaps his mother had sent

him out on a dawn errand, and he'd been delayed somewhere. She would go in and chat with Hannah. Then,
having cleared up the mystery, she could enjoy a cup of
Cicero's good, strong coffee.

At her own back door, Charlotte went in to find her
kitchen deserted. While shafts of sun reached through the
windowpanes, she revived the fire, first stirring the ashes,
then adding split sticks. That raised a little smoke and finally a burst of flame. Leaning over the hearth, she pulled
the hanging kettle forward.

A cup of tea would be welcome to all, she told herself
as she made her way with a pail to the keg of spring water
outside. She scooped up and drank a dipperful, thinking it
would be another fine day. The month of May was surely
one of the prettiest, before the dust and haze of summer
began to rise. There were some, like Hannah, who disliked
new buds and flowers, for they brought tickling noses and
scratchy eyes. But for the rest, they were a welcome sight.

When the water had boiled and the pot was brewing—
and Hannah still had not appeared—Charlotte thought
of taking up a cup of tea. Then she decided against it.
Phoebe would better enjoy being awakened to the new day.
Mrs. Willett set a china cup onto a saucer, filled it, and
found a spoon for the sugar pot. Sensing a presence behind
her, she turned to see Hannah standing in the doorway,
eyes red with sleep or perhaps the effect of the spring air.
Whatever the reason, she seemed loath to speak.

Charlotte handed her the cup and saucer with a warm
smile. "This was for Phoebe," she said, making conversation, "but you may need it more. Are you quite well?" she
asked with sudden concern.

Hannah only nodded as she raised the teacup to her
lips, a noticeable tremor in her thick arm.

"It's difficult, I know," Charlotte continued. "I suspect
Phoebe feels much the same, being away from her family.

Still, she has you here. And Will, of course, outside—though he isn't in the garden now, and he didn't come to help me with the milking. I wonder if you told him last night to run somewhere early?"

"No," said Hannah, her eyes now brighter.

"Well, we'll see when he returns—from wherever he's got to. I'll take tea in to Phoebe, and ask her where he is. She's probably the last to have seen him. And fairly late, too, I would guess."

At this, Hannah coughed, but made no further comment on Will's unusual devotion to his fiancée. Mrs. Willett picked up a second teacup and crossed to her study. Once there, she knocked softly on the closed door. Receiving no answer, she lifted the latch and stepped inside.

Though one set of curtains was open and the room was filled with light, Phoebe lay asleep under her covers. Arms close by her sides, she looked like someone from a book of stories. It was a sight Will would soon have to treasure, no matter what else might happen . . . through a life that would surely include sickness, childbirth, and countless other worries. But for now, Phoebe lay safe in sleep. So peaceful, so pale. So unmoving.

Charlotte felt a sinking in her stomach, and heard the cup in her hand tremble against its saucer. There was no movement at all in the room—not even the sound of breathing.

Slowly, she set the cup down on the small table beside the bed, and bent to press her fingers against the girl's smooth throat. The skin was cold. Though impossible, there was no doubt. Phoebe Morris had died in the night.

Charlotte inched down the length of the bed, and finally turned to plant both hands on the windowsill. Then she pressed her forehead against a pane of cool glass, suppressing the moan rising from deep within her. With numb fingers, she somehow managed to raise the sash, then thrust her head outside, while her mind continued to cry out for answers for what lay behind her.

How could it have happened? Phoebe's condition yesterday had given them little cause for fear. And Will! What would the boy do, when he learned of Phoebe's death? Unless—unless he already knew ... ?

The air before her shimmered, and she seemed to see the young girl standing in the garden once more, a hand extended toward the window. Deliberately, Charlotte drew back, turned, and took a long breath; she blinked, and ignored what reason told her must surely be nothing more than a memory tricking her eyes.

Then she forced herself to consider carefully. What could be done? For Phoebe, nothing. Nothing! Yet it would be wise to do *something* to make sense of this tragedy, and quickly. Word would soon spread, and wagging tongues would no doubt begin to craft curious tales. After all, if suspicion already grew in her own mind ...

Gathering her courage, Charlotte returned to Phoebe's side. There *was* a bruise above the girl's cheek, as a child might show for having been at war with another. A small injury, though one she could not remember seeing the day before. But beyond that ... ?

In another moment, she reached out to fold back the smooth bed coverings, wanting to look more closely at the girl's arms and hands. Then she stopped, deciding to leave things as they were for others to see. She looked about the room for anything else, but there seemed to be nothing out of place. On the small table, next to the still-steaming teacup, stood an empty glass and a closed volume, neither of which told her more.

Again, her eyes sought the purple bruise. Could Phoebe have been struck by someone who had seen her last evening? What if she had also been hit from behind— by a much harder blow?

Gently, Mrs. Willett reached down and moved the girl's fair hair away from her neck, then lifted the head slightly, and bent to look below. No sign of blood or swelling, but the pillow beneath was damp to her touch. She lowered the head, feeling some resistance, knowing from experience that this would soon increase.

Of course, there was one idea much of Bracebridge would be sure to embrace, and it was this: Inoculation had been at fault. But Phoebe had seemed hardly ill at all, while she lived. Though what if the powder she'd inhaled had acted not only as a carrier of the smallpox, but as a poison, perhaps to the lungs, as well?

Almost immediately, Charlotte was struck by a second horrible idea. What if Diana, too—! She whirled toward the door just as Hannah Sloan tried to enter, apparently to speak to the girl herself. Seeing the look on Mrs. Willett's face, Hannah flung her hands up into the air and fell back.

"I must see Diana!" Charlotte cried, racing for the stairs. In seconds she was outside the bedchamber. Bracing herself, she opened the door and peered inside. Nothing! But then, with a small moan, the quilt-covered body on the bed tossed from one side to the other, before it settled. Greatly relieved, Charlotte crept back down the stairs.

In the kitchen, Hannah Sloan sat hunched before the fire. At Mrs. Willett's return she looked up mutely, waiting for direction.

"Brew another pot, Hannah—and toast some bread. Have some yourself, with plenty of jam," Charlotte added, for she had seen the effects of shock to the nerves before. "Stir extra sugar into your cup. I'll be back!"

Outside, she flew down a twisting garden path, past herbs and flowers that sent sweet scents into the morning air. In another few moments she reached Longfellow's kitchen door, and soon found her neighbor taking coffee in his study.

"Someone is ill," he concluded immediately, alerted by her strained expression.

Charlotte nodded. "Please, Richard—call Dr. Tucker."

"Fever? Is it Diana?"

"Phoebe Morris is dead."

"What! But how?"

"I supposed you would want to see her before anyone else . . ."

Longfellow hesitated, opened his mouth to speak, then turned his head away.

"Cicero!" he bellowed. Unable to wait, he leaped to his feet. The two soon came face to face at the study's door. "Get Tucker up, and be quick! There's been a death—Miss Morris! He'll probably take some shaking, and help him to dress if you must."

The spry old man took the stairs as fast as he could, while Longfellow returned to his study.

"Was it the smallpox?" he seemed to ask himself, while looking to Charlotte with eyes that revealed his disbelief.

"She has no sign of it, that I could see. But must there *be* signs?"

"I've been told no two cases are alike."

"There's another thing . . ." Charlotte began.

"Yes?"

"Well, she seems almost ready—"

"For burial, do you mean?"

"For sitting over, at least."

"Hannah probably saw to it earlier."

"No, she was beside herself when she saw the girl, after I'd found her. Hannah slept quite late today—"

Mrs. Willett broke off abruptly, and there was another long spell of silence between them.

"Tucker should tell us something when he sees her," said Longfellow, beginning to drum his fingers rapidly on the arm of his chair.

Charlotte nodded. But as they waited, she found herself feeling less than certain that her neighbor's confidence in Dr. Benjamin Tucker would be well rewarded.

HANNAH OPENED THE door at their approach, this time with eyes surely red from weeping. All four went directly to the study. There, the doctor bent over the peaceful corpse, flexed its fingers, examined its skin, looked under the eyelids, sniffed about the face, and then rose from his knees.

"What was it?" Richard Longfellow asked, obviously moved, yet also impatient. He saw Dr. Tucker shake his head, wincing as he did so. It *should* hurt him this morning, Longfellow reasoned, considering all he'd seen the old tippler pour down his gullet the night before.

"It is difficult to say . . ."

"Could it have been the smallpox?"

"It could have," the physician replied, seeming to weigh the idea. "A few do die without the rash, though usually in the second week, and with a high fever. When I examined her yesterday, I thought perhaps she was a bit warm. Yes, it is possible it was the smallpox . . ."

"Though not certain."

"Not certain at all. In fact, I think it unlikely."

"Could it have been a weak heart?" asked Charlotte.

"Again, that is possible. But her heart seemed strong enough only yesterday. You do remember, Mrs. Willett, that I examined each of my patients carefully? This could also be the result of a failure of a vessel carrying blood somewhere within the body—something none of us can predict."

With a frown, Longfellow looked away from the girl's still figure to the untroubled world outside the windows, where the road had begun to see movement. "What about burial?" he asked abruptly. "We'll assure the village we've taken all precautions, but with no clear cause, they're going to think the worst. I doubt they will be happy with either of us, Tucker."

While the men spoke further on the subject, Charlotte wandered from the bed to the open window, feeling increasingly ill and looking for a distraction. There was her rosemary, and next to it the young cherry tree she and Aaron had planted, which now required a light pruning. She set her hands on the frame, then removed them with surprise. Though Lem had recently repainted it, a few scratches already marred the sill down to the wood, in an arc suspiciously like the width of a large paw. With a slight smile she fingered the pattern, deciding they would have to take care of it before the weather got in. Some things, at least, could easily be fixed, and forgiven. Others could not.

Mrs. Willett's mind wandered farther, drawn out into the garden by the beginnings of the same shimmer she'd seen earlier. It was an effect often noticed during an afternoon of high heat, yet it did seem out of place now, with the morning so cool. She peered more closely at the pot of rosemary lately moved to its summer home, after spending the coldest months in the glass house. Rosemary, for remembrance . . . what was it she sensed as she stared at the green plant, the light, the garden beyond? Surely, there was something. . . .

She heard her neighbor speak behind her. "We'll wake the boy first. But say nothing," Longfellow warned as he led Dr. Tucker from the room.

Lem was soon brought in. At first, he yawned and wondered at the advanced hour of the morning. Then he saw Phoebe, and his mouth worked as he tried to speak, but could find no words.

"She's been dead several hours," Mrs. Willett told him softly, reaching for his hand. "Did you hear anything last night? Did Phoebe cry out?"

"I heard her talking to Will . . ."

"Loudly?"

"No, but I didn't want to listen, so I closed the window and went on reading . . . until I forgot to cut the candle wick. When it guttered out and I didn't want to get up, I went to sleep."

"You remember nothing else?" asked Longfellow.

"I remember the moonlight when I woke later. Just after the clock struck three."

While the boy spoke, Hannah had crept into the doorway. Now, gasping, she fell back against the wall in a swoon. Charlotte hurried to console her.

Lem then found a question of his own. "Has anyone told Will?"

Charlotte looked to Richard Longfellow. "No one's seen him this morning."

"Hannah, have you sent him on some sort of errand?" asked Longfellow. The boy's mother only moaned softly, and brought her apron to her face.

"He'll be able to take care of himself," Charlotte assured her gently, with as much conviction as she could muster.

"Oh, Will!" Hannah wailed.

"I will go and wake my sister," Longfellow decided abruptly, turning on his heel.

"There's no need to bring her down," the doctor called after him, but as the others could have told him, Diana Longfellow made such decisions for herself.

Sure enough, in two minutes the young lady sailed into the room, expressing disbelief that they all should have misread the situation so—for it clearly could not be as bad as her brother believed. When she had truly looked at the girl on the bed, she fell silent for several moments—until she found a reason to doubt even her own eyes.

"There is an illustration in my book of plays upstairs, Charlotte, of Juliet. She appeared dead, you know, but she wasn't—she'd only taken a sleeping potion. Have you given her a good shaking? No—I suppose—but perhaps—if she is dead . . . could it be she swallowed something far worse?"

"I don't know why she would," Richard Longfellow finally answered. "Do you?"

"No, I don't *know* why, but—"

Diana pointed to the empty glass on the table next to Phoebe's bed. Her brother picked it up. Carefully, he examined its dried brown dregs, first with his eye, then with quivering nostrils.

"Cider," he pronounced, setting the glass down again. "Diana, did you talk to Miss Morris last evening?"

His sister nodded. "Some time before dinner, and she did seem quite agitated—as, of course, we *all* are! But then she went into her room to rest, and Mr. Pelham came, so I talked with *him*, alone. We sat there in the large room. After Mr. Pelham left, I went to see what Hannah was cooking. After *that*, I went upstairs, and called for only a little rice pudding. I meant to come down again, but I never did. Richard, might she not have done something extremely foolish? What is it she was reading?"

Longfellow picked up the volume from the table.

"Only Pope," he answered. "Hardly the sort of thing to excite a modern young woman unduly."

"But . . . if I had only come down again and talked to her . . . do you suppose she'd be alive still?"

Something new in her eyes decided him. "No sense staying here any longer," said her brother, taking Diana by the shoulders and turning her around. He had soon marched her into the sunny kitchen, where he sat her down, found the pot of tea, poured one cup, and then another for himself. Recalling her own duties, Hannah wiped her eyes and set out toasted bread and preserves, with more chunks of sugar to pound down for the tea.

Then, officially, Longfellow instructed them to close

the study door, and keep it closed until a decision was made by the selectmen and the constable.

"Are you going to look for Will?" Hannah asked tremulously, for Longfellow had said no more of her son's disappearance.

"I'll ask if anyone has seen him, Hannah. Since he's gone, I have to assume he's aware that Phoebe is dead— and he must have felt her death more keenly than we. He'll be better off by himself, while he finds his way through the beginning of the suffering that must come."

Knowing that he understood a lover's sorrow, Hannah forced herself to agree with Longfellow's conclusion.

"As for the girl," he went on, "I will go and inform Reverend Rowe—though God knows I don't relish the task. Do you wish to join me, Mrs. Willett?"

"I'll stay here," Charlotte decided, "and do what I can."

Dr. Tucker voiced his approval. "Make sure everyone keeps warm and continues to eat. We should be able to move her shortly," he added quietly.

Promising himself a large brandy long before then, Richard Longfellow led the doctor out of Mrs. Willett's kitchen door, and back across the garden to his own.

Chapter 7

ALONE IN HIS study, Richard Longfellow found himself perplexed, as he felt his active mind sink once more into a black humor. That was to be expected, he supposed, with a young woman lying dead only a few yards away.

But there was more to it than that. With no immediate answer to the question of cause, he could not help but wonder if he himself might be at least partly to blame. After all, he had chosen Benjamin Tucker to perform the inoculations. Had the man somehow failed in his duties? It was clear now that Tucker had a tendency toward excessive indulgence, at least in drink, which must indicate a weakness. Yet, regardless, physicians could not always be successful—as he knew from bitter experience.

But what if his own idea had been a dreadful mistake? No, there was no reason to suspect the powder, and he refused to think of it, at least for the present. After all, Diana was well, and she, too, had been given the stuff. But he vowed to watch his sister's condition more closely, as long as she remained in Dr. Tucker's care.

For a moment, as he looked about the familiar room, Richard Longfellow pondered something even more strange. He sometimes suspected that Cicero had a queer idea about the Howard farmhouse. It did seem that Death stopped there more often than he visited others. Could the place be some kind of infernal magnet? His sister was still in the house—with Charlotte. Dear God—might they, too, be yet in danger?

Swiftly berating himself for even imagining such superstitious nonsense, he set down his brandy. Then he returned to what he knew to be the facts of the matter before him, though they were admittedly few.

Was it to be death by natural causes, then? He, Tucker, the other selectmen, and Constable Wise would have to decide upon an answer. Everything, after all, had to have a reason, for the physical world did not operate by magic! It would be well, though, if the girl's father could be given something beyond condolences, when he found his daughter had died in Bracebridge. But what, exactly, could they tell him?

Rowe, he suspected, would be quick to blame the inoculation, having made his opposition clear from the pulpit. But if smallpox was not the cause of Phoebe Morris's death, and if no other natural morbidity could be discovered during a closer examination of the body (which the doctor had promised to undertake that afternoon, after they'd moved her)—then what other reason could there be? What was most often considered, he asked himself, in the case of an unexplained death?

Human agency, of course, was one possibility. Diana's feminine mind had immediately suspected that Phoebe took her own life, perhaps while affected by some sort of romantic madness. But had they knowledge that might lead them to believe the girl had any such desire? And where would she have found the means? On the face of it, the idea seemed implausible.

Mrs. Willett was concerned that Will Sloan was nowhere to be found. And the boy's own mother clearly seemed to fear his involvement. High emotion between lovers often enough did turn deadly. It was something to consider.

But if it had not been Phoebe's wish, or Will's, could someone else have wanted her dead? Might an unknown person have walked into the girl's bedchamber last evening, and helped her soul out of it? No, even more absurd! For who would have wanted to harm her?

Finally he groaned aloud, forced to admit that none of his theories could be easily sustained, nor could any of them be disproved. And so, when Reverend Rowe's knock sounded on his outer door, Richard Longfellow rose to answer it with a feeling of relief. Another disconcerting problem was approaching—but at least this was a devil he knew.

Christian Rowe entered as usual, his long-tailed coat of black broadcloth clinging to his frame like a wrinkled skin. Barely thirty-five years of age, he dressed as an old man in mourning. Yet there was an ageless arrogance in his manner, something that stifled compassion and nettled more than a few of his flock. Longfellow had long supposed Rowe expected to find no goodness in anyone; clearly, he preferred to hunt for evil—softly, though, at first, without alerting his quarry.

"I was told I'm needed to discuss a matter of great importance." His stern face implied that it had better be so.

Longfellow stood his ground and spoke with an authority of his own. "As a selectman, I must tell you that Phoebe Morris, a young woman staying in Mrs. Willett's house, has died." He saw the reverend's demeanor alter immediately.

"Dead, sir? Who is responsible?" Rowe demanded.

"There is no obvious cause," Longfellow returned, surprised that the preacher appeared to feel more outrage than shock.

Reverend Rowe sat down, taking off his hat, paying some heed to the state of its round brim before setting it on a table. By uncovering his head he showed a quantity of wispy golden hair, said by a devout few to resemble a halo.

Longfellow smiled as he remembered a whispered rumor he'd heard from Cicero, the gist of which was that there lived inside Christian Rowe an angel, revealed when the fearful black suit and ivory stockings were removed, and he stood in his long white shirt. Then, according to at least one witness, the reverend had a desire to please more than the Lord. Perhaps, Longfellow thought again, the fellow was not entirely deficient in normal human feeling, after all.

"I see by your smile," the preacher finally replied, "that you are not displeased to give me this news! So I presume you do not believe the pox is to blame?"

"Yes, and no. The news of Miss Morris's death is something I heartily wish I did not have to give—but as for the smallpox bringing it about, I don't see how it could have. Nor does Dr. Tucker."

"No, I would imagine not. But can you *prove* that it was not responsible?"

"No more than you can prove the reverse," Longfellow replied, unable to mask his impatience. Hearing it, Rowe pounced.

"Have I not warned you that inoculation is the work of Satan? Through your foul ministrations, you may well have helped this child to become his victim! For she has surely been snatched from the world before her time, with no chance to prepare for the next!"

"I don't yet know *whose* victim she might be," Longfellow interposed, "but does it not seem strange to you that

Satan routinely takes only a few of the inoculated, while far more die of the disease among those who remain as the Lord made them? I would think a man with a God-given brain and a wish to preserve himself could see what is obvious."

The preacher grew rigid with righteous anger. "If a man dies in a natural state, we can at least be certain his death is a part of Jehovah's Plan!"

"Yet Cotton Mather, surely one of our most celebrated preachers, encouraged inoculation," Longfellow volleyed.

"Yes, Doctor Mather did," Rowe returned with a sneer, for he had little sympathy for the old Puritans or for their learning. "But Jonathan Edwards, a *greater* man of God, refused the practice, even while he ministered to the savages on the frontier—heathens, it should be remembered, whom God chooses to destroy by smallpox *in far greater numbers* than our own people! Reverend Edwards rightly labored to save only their souls, while their lives were taken in a part of the Great Design. Yet the Lord chose to preserve *him* from smallpox! I will admit Edwards later fell from grace—he should never have accepted the presidency of that renegade college, at Princeton—but when he met his fate, it was a result, you may recall, sir, of *inoculation!*" Reverend Rowe's voice boomed in triumph.

Longfellow slouched back into his chair. "Tell me, Rowe," he finally asked, staring at his guest, "have you had the smallpox yourself?"

"When I was a boy. Through God's grace, I recovered."

"Why do you think that was?"

"I cannot say. I imagine He had good reason."

"Reason! And now, you think it His judgment, His justice, when anyone else who sickens from an illness does not recover?" Yet again, Longfellow painfully recalled the pitifully swollen face and dark, matted hair of his fiancée, Eleanor Howard, as she lay dying.

"His ways are beyond our knowing," Rowe returned, pleased with this ultimate answer.

Longfellow closed his eyes. The man was insane—further argument would be pointless. Years ago, he had seen this particular minister for what he was—something far worse than the average, which was bad enough! Here was a zealot skewed by the rumblings and bleatings of the Great Awakening . . . a reformer who loved the idea of Hell even more than the Puritan founders of the Bay Colony had enjoyed their hopes of an orderly Heaven. Most of the descendants of those paragons of old Boston no longer spoke of Predestination, of course. Instead, modern men proved their worth by seeking material things with which they adorned their inherited City on the Hill. They had grown powerful and secure, on earth at least—even if they were arguably less prepared to enter the world beyond.

Rowe's kind had taken a different path. They craved power that sprang from fear, while they sought out and preyed upon human doubt hiding beneath many a modern veneer, in many a guilty heart. In this, they opposed rational, mercantile, and scientific beliefs—things all men of good sense in the community revered. Flying in the face of Reason, these smoke-belchers were men quite capable of anything. Rowe, angelic? Ha! Although Satan, he suddenly recalled, had once been an angel, too . . .

"What about the boy?"

"Mmmm?" said Longfellow, called back from distant fields.

"What about young Sloan? What does he have to say?"

"Will? At the moment, he's not here."

Rowe's interest increased. "An evil sign," he concluded, his eyes roaming around the room. "I recently spoke to them both, prior to their nuptials, and I cannot say the pairing seemed likely to fare well. *If* you believe the death of Phoebe Morris was *not* caused by the inoculation . . ."

"You think Will could have murdered his own intended?"

"From what I knew of her, she might well have driven a man to acts of shame. Young women do kindle men's passions, and Sloan is a fiery youth, as we all know! They must have had a quarrel. It's likely she didn't respect him as she should—these days, a fault increasingly common among women. If she rejected him, he could well have lost his reason! For even the most vigilant—" Rowe stopped, and looked searchingly at the man before him.

"Yes?" asked Longfellow, waiting.

The reverend wiped his lips with a handkerchief, and dabbed at his forehead, before he concluded.

"When you find him, Will Sloan must be questioned thoroughly, for as long as it may take."

"As long as what takes?"

"As long as it takes to get him to admit to his sin! For if he has fled, he has all but admitted his guilt."

"You think so? Unfortunately, I have little experience with interrogating men, especially to discover their souls. Perhaps what we need is a Grand Inquisitor. I am only an elected official, trying to do my duty. To that end, I'll confer with Constable Wise and ask him what *he* plans to do. I shall also call for a meeting tomorrow of the other selectmen and Dr. Tucker. If you come to the inn, you will find a seat. That's where I'm bound now. I will walk you to the road."

Reverend Rowe had been notified, as the village would expect. And that was that. Longfellow would be damned before he would give the man more. In fact, he thought ruefully, he would most certainly be damned by Rowe anyway—in the village, and quite possibly in the preacher's prayers—no matter what he did.

Soon Richard Longfellow watched the minister scurry away toward Mrs. Willett's house, probably to inflict as much unease there, too, as he could. Meanwhile, Longfellow strode across the road to Jonathan Pratt's establishment. Inside, the innkeeper bustled toward him, a look of sympathy on his round face.

"I've just heard. A customer from the Blue Boar came and told me, after Cicero called for Phineas. I'm sorry, Richard. I know you did your best for her. This is most disturbing! What has happened, do you think?"

"Who knows? But, we may yet find some physical evidence. Beyond that, I suppose we'll need to question a few people concerning the girl's state of mind, and seek out anyone else who might have information about her recent behavior. I believe that's what's expected."

Behind them, the chatter from the taproom erupted into laughter, but it had no cheering effect on the two men.

"It puts you in an uncomfortable position."

"It does. Though I hope to have some company quite soon. Can you find Tim for me?"

"Certainly. What would you like him to do?"

"I want him to take a letter north. I'll write it out now. Send him off right away."

"He'll leave at your pleasure."

"Pleasure," Longfellow repeated darkly, as he sat down in a hall nook at a baize-covered table. Its single drawer contained paper, a few split and sharpened feathers, and a bottle of ink. It only took him a moment to scratch out a brief message, after which he leaned back with a deepening scowl.

IN HIS BEDCHAMBER across the road, Benjamin Tucker was finishing a much lengthier epistle of his own. Perhaps the letter would never be opened, and its contents would make no difference. He still hoped to keep worse from happening.

And yet, this morning, Phoebe Morris was dead! The horror of his situation continued to grow, as some of the confusion in his spirit-addled brain ebbed away. The cause of death was, after all, unclear, but he grew more afraid. Three years ago, such a beautiful child . . . no, that was all finished! But how could he have convinced himself that she needed no help? Why had he allowed her to return to Concord?

Hadn't she looked fine, though—better than before, even, when he was with her only yesterday? After that, he had to act . . . for she was about to marry! How could he allow it? *How?*

He had told her at last . . . but had he done far more? Even now, he wasn't sure. If he could only remember!

If only he had disengaged himself, when he first saw her again—but how could he be expected to live in disgrace, with no clients, no work, so few pleasures to lighten the eternal pain? What would they have thought of him, had he told them? Would he *ever* be able to give up his final hope?

The doctor's head throbbed. Last night he had talked with Longfellow in his study, peering into his host's microscope until the small hours while gulping down brandy. It had been a long while since he had been able to afford his fill of anything so costly. And yet, on top of the opium he had swallowed for his twisting gut, had he been wise to drink at all?

He did remember going out for air, and barely recalled coming to the greenhouse. The climbing roses at its doorway . . . surely, they must explain the carefully hidden scratches on his wrists. . . . Though how he had ended up in his bed fully clothed this morning, he could not tell.

There *was* still time to warn Longfellow's sister—but would she listen? Even if it came from his own lips, could she bring herself to believe such a ghastly thing possible? Such weakness—such madness? Frequently, women refused to see what stood before them. Yet Phoebe had been terrified enough, when he spoke with her! At first, she had only dreaded her young man's reaction, should he hear the worst about their shared past. But then—

The question was, how much did the boy know *now*? Had she told him anything? Had she confessed *everything*? Or had this Will Sloan been the one to kill her, after all? Oh, if only he could *remember*!

How Benjamin Tucker longed to tell what he suspected, and confess to what he'd done, whatever the consequences. But if, in the end, he found himself unable, they would at least have his letter.

Scratching an address on the outside, he lit a candle from the embers in his hearth, dripped on a wax seal, and impressed it with a finger ring. Soon, horribly, he would have to look over what remained of Phoebe, to see if there was anything that might give the game away. How ironic that he alone would examine the corpse closely. He must tell them, he decided, that she was still a maiden, even though . . .

After all, there was still her family. Why should they suffer, as his own already had? As for himself, he would take another drink, or two, for health's sake, before he attempted his final visit with the dear little thing.

But first, Dr. Tucker took letter in hand and walked briskly across the road to the Bracebridge Inn. There, he left instructions for his communication to go into Boston first thing in the morning, along with the fresh vegetables, and several kegs of fermenting cider.

LATE THAT EVENING, Charlotte Willett sat in her borrowed chamber, between those of Dr. Tucker and Cicero, where she and her faithful dog kept each other company. Orpheus sensed that something unusual had happened, and was full of concern for his mistress. While she walked about, he watched her carefully, moving out of her way when she forgot he was there, looking into the hallway as steps came and went, or when the front door banged below. He watched, too, as Charlotte sat motionless in the Windsor chair next to her bed, still recalling the events of her exhausting day.

First she had discovered Phoebe, and had gone for help. After the initial investigation, she'd stayed to do what she could for Diana and Hannah, while Lem, pressed into a window seat, watched for passersby along the road, wishing, Charlotte imagined, that his friend Will Sloan would suddenly reappear.

Later, Reverend Rowe had paid them all an unwanted visit. Before he left, he had scared Hannah half to death with his questions and suspicions, anxious to pin blame to someone, though he had no proof. Fortunately, Diana had been more than a match for him, and her chilly manner soon drove the reverend to the door. They might have welcomed him had he anything useful to say, or any comfort to give. But as far as Charlotte could determine, Reverend Rowe brought nothing to the situation that helped settle matters. Though of course, thus far, neither had anyone else.

After that, Richard Longfellow and Phineas Wise came in with two others who carried a pine box. When the constable had seen Phoebe for himself, from a distance, the young men carried her away to a cellar in Longfellow's barn, where she would await her eventual interment. Then Longfellow and Wise went outside to examine the areas beneath the windows of the house, but found nothing beyond a wealth of spring grass, nor any further indication of what might have happened during the night.

Tears now came to Charlotte's eyes, as she remembered Phoebe whirling with joy only days before, when the path of her young life had seemed clear. How she wished she'd been more inquisitive while the girl was still alive! Hannah, too, had obvious regrets—though she was as yet unable to weep for one who would soon have become her daughter. She could not even speak Phoebe's name; rather, she seemed to be brooding, enough so that Mrs. Willett feared for her well-being, and suggested a dose of valerian from her simples chest, for sleep. The idea had frozen the distraught woman further, as if she somehow dreaded the prospect. Yet sleep would be needed, Mrs. Willett knew, before any of them could begin to forget. Time must pass: there was no other hope. For Phoebe had left them, never to return.

A short while later, seeking comfort in her own bed, Charlotte lay grateful under a warm quilt. But as she felt the clarity of the day fade, she continued to think. Lem said he'd been awakened, he supposed by moonlight, long after he'd gone to bed. *Something* had lifted him from sleep—a noise, or the light, or a moving shadow. And well out of hearing, she had been roused at the same time, for she had heard a different clock strike three.

Could it possibly be, she wondered, tingling at the thought, as it was with Aaron? For years there had been that occasional brush of a hand on her cheek, with no one there; the echo of soft steps, which Orpheus, too, seemed sometimes to hear; a recurring scent of horehound. Lately, such impressions had lessened, but Aaron Willett was with her still. Now, could there be another? Last night—could Lem have heard a life end, while she woke to sense a new beginning?

She hardly liked the idea, which went against her faith in Nature, and her trust in Reason. If others were to suspect such a thing, it could certainly give encouragement to those who accused her of being willful and dangerous—including Christian Rowe—even though spirits had long been a part of religious belief. In fact, she knew some of her most pious neighbors feared the walking dead. When the day ended, and fires burned low, there was more than entertainment, she felt sure, in the ghostly tales they continued to tell their children.

But were not even the most learned inclined to believe in such things, given a proper incentive? Who was not moved by the shade of Hamlet's father, or Banquo's ghost? Charlotte hardly knew what others might believe, but she suspected it was probably more than most would be willing to admit.

At any rate, she decided, she would continue to keep her own counsel in this, for she had, after all, grown used to discovering things for herself. Unnatural or not, death required a sorting out, before life could move on. In that, she might help. She would start by sifting quietly, employing her intelligence. Soon she might ask a few more questions.

After that, thought Mrs. Willett, she might, perhaps, go just a little farther.

IN HER ROOM on the second floor of Mrs. Willett's farmhouse, Diana Longfellow sat in a tin tub full of water that covered all but her knees, face, and hair piled high. It was the only calming refuge she had been able to think of, and it had the added pleasure of keeping Hannah busy in the heating and hauling, with a little help from Lem. It also kept them from noticing that they were one less, tonight.

Once again, by the light of a candle, Diana raised first her limbs and then her torso, looking carefully over all she could see. No, there were no spots. Nothing marred the smooth beauty of perfect skin. She picked up her hand mirror and scrutinized her face.

Wait! A small red spot—but couldn't it be a hive from the heat of the water? Her anxious fingers felt nothing suspicious beneath the skin. Still, a blemish was a blemish, and horror enough on top of everything else! Determined to be brave, she settled more deeply into the tub. At least, she thought, she was still alive.

But Phoebe—Phoebe! What had the girl done? Had

she really taken her own life? It was unfathomable, though not unheard of. But why would she *do* such a thing? She already had a promise of marriage, so the usual unspoken answer couldn't explain it. Of course, she was an artist, and rather highly strung . . . but given their circumstances she'd seemed reasonably content only the day before. Will Sloan was gone, so they might have quarreled, but she certainly couldn't have died from a broken heart, at least not so soon!

Diana was puzzled by something else. When she had seen David Pelham yesterday afternoon, he had asked if she or Miss Morris might be alarmed by anything in their confinement, or if they had yet felt very unwell. He also asked if they had been given any pills or powders. She had answered they were both well enough, and that she, at least, had been given nothing—but she had felt surprised at his kind concern for a stranger, and his obvious worry for them both. In fact, David Pelham had seemed about to say more . . . perhaps of a passionate nature? She had hoped . . . but instead he'd set his appealing lips, while his eyes took on a pensive sadness that was quite becoming.

Yet it had later become apparent that Mr. Pelham was hardly Miss Morris's ideal in a visitor. The girl had given him such a *look* yesterday, when she stepped out of the study, just as he left by the front door. It was as if he had been a gargoyle from one of Richard's folios of European architecture. She had once seen some herself, in the place with the cathedral, outside of London. What a charming visit that had been, and a lovely voyage, too.

Closing her eyes, Diana let her memory take her far away, while she patted beads of moisture absentmindedly from her high, clear forehead.

Chapter 8

—♦ Friday

FIVE DAYS AFTER he had returned from Boston, Richard Longfellow stood at the edge of his land, surveying his surroundings.

To the north, the morning sun played on the Musketaquid as it flowed on to the town of Concord (where Phoebe's family must now be making their peace with the Almighty, he thought with renewed discomfort). Nearer home, the marshes reflected patches of water among the rushes like scales on a snake. Ducks were plentiful again, too, some building nests, some resting on their way toward the boreal pole. How much better it would be, he decided, if humanity were as well ordered and dependable as the fauna and flora with whom they shared their planet. But humanity was a hodgepodge, at best. For men, who could see far more than other creatures, rarely looked beyond the tips of their noses, or past their grasping fingers. Few suspected they were in any way related to the rest of the natural sphere. It was incredible, but true.

Turning again to the west, Longfellow gazed through a light haze of woodsmoke, and distracted himself by picking out structures on both sides of the river. There at the edge of the elm-lined Common stood the meeting house, clean in a new coat of white paint. Beside it was Reverend Rowe's pile of weathered stone, cold and forbidding but for the vines that clung to its sides. Scattered around these familiar landmarks, beneath fruit and shade trees, other houses and cottages sheltered families and small shops. And there, across the bridge, the grist mill stood at the edge of the dark pond fed by water that descended from southern hills.

The Blue Boar sat just beyond, at the junction of the two roads connecting Boston and Worcester, Concord and Framingham. He hadn't set foot in the tavern for some time. It was something its owner would no doubt remember when they met that afternoon. This made Longfellow uncomfortable, for he genuinely liked Phineas Wise, and wished he could say he'd given the place more custom lately. There was nothing wrong with the Blue Boar's cider, and talk there made a change from conversation at the inn, since it came largely from the mouths of farmers, artisans, and tinkers. Perhaps it was the reputation of the stews Wise made that tended to keep less hardy folk away.

But now, up from the village, came a horse ridden to the breaking point. Its blue-coated rider looked as if he'd come far, probably through the night. In fact, he looked familiar. In another moment, Longfellow realized who the man was.

Edmund Montagu knew better, but still dug his heels into his mount's side as he urged the animal, nearly faltering, up the long slope from the river. Then the captain leaped to the ground, nearly tripping on his sword while he left his reins to trail in the grass. He strode to Longfellow's side and grabbed the other's arms with gloved hands.

"Where is she?" he cried out.

"Who?"

"Diana! From your scrap of a letter—! And after what I'd asked you earlier, should the occasion arise, I have to assume—but you were so certain she would be spared the worst!"

"There's nothing wrong with Diana. I'm just going to see her now."

Montagu took a breath before reaching into his coat to produce the paper Longfellow had sent him the day before.

"Then what is the meaning of this?" the captain shouted, his eyes sending out a terrible message of their own. Longfellow took the letter and read it aloud.

"There has been a death. Come immediately, if you would see her. Circumstances unclear. We might use your assistance. Richard Longfellow."

"Well?" asked Montagu again.

"Well, there *has* been a death. Phoebe Morris, a young woman from Concord, staying in the same house. Good Lord, man, if it were Diana, don't you think I would have explained that to you in slightly greater detail?"

Montagu sank down onto the wet grass, careless of his coat and silk stockings. His cocked hat popped off and rolled to the side, and his tie-wig fell askew, revealing short brown curls below.

Richard Longfellow sat down companionably. He set the black hat upon his knee, away from the dew that would soon cause its felt to buckle. It was all he could think of, at the moment, to make amends. He now realized he'd put Edmund Montagu through a good deal of suffering; yet he could hardly help being amused by the man's agitated state.

"I'm afraid I had no idea how far my sister had rattled you. I beg pardon, Edmund . . . though I would imagine Diana will be decidedly pleased, when I tell her—"

"You will not!" Montagu stated each word firmly, forming them into a threat.

"Come and tell her yourself, then. You have had the smallpox?"

"As my face would have told you, if you'd ever bothered to look at it closely. But no—your thoughts are always in the clouds, aren't they? Or off to some other world entirely! However, you needn't worry; I will accompany you. The girl's body is still in the house?"

"We've moved it to a cellar, where you may see it later. Along with Diana, Miss Morris was exposed to smallpox three days ago, but you'll find there's no clear reason for her death. Which gives us something of a mystery—beyond the tragic element, of course. Since you know how my neighbors take that sort of thing—at least you should know, after your visit last fall—I'm sure you'll agree we'd do well to declare the cause of her demise as soon as possible. Especially since the whole inoculation business has been a point of considerable contention! There is one other thing I think you should be aware of . . . but you'll find it out soon enough."

"You have at least one more on your side, I would imagine," the captain said as he watched a woman in simple country attire walk toward them, a basket under her arm. "Madam!" he called out as she approached. Charlotte Willett hurried forward, true pleasure on her face, now that her ears had told her what her eyes were unable to be sure of.

"Captain Montagu," she cried, extending her hand. "How is it that you break your visit to New Hampshire?"

"You might ask that of Mr. Longfellow some time, and see what he says. He has just invited me to visit Diana. I will guess that is where you're going, as well."

"We'll lead your animal to the inn's stables first," Longfellow suggested, "for a rub and a much-needed rest."

That task accomplished, the trio proceeded toward the road again. But they were soon halted in the yard by an arresting figure.

By now, Mr. Pelham had abandoned his city coat for a loose, collared frock-coat made of black linen, worn today over a yellow waistcoat unbuttoned to display drooping silk ruffles at the front of his shirt. Instead of the shoes with thick gold buckles he'd worn when they last met, he wore high boots of soft, slouching leather. In one hand he carried a tapered walking switch. A leather volume reposed in the other. Contrasted with the captain's grander but travel-sullied attire, David Pelham's looked both easy and romantically affected—much the same as his smile, Montagu thought with some distaste.

"Mr. Pelham," Longfellow called out, stepping forward. "You are on your way out?"

"I'm on my way to see your sister, sir! She's asked me to bring her something to read, and I believe I have just the thing. See here—I've brought one of two volumes by Dr. Oliver Goldsmith, which I believe she will enjoy. Have you read it? The work is called *The Citizen of the World*. Goldsmith mocks Londoners through the eyes of a man of China, of all places—quite amusing, since everything stylish in London lately seems to come from the Orient. It is the new Olympus!" Pelham concluded with a chuckle.

"I find myself intrigued," Longfellow replied, "by what I have heard of Eastern medicine and philosophy, which I plan to give more study—but have you read the account of Montesquieu's fictitious Persians in Paris?"

"I haven't. Sorry. I can tell you, though, that Goldsmith, by reputation at least, is a poor Irishman with a lurid taste in clothes. He does seem to have an admirable wit— in that he is like your sister, although I think she dresses rather well," Pelham finished, with what Captain Montagu supposed was a smirk.

"As my correspondence with her dressmakers would suggest," Longfellow responded.

"But I doubt," Mrs. Willett said softly, "that Diana will be up to a literary discussion today, Mr. Pelham. And none of us, I think, can forget that the house has seen a death."

"What?" cried David Pelham. "But sir, your sister—?"

"She is well—it's Phoebe Morris who has died. She is—was—the young woman from Concord whom I mentioned earlier. We discovered her yesterday morning—but I am surprised that this is news to you."

David Pelham had first appeared stunned, but rapidly recovered himself. "Yesterday, I was alone . . . taking a healthful journey on foot. Then when I returned last evening, I had supper in my room, where I stayed to finish this volume. I will admit it does seem strange to miss such a thing in so small a place—but I did not hear of it. And I am truly sorry to hear of it now."

Listening to his explanation, Mrs. Willett asked herself if country walks could agree with Mr. Pelham, for he looked on close examination rather more worn than he had the last time they'd met, no matter how much his high spirits suggested otherwise.

"You must have met the young lady when you went there on Wednesday," said Longfellow.

"I'm afraid I did not have that pleasure, yet I am saddened. Life—life can be a most fragile voyage. It may be as Defoe has said, that the good die early . . . but do you know what caused her to die?"

This time, it was Longfellow's face that revealed a certain strain. "No one knows for certain. We are making investigations, of course."

"But then, we have all the more reason," cried Pelham,

"to offer comfort to those who remain in the house—for they, unlike ourselves, are hardly free to escape it!"

"Mmmm—yes," Longfellow admitted unhappily. "Let us all go on, then. Captain Montagu and I have other business before long. Oh, allow me to present Edmund Montagu, who is an officer of the Crown. And a great favorite of my sister."

Longfellow was pleased to see David Pelham's eyes, which previously suggested rounds of toffee, take on a glint of something far harder as they locked on to Montagu's own. Though words were not exchanged, each man gave the other a grudging bow of recognition.

"Come along, Mrs. Willett."

Richard Longfellow took the basket from his neighbor with a peculiar smile and offered her his arm, before propelling the little party up the hill.

"AND THEN," DIANA Longfellow sighed, "we spoke of things beyond our fears, and our prayers for getting safely through this dreadful ordeal. I remember Phoebe talked of her family, as did I of mine." Diana sent a brief look to her brother and decided to move on to another topic, while she reclined on a day-bed made up with quilts and pillows, on a settle in the large room downstairs.

"We also compared stories of the people we knew who had taken the smallpox . . . but that was unpleasant, so we went on to speak of her drawings. I told Phoebe I had seen many great paintings while in London—as well as most of those worth anything in the better homes of Boston. A few there should not be sniffed at, you know. It seems all who can afford it now want their families painted, surrounded by their possessions—though why they insist on wearing their quaintest clothing for these sittings, I have yet to discover! Would you not think they would be proud to display more of the current fashion?"

Charlotte watched Diana's bright silk turban swivel and bob while the monologue continued. She also saw that the young woman's conversation was well below its usual quality, and guessed Diana was not as blithe as she pretended to be. Captain Montagu was concerned as well, she supposed, for he did seem to stare.

"But you must have talked about her feelings on her coming marriage?" Longfellow inquired again.

"Ladies will seldom mention it to you men, when we do," Diana reminded her brother. "But I'll be truthful, Richard, in this case. She spoke of Will Sloan's trips to Concord when they first met, and I asked her to describe his proposal. I thought it sounded rather dull, at least the way Phoebe told it. Her ardor for him was hardly dramatic, though she seemed quite constant. I did think it all a little strange, somehow."

"Constancy *may* seem strange, these days," Montagu replied gravely, crossing his legs and turning to stare now at David Pelham. Clearly, Diana had encouraged this fop to visit, and had preened herself to receive him. The surprise of his own entrance had hardly given her a moment's discomfort. And though she must see his state of disarray, she had not bothered to question its source. Was *this* the young lady he had ridden his horse half to death through the night to see, one final time?

"At least, more colorful emotions may seem the fashion now," Mr. Pelham offered cheerfully, "for there is, I believe, a more romantic view toward love these days. But are young ladies really much changed, at heart?" he queried the ladies present.

"I would say," the captain interjected coldly, "that the flirtations that now seem acceptable in Boston society are a far cry from its former standards of modesty—and even decency."

"Perhaps they inch closer to what has long been hoped for by Boston's young men," Diana tossed back.

"For it is you men, is it not, who boast of making most of our rules for us?"

"But surely, Miss Longfellow, you would not have *those hopes* influence a lady's behavior?" countered the captain with some warmth. "And do you suppose fathers—or brothers, for that matter—can be expected to forgive serious trespass against the females in their families, which may well result from flirtation?"

"We realize, Edmund," said Longfellow slowly, "that in England, poaching a deer can be a hanging offense; but in Massachusetts, game is less often confined to hereditary preserves."

"Hanging is one solution to poaching," Montagu returned. "Though we have evolved one or two more subtle ways of influencing courtship. We *must* uphold standards which protect the weaker sex from the stronger, due to their entirely different natures—a difference that must be obvious, even here!"

"I fear that the sexes are still alike in their human nature. And as for protection, I find it difficult to say which gender most needs protecting from the other."

"Then answer me this: Do you say there is hope for a woman who has lost her honor, in your society?"

"That sort of thing," Richard Longfellow replied with a smile, "is something best left to poets, rather than to simple farmers."

"Here are the words of a poet, then:

> When lovely woman stoops to folly
> And finds too late that men betray,
> What charm can soothe her melancholy,
> What art can wash her guilt away?
> The only art her guilt to cover,
> To hide her shame from every eye,
> To give repentance to her lover,
> And wring his bosom—is—to die."

"How droll," Diana remarked, after a sharp little laugh. But Captain Montagu, imagining a still body he had yet to see, focused his eyes on Mrs. Willett while he waited for her to comment.

"If, Captain, a young woman is overly sensitive to opinion, and if she is willing to injure others," Charlotte answered at length, "then she might consider such a thing, I suppose. But I don't believe in Bracebridge, at least, death could be seen as necessary. Here, I think, most *do* plan to marry, who tread where they have been told not to. But if they do *not* marry—and the frequent result becomes obvious—then pity will still come from many . . . though shame is called out by some, who should know better."

"I see," the captain said thoughtfully.

"Do you imagine someone in particular?" Charlotte asked.

"Two, in fact."

"Is that clever composition your own, Captain?" asked Mr. Pelham, looking away from Miss Longfellow.

"The song belongs to Oliver Goldsmith. It is unpublished, but more than once I've heard 'Nol' repeat it for a glass of spirits. It is found in a novel soon to be published."

"How did you come to meet Goldsmith?" Pelham demanded, smiling as if he were inclined not to believe the captain's answer.

"That is a long story, best left for another time. I can only say that he and I have frequented the same waterfront streets and London dens, where one may observe the lot of the fallen. And we both have seen tainted, diseased women of the town who are the equal of any man in depravity—although they often arrived there through little fault of their own."

"But how came you to be in these low places yourself, sir?" Pelham inquired doggedly.

"Again, I must decline . . ."

"The captain is a charitable man who often seeks to assist those in distress," Charlotte answered for him.

"It's quite true," Diana replied, flouncing her skirts. "And apparently he's come to do me that favor during my quarantine, even though he might be enjoying more splendid entertainment with well-to-do ladies in New Hampshire. Is that not charity, toward a poor, suffering, weak, misguided woman?"

"If Captain Montagu has come here to see you, Miss Longfellow," said David Pelham, "then I will admire his taste for beauty, at least. However, I'm not at all sure I can applaud his idea of acceptable conversation for gentle ladies."

With a glower, Montagu rose to his feet. Fortunately, more serious wrangling was prevented by the sudden entry of Hannah Sloan. She looked at the group with some confusion until her eyes found Richard Longfellow.

"Have you heard anything at all of my Will, sir?"

"No, Hannah. If I had seen you before—"

"I've been tending Lem. He's become feverish. Shouldn't Dr. Tucker be called?"

"I'll go now. As to your son," Longfellow added, rising to continue quietly at her ear, "I've made attempts to learn if anyone's had news of him, but I'm concerned that calling for a full search might lead to even more trouble for the boy. It would be wise to wait a while longer."

"He is a good boy, truly," Hannah insisted. "We all thought he would be a blessing to Phoebe, since the girl had such ideas . . . from too many books, and those drawings of hers. She wasn't a sturdy girl, either—up and down in her feelings like a candle, she was. Not at all like my Will."

"Mmm," Longfellow began uncertainly.

"But there is one more thing. You do know, Mr. Longfellow, that Will has not had the smallpox? Nor have any of my children. And I know he would not want to infect them, or anyone else."

It was said with little emphasis, but Longfellow immediately realized the woman's meaning. He felt his scalp tighten. Despite what his mother was inclined to believe, Will was not known for a level head. Now, Hannah seemed to tell him the boy might indeed have approached Phoebe during her final hours. And if, somehow, he had taken the disease himself . . . ?

"When I speak with the selectmen this afternoon, I'll bring up the point," he told her. Hannah Sloan extended a hand as if to touch his coat sleeve—but let it drop.

"I believe I will go upstairs," Miss Longfellow decided, drawing attention to herself once more. "To rest. But if you please, Charlotte, come and talk with me later."

"Edmund," said Longfellow, "before we go, perhaps you would like to help my sister take herself back up to her bedchamber. I see she's moved quite a lot of paraphernalia down here. She may also wish to speak to you alone."

"Richard," Diana responded quickly, "I'm sure I would not wish to—"

"The man's ridden all night from New Hampshire, Diana! Would you not extend a little charity to him? And if he's not back down the stairs in five minutes, by the tall clock there, I will send Mr. Pelham up after you both."

"Richard!"

"I hope I have shown the captain that I have *some* concern for your honor, after all," said Longfellow pleasantly, before he turned and led Mrs. Willett through the kitchen door.

CHARLOTTE KNEW LEM was seriously ill when she saw him lying under his blanket with no book in hand, his eyes studying only the ceiling. The boy turned his head to watch them enter the tiny room—an effort that clearly caused him discomfort.

"Now, Lem," said Longfellow, looking him over, "I see you've met the enemy."

"I suppose I'll survive, sir."

"Let us hope so. Feel anything besides unusual warmth?"

"My stomach's been upside down for half the morning."

"Have you begun to sweat?"

The boy nodded. In another moment, he shuddered with cold.

"You should improve in a day or two. We'll soon have you out chopping and milking again. I'll send Tucker over, and I'll be back tomorrow."

"Is there anything I can bring?" Mrs. Willett asked. "We have some ice left in the sawdust. Would you like a sherbet with preserved cherries, do you think?"

"Tomorrow," Lem whispered, as he felt his stomach rebel once more.

"All right."

Charlotte reached out and stroked the boy's still-smooth cheek. Kindness could do far more, she knew, than most medicines. And for a moment, her effort was rewarded with a heartfelt smile.

LATER, IN THE room full of stores and notions that occupied a part of the home of Hiram Bowers, reaction to Mrs. Willett's proximity was less favorable. She had walked down to the village to purchase a few items, including Virginia brittle, which she knew Lem enjoyed. In a few more days, she hoped he would like the taste of some again.

Leaving the road, Charlotte approached a Dutch door whose top was already ajar to let in the air. Humming, she entered and looked around as her eyes grew accustomed to the dim light inside. Before long, she realized that three women stood in various parts of the shop, though not one had greeted her.

Indeed, the acting proprietor, Mrs. Emily Bowers, seemed frozen with indecision. Over by a barrel of coarse sea salt, an older woman finally made a clucking noise, then turned her back. Charlotte had known Mrs. Proctor from childhood, and admired her as a pillar of good works in Bracebridge. And wasn't that Mrs. Hurd beside her, holding a piece of lace? Yes, it *was* Jemima, whose aches and twinges she had politely followed for years—but Mrs. Hurd, too, looked away without speaking.

Emily Bowers managed to clear her throat.

"What is it that you need today, Mrs. Willett?"

"Peanut brittle, please."

"How much for you?"

"A quarter-pound will do."

"I'll have my husband bring it over to Mr. Longfellow's house this afternoon."

"Thank you. I planned to take a few more things, but it seems I may not be welcome here today."

The other ladies moved slightly, in a way that reminded Charlotte of her hens when they suspected someone might soon take an egg from beneath their feathers.

The distress of Emily Bowers increased, for she knew Mrs. Willett was genuinely liked and respected by more than a few of her female clients. Beyond that, she paid swiftly.

"It's only that this morning," the woman explained, "as we've been speaking of Phoebe Morris . . ."

"But I don't see—"

"People wonder what's happened, and they want to know who's at fault," Emily Bowers hurried on. "We've heard talk these past weeks that inoculation is safe—yet I can't say all of us believe it. If the talk is wrong, then such a thing should never have been tried on the poor girl, especially not here in Bracebridge! People fear others will soon be contaminated, because of this Boston doctor's efforts. But now let's suppose inoculation *is* safe. Then, people are bound to blame the man for doing something else to Phoebe . . . and, perhaps, they may find fault in those who caused him to come here in the first place . . ."

"Think of how Will Sloan must feel!" Jemima Hurd fluttered, "to lose his young bride! Though you know," she reversed herself, "that boy has been a trial to his poor mother. As Hannah Sloan was saying only last week—"

"Reverend Rowe may be correct, as well," Mrs. Proctor interrupted sharply, "in suspecting both young people of wrongdoing, for there is far too much laxness, these days."

"I see," murmured Mrs. Willett. "But shouldn't we wait to hear what the constable and our selectmen decide?" she asked mildly.

"Fools!" old Mrs. Proctor exclaimed, drawing a nervous titter from Mrs. Hurd. "Count on them to get everything wrong—though they will rarely tell *us* what is going on, so that we might straighten them out! In the meantime, people are afraid *you* might carry the contagion, Mrs. Willett, coming and going from your house. Some say it's simply a matter of time before you take the smallpox, which I've heard you admit you have not had."

"And a woman's first duty, before all else, is to think of the children! What of their safety? What of their future?" Mrs. Hurd's face was uplifted while her cry rang out.

"It was to protect the future of three lives," Charlotte countered, "that the inoculation was arranged, for it is widely believed to be a wise precaution!"

"I don't know about that," Sarah Proctor retorted. "But I do know people have died both of the smallpox, and the inoculation. And do not forget, most in our village are not protected! Only a few have money enough to bring physicians from Boston, as you well know. Who will help when one of us is stricken, as a result of your encouragement of outsiders?"

"I'm sorry for you myself, Mrs. Willett," Jemima Hurd admitted, "but what can we do? The village has decided. You should go into your home with the others, and pray that things become no worse. Go home, and stay there!" she finished shrilly.

Charlotte had no wish to hear more hysterical twaddle. "I'm sorry, Mrs. Bowers, to have troubled you today," she said, turning to leave as another walked through the doorway, dressed in well-worn, though newly ironed, garments.

"Mrs. Willett! How good to see you," the woman exclaimed, offering her hand. "Are you keeping well?"

"Yes, indeed!" Charlotte answered with a force that surprised even herself. "How are the children?"

"Well occupied," replied Rachel Dudley, "with the garden growing. Winthrop's father is now letting him chop wood. And Anne lost both of her front teeth this week."

"That will make life more interesting, when apple season comes again."

Mrs. Dudley smiled, but Charlotte suddenly recalled a mother in tears. Last October, the Dudleys had lost their eldest son. The memory reminded her now that life did go on, despite great trials, and petty fuss—even though none of them were far from the encircling arms of Death. It called for much courage to recover from the loss of a loved one. Yet most families managed somehow, with the help of friends and neighbors, while each wondered who among them would be the next to go.

Mrs. Willett looked back to the three older women who had been silenced by the hard-pressed mother they knew to be struggling to keep her children fed and clothed—a woman who had just held out her hand gladly to another—someone they had refused to welcome.

"Are you leaving?" Rachel Dudley asked wistfully.

Charlotte thought for another moment, and then shook her head. "I'll stay awhile, for I could use your advice on mending." The statement was not exactly truthful, for she always avoided that particular task by bartering with one of Hannah's girls, all of whom were handy. But Mrs. Willett proceeded to ask about a selection of needles soon put before her, knowing Mrs. Dudley to be a fine seamstress.

Before long, Mrs. Proctor and Mrs. Hurd again began to take up their own business. And Emily Bowers bustled about the room, beaming as she offered her wares to all.

Chapter 9

IN THE LARGEST dining room on the second level of the Bracebridge Inn, eight individuals sat over Madeira, sherry, cider, and ale, sharing a plate of bread and English cheddar while they discussed the latest dilemma of the village. Four of the men, including Richard Longfellow, were selectmen. Phineas Wise came as their appointed constable, having begun a year's term (rather than pay the stiff fine for refusing) several months earlier.

Reverend Christian Rowe, legally kept by his godly office from any position in secular government—though stating he was an earthly representative of a higher authority—also claimed a chair. Benjamin Tucker had been called as a medical witness. And Captain Edmund Montagu sat invited as a friend of the village; this was partly a bow to the captain's somewhat vague connection to the Crown and its Boston representatives, as well as a recognition of his past service to Bracebridge in a matter of murder.

"So, then," said Longfellow, putting down his glass, "are we agreed that the remains will be moved today to a better resting place? I suppose Miss Morris can be buried in what she wears."

The reverend reddened, then answered. "Certainly, for it would be unwise for the village to be further exposed to contagion . . . by touching her again. She should be interred immediately."

"Her family may wish to move her to Concord later."

"Could we not send her there now?" another of the selectmen asked with faint hope.

"I hardly think we can, without her family's approval. The father and two uncles are away to the north, at Penobscot, seeing to some timber. I take it the mother is too ill to travel, after hearing the news. A sister has written she will come when she can. For now, they leave it to us. I suppose they feel Will Sloan has some claim, and expect his family to see to the girl's immediate needs."

"The poor child," Dr. Tucker whispered, lifting his glass once more.

Odd, thought Richard Longfellow, that Tucker appeared to be more moved than anyone of the village, except perhaps Reverend Rowe. "But now," he continued, "what about Will Sloan? Has anyone had news of his whereabouts?"

When no one spoke up, he rose and went to one of the tall windows.

"When a man runs away from a thing like this," said Phineas Wise haltingly, "some say it's because of guilt. How do you gentlemen feel about that?"

"If," said Longfellow, turning back, "a man were to see his fiancée lying dead, do you not suppose he would want to be alone, until he could sort himself out? If that is the situation here, Will Sloan's absence is understandable.

And we might find him before we accuse him—especially as we haven't any clear idea of what has actually happened. But," he added, looking from face to face, "we do have another concern. Will may be innocent of harming Phoebe, yet still a threat—if, for any reason, he went into the room to the girl. We all know that only those who have had the disease, or one very like it, can be trusted not to carry it. Will Sloan," he finished bluntly, "never had the pox."

"Then if we do find him," asked Phineas Wise, "exactly what are we to do with him? I myself haven't had it, either!"

Dr. Tucker answered, his voice weary. "I would suggest keeping young Sloan away from anyone else for a fortnight, at least, until we can be sure he's over the risk of contagion. Any of you who have not had the smallpox should obviously refrain from looking for the boy in the first place."

"I would like to add . . ." Captain Montagu began. While the others looked his way, and Longfellow again took a seat at the table, the captain waited. Then he went on.

"None of us knows exactly how smallpox is spread. But it has come to my attention that handling clothes, and particularly blankets, may be as deadly as making direct contact with a body, or with its gases."

"I am aware of that, Captain," Dr. Tucker said slowly. "There may also be a danger of effluvia carried on the air, which could ferment the blood of someone who has not been made invulnerable to infection. The medical community is still vague on that point—but I would be interested to hear of the circumstances on which you base your own conclusion, sir."

"Recently," Montagu replied, "during a parley with the Indians, one of our generals suggested to a certain colonel that he give blankets and handkerchiefs infected by smallpox to Pontiac's warriors. The colonel followed this suggestion, which had the desired effect. Many died—though some by drowning, as they tried to cool their burning bodies in the waters. In fact, few were spared, even among their women and children."

There was a moment of silence at the table.

"A shameful thing," the doctor returned with a shake of his head.

"But we know war's not always as tidy, sir," said one of the selectmen, "as might be wished—"

"Pretty maids all in a row, marching with fine red coats on," growled another, "may be marching to Hell, I tell you, for I've seen an Iroquois raid! And it's not over yet for the brave men across the mountains—as these savages will honor no French treaty!"

Several others muttered their agreement, while Montagu felt his own blood rise. He, too, had known and admired men recently massacred in frontier garrisons: officers who had given their lives for their King, and to protect these very colonists! Yet could the sly murder of even women and children by infection ever be condoned?

The captain eyed the men about him carefully, before he spoke once more. "There are, you will agree, gentlemen, such things as rules of war, and of honor. I would imagine more than one of you has spoken lately of the Natural Rights of Mankind—"

Instantly, the muttering increased, and the conversation of some easily returned to the frequent topics of taxation and Parliament, and the dreaded stamps.

"Only tell me," continued the previous speaker, banging a fist upon the table, "what rights the Indian may have, after he consorts with our enemy, and that enemy is defeated!"

"I've heard your story of blankets myself, Captain Montagu, but I will not believe it of Amherst," came a different challenge. "For my brother followed the general to

Ticonderoga, and swears he is as fair a man as you'll meet in the King's service."

"In the King's service," echoed another suspiciously, casting a glance in Montagu's direction.

"The question, gentlemen," Richard Longfellow broke in, "is, should we instruct that the coffin be moved from *my* cellar to the churchyard, and buried *this evening*?"

At last, there was general agreement.

Hoping to move things along, Longfellow looked once more to Benjamin Tucker. Again, he was surprised to notice how the fellow's face had aged. The man, he thought, did not look well at all.

"Dr. Tucker, you have now had a chance to examine the body of Miss Morris more thoroughly."

"Ahhh—" exclaimed Reverend Rowe, as if struck with a twinge of toothache.

"I have done so," the physician replied, his eyes on the table before him.

"Have you found anything there to help us?" Longfellow asked, though having spoken with Dr. Tucker earlier, he knew the answer.

"Nothing at all. She was unblemished, as we both saw; her limbs were unbruised, as was her face, except for a mark that amounted to nothing. She also lay, when found, in a composed manner. I assure you there was no sign of any other . . . interference, recent or otherwise. It is quite possible that she merely fell asleep, and never woke. It does sometimes happen, even in the young."

"*No* interference, good sir?" Reverend Rowe wheedled softly, seeming to desire more on the subject.

"It is also possible," said one of the others, "that the young man flew into a rage when he found himself not the first in her *affections*."

"She may indeed have had other suitors," Phineas Wise had to agree. "She was a pretty enough lass."

"Though she had none recently," Longfellow returned.

"My sister has informed me of this, as did Hannah Sloan—and as the doctor tells us, there was no *indication* . . ."

"But do you mean to say that he actually—"

"This is altogether too much!" cried another select-man, who had heard enough of speculation. "Are we to guess about these things like gossiping women? Or will we speak of what we *know*? *He* may have done this, *she* may have done that! Is there nothing we cay say for sure? Or must we try our best to ruin both their good names, with fancies no judge would think twice on?"

"The girl is dead," Longfellow said curtly. "We know that well enough."

"A violent death, which no one in the house heard, seems to me highly unlikely," Montagu now decided. "But there is still the possibility of suicide," he continued, look-ing meaningfully at Benjamin Tucker. "Though it is an un-kind accusation—one that might even be avoided, by a man of feeling—"

"Suicide!" Reverend Rowe hissed, his appetite for sin receiving new relish.

"—for obvious reasons," the captain concluded.

"That thought occurred to me, as well," Longfellow said. "For if the tables were turned—"

"—if, in fact, Miss Morris had been scorned by Will Sloan, and if she had access to some sort of poison—"

"—then she might have done away with herself. But for so little reason? Surely, that would indicate a weak and sickly mind, and I don't believe anyone noted these symp-toms in Miss Morris before her death. Doctor? No, I thought not. And just where would she have to come up with this poison, locked up in Mrs. Willett's house?"

"It would appear," Montagu had to admit, "that we cannot be certain of how or why the girl died. But we might at least look at who might have had an opportunity to influence her. We ought to learn who else might have been nearby, on the night of her death."

"There's something in that," Phineas Wise replied, scratching the stubble on his long face. "We could question everyone who may have visited Mrs. Willett's house. Or yours, Richard, which is the only other close by."

"Perhaps," said Reverend Rowe in an unctuous voice, "I should help Constable Wise with his questions. Mr. Longfellow has suggested to me that we might find a Grand Inquisitor to be useful. I am no Torquemada, I'm sure, but I know my duty to my congregation. Do you know," he went on smoothly, "it occurs to me, Longfellow, that if it should be decided Phoebe Morris did away with herself, as the captain now suggests, then a court of law could hold you partly responsible. After all, you are the nearest householder—a thing Mrs. Willett herself cannot claim, since she remains on the property at her brother's pleasure."

Reverend Rowe was gratified to see small nods among the others, who felt obligated to bow to the law first, and to logic second. Thus fortified, the preacher went farther.

"I must say, sir, that I, and others in the village, have long been uneasy with the living arrangements you have lately engineered. For there was always a potential for great mischief in them, which you seemed to find of small concern."

"You would do well to be wary of village opinion yourself, Reverend." Richard Longfellow stood slowly, drawing himself to his full, impressive height. He had kept his temper in check, but had no hope, or desire, to keep it that way forever. "There might be more who believe there is also, in the arrangement of your own words, sir, a great potential for slander!"

Longfellow now had the satisfaction of seeing Reverend Rowe cringe before him. For the law in general, and lawyers in particular, were known to cut both ways. Then, summoning his wits, the clergyman forced himself to rise with a chilly smile. The others, too, stood with a clamor, hoping to ward off the storm that had begun to build around them.

With that, the meeting was adjourned, allowing the gentlemen to hurry out into the sunshine, where before long they offered others, unofficially, the benefit of their few and dubious conclusions concerning the sad death of Phoebe Morris.

AT THREE O'CLOCK, after an unceremonious dinner at Richard Longfellow's house (during which politics, rather than Miss Morris, were discussed), Charlotte Willett sat down to think at the desk in her study. Beside her, Diana lay on Phoebe's mattress, now stripped of its bedclothes, letting her fingers pull out some of the sweet straw that peeped from the stitches along the ticking. She had removed her turban, and her auburn hair fell from a gathering held up in the back by combs.

From her seat, Charlotte examined a portrait of her parents, drawn in charcoal by her sister Eleanor, which hung in a gilded frame.

"It's difficult to lose someone—even someone you have barely met," said Diana pensively. "It's difficult to know how to feel, or even what to say. Not that there's anyone to say much to, except for you, of course, Charlotte," she added. "And one can say nearly anything to you without worry."

"I am glad that you, at least, believe I will not bite."

"What was that?"

"It sounded like thunder, still far away."

"I'll go upstairs and have a look from the window."

Diana rose rather ungracefully, then unbuttoned and threw off her brocade bed gown in exasperation. Freed from its weight, she walked quickly and lightly to the door in her cotton shift.

"That's better," she said as she disappeared. Charlotte thought of taking up a pen, but decided Diana would only interrupt her when she returned. Instead, she rose and took a book from a shelf that held a variety of volumes from her own time, and those of her father and grandfather. Would a translation of Livy do for the evening? She thought not. Looking further, she saw a flowered cloth cover, a stranger among the rest. It sat behind the narrow bed that Phoebe had lately occupied. Charlotte reached over and pulled the volume out. She was surprised to find it was another sketchbook, much like those she had already seen. And the young woman's name was written inside the cover, with a date: 1761.

Leafing through the images, she saw that Phoebe's skills had improved in the intervening years, although her early work was quite detailed, and uniformly charming. There were several portraits of children, probably her brothers and sisters, as well as a rather severe older man, and a weary looking woman—no doubt her father and mother. How different from the couple on Charlotte's wall, who regarded each other with a love they'd long enjoyed. She thought for a bittersweet moment of her own brief marriage, and wished the miniature of Aaron was in its usual place on her desk, instead of across the way in her temporary bedchamber.

Looking farther into the sketchbook, Charlotte saw that at some point Phoebe had decided to try her hand at landscapes, in which a river and its surrounding fields and foliage played a large part. There were also expanses of grain, gold in the sun, drawn in colored crayon beneath a blue sky. Surprisingly, the sketches then changed to include scenes of Boston: crooked lanes with cramped houses, tiny front gardens, brick and cobbled streets. There was Faneuil Hall, with repairs being made after the fire; Long Wharf, with its mass of ship masts and rigging;

majestic Town House; a view of the harbor, and another of the green hills across the Charles.

Then there were other faces, more stylish poses. Here was a sketch with "Aunt Mary Morris" written below. It showed a woman who appeared to be kindly, holding a small dog on her lap. Another quick sketch showed a kitchen maid polishing silver. After that came an attractive, bewigged gentleman who looked familiar.

Charlotte sat down on the bed and closed her eyes. Then she looked again at the drawing of David Pelham. The fair complexion, the full lips, the soft expression of the eyes—these things were nearly the same today. In the sketch, he gazed at the artist with a look that seemed to express admiration, at least.

"There's a storm coming, I believe," Diana commented as she walked back into the room. She stopped in front of Charlotte. "The hills to the north are nearly purple, and there's a different kind of cloud overhead, which I'm sure Richard would bother me with the name of, were he here. What have you there?"

Charlotte pulled in her skirt and Diana sat, looking to the book in her friend's lap.

"It's David Pelham," Diana said softly. "Isn't it?"

"I think it must be."

"I haven't seen this book before." Taking the volume and scrutinizing its cover, Diana then turned through the first several pages. "It's earlier than the others Phoebe showed me. She probably thought it wasn't as good—it is quite good, though, isn't it? He almost looks as if he's dreaming."

"Like a man in love, do you think?"

"Possibly," Diana replied. "She certainly took great care in her work . . ."

"And yet he claimed not to know her."

Diana sat back, folding her arms. "When was that?"

"This morning, before we came to visit you—" She

stopped, remembering an earlier meeting when she had noticed David Pelham's clenched fist, and his sharp look to Dr. Tucker as soon as the physician had spoken Phoebe's name.

"I don't see why he would say that. He must have realized he'd soon see her again."

"I wonder," said Charlotte uneasily.

"Though I'm certain," Diana went on, "that I mentioned Phoebe to *him*—and of course, he said he'd come and see me often, as long as we both remained in Bracebridge. Oh—and he did inquire as to her treatment . . ."

"Are you sure Phoebe never mentioned David Pelham to you?"

"Quite sure! Since I'd recently seen him at the inn, I would have enjoyed telling her he was here—which I did not. *That's* why she gave him such an odd stare, standing there in the doorway, when she saw him leaving! She must have had no idea he was in Bracebridge. Judging by her expression, I suspect it wasn't an altogether pleasant surprise, either. After all, she must have realized he had come to see *me,* and not her."

"So he knew, and yet— well, it would seem they had a falling out, if he no longer chose to claim her acquaintance."

"Perhaps I should ask him. And I hope he has a good explanation!"

Both women were silent for several moments. Indeed, they were so deep in their separate thoughts that each was startled to see Dr. Tucker walk into the room, quite without warning.

"Ladies! I hardly expected to find you both in here; but when you were nowhere else—"

"Dr. Tucker!" cried Diana, sending her fingers to her hair.

"We were just speaking of Miss Morris," said Charlotte, "and we are unsure. Perhaps you might enlighten us."

"Yes, madam?"

"When you spoke with Phoebe, did she tell you she was acquainted with Mr. Pelham?"

Dr. Tucker's eyes darted to Diana's face.

"We ask," Diana explained, "because there is a drawing of him in one of Phoebe's sketchbooks." She picked up the volume in Charlotte's lap, and passed it to Tucker.

The man's response, thought Charlotte, was a perplexing one. As he looked down, his expression was grave; then, he seemed to wheeze, though from something other than mirth. Finally he looked up to Diana again. This time, there was determination in his eyes.

The moment he began to speak, a gust of wind blew in several curtains, upsetting a jar of violas Mrs. Willett had brought in earlier. Their water fell across the floor, and rolled toward a pair of satin slippers Diana had left by the hearth. She gave a piercing cry as she leaped forward to lift and shake them, fearing they would never recover; then, she danced about with the slippers at arm's length.

"Miss Longfellow! I must tell you—warn you!" the physician tried again.

"Yes?" asked Diana impatiently.

"You must know—"

"That I should be in bed? But I feel fine! In fact, I'm afraid if I lie cooped up in that room any longer I may lose my good nature entirely, and have to resort to rum, or worse! Do you know, Charlotte," she mused as she sat down once more, "I like this bed far better than my own. Perhaps I will move down here, and be closer to everyone. The scent from the garden is so pleasant. Yes, I *will* move down; I'll get Hannah to help me. She can carry in the folding screen from the next room, so I may also have a small dressing area, there in the corner. I hardly think anyone will object, since I've had the same treatment as Phoebe—although I hope to avoid the same result," she added, looking obliquely at Dr. Tucker.

"Miss Longfellow!" he cried again, extending both arms in supplication.

"I suppose it was not your fault, Dr. Tucker. In fact, I am almost positive of it. But I think I'd better move down here, you know. It will give me something new to do."

"It might be easier for Hannah," Charlotte agreed.

"But I beg you," the physician said with renewed effort, "if you insist on this move, to keep your window closed! The air, at this time in your treatment, may be harmful—quite harmful indeed! Keep your windows closed, and perhaps your door open. That way . . . you will benefit from the heat of the kitchen."

It was a strange idea considering the fine spring weather, and Charlotte began to feel some concern for the state of the doctor's nerves.

"We might all benefit from a return to rest and quiet," she suggested. "I'll take mine while visiting my cows, since it's nearly time to milk them again." Off to the north, she heard thunder echoing among the hills, while outside the windows the trees had begun to dive and thrash, exposing the silver undersides of their leaves to the dusky sky.

"A storm will perhaps clear the air," she added.

"I certainly hope you're right, Charlotte," said Diana, her expression an unusually thoughtful one. Staring at the leaves as if under a spell, Dr. Tucker made no reply at all.

CHARLOTTE WAS SLIGHTLY out of breath when she arrived at the dairy's door, and her hair, which she had neglected to cover, was in great disarray. She reached up to adjust its pins, while her eyes became used to the low light that filtered through a line of small, high windows above. Henry Sloan was waiting inside. Henry had recently reached the age of twelve and manhood, at least in his parents' eyes.

"Any word from Will?" she asked. For reply, she received only the ducking of a fluffy head. "Have you been told what to do if you see him?" This time, a nod, while the eyes beneath the light blond mop shorn straight around rose to watch her cautiously.

"It's very likely he's fine. If he's not, though, you'll have to think first of your brothers and sisters, Henry. He can come to my house—but *you* mustn't go in there, except as far as the door. But don't worry—even if he's ill now, he'll be home soon. And he might not mind resting from his chores for a week or two, while your mother brings him soup and biscuits in bed!"

"My mother says we aren't to talk of him. She says she can't bear it."

"Oh? Well, now, do you know what to do with an udder? Show me, and then I'll go to the next one, and while we work, we can talk."

Wondering if his mother or the rest of the family yet allowed young Henry to speak his mind, she watched the silent boy pull industriously at two teats, until a smooth flow matched his even rhythm. This was far better than the work of his devil-may-care brother, she quickly realized. A few years younger than Will, Henry already seemed to possess more sense, and appeared not to be the kind of boy who would find himself in trouble often. Charlotte thought of Lem, lying in bed, who had started in her dairy in much the same way. Then she imagined Will, out in the world alone, suffering terribly for the loss of his first true love—no matter what, or who, had caused it. Or was it just possible that Will Sloan, too, lay cold and still, like Phoebe? Was this what Hannah truly feared?

With a heavier heart, Mrs. Willett started up a rhythm of her own. Soon she was comforted by the patter of milk as it went into two pails, a pleasing staccato from four hands, against the placid chewing of the warm and gentle herd.

• • •

DR. BENJAMIN TUCKER stood alone in Longfellow's darkening study. He set down his empty sherry glass, and recrossed the room to look down again at the open rosewood box that held two matched pistols. He picked one up and examined it closely. It was not the first he'd seen; in fact, he'd watched similar weapons being loaded many a time, by young gentlemen showing off their toys together. He knew black powder from a small container went into the barrel first. Then a paper-wrapped, round-cast ball was seated firmly, tamped with the ramrod. After that, the curved steel plate on top was pulled back to half cock, and a smaller amount of powder was placed in the shallow pan beneath. Finally, the plate was lowered to cover the priming pan once more.

When he was done, he inserted the loaded pistol into the band of his breeches, so that its handle came up at the vent of his waistcoat. After he had settled his larger coat, he studied himself in Longfellow's Venetian mirror. How worn his features had become, he thought. How haggard, and how like his soul. He hadn't looked this way a week earlier, in Boston. But that had been before he'd seen David Pelham again. Why was there always something going wrong in his chaotic life? Money, rumor, bad luck, and, like a bad penny, Pelham, putting his nose where it did not belong. If only he had never run into the man again! And, of course, the irresistible child. She was the key player in their little drama. Was it coincidence that had brought them all together here? Or Aphrodite herself? He could easily blame Pelham; but who had done the worst, of the three of them? How could it have been helped, after all? And where would it all end, now that another prize, another beauty, was in sight? *Love sounds the alarm,* he heard again. But could anything make up for what had already occurred? Only one thing, he again decided.

Dr. Tucker poured and downed a final glass of sherry,

then turned and left the room, walked through the echoing entry hall. Outside, the trees whipped themselves into a frenzy. Long waves of wind raced down the meadow grass. Before him, the inn beckoned. Inside, there would be men and a few ladies having wine and punch, arranging for a little entertainment of some sort at the end of a long day. The heavens might provide them with their own show, he thought, looking up at the swirling clouds. But that was of little concern to him. He had something else to do with his evening.

Somewhat unsteadily, he walked across the lawn, then onto the road. Angling to one side of the inn, Tucker moved with purpose along the building, saw the side door, and stopped. Above him, safe on the second floor, David Pelham probably sat with a book in his hands, digesting his dinner. What plans had the man made to take himself into the night?

Dr. Tucker felt the weapon at his waist. He put one foot forward, then turned his head. Finally, pulling himself away, he continued to walk until he had left the inn and passed by the carriage yard behind. Increasing his speed, he went on to climb a sloping field. Eventually, he reached the trees. He took a small footpath that led into the forest. As he walked, he was aware of the whoosh of fresh leaves churned to a froth above him, as well as the menacing clouds overhead.

Suddenly, he stopped. With a last look down the hillside, he reached into his belt, and removed the pistol. He pulled back the cock as far as it would go, and positioned the barrel carefully against his temple. For a moment, he watched the tempest building above his head. Then, while Nature continued to moan all around, Dr. Benjamin Tucker let out a groan of his own, and pulled the trigger.

Chapter 10

—⌐ *Saturday*

FROM BENEATH THE works of an iron grinder, Cicero
slowly removed a box filled with a soft cone of fragrant
powder. As he lifted it to his nose, he enjoyed the pungent
aroma that marked the day's official start. Shuffling in his
slippers, he went to the hearth, lifted the boiling kettle,
and continued the unvarying routine for creating a heavy,
black elixir that made pale-tea drinkers quiver in their
shoes. How one could expect tea to clear the eye, let alone
wake the brain, was beyond understanding.

He decanted the liquid away from the sediment into a
warmed pot, slipped on a squat cozy, and set both on a tray
near bread for toasting, next to a block of butter. After
that, he moved the whole of the operation to the study,
where he knew Longfellow would soon be drawn by the familiar aroma.

Cicero poured some coffee into a bright Indian cup.
He sank into one of the two cushioned chairs that rarely

left the middle of the disordered room. A first sip revived him—the second he was actually able to taste—the third was ambrosial. He had heard the rain end in the night; now the air outside the tall windows sparkled with new clarity, as the sun played over shining leaves. It would be another lovely day.

Content with the progress of things so far, Cicero let his gaze run fondly around the study as he took his fourth sip. The leatherbound books with their gold-stamped spines awaited his choice; he'd finished one of their companions the night before. Perhaps, this evening, he would look into Pope again. The twisted little man had known what it was to suffer—although he usually got a bit back in the end. Yes, Pope would do well for a Saturday night.

Unexpectedly, Cicero's eyes spotted something not right. Specifically, they rested on a space where something should have been—but wasn't. Where, he asked himself, was the rosewood box?

When had the pistols last been moved? Longfellow rarely touched them, but he'd mentioned recently someone had found them interesting. Wasn't it David Pelham? Cicero looked around, then with some relief saw the box sitting on top of the piano. He would move it back to its place later. Still . . .

The old man walked to the box and opened it. Like a funnel of dust in a hot field, fear rose within him. One of the weapons was there. The other was gone!

Cicero set down his cup quietly, and went from the study into the hall. He climbed the broad steps to the second floor. Reaching the physician's door, he cocked his head to listen. He knocked, but received no answer. Gently, Cicero opened the door to peer inside. No one was there. He went in a few feet and looked around. Everything was tidy, all was orderly. So orderly, in fact, that he knew the chamber was just as it had been the day before, when he'd walked by and seen young Martha Sloan pulling the bed together. It hadn't been slept in since.

He considered for a moment more. Perhaps, since someone else had recently admired them, Longfellow had finally decided to try one of the pistols himself. It could be he'd gotten up early and taken one into the fields. But Cicero had heard nothing along those lines discussed the night before.

Stopping next at Longfellow's door, he heard a rustling. He waited. Richard Longfellow emerged almost immediately, wearing his usual linen trousers, a cambric shirt, and a colorful waistcoat, as yet unbuttoned.

"Umm?" Longfellow exclaimed with a start. "What are you up to? You can't have had more than one cup, since I only began to sniff it a moment ago. The house isn't on fire, I presume, or I would have smelled that, as well. What disaster has disturbed your morning routine? Ah! Another rat in the pantry. Did you think to call the cats?"

"One of your pistols is missing."

"Is it, indeed? Where do you suppose it's got to?"

"Dr. Tucker is not here, either."

"He is up this early?"

"I'd be surprised if he even slept here last night."

"Unusual," Longfellow commented, starting off down the stairs, although his shoes were as yet unbuckled. "What do you make of it? And when did you see him last?"

"Before he went to Mrs. Willett's to see his patients, and you and the captain walked off your tempers in the pasture."

"When we came in, after the rain started, I presumed Tucker had gone to bed early. After all, we can't be expected to amuse our guests all the time, nor they their hosts," Longfellow added, although it did seem to him now that he may have been remiss in his hospitality.

"He could have gone out later to visit Mr. Pelham at

the inn, and slept there," Cicero offered. "Or possibly, he met someone else he knew."

"Possibly. Or he could have wandered off to study the stars, I suppose, taking a weapon to counter his fear of the countryside."

"In the rain?"

"Well, he might have gone somewhere, and then decided to try his hand this morning at shooting waterfowl. Unlikely he'd hit anything with a pistol, but not beyond belief for a man from town to try. He did point out that he didn't like the things."

"Waterfowl?" asked Cicero with surprise.

"Pistols. He said they made him worry. Seemed to feel they were sinister."

When they regained the study, Cicero poured out two cups of coffee. "Should I wake Captain Montagu?" he asked.

"Let him sleep. He had no rest the night before this, and you and I kept him rather late last evening, as well. But I think . . ." said Longfellow, barely tasting the coffee as he gulped it down, ". . . I think I'll take the air." He quickly took the silver buckles for his shoes from a pocket, scowled as he realized the advisability of sturdier footwear, then put the buckles on anyway.

"Shall I come with you?"

"Let your toes uncurl at their own pace. Tucker may come back and require breakfast."

"We can hope for that," said Cicero, though without much conviction.

As soon as Longfellow finished buttoning his waistcoat, he lifted his coat from the back of a chair where he'd left it the night before.

"Yes. Let us *both* hope," he called back, dashing off through the study's doorway.

• • •

A FEATHERY TAIL swished back and forth as Orpheus moved over wet field grass, nose working, ears alert.

Charlotte Willett walked behind with her skirts raised, exposing high boots that might have been mistaken for her brother's, had they been larger. In truth, she had been fitted by a rough cobbler who lived in the village. Most Boston ladies she knew wouldn't have admitted to owning such things, but she greatly preferred them to Diana's iron pattens, or to wooden clogs, or certainly to getting her lighter shoes soiled and bedraggled while she explored the countryside.

Today, Charlotte had put on her boots and braided her hair to go on a search for mushrooms. She had already found several clusters that had sprouted overnight in a pasture, on mounds of rotting dung. They would be tasty in a stew. But after the heavy rain, she hoped, too, to find some forest mushrooms growing between the trees on the damp slope. Fried in butter, these would be a special treat.

With her braid swinging under a straw hat and a deep basket dangling on her arm, she led Orpheus back to the road, crossed it, and climbed the forested hills behind the inn. From a higher spot she could see sections of fields and fens to the north, where a light mist still rose into the sunshine. Her own way was yet in shadow. Even the birds had deserted the chilly shade to search for food in the brighter air below. She shivered again as the wind brushed by through weeping trees. The drops caused her to hurry on toward a glen where she had often had successful hunting.

Before Mrs. Willett reached her destination, Orpheus had overtaken her. The old dog suddenly turned and ran down a path that came up from below. She followed him with her eyes, then she was startled to see something brightly colored several yards off through the bushes, quite low to the ground. Too low, she thought with sudden unease. When nothing stirred after the dog's intrusion, she turned and followed the path through a thicket of elder-berry. At last, she recognized the russet coat, and the fa-miliar waistcoat. Though his head was hidden by ferns, it was surely Dr. Tucker. He continued to lie still, even as Orpheus snuffled at his ear.

The piercing cry of a flicker from the top of a high pine startled her, and made her swing around. Then she saw the wig, a few feet from where his hat had landed. Both were sodden and stained.

He must have tripped and fallen—but the physician lay on a fairly level spot, his feet seemingly free of vines or runners. She took another few steps forward to nudge a cluster of fronds away from the balding head, with its few short strands of damp hair. In another moment, she real-ized that a part of the doctor's skull had been lifted away. The ragged material around the larger of two holes had been washed clean of blood; some of the pale stuff inside had later been covered by a delicate new leaf partly de-voured, perhaps by a caterpillar, or some other treetop creature. Charlotte shuddered from head to toe. Yet as this passed away, she felt a new surge of curiosity. Finally, she forced herself to bend down.

She slipped tense fingers under Dr. Tucker's coat, wanting all the while to pull away. But she soon learned that the earth beneath him was dry. He must have died be-fore the rain, she reasoned, and remained there through-out the night. How sad to die alone—even when death was not unexpected. A few feet beyond the body lay Richard Longfellow's pistol. There had been no attempt to hide it, or to take it away; and who else could have bor-rowed it? She had to suppose something incredible—that Dr. Benjamin Tucker had taken his own life.

But she had seen him only hours before! How, she now asked herself, had he behaved? As the storm ap-proached, he'd become quite distraught. It had occurred to her at the time that the wretched man felt some

blame for Phoebe's death, and was greatly affected by it.
Yet hadn't there been more? She recalled the doctor's last
instructions. He was obviously concerned for Diana's
health. But hadn't he also urged her to have a care for her
safety, as well? He had told her to be careful of drafts . . .
and of windows! In the event that someone might enter?
But who? Could it have been—?

No. Oh, no! And yet—could it possibly have been
himself? Abruptly, she remembered the way Dr. Tucker
had gazed at Phoebe, the afternoon she'd left them alone.
His tender look had seemed to reveal both pleasure and
pain . . . perhaps even a sickness of the spirit . . . but surely,
he couldn't have been such a man? One who destroyed, after enjoying forbidden pleasure? Enslaved by amorous desires, yet perhaps inclined to warn, like a hissing snake,
before he struck?

Or, she asked herself after further reflection, what if
her own vivid imagination, inflamed by unhappy novels
that had lately come her way, led her now to conclusions
based on nothing but foolish, melancholy fancy? Was this
tendency not something she had often regretted in Diana's
dramatic and too quickly made pronouncements? Did not
this unfortunate man deserve something better, after all?

Again, the wind slashed through the branches above,
sending down more drops. Charlotte rose and stood looking out over the sunny landscape beyond. Then Orpheus
pressed against her, trying to move her away from the thing
that lay so still before them.

Mrs. Willett left her basket where she'd dropped it,
and hurried down the path. She might, she thought, stop
to ask for help at the inn. But what help could there be for
Benjamin Tucker now?

And so she continued on, out of the trees and across
the sloping field, skirts flying, past the gaze of landlord
Jonathan Pratt, who sat at his desk.

What could Mrs. Willett be up to now, Pratt asked

himself, straightening sharply. Craning his neck to the window, he saw her reach the road and cross it, gain the lawn, and leap past the trees that stood before Longfellow's house, before she vanished inside.

Sitting back, the landlord tried to imagine what this was all about, with little success. However, he assured himself, he could expect to hear more of whatever had happened soon enough.

RICHARD LONGFELLOW, HAVING seen Mrs. Willett running, hurried in from his own unsuccessful search. Upon learning the shocking news he sent Cicero to alert Constable Wise and Reverend Rowe. He himself woke Montagu. The two men then started out together, leaving Charlotte alone in the house while they went to recover the corpse—something, after all, hardly fit for a woman's eyes.

They found the physician lying as Mrs. Willett had described. Both stared into the jagged crater in the left side of his cranium, and at a small, powder-blackened hole opposite. Beneath the two, the all too familiar features remained—features that had been animated only the day before, when the doctor had joined them in conversation— kindly features now sadly stilled by the hand of a tormented soul.

"It is hard for me to understand," Longfellow admitted, "that a man would do *this* to himself, when surely he knew of far less unpleasant ways to leave the world."

"Perhaps he wanted to call attention to whatever drove him to the final act."

"I would imagine, then, that he's left some kind of explanation behind . . ."

They searched the doctor's clothing, but came up empty-handed. Longfellow next rose to retrieve his pistol, which still lay on the ground. With a frown, he put the thing into his pocket. Then he turned to study the corpse once more.

"It was thoughtful of him to come away," he said finally.

"Rather than do the thing in your parlor?" Montagu replied, sitting back on his heels. "Yet I think your villagers *will* be suspicious of you, Richard. From what I hear, you've lately taken on the characteristics of Beelzebub."

"Surely, they don't believe I am the very Devil?"

"I would be inclined to imagine Dr. Faustus myself," the captain replied with mock seriousness. "Unless, of course, our old friend here better deserves the role."

Longfellow unfolded a large piece of canvas he'd brought along, setting it down next to the corpse. "One tries to assist a fellow being out of kindness," he grunted, while both shifted Tucker onto the tarp, "thinking, too, of the good of his own family—and what does he get for his pains?"

"Involvement in the lives of others quite often forces distasteful tasks upon us." They lay hat and wig on top of their former owner, and rolled all up together. "Fortunately, Richard," the captain added, as he picked up his end, "no one can expect you to carry this sorry burden alone."

"We'll see about that," Longfellow returned skeptically.

Captain Montagu paused to pick up Mrs. Willett's abandoned basket. Then, lifting the heavy bundle to their shoulders, they started off together down the trail, finally gaining the meadow below.

Again, Jonathan Pratt stared out of his window; this time, his eyes protruded even more at what he saw. What were Longfellow and the captain doing with a rolled-up sheet, looking for all the world as if it contained a body? And with a picnic basket, as well?

The landlord stood just as Lydia Pratt came into the

room, searching for a copy of an order she'd recently sent to Boston. Fortunately, her husband's wide girth blocked her view.

"My dear," he said, offering her his chair, which he had turned from the window. "I believe I'll go out for a while. To take the air."

"And leave me to do your work," countered his spouse. "Go, then. I can do what needs to be done here, and you could certainly use the exercise! While you're out, go and tell Mrs. Willett she may have the lamb quarter she requested for their dinner tomorrow. It will be sent over this afternoon."

"Yes, my dear," answered Jonathan Pratt, smiling at what his wife did not know—and feeling an additional surge of anticipation.

ALL THAT REMAINED of Dr. Benjamin Tucker was deposited in a dim laundry shed behind Richard Longfellow's house. As sunlight struggled to penetrate small, bubbled sheets of glass, the corpse was viewed by Jonathan Pratt and by David Pelham, who had happened to observe the others and followed them. Mr. Pelham's acquaintance with Dr. Tucker led Longfellow to hope that he might assist them in setting this strange story right.

Next, having been summoned once again by Cicero, Reverend Christian Rowe appeared. The preacher glanced down with distaste at the mutilated head, before producing a handkerchief and carefully wiping at his fingers. Finally, Cicero himself returned with Phineas Wise. The constable lowered his eyes to the body, and raised them with a grim nod.

Richard Longfellow then ushered the men back to his house, and into the little-used great room. Charlotte and Cicero trailed unnoticed behind the rest. Two small cherry wood tables that had flanked the tall hearth were soon united, and chairs pulled from a set of two dozen standing along pale yellow walls. Longfellow himself threw open blue velvet curtains; suddenly, the sun streamed in, illuminating a blizzard of dust and a pair of crystal chandeliers. When he walked back to join the others, his steps echoed across the polished wood floor.

Partially hidden behind a screen, Mrs. Willett sat on a sofa once meant to be her sister's particular seat, well away from the rest. This she found rankling, for she might have taken a chair by any of her neighbors on a social occasion; however, the arrangement had the advantage of allowing them to overlook her presence, and of letting her stay to observe what females were usually not permitted to see.

When he had sent Cicero off for refreshments, Longfellow examined the four faces around the table. "It appears," he began, "that we have yet another body, with little to account for it."

"This fellow, though, wasn't about to become a member of our village," said Phineas Wise.

"He is our responsibility, I think, nonetheless."

"Well, it's obvious to me that the doctor arranged his own end, though for unknown reasons."

"I only wonder that he carried no written explanation, which I believe is the usual thing. And Tucker seemed quite content when he first arrived. He told me he looked forward to renewing his practice in town, once the smallpox abated. What do you say to all this, Mr. Pelham?"

"He told me the same." David Pelham leaned back, fingering the indigo scarf of a workman, which hung today over his frock-coat.

How like human nature for the rich (and lately even the royal) to enjoy dressing as if they were laborers and milkmaids, Longfellow observed, while the lower orders attempted to imitate dukes and duchesses—at least, those who could find the coin to waste.

"Did you speak with him last evening?" he finally inquired.

"No—though we spoke the other night of the slowing of business in the colonies, as well as his own misfortunes. And I agreed to help him, if I could. We'd not seen each other for many months; yet I supposed he was frequently despondent. I found Tucker to be a scattered man. One of many moods. Though not a bad sort."

"Nothing else?"

David Pelham looked carefully at Longfellow, seeming to weigh something in his mind. Then he answered quite firmly, his face becoming smooth again.

"Nothing else."

"I suppose there is little doubt." Longfellow sighed deeply, considering human frailty for a moment before returning to his duty. "Phineas, how is your other investigation proceeding?"

It was Reverend Rowe who answered. "As well as can be expected, when few will admit to knowing or seeing anything at all. At least to us—yet they break off talking of it among themselves as soon as we appear!"

"Thus far," the constable went on, "we have been unable to discover if the girl had another lover, or that Will Sloan had any desire to abandon his wedding plans. His mother will say little—but it seems the girl's time is well accounted for, and she received no letters, apart from those that came from her own family."

"But something here is not right," the reverend insisted. "I believe there is still strong reason to suspect evil in our midst." He then gave a terrific start, and his head ducked under the table; in a moment, his shout sent a spitting cat flying. More than one set of eyes was averted as Reverend Rowe rose up, glaring.

"As to Will Sloan," said Longfellow mildly, "I've now sent queries to Worcester and Concord. Thus far I've heard nothing. I suspect Boston would be too big a jump for the lad—at any rate, with the state the town's in, few would have noticed him there. It is a shame, Reverend, that you've received little for your trouble here, though I find it hardly surprising."

Jonathan Pratt quickly added his own thoughts. "I do not see the point of explaining my whereabouts every hour of the evening, from dusk to dawn—which we only *suppose* to be the time something might have been done to Miss Morris. I wonder, Reverend, if you would answer such questions *yourself*, another time? No, I thought as much."

"I expect to keep at least some things my own business, as well," said David Pelham.

"Yet Mr. Pelham has given us his oath," said the constable, "and has sworn that he remained in his room all the evening, reading an improving book with a bottle of Madeira for company. If I'm not mistaken," he added, his face showing a Yankee's pain at a profit lost, "here is more of the same."

Cicero came in with a tray that held two bottles and a half-dozen glasses, one of which he filled and took across the room to Mrs. Willett.

"As for last evening, Mr. Pelham," Reverend Rowe asked, obviously hoping to add to his meager arsenal of blame, "where were you then?"

"Last night? I recall that I had a supper of oysters and ale; then I sang lustily with a handful of others in Mr. Pratt's taproom, to counter the thunder, until well after the storm broke. The old fellow must have been dead then, for I cannot see a physician risking his health by walking out into the pouring rain, even to shoot himself."

It seemed to Richard Longfellow that Mr. Pelham was somewhat deficient in feeling, so odd was the latter's mood, given their grim discussion. He seemed to go from sense to rattle with little warning—one of the many annoying symptoms of courtship. Ah, well. Considering what

Diana had done to her other suitors, Pelham would soon become sober again. "Just where does this leave us?" he turned to ask Phineas Wise.

"In my official capacity," said the constable, "given what you have told of finding the body and the weapon, I believe Dr. Tucker to be a suicide. Doubtless his action stemmed from melancholy, due to the unfortunate death of the young woman in his care. I would add that I believe the death of Miss Morris to be the result of natural causes, influenced by the inoculation, perhaps, but also by the delicate nature of many a female constitution. I suppose the village will see it that way—and that they will accept our verdict in both cases, if the selectmen concur. This should make an appeal to the Middlesex authorities unnecessary. But, we should wait a little for Will to show up, I think, before we tell the world our conclusions. Just in case we're all wrong," he added under his breath.

"I agree it's what the village would prefer to think," said Longfellow. "And most of us would rather not bother the sheriff in Cambridge! If we have reason to suspect anything more after Will's return, then we might still take the matter to a justice of the peace. But I doubt it will come to that."

There was a chorus of relieved approval. "Unless, of course," Captain Montagu suddenly suggested, "there is one among you who will press for further action, for his own reasons."

"Who? Who would do such a thing?" Phineas Wise looked about with alarm.

"Last autumn, I watched as one of you rallied the village to threaten the life of an innocent man, while asking others to imagine the worst of one of the gentlest among you. Did you not, sir?" Montagu concluded, pointing a finger across the table at Reverend Christian Rowe.

There were gasps at the audacity of the remark, for Reverend Rowe, as a representative of the church, enjoyed a position of moral leadership even among those who often found his words distasteful. But the preacher replied with a smile that was politeness itself.

"I was glad to admit my error," he owned easily. "But we are all under the eye of the Lord. And none should fear honest inquiry on His behalf. Such inquiry is never a personal matter, for I am sure we are all friends here, and fellows in God. In the same spirit, however, I might remark that once again we find Mrs. Willett and Mr. Longfellow involved in a most peculiar death—this time, while they both reside under one roof. As I have said before, that fact has already aroused the suspicion of others . . . but I will keep an open mind, and say no more."

In the silence that followed, Constable Wise blew his nose loudly on a not too clean piece of linen, which he then stuffed back into his breeches. "For now, then, we're in accord," he told Longfellow. "The week's events are tragic, but they require no charges. However, we have one more problem that needs solving. Who will be responsible for Dr. Tucker's body?"

"A suicide cannot be laid to rest in the churchyard," Rowe stated flatly.

"Then," said Longfellow, "as I brought him here to Bracebridge, I'll take the responsibility. I shall send word to his household this afternoon, though I doubt it will do much good. For the moment, Tucker can stay where he is."

After addressing a few more details over another fortifying glass, the men rose to their feet. Longfellow moved to Mrs. Willett, bottle in hand, and sat down beside her on the sofa. "I've been asking myself," she began, after accepting a second glass, "who will see to Lem and Diana, now that Dr. Tucker is gone."

"Thankful Marlowe at the Three Crows once recommended a Worcester man. But I suspect we can do as well ourselves."

"Richard, do you suppose people *are* talking . . . about the two of us?"

"People are always looking for something to worry them, Carlotta. But we might discuss that thrilling possibility tomorrow, at our leisure—for Rowe has ordered my entire household to stay away from Sunday meeting until we lift the quarantine. Remind me, too, that I should discuss village etiquette with Captain Montagu. Now, I shall go and break the news of Tucker's death to Diana. I'm sure Edmund will want to join me. But I'd better show my other guests out, first—or they might decide to take a tour of our bedchambers, and stay to dinner!"

There was little point or reason, Charlotte told herself, to argue with the conclusions she had overheard. And yet, every man present had neglected several muddy questions. Exploring them further herself, she decided, might allow her mind to rest more easily. And then there was the question of Phoebe's final rest, as well. . . .

Warmed and fortified by the wine, Mrs. Willett went forward to gather what she could. She had no notion of where her inquiries would lead. But at least she had an idea of where they might begin.

Chapter 11

CHARLOTTE RETREATED FROM the bustle of the hall and climbed to the second story of Richard Longfellow's house, where four bedrooms stood in a row. Here, she usually went left toward her own chamber, just before Cicero's at one end. But this time she stopped, reconsidered, and turned the other way.

Longfellow's was the last room of the east corridor; she knew it had the advantage of the morning light. The nearer of the two, next to her own, was usually given to Diana on her visits, though lately it had been the temporary home of Dr. Tucker. She turned the brass knob and walked in. The bed still had its coverlet in place, over a freshly mounded featherbed. There was a large trap standing open on a chair; at the foot of a bedside table stood another bag she'd seen before, which held medical supplies and instruments. On the table itself, she saw a red volume—a recent publication on wildlife in the southern colonies.

After studying a startling engraving of a leaping panther, Charlotte put the book back by the oil lamp. Then she attacked the larger of the two leather cases. It revealed only stockings and shirts, another coat, and a pair of satin breeches. But she soon discovered something of far more interest in the drawer of a writing desk that stood against a wall, across from the four-poster. In a dimpled pigskin wallet she found four letters, each one dated months before. All were from Williamsburg, and written by someone named Jeanette, apparently a charming young woman with a wealth of family anecdotes. In a few moments, Charlotte realized that Dr. Tucker had been Jeanette's father.

The girl gave information of a brother at sea, and a smaller sister still at home. It seemed both girls, as well as their mother, lived with friends, rather than in an establishment of their own. A final letter dated the previous autumn was especially affecting, as it foresaw her father's return.

Dearest Sir (Charlotte read with growing unease), if You are doing well in Boston, and are regaining some of what should rightfully be yours for your Skills and Efforts, I am sure we all encourage you, for we know you will send for us when you feel ready. But if, as I begin to fear, You are not entirely well, and your Work and its Rewards do not come as you expect, then I wish you would return to a place where we can at least offer you comfort, and give you Happiness through the closest ties Heaven bestows. We will not heed, I promise you, what others say, for we refuse to believe you have anything with which to reproach yourself, or to hide!

I must sadden you by writing that my Mother

is not well. Most of the time, she keenly feels the great distance between Herself and her Husband. There is a good chance, however, that we will soon have access to a little money, if I am joined to a Gentleman who is always in my heart. He is not wealthy, but his chandlery is growing. I will learn to help him in his Shop. If what I hope occurs, you may yet be able to return to your own dear house again, as I will be able to discharge, each quarter, a little more of what is owed to our creditors.

Dearest Papa, I cannot imagine that the Lord above, who has somehow allowed your Home and your Reputation to be lost to you, has no plans to again raise a Man so valued by the many sufferers to whom he has given assistance. I am sure it is only a matter of time before the world sees you in a truer light, and you are freed from your burdens. It is a thing I pray for daily.

With every hope of seeing you soon, and love from us all,

Jeanette

Charlotte refolded the letter and sat down to think. What, exactly, had Dr. Tucker done, that forced him to abandon his family and seek a new practice in Boston? Was it something to do with his medical treatments? Then again, it may have been something more personal. It could have had something to do with the physician's fondness for the bottle; she'd begun to suspect he often drank far beyond good sense. Perhaps it was gambling. She had heard this was a pastime often practiced to extremes, with sad results, south of New England. Clearly, whether he was at fault or not, Dr. Tucker had felt his situation deeply. Still, his hopes were high when he arrived. Perhaps that was because he had a new chance to attract clients, and believed his life would soon improve, and his family be reunited with him. Had something occurred to end those hopes before his plan had a chance to succeed? His own death must have had something to do with the death of Phoebe Morris. But what? It seemed his daughter did not believe him capable of any serious error. But of course the whole truth might have been kept from her, for good reason.

She thought of Jeanette's future, clouded by Benjamin Tucker's suicide—and then of Phoebe, today lying under the churchyard sod, though none too permanently. One's fate might be unbearably cruel. It was no wonder some pinned their greatest hopes for happiness on Death's mercy, rather than the Lord's help for the living. Yet death was surely a part of His plan for all—and since it was inevitable, should any of them be greatly blamed for hoping to hurry it along?

Amazed at her own presumption, Charlotte closed her eyes, then glanced about the room once more. In a basket she spied crumpled paper, but closer investigation revealed only two wine corks, a few scribbled drawings, and the first lines of a poor attempt at poetry. Then, with growing curiosity, she opened Dr. Tucker's bag of medicines and examined its contents. Most of the things inside she did not recognize, for there was little in the way of herbal remedies. But she made a note in her mind of the labels on the containers of liquids and pills she did find, apparently compounded by a Boston apothecary, although the labels indicated not their contents, but their uses. Sniffing told her little more, beyond the fact that some were highly flavored, and a few smelled thoroughly vile.

Finally, Charlotte repacked and closed the doctor's friend of many a hard campaign, and left the small, worn bag beside the other. They were, she thought with pity, the last useful remnants of a man who might have been pathetic, but had not been entirely unloved.

• • • •

MRS. WILLETT TRIED to rest on her bed for three quarters of an hour. Finally she gave it up; but when she rose, it was with a new idea in mind.

Swiftly, she modified her earlier walking outfit by putting on a fresh blue apron. She unbraided her hair and twisted it into a knot, which she covered with a small lace cap. Finally, she changed into prettier slippers, knowing she would not be walking far.

Minutes later, Charlotte crossed the road and entered the front hall of the Bracebridge Inn, where she looked around to see if she would be successful in avoiding Lydia, and fortunate in finding Mr. Pelham. Peering into the fragrant taproom, she saw her quarry sitting by a window, sipping ale and eating crisp rolls. Amazed at her own boldness, she walked over and stood near his table until he looked up.

"Mrs. Willett! I'm enjoying a late breakfast, after our disquieting morning. Would you join me?"

"I only wished to remind you, Mr. Pelham, that we'll be pleased to see you at dinner on Sunday . . . if you will still come."

"Nothing could stop me! Did you believe something might?" he asked in a softer tone.

"I have heard some say lately that they would prefer other company to ours, at least for a few weeks more."

"I can think of no company I find more pleasant," he replied, helping her into a seat across the small table.

"In fact," she went on, "I have been hoping to talk with you, especially after what happened today—or I should say last night. May I ask you if you knew Dr. Tucker well?"

"I suppose I did," replied David Pelham, folding his hands before him. "Let me see. I first met Benjamin Tucker about three years ago, when I had need of a physician and little money to pay one. Tucker had just come to Boston with funds to set up a new practice. But sadly, he tried to increase this amount by investing in a land company. It was the old story. Wanting more, he lost all that he had. I must confess I introduced him to some friends, engaged for a time in speculation . . . though only after he pleaded with me to do so. Unhappily, their holdings became worthless the moment the King's Proclamation forbade further settlement in the West. Bad luck, I thought—though shortly before, I was unhappy at having no money to invest myself! But there is Fortune for you. Well, after that, inevitably, Tucker and I saw less of one another. I soon married, and then employed the physician recommended to me by my wife; she already had him about her much of the time, as he treated her for a chronic complaint. Her life was an unhappy one," David Pelham added gently. "Dr. Lloyd did what he could, but in the end she was taken from us. Though I'm sure you have little desire to hear of any more misfortunes, at the moment."

Charlotte took the hint, and found another topic. "Did you and Dr. Tucker once count Miss Morris among your mutual friends in Boston? Oh—but I forget you told us you never knew her. . . ."

Pelham sat quietly, and studied her face closely before he replied.

"It is what I said, madam, and for that, I must apologize. It wasn't quite the truth—as I suspect you know."

"I found your likeness in one of Phoebe's sketchbooks."

"I see! You must understand, Mrs. Willett, that my circumstances have altered greatly since the day I sat for my portrait. With a very meager income, I struggled then to make ends meet. I also found myself living near a good lady by the name of Mrs. Morris, who seemed sympathetic to my circumstances; happily she considered my name to be a truer indication of my worth than the poor state of my purse. When her young niece came to visit, the aunt introduced us, and after that day I spent several pleasant afternoons with Miss Morris. I posed for her pencil; we walked about the Common. She was, of course, barely sixteen. I offered her my protection, as she was one of the family of my friend and neighbor. But you will imagine my distress— how can I tell you?—when Phoebe presumed to offer me more than I could accept. I had no wish to encourage the young lady, and so I began to avoid the house. Then, Miss Morris went back to Concord. It was the last I heard of her."

David Pelham drew himself up with a deep intake of breath and looked down, as if offering a silent prayer for the unfortunate girl.

"I do know," Mrs. Willett replied with sympathy, "that young women can imagine attachments, even to gentlemen who only show them kindness. But surely, by now . . . ?"

"There *was* more," he replied unhappily. "Although, for the sake of her family, I'd hoped to keep it to myself. We all become world-wise, with time . . . yet I think, in this instance, there was something in Phoebe—which may be unfair to tell of," he decided abruptly. Then, as suddenly, he changed his mind again. "But no, I will go on to you, madam—though I will confess it still gives me great pain to think of it! You see, I had begun to suspect I was not the first gentleman for whom Phoebe had developed a strong liking. She seemed to have a knowledge of amorous behavior that I found unsettling, in one so young. Something in her eyes reminded me, I'm afraid, of what I had seen on the faces of those girls who so often approach one in the low streets, by the docks. I hope I do not shock you, but when I heard Captain Montagu describe such a scene lately, I was again reminded of that penetrating look. The aunt did hint—she even attempted to warn me, I believe, after she'd seen us both out walking—for Phoebe was always quite gentle and well-mannered while in Mrs. Morris's home. But I had to believe there was some added spark, something unnatural, in fact, in the girl's constitution.

Something I supposed she could not control. Perhaps, she never even saw it as wrong! I felt I could not blame her; but this week, I was appalled to see her here, in a house with Miss Longfellow!"

"Oh?" Charlotte asked, smiling without quite meaning to.

"I blush to admit this, for I suspect she hardly knows—but that beautiful young lady has made a strong impression on my own poor heart! You must understand, Mrs. Willett. I feared my visits to your house might encourage Phoebe once again, especially as I am now considerably more eligible. I had also heard that Phoebe was about to marry, having made an appropriate match. And Heaven help the man who steps between a country lad and his maid! I would imagine that these fellows have a number of likely weapons at their disposal. And I saw that this boy, Will Sloan, might well resent me."

"Some do suffer, when they find they're not the first to stir a girl's heart," Charlotte responded. Then she stopped and looked across the taproom, listening for a moment to her own thoughts.

"Would you like a glass of cider, Mrs. Willett? Or perhaps a sherry?"

She seemed not to hear him. "And the doctor's death?" she went on. "Had you any idea he was capable of such a thing?"

"Well . . . I realized he had a problem with drink, of course."

"More than most?" she asked, knowing befuddlement to be a common occurrence.

"Oh, yes. I'm sure Tucker couldn't drink steadily, because of his work. But occasionally, as I recall, he drank to great excess, which tends to unbalance the best of men. And most especially those who have fallen into sad circumstances. I hope I've not alarmed you with my frank answers, Mrs. Willett. But I did want to set your mind at ease. And perhaps, in doing so, my own."

"I'm afraid you may feel I've been too inquisitive, Mr. Pelham."

"A characteristic of ladies of intelligence, well worth the pain it sometimes causes. And you never know when you might hear something interesting from such a person, even about yourself," he added, seeming to invite her comment. When none came, he continued. "Now, I have a question for you, madam."

"Of course."

"Will you be seeing Miss Longfellow today?"

"I'm about to go and see her now. Would you like me to take a message?"

"You might ask if she will allow me the pleasure of a visit later this afternoon, to express my sympathy for the sudden loss of her physician. I'll also inquire of her maid if Miss Longfellow is well enough to see me, when I arrive."

"Hannah?" asked Charlotte, picturing the woman's reaction to her new title. "Certainly," she said with a smile. "I'll tell them both of your intentions."

"I would be obliged. Now, if you'll excuse me, I must go up and answer some correspondence. I'm afraid I haven't had much time to think of my own affairs lately. Life in the country is hardly what I had imagined," he concluded as he escorted Mrs. Willett to the inn's front door.

"It does often hold surprises," she agreed, with a growing interest in the handsome, and most considerate, Mr. Pelham.

IN MRS. WILLETT's study, Edmund Montagu remained with Diana Longfellow after her brother had broken the news and gone away again. She soon adjusted herself to the dreadful surprise; then, rather than dwell on the tragic nature of the doctor's death, she began to decide how it was likely to alter her own future.

"Though I doubt he'll be missed, really," she declared, fanning herself. Today, Diana sat at Mrs. Willett's desk, leaning with less than her usual perfection of carriage. The captain, too, seemed somewhat more relaxed than usual. "For I am quite well," she continued, "and Charlotte makes Lem more comfortable than Dr. Tucker ever could. I've asked myself more than once where Richard found the man. He was not at all successful, I'm sure of that—otherwise, I would have heard of his practice long ago. He did express a high opinion of Boston; but I suppose he *would* admire our society, though he was hardly a part of it. Society is often a useful beacon for the lower people."

Captain Montagu merely nodded.

"Only imagine what would happen," Diana continued, suspecting a lack of agreement, "if popular tastes had no check! If some of the North End had their way, we might see the drinking of rum in the streets—as one sees gin consumed in London! Then we would receive even less respect from people of that place, than we are grudgingly given now!"

"I hadn't realized you found British respect worth cultivating—or that you had ever found it difficult to obtain."

"I speak not of myself, of course, but of the colonies, which London seems to think are something less than civilized."

"I myself have lately found a lack of fastidiousness here in Boston, compared with that of London society," the captain rejoined.

Diana's look became a frown. "And I assure you, Captain, it is just the opposite! Most here are daintier than those I have seen at Court! London ladies do seem to have a great problem keeping their necks and faces clean. Though there's little surprise in that, as they live under a constant cloud of smoke, which has given the entire city a shopworn appearance."

"I refer to fastidious behavior, rather than appearance," the captain corrected, "having lately been assured that females on this continent expect far greater liberties than do our own. At the same time, they seem less likely to strive to earn them, I think. Which could explain why women are respected less by colonial men, than by British gentlemen."

"Surely, now you're trying to make me laugh!"

"For instance, I sometimes witness simple flirtation in Boston gatherings, but I believe it is a rare American who expects to find either wit or learning among the ladies here. Can you imagine your brother willingly attending a Boston *salon,* if you had such a thing?"

At this, Diana did laugh, but there was a certain edge to her reply.

"We have little need for *salons,* Captain, for most of us prefer the company of friends and family to hobnobbing with near-strangers, in the hopes of swooning at a *bon mot!* As for our character, you must admit Americans are satisfied enough to find fewer mistresses than those in London generally do. I gather they are *de rigueur* now, among those of high standing in the capital."

"What is done by a few differs greatly from what most of us expect of our sisters, and our wives. The King, you must admit, is known and praised for his virtuous behavior—"

"And has a large family on the way, I'm sure!"

Miss Longfellow feared for a moment that she might have gone too far, but the captain did not seem perturbed.

"It is to be hoped. What is most peculiar," he continued, "is that in Massachusetts, though some of you imagine yourselves part of a society of your own, you are all cut from much the same cloth, and none is entirely sure of his, or her, place. Consequently, when your people hear the theories of Rousseau, and the other levelers—too often published in your press, and even preached in your streets!—then the men become encouraged to go out and practice an equality of behavior which those of real breeding must find confusing, and even abhorrent. Meanwhile, many women begin to believe they can behave much as a man might, with little regard for what is proper."

"To whom, specifically, do you refer?" Diana countered coldly, both hands now on her knees as if she might spring.

Montagu fixed her with piercing eyes before he replied. "To the girl who died here this week, for one. Phoebe Morris should serve as a warning to others, if it's found that she drove her explosive fiancé to a murderous passion by her light behavior, which I think quite likely . . . though I realize it is not your own view of the situation."

"Phoebe! And Will Sloan? I hardly think—!"

"Ladies sometimes don't, until it is too late. But when dealing with certain kinds of men, there is always a chance flirtation may lead to disaster."

"That can be true, if one is not careful, Captain. But tell me, do you also insist that young gentlemen spend their entire youth being very, very good?"

"I insist that a gentleman should have a conscience, and refrain from helping any female to pursue desire to its ultimate end, if that might bring about her ruin."

Diana gave him a peculiar smile before going on.

"Well, Edmund, just how should a man obtain a certain knowledge, then? For I am sure most men feel it their right—even their duty—to learn something of life before marriage. For instance, have you never . . . ?"

Montagu blinked at the directness of her query, but kept his composure. "A better question would be, has my sister ever . . . though I hardly think there is any possibility of that! Young men, of course, may also ruin their health and happiness, for too often they become—"

Montagu stopped abruptly, then adopted a gentler air. "Today I warn, of course, of lesser liberties than the final error . . . yet that end often comes from very small beginnings."

"Like the mighty oak? But let us return to my question, Captain. Let us rule out sisters, then—and wives, of course! That leaves only someone's aunts and cousins, I believe, on which the great burden of educating young men must fall. Unless it is possible that you have one or two of *those*, as well? You'll notice I spare us both embarrassment by leaving our mothers out of the discussion."

"Miss Longfellow!" This time, he thought, she *had* gone too far.

"Oh, I really don't look for much in the way of liberty, Edmund," Diana pleaded. "But as you have a sister, I believe you are obliged to look on our sex with more compassion, and give us just a little room to breathe—and to explore life's many possibilities! We are none of us, I am sorry to say, made of the same material as the angels. And after all, what is a little talk?"

"A little talk, madam, has been known to lead to ostracism from honorable society, even in America!"

"It might, I suppose, in extreme circumstances. But do you suppose no man can be discreet?"

"Men who are not are common enough."

"Exactly. And I make it a point to have little to do with such common men. I thought you might know that of me by now," she added, pouting prettily.

"Then do you seek out one with high ideals—so you can encourage him to leave them behind at your pleasure? It would seem you play a game of paradox, Miss Longfellow."

"Let us just suppose," Diana tried carefully, "that a young lady warms to a man she believes to be worthy of her trust. Even if he should disappoint her, and their intimacy is spoken of, it will be her word against his. But would not the lady be believed? It is universally held, after all, that we are the more truthful sex."

"If only one man's story of shared passion is whispered to the world, a lady might be safe—although she would no longer be honest."

"At any rate once she has aged—say, to thirty—none of it will matter. As long as she has had nothing proven against her, then her understanding of life will be assumed—especially, sir, if she should live in London! But her own knowledge will have made her more sure of her choice when she *does* marry, and will have done no real harm as long as nothing obvious has come of it. When she marries, all must give her due respect—or face the consequences of dealing with her husband!"

"Do you mean to tell me Phoebe Morris could not have been compromised, or felt the effects of such an event, unless the fact reached the world's attention? Could not its falling on one beloved ear have been enough to ruin her happiness?"

"Well—" Diana replied uncertainly.

"I'm quite sure you say these frightful things to amuse others, or to please yourself. But you may be in greater peril than you know. I have no idea how far you will choose to walk out along a garden path. But I have a good idea of how far you might be led, Diana, or even dragged, and to what object."

Miss Longfellow blanched at having such a crude warning laid directly at her feet. "Do you refer to yourself, Captain Montagu? For we all know what *soldiers* are capable of. They have their own reputation, which I believe many of you even boast of, do you not? And you are, you know, alone with me now. Yet I must say I see no dangerous passions in you! Nor have I since last October."

"I only wish to say that a person of beauty and worth should be careful in this world. Caution is especially necessary when one has left the city, where forms are more likely to be maintained, and has come into the wilder countryside."

"To set your mind at ease, I'll promise to refrain from frequenting haystacks in the fields, as soon as I'm let out of this accursed house! For now, I really don't see what harm can come to me here."

"Do you not?" he replied so seriously that Diana squinted slightly, to better study his expression. What she saw displeased her less than it unsettled her.

"But you don't think—you can't mean Mr. Pelham? How unfair of you to try to sway me, Edmund. For you must know he is your rival for my affection!"

"As you'll recall, I have never professed love to you, Miss Longfellow . . . although I will admit to an admiration that has grown quite strong, in the company of your brother, your mother, and others of merit."

"Well, he is," said Diana to herself, thinking that the captain held his affections quite high above his head at the moment—like a man crossing a rising stream. Why was it, she wondered, that he withdrew whenever she began to refer to his feelings, or to her own?

Montagu stood, picked up his hat, and bowed over it. "I'll go and see how the boy does, and then take my leave. I must allow you to rest and regain your composure— especially when I remember the news you've had today. It can't have been pleasant for you, and for that I'm truly sorry."

"No, it wasn't, indeed," Diana replied.

"It's not necessary for a woman to be an angel," the captain added when he was at the door, "but it does her no harm to be wary."

"Perhaps I should keep a sweet old dog around me, like Mrs. Willett does, to discourage the more dangerous variety. Do you think you might enjoy performing that sort of duty, Captain?"

"Possibly," said Montagu, turning with what seemed

to Diana to be an almost brotherly smile, which she thought was rather horrid.

MUCH LATER, ACROSS the garden at Longfellow's house, Mrs. Willett again lay upon her bed, while Orpheus stretched on the floor at her side. It had been another difficult day. Shortly after dawn, she had found Dr. Tucker. Then she had watched a group of men, most of whom she admired, in one way or another, struggle to organize their thoughts while trying to decide what could be happening in Bracebridge.

She had wished to ask a few questions on her own, but of course, at the time it had been impossible. In the morning she would be able to speak more about what had gone on, with Richard Longfellow. For now, she reached for the hand mirror by the side of her bed and examined her face closely, pulling back her soft hair and trying to see under her chin. Satisfied, she also looked carefully along her arms and under her shift, then lifted each leg from the covers for a final perusal. Since Dr. Tucker's warning, she was less certain of her own safety, and of the benefits of cowpox. And then there was the prophecy of Mrs. Proctor, as well as the parrotlike concurrence of Mrs. Hurd. . . .

But nothing alarming had appeared on her face except for a worried expression, and two reddened eyes. Sleep would be welcome. Thankfully, she blew out the candle.

Yet sleep was clearly not going to come until she addressed some of the things that capered together at the far reaches of her brain. At least, Diana was still feeling well, and Lem's illness was progressing as expected. His face had several blisters, which had started to open and tickle him. He was forbidden to scratch, for that would only make the pocks worse. But his fever was broken, and he had enjoyed the sherbet she'd taken him in the afternoon.

Diana now seemed more upset by Captain Montagu's

latest visit than by any fear of the smallpox. Charlotte had heard one participant's version of what had been said between them, which sounded less than flattering to Diana—though Miss Longfellow herself had repeated it! She knew Diana was often more reasonable than her quick words would lead one to believe, and that her sense was not at all deficient. But she might be easily angered, and in that state, who knew what a woman might say, or do? Especially now, it would be far better for Edmund to soothe, than to annoy. It was something she might mention to the captain tomorrow. At the moment, however, she wished only to roll over and go to sleep.

Diana had seemed far more pleased to talk of David Pelham, who made his own brief but adoring visit after Montagu had gone away. Mr. Pelham, too, was concerned for Diana's well-being, threatened as it was by the illness he himself had recently suffered. According to Diana, Pelham had cheered her by telling rollicking stories, after she'd insisted—stories traditionally told by ladies and gentlemen in strange houses, while being "done" together for the smallpox. Apparently, it could be a very amusing time. It was too bad, Diana had decided, that her own group had been reduced to such a pitiful thing. But then, it would all be over soon.

(Perhaps, Charlotte considered, she might ask Richard to send over a volume of the *Decameron*? But no, perhaps not.)

She had then related to Diana her own conversation with David Pelham, held earlier that afternoon. Diana had been interested to hear how Pelham had confessed to meeting Phoebe under circumstances that were honorable, after all. His answer for why he had first refused to admit his acquaintance with the girl caused Diana to nod with approval. There was no doubt Mr. Pelham was considered a catch by many of the Boston ladies, now that he possessed not only an old name, but money, too—as well

as a casual charm that had taken generations of family influence to develop . . . according to Diana. All in all, she
felt he was right to avoid contact with the sort of person
who might take advantage of his situation, while unable to
give anything of value in return. It only made sense, to
Miss Longfellow.

(Would that owl never stop?)

And a gentleman would, of course, be suspicious of a
young woman who had once thrown herself in his way, and
was now promised to another. That was only natural. Diana was sure Mrs. Morris of Boston, the lady with the lap-
dog, could hardly have known what she had on her hands,
when her niece arrived with sketchbook and crayons.
Why was it, Diana had asked Charlotte, that country folk
often supposed those in Boston to be dangerous, when it
was more often the other way around?

(Perhaps, if she rolled over again . . .)

She was less sure than Diana of the relative dangers of
country and city. But Charlotte did think she understood
some of what lay behind the captain's warning against
David Pelham. Early in their acquaintance, she remembered, Captain Montagu had spoken of being sent to save,
or at least to remove, young men of good family from bad
surroundings, after they had found the temptations of
military life too great. He must also have seen young ladies
of both high and low birth (and, presumably, virtue) injured by the disgraceful behavior of the well-born. Montagu himself answered to higher standards; in fact, Charlotte
suspected the captain was, by nature, somewhat over-
critical of his own behavior. His aristocratic upbringing
had no doubt taught him the value of control, and of maintaining an impenetrable façade—while Diana's childhood
had given her feelings that were exactly the opposite. At
the moment, he must view her abrupt displays of willful
behavior as an embarrassment for them both—and one
he could do little to avert. Was it any wonder, especially

since Edmund Montagu seemed to be truly fond of Diana, that he wanted to protect her from herself, and from others? He feared she might be injured—but he, too, was liable to be hurt, thought Charlotte with a sigh.

Now, her eyes were open. Lit by starlight, she clearly saw the Windsor chair, the desk, the oil painting on the wall, her skirt hanging from a peg. . . .

All at once, she tensed as she watched the door to her room begin to inch inward. What reason could there be, at this hour of the night, for anyone to enter her bedchamber? A lithe body answered the question as a striped cat stalked in. Surveying her territory, Tiger walked over to examine a plumed tail much more substantial than her own. When Orpheus opened an eye, Tiger put out sharp claws and briefly combed the tail—before surprising them all by pouncing on its tip. Charlotte's old friend sat up and yelped; then she, too, sat up and scooped the huntress into her arms. She held Tiger against her chest until the cat began to purr. With a grateful whine, Orpheus settled back to his slumber.

Sometimes, Charlotte thought while stroking Tiger's taut, rumbling sides, it helped to step between friends, especially when one of them enjoyed pretending to be something of a danger to the other. The thought made her smile as she put her head back on the pillow, and finally drifted off to sleep.

DIANA FOUND HERSELF staring at the folded fire screen positioned in one corner of Mrs. Willett's study. Its japanned surface gleamed with several flowers of some kind, large and golden, as well as a pair of pheasants whose feathers reminded her of a hat she had at home.

Too restless to sleep, Diana took a pen in hand and began a letter.

•   •   •

Saturday evening, Bracebridge
From Mrs. Willett's house, still!

My Dear Lucy,

I have now been away from Boston for Six Days, and find that life in the Country can be interesting after all! Since I last wrote to you, we have had Two Deaths in this small place, both of them Closely Related to Me! I find it all quite Affecting.

The First was the sad Girl of whom I wrote; you will remember she was to draw me while we both recovered from the Smallpox. So far, I have shown no Symptoms at all—but poor Phoebe is Dead! Not of the Inoculation, one supposes, although no one is quite Sure. My brother thinks her Constitution was unable to stand the Strain, which you would think her Physician should have Discovered before he gave her such Treatment. Still, the man did well enough by Me, for I have nothing to report there at all. It was quite a Blow to see Phoebe lying there, on the very Bed I have since moved to, in order to be better able to receive Visitors. I find this Downstairs Room makes a far better *boudoir*. And you know that I am not one to be Squeamish, at least without Good Cause.

The Next thing that happened was that my doctor Shot Himself, so now there is no Physician here to look after Lem, who *has* become Ill—and there is no one to care for Me, should I need help after all! Why Tucker chose this Time and Place to end his Life with one of my brother's Pistols is a great mystery to Everyone, and I think he must have been thinking only of Himself—but I expect all will be Explained, eventually. I would say More on the subject, but what is there to Say?

You remember I wrote that David Pelham showed up at the local Inn? Well, he and Captain Montagu have met, and Disliked each other Immediately. You may ask yourself the Reason for this, Lucy, and find one without Trouble! I believe Captain M. to be a Better Man in both Looks and Sensibility, although he does lack the Warmth one wishes for in a Lover. Curiously, he vows he is Not one, at the moment! I think he Truly Believes only hardened women should be the Recipients of his Caresses, although he is naturally Ashamed to say it—and he feels I am entitled only to a man's Merest Touch, before taking Eternal Vows. Though in all fairness, I suppose No One can be Expected to approach me, at the Moment! At any rate, M. apparently suspects P. is up to No Good, which made me feel a little uncertain when I entertained P., after the captain left this Afternoon! But Pelham was exceedingly Charming, and it is pleasant to have One *Attentive* admirer here. I will be almost Sorry to have to disappoint him, one Day—though I am also Sure that before long, *Another* will not. And, perhaps, I will change My mind!

I must retire, for it is getting Late. Write to me soon, Lucy. You know how I long to hear News of the Town!

When it was finished, Diana folded her letter and got into bed. Upon blowing out the candle, she thought she heard a noise outside. She pulled back the window's curtain. But nothing was to be seen, beyond vague forms of plants lit by starlight, for there was as yet no moon.

It was probably only an animal; an owl, a skunk, or even a porcupine—the last an animal that she had never encountered, and hoped to avoid in the future. But it could also have been a person, she imagined. Someone might even have been peeking into her window, from the garden.

Closing the curtain and lying back with a soft moan, Diana Longfellow spent some time trying to decide just which of her two Bracebridge gentlemen it might have been.

Chapter 12

— Sunday

ON THE MORNING of the Sabbath, little was planned by the Longfellow household beyond a simple breakfast. When that was over, Richard and Charlotte shared coffee with Cicero and Edmund Montagu, speaking little, and that softly, until the meetinghouse bell roused them. Mrs. Willett and her neighbor then walked arm in arm out into the sunshine, making their way to the glass house to praise the workings of Nature. Orpheus came along, savoring the air. And the two cats trailed behind, making occasional forays into clumps of grass.

"It's a shame Diana can't be out with us," said her brother, pausing to tie his hair ribbon more tightly against the breeze. "This would be just the thing for her nerves." Mrs. Willett smiled at this, realizing her neighbor had begun to miss his sister, after all.

"Do you think I could take her some strawberries today?" she asked.

"A good idea! A few were reddening, the last time I looked."

At the greenhouse door they were met by moist, rich smells of humus and living fauna like no other in the neighborhood. Though the light inside was filtered, the lack of shadow under newly whitewashed panes made the place seem oddly bright, while the hues of many plants, arranged in pots along the tables and on the ground, were cheerfully heightened. At the moment, wind activated a wooden ventilating fan set into the roof, but it was still several degrees warmer within the enclosure than without.

Charlotte reached through a slit in her skirt and took a folding fan from a pocket that hung around her waist. As Longfellow paused at a collection of wild orchids, she waited another moment to compose her thoughts, cooled herself a little, and opened with one of several questions she had formulated the day before.

"You and I, Richard, have had more than one clear look at the Grim Reaper—"

"Too clear."

"—and we both know that his face can change a good deal, from one appearance to another. But with Phoebe, her illness, if that is what it was, left no mark behind at all. I suppose Dr. Tucker did what he could—but do you think he was clever enough? Could someone else have examined her more carefully, to learn what happened?"

Longfellow looked up with surprise. "I suspect not. Most physicians merely guess at what bothers their patients, while listening to them complain; once a patient is dead . . . some will occasionally cut into a body to look for something more. But that was not a thing Tucker was prepared to do, especially with a corpse infected by smallpox.

"A gentleman in Padua," he continued, looking up from a stem of white *phalenopsis*, "recently published his thoughts on some seven hundred autopsies which he had performed over sixty years. Quite a life's work! But we are hardly in Europe. We are not even in Cambridge! While examining a body might bring a little peace to a few of the living, it would surely lead many more of them into warfare with one another. Unless, I suppose, one wishes to dismember the corpse of a felon, for the law is not far beyond doing that itself, in drawing and quartering. But what would you expect Tucker to *find* inside, with no sign of anything suspicious on the outside?"

Charlotte looked up into the palm fronds that hung like fingers from the sky, before taking another tenuous step. "What," she asked, "actually causes death, Richard, in someone who becomes ill? What lies beneath the changes the body goes through?"

"An excellent question, Carlotta. To which I haven't much of an answer," Longfellow went on, walking over to examine his pots of cabbages. "Wise men—those who believe in earthly causes of disease, rather than in spirits, or heavenly whim—these men are still split into several factions. They may diagnose an illness, and even cure it; but when asked to consider the question of what unites a symptom with its actual cause, they are rarely in agreement. Even in this great scientific era, there is no one Grand Theory to link cause and effect in healing. Some look for answers in numerology, or in observations of the sun and moon . . . some in climate, and atmospheric change. Expose yourself to cold and come down with the ague, you see. Others blame illness on our internal chemistry. They conclude some of us become too acid, or too alkaline, until we are encrusted in our vessels, or eaten away in our joints. But what, exactly, causes the ague, or the gout, or even a common fever? We worry when we're feverish, but can we be completely certain that fever is an evil, when it often precedes recovery? In Leyden recently, the famed Dr. Boerhaave taught that fever is the body's attempt to fight off death. But then, Boerhaave also held that we're all little more than machines full of fluids, whose conduits clog up from time to time—rather like clay pipe stems. Others have their eye on tiny worms found in tooth scrapings, or even in the blood; I've shown you some, you'll recall, under my microscope. Yet none know what they are, or where they come from, though some do attempt to explain them with the old chestnut of spontaneous generation."

"Which is—?" inquired Charlotte as she watched the cats play among the empty pots in a corner.

"Ah, so I *do* have your attention! Well, it's long been believed, by men who otherwise seem intelligent, that living creatures can spring from non-living matter. It's said they generate in corruption of some sort—mud, for instance. Frogs, flies, maggots, that sort of thing. Would you care to hear a recipe for creating mice?"

"Certainly, but I wonder that anyone would want to," Charlotte replied, waving her fan at white flies rising from a bed of seedlings.

"One has only to put dirty linen into a willow basket with a little wheat, or a piece of cheese," said her pleased instructor.

"I imagine that would work, eventually."

"Yes, but you're a farm woman, with enough sense to see how reproduction must occur, and that it does so without any kind of magic. Sadly, some of our great men are unable to grasp such a simple-minded idea."

"You do flatter me."

"Well, whatever else they may say of you, Carlotta, it is not that you lack a brain. The point is, anyone claiming to know the entire truth of disease and its cause is either seeking his own fame, or after someone else's fortune."

"Then you don't believe in any of the theories you have mentioned?"

"I do not. I am convinced that most philosophers, natural or otherwise, are fools. I'm also certain that their theories tend to drain away much of our common sense, especially when their theories are honored above observations that prove the exact opposite! To learn, Mrs. Willett, one must see for one's self, without prejudice. Here's a curious thing," he added, lifting a finger as if sampling the wind. "It's possible that all life is merely a chain of Eaters and Eaten. Dean Swift put the idea quite neatly, some years ago.

> So naturalists observe, a flea
> Has smaller fleas that on him prey;
> And these have smaller still to bite 'em,
> And so proceed, ad infinitum."

Mrs. Willett smiled at both the wit and its presentation, though she found the idea somewhat distasteful. "Is that why you've moved from telescope to microscope, lately?" she inquired.

"The microscope, too, has the ability to reveal amazing sights, which are nonetheless real for being unobservable with the naked eye. A Swede who now calls himself Linnaeus has just classified some of the world's tiniest beings into a group he calls Chaos. I think we can do better than that, before long. It only requires lenses that go a bit deeper."

"And what," asked Charlotte thoughtfully, "if your chain were reversed, or some of its links jumped over?"

"How so?"

"Well, a carcass in the fields might feed a bear, or buzzards, and it will soon attract weasels, voles, horse flies, and so on; but it is the tiny worms that will finally dispose of it, and the rest of us, eventually. Of course we do not think they will feed on us while we live—but we know that leeches, and mosquitoes, surely will! What if—what if we're also being bitten, while we live, by things far smaller, and unseen . . . whose bite carries an insect's poison, like certain spiders, or scorpions? Could this poison cause the smallpox, do you suppose?"

"I doubt it, Carlotta! For one thing, the blood worms you have seen, though they do multiply in those who have certain illnesses, are not observed to increase greatly in those who clearly have other illnesses, including smallpox. Or the Great Pox, for that matter."

"The French Disease, do you mean?" Charlotte asked quietly.

Longfellow paused to consider propriety, which naturally forbade the discussion with a woman of diseases that pass between male and female, before he decided in favor of knowledge. "Or *syphilis*, as the Italians have named it. Something we rarely speak of, yet since you have an admirable interest in healing, Mrs. Willett, I will go on, if you like, while doubting you will encounter it in Bracebridge any day soon."

"Why is that?" In fact, Charlotte did know something of this old malady, which cleverly mimicked many others, from a medical treatise her brother had brought back with him on one of his visits. But she hoped now to hear something new.

"Because," Longfellow continued, "it is said to be a disease that originates in poverty and immoral practices. So, of course, one discovers it most often among Europeans, and in cities. There is, unfortunately, no inoculation for the Great Pox as there is for the Small. And contracting it offers no protection, for the future is the victim's greatest fear—though more often than not, time will bring no change. When it does, however, it can take the form of deafness, blindness, paralysis—as well as delusions and, finally, insanity. When this phase begins, some of the symptoms may come and go, but death is the eventual end—and by then it is a blessing."

"Richard, if the Great Pox is so deadly, what keeps it from killing outright, like the smallpox? And is there no hope for cure?"

"No one knows why, Carlotta. And there is no cure. Some believe there is hope of avoiding symptoms in the application or ingestion of certain salts—but these are not without their own peril. I suspect it is likely that most treatment does nothing. Nature herself seems to spare a good half of those infected from any further problem. Fortunately, after a few years there is little risk of spreading the infection further, except by giving birth. Then, as the Bible tells us, the child will suffer for the sins of the father. As we are speaking of the Bible," Longfellow went on, deciding Mrs. Willett should be given something else to ponder on the Sabbath, "I'm curious about what our own preacher said to you and my sister, on the day of Phoebe's death."

"Why do you ask?" Charlotte countered uneasily, hoping she would not have to reveal her uncharitable thoughts about Reverend Rowe.

"Because I sent him up the hill, after I gave him the news. For that, I suppose I feel some remorse; but the more I think of it, the more I'm disturbed by his quick condemnation of the girl. After all, I said nothing to suggest Phoebe played any part in her own death. Do you yourself suspect that Will was led, for one reason or another . . . ?"

"No," said Charlotte, though her look was not entirely convincing.

"You're sure he did nothing to her?"

"Possibly he did give her a slap. But more . . . ? Richard, her pillow was wet when I found her."

"Was it?" Longfellow asked uncomfortably.

"Which suggested to me," she explained, "that when Phoebe spoke to Will, something that was said set her to weeping. He couldn't have stayed and argued for long; someone would have heard them. So, she must have been alive long after he left her. The young do tend to suffer excessively, I think . . . for they are still tender-hearted."

"It is an interesting theory, though youth, in my experience, is a poor indicator of innocence. But what if Will returned later?"

"Have we reason to suppose he did? Do you think he could have planned to harm Phoebe, and done it quite coldly—without the heat of aroused passion? That, too, strikes me as unlikely."

"Have you seen a wound fester, Carlotta? Does it not look angrier then, than before? I do see one thing that could be in the boy's favor. An explosive temper will let venom out, before it has a chance to work itself deeper into the soul. So perhaps you're right, at that."

"Let's suppose, though, that the girl actually *wished* to die, Richard. Someone should at least ask the question. Even though it is terrible to imagine that Phoebe—but would it have been *possible?*"

"I presume she brought no poison with her, for why would she choose death, when she had agreed to the inoculation to ensure her future? And do you keep anything of the sort in your house? Bear in mind, such a poison would need to be subtle. Foxglove? No, your own heart is quite sound. Or henbane?" he asked, smiling at a memory they shared.

"I can't think of anything—"

"But what about this?" Longfellow hurried on. "A firm wish for death may in itself achieve that end, and in a relatively brief time. Take an aging spouse, whose dame has passed on. How often will he follow at her heels? This sort of thing has led me to suspect mind and body are more closely related than scientific thought would have us believe . . ."

"Actually," Charlotte replied, "I did wonder, since Phoebe sometimes seemed less than content—"

"But I wouldn't say that kind of thing is likely to occur overnight, as we saw here. And those who exit life in this peculiar fashion are usually those who have developed great strength of will. Now, fear can be another danger, and some peoples can wound one another with curses. We have only to look to the sugar islands, where what they call *voudou* can bring on a wasting sickness, or even a violent death. Nervous energy alone will encourage many maladies. Among our own young ladies, emotions are often believed to stimulate illness—though few die of their swoons and palpitations. Give them new gowns, and women will be greatly changed for the better."

Mrs. Willett saw that her neighbor's interest in her original subject had degenerated. "I only wish your sister were here to answer for our sex," she countered. "For I hear she has begun to meet with some of the town's intellectual ladies, including Mr. Otis's sister Mercy—

"Diana, interested in things of the mind? And with Mercy Warren? I tremble to imagine it! You would never join such a movement, I hope, Mrs. Willett? Would you discuss philosophy or even politics, with a group of Amazons? Or perhaps you do so already, with your cows?"

Charlotte endured his teasing while she fanned a scented breeze through a tall *pelargonium*.

"I'm afraid," she said, "that my hands are full at the moment. For I'm trying to keep one of my scientific acquaintances from being the first in the colony to be burned at the stake."

"What have you heard?" demanded Longfellow.

"Nothing sure to convict you. But there is grumbling . . ."

"Is there, by God? That's a nice turn of things, after all I've done for this blessed village!"

"If you were to do any more in the next week or two, we might both consider making an extended visit to Maine—or one of the sugar islands you mention."

"I wonder how Cicero would take the idea? He says he's heard talk of fining me at the next meeting for encouraging inoculation, with no license to do so."

"Can that be done?"

"I'm not sure. I have half a mind to consult a lawyer myself, if I hear anything more. Blast them all! They rob me of my peace of mind!"

"But, Richard, seriously, there is one thing more that has been troubling me—"

"One thing, Mrs. Willett? You *are* a fortunate soul."

"—and it is this. Dr. Tucker has died; and I wonder, for what?"

"How do you mean?"

"Could his death have had some unrevealed purpose? Or was it simply that he believed Phoebe's death to be the result of his poor treatment? Surely, he must have lost patients before this?"

"He did tell me a curious story one evening, after consuming a large portion of several bottles that we shared. It led me to suspect his earlier experiences in Virginia might have been enough to have driven him, in the end, to despair."

"What did he say?"

"That he was turned away by his influential patients in Williamsburg, after the daughter of one of the wealthiest among them died. It seems the girl was secretly with child, but refused to be examined when another complaint, probably a pellagra, became quite obvious. He prescribed a compound for this which tragically killed the child in her womb. And that soon resulted in the death of the mother, as well. The father was never discovered—but it was assumed Tucker had knowledge of the girl's condition, and that he tried to help her lose this child, to keep her own father from discovering what she had done. This belief ignited the entire family, and a duel was arranged before the doctor fled with what funds he could scrape together, leaving his wife and children to the mercies of the few friends who stood by them. Tucker came to Boston, where he lost all he'd brought with him through land speculation—as did many others. Though none of this appears to have been entirely his fault, how it all must have weighed on him! No wonder the fellow's mind was finally shattered, when he saw his last hope decline with the death of yet another young woman. Of course, this is something I hardly felt it necessary, or wise, to make known."

Her own mind now nearly overcome by their far-flung conversation, Mrs. Willett longed to be gone from the closeness of the glass house, and out in the freshness of the morning. She gave a final thought to the letters from Jeanette she'd seen in Tucker's room, but decided to leave her curiosity about the disposal of these, and the rest of the physician's possessions, for another time.

"Richard, the strawberries—?" she asked.

"Let us go and see. Tiger? What—*what* have you done?"

The cats had already discovered the first of the season's piquant fruits; even now, Tiger could be seen slavering over the remains of a succulent specimen lodged firmly between her sharp teeth.

"Debaucher!" Longfellow shouted, lunging at the unrepentant feline as she bounded away. Eventually, she slunk under the cover of some fat squash leaves, imagining herself safe, while Tabby darted up the trunk of his master's precious palm.

It would be best for her neighbor to deal with this latest dilemma alone, Charlotte decided, as she left Longfellow to rail against his own demons, and went to see to Sunday's dinner.

Chapter 13

DIANA LONGFELLOW SAT in a winged chair in Mrs. Willett's great room studying David Pelham, who honored the Sabbath by again wearing his most splendid attire. As he sipped a glass of sweet wine, she offered him some Scottish shortbread from a tin Charlotte had earlier provided.

"I imagine you've noticed she is a plain person, Mr. Pelham, at least in terms of fashion; but you know Mrs. Willett has spent nearly all of her life in the country. Her husband was what they call a Friend, from Philadelphia. They are prevalent there, of course, though I know we have a few in Boston, too. She fell easily into his ways—it seems they were mostly her own, anyway—but she doesn't make a religion of it. Still, Charlotte is unusually plain," Diana repeated, glancing down at her own fine gown.

"Plainness may serve to enhance native beauty," Pelham replied kindly. "It must also save a great deal of time. Imagine not being obligated to be at one's toilette for an hour or two, before going out the door! Yes, I think there is much to be said for the plain life, Miss Longfellow. And I suspect Mrs. Willett's friends care little how she looks, of an afternoon," he added with a roguish smile.

"Perhaps you're right. I know I often feel a martyr to the requirements of town. My lady's maid is forever complaining about the trouble it gives *her*! Patty especially hates to groom my animal, but one can hardly show one's self to advantage, with a dog that is unkempt."

"Is it a large dog?"

"No, quite a little one. That's why I cannot understand why the foolish woman objects to bathing it, and fixing on its ribbons. Though I do recall she has received one or two small nips."

"She should expect that, as a part of her job."

"Exactly. She's only required to walk him when I'm not at home, or when I don't feel quite up to doing it myself. But this gives her plenty of time to see other servants who are out doing the same thing. I would think she would be grateful for a chance to improve her social life, which I don't suppose is a very full one. Yet I have heard her curse the little dear, and call it a monster!"

"*Quite* beyond belief."

"When I've returned to town, you and I might enjoy a walk with Bon-Bon, out on the Common."

"A delightful prospect," said David Pelham. He quickly turned the conversation back onto an earlier path. "You say your friend is plain—yet I would guess Mrs. Willett's thinking is far from simple."

"One could say that," Diana agreed.

"In fact, I suspect she's interested in many subjects."

"Much like my brother, but Charlotte is far less critical. And a great deal more pleasant."

"From what I gather, most people are."

"Do you criticize my brother, now?" asked Diana, a little pleased at the idea.

"Only from a suspicion that he sometimes neglects you, my dear Miss Longfellow."

"That's so true," the lady sighed.

"Do you know, your friend Mrs. Willett came and spoke with me yesterday, at the inn. I must admit I was intrigued when I realized she had told me almost nothing of herself."

"Oh, Charlotte rarely tells much of what she knows about *anyone*. Unlike many women I could mention."

"Reticence is, I believe, a fine quality."

"Perhaps. She usually gets to the core of a question, once she puts her mind to it. She's made things unpleasant for several villains, you know. Last autumn, for instance, when she discovered a murderer in our midst, here in this very village! Who ever would have thought such a thing possible?"

"Who, indeed?" Mr. Pelham asked thoughtfully. "Although yesterday, I felt she may wonder if there is a murderer here now. At least her questions made me suspect it."

"Charlotte has not spoken anything of it to me! But other than the doctor's undisputed death, I know of only one other here lately. Do you think it possible *Phoebe* was murdered, Mr. Pelham?"

"As you say, that would seem quite unlikely, in as small a place as Bracebridge. I suppose Mrs. Willett did mention that we spoke of the girl?"

"Yes, she told me."

"As I confessed, I knew Miss Morris in Boston . . . briefly, and when I was more able to move about society without fear of being loved only for my fortune. I'm afraid Phoebe had some hopes for me, even when I could have none. And I believe she really did care—" He paused, his eyes becoming distant. "Do you know, in a way, I'm less happy now than I was then."

"How can that be?" asked Diana in disbelief.

"When you are envied, as I am, people you once considered friends will find fault with what you do. Whatever it is, they will call it fine to your face, but then say otherwise behind your back. In my own case, I began to hear rumors—perhaps even you have heard them—which were quite untrue."

"Rumors?" Diana repeated with a twinge of shame.

"Such lies worried my wife, and I believe they encouraged her decline. For that, I can never forgive them. Now it seems I have been targeted for marriage again, by these same heartless women. I sometimes feel that I am pursued—and from the reports I hear, several ladies have sworn to see me attached before the year is out. The truth is, I hardly feel I could marry again, Miss Longfellow. Not in twice that time," he finished gloomily. "Unless . . ."

"It is a difficult situation," said Diana, her eyes wide with newly discovered sympathy.

"Yet I must admit that I've found having no lack of funds can make life enormously pleasant, in some respects. Now I am able to plan, and to build. I can also travel with more ease than a poor man, or woman—especially one who must always count on someone else."

Remembering her own difficulty in extracting her brother's promise to take her to New York, Diana nodded. She leaned forward on the arm of her chair, in a pose of rapt attention. "But Mr. Pelham, isn't it far more pleasant to plan, and to travel, with another? Rather than by one's self?"

"Sadly, one's first choice for a traveling companion is not always possible. And a second invariably seems not good enough. Someday, I may try to interest a particular young lady of truly superior charms and accomplishments in sharing my journeys, and my home. But as the usual lament goes, the most desirable partners are often out of one's reach."

"Often, but not always."

"No, not always," replied David Pelham earnestly, his tone expressing an unusually swift return of high spirits. "Do you ever wish to travel yourself, Miss Longfellow?"

"Lately, it's almost all I ever think about," Diana replied as she scanned the walls of the small room.

A bubble of amusement burst from Mr. Pelham's lips. "I predict we will soon discover we have much in common, Miss Longfellow, and much to share. But as you are unable to leave just now, let me ease your wait with a story or two from my own travels on the Continent several years ago. At the time, you may well laugh to hear, I went about as something of a happy vagabond. . . ."

Once again, the conversation veered. And soon, Diana had forgotten the small seed of discomfort that Mr. Pelham had planted in her active mind.

TWO HOURS LATER, David Pelham sat at a table in a small, cheerfully papered room next to Richard Longfellow's study. By him sat Mrs. Willett; Longfellow and Captain Montagu shared the opposite side of the board. They had Cicero to serve them, yet Charlotte often found it necessary to help in the kitchen, which allowed the men to take their conversation into areas found to be of mutual interest.

The first half of their meal had featured lamb roasted on a spit; Longfellow explained how the spit had turned neatly by itself, attached to a clockwork mechanism needing only to be wound and set to a proper tension for the desired rate of rotation. Cicero had also brought them young peas in a creamy sauce, as well as some fritters made with pounded and whole soaked corn, served with thick maple syrup. Now he and Mrs. Willett had disappeared again, and the talk settled on politics.

"Of course, Grenville is still looking out for money to pay off the debts caused by your defense during the last war," said Captain Montagu, as he circled a bit of fritter in the juices on his plate.

"*Our* defense?" Longfellow stopped a bite in midair. "Did you arrange for a passport, Edmund, to come to this place? You might recall that we are *all* a part of this grand new empire . . . which you apparently hope to maintain for your own gain."

"My gain?" Montagu returned with a faint smile. "I'm afraid I have derived little beyond trouble out of it, thus far—especially while in Boston."

"I refer to Grenville's lack of concern for the financial trouble of the North American colonies," Longfellow went on, while David Pelham nodded his agreement before adding his own thoughts on the matter.

"The Chancellor can have no idea of the consequences of levying these higher duties. Things won't be pleasant, Captain, I can assure you, when you attempt to clamp down on the rough legions who trade in molasses and rum."

"Consequences?" Montagu countered. "Do you imply that these men could become a threat to Britain, Mr. Pelham? But what else would you have Grenville do? His sole interest is to repay the treasury, for that is his duty! And the new Act was surely not made to punish the colonies, as most men here seem pleased to believe—"

"—yet that will surely be its effect!"

"But sir, the sugar trade is now required to pay only one-half the duty expected of it before! According to the new revenue legislation, this so-called Sugar Act, they are asked to pay three pence to the gallon on molasses, rather than the six formerly required—"

"—which, as we all know, has rarely been paid to the Crown . . . though part of it may have wound up in some Customs Johnny's pocket," Mr. Pelham added with a twist of his lips.

"I am quite aware of that. However, new requirements

for selecting those customs agents, and for paying them with Crown money, rather than the Colony's, should alter things. I am truly sorry, of course, to hear of the increased cost of importing your Madeira," Montagu added in a more conciliatory tone, raising his glass, "but there is another proposal being discussed in London that may soon reverse the rest, and bring us all into harmony again. I heard, while in New Hampshire, that Grenville may soon ask Parliament for a stamp tax—"

"Stamps!" gasped Pelham. Massachusetts had, indeed, heard of the idea before.

"Then the rumors were true," Longfellow commented coolly.

"Taxes, instead of duties, will anger far more people!" David Pelham sputtered in a thick voice. "Their revenge will be non-importation—and as my own business involves the shipment of general goods from London, that is bound to bring trouble to my own doorstep! Where will this insane revenge end, Captain? Where will it end? In killing us all!"

Richard Longfellow sent a warning look to Pelham, whom he suspected of having gone beyond civility, and quite possibly against his own interests. For Longfellow knew Captain Montagu to be a man of untested powers, at least in his official capacity, whatever, exactly, that was. "I hope you've enjoyed your tender lamb today, Edmund," he continued pleasantly, "since some, you know, have already advised us to stop eating the animals—for a year, to start. By that time, they say we will have more grown sheep and thus more wool, for the increased manufacture of our own cloth."

When Captain Montagu said nothing, his host went on.

"I tend to agree that self-sufficiency is a fine thing, as a rule . . . and I'll admit I've often thought of raising a few of my own creatures. Old mutton is less palatable than what we've had today—but it can be acceptable. Especially when the kitchen is intent on making a stew," he added, his look strongly suggesting another meaning.

"Surely, sir," came a new plea from David Pelham, "British manufacturers won't accept such a state of affairs? For must they not stand to lose several fortunes, as well?"

"Losing the custom of two million colonists would make quite a difference to their profits," Longfellow agreed, "if all of America should become a reluctant buyer."

"The real question will be, can British merchants sway the most powerful in the current government, who have had little training in trade?" was Captain Montagu's pensive reply.

"If they cannot, then we may see a new government, before long."

"And what," asked Mr. Pelham, "if no one here will buy these ill-conceived stamps? Do they propose to cram them down our throats? If so, I will warn you that Americans can be stubborn, too!"

"That, I know," Edmund Montagu assured them. "But it will be far easier to sell a stamp than to enforce current navigation restrictions and duties. And only think of the benefits to you! There will be no more need for coastal cutters to chase your forgetful captains for their unpaid duties, nor for writs that allow peering into a man's business. With the stamps, evasion will be difficult, for they'll be seen on every document of law, every newspaper, all papers used in ordinary commerce . . . stamps going quite reasonably from a pittance to a few pounds each, depending on their use. Unless you plan to stop recording your marriages, reading the news, shipping goods, and romping with each other in the mock battles that fill your courts, you will *all* pay—for each of these activities calls for paper, and all official papers will need stamps."

"Well, it will be a pretty unpopular fellow," Longfellow countered, "who consents to sell them."

"Yet you will have to admit to the fairness of such a plan, Richard. Its burden will fall on all levels of society, and on every colony, in the same way. And by easing the official eye on your imports and exports, it should even please the rebellious Mr. Pelham."

"But, sir, I have little wish to rebel," said Pelham, now suddenly shifting to a smoother tone, "and I assure you, Captain, I pose no threat to your titled friends in London, who will surely decide our fate. Yet have you yourself considered what our many lawyers will do, when they find they are the special target of the Crown's revenue men?"

Longfellow grinned. "Not only lawyers, but news printers as well, by God! Think of what that might mean, Edmund, and of all of the bombastic words and sentiments in the arsenals of these gentlemen who thrive on strife—who will most certainly become your enemies. Of all men, these enjoy inflaming others most, for in this they find their usual profit. I wouldn't care to be in your shoes, if they're forced to abandon their presses and the courts, and take to the streets! Jemmy Otis, for one, will not fail to find something interesting to say."

"Something, but will it make any sense?" asked Montagu. "I'm sure you know most men in England value liberty, and so applauded Otis's arguments against the search writs some years ago." This brought smiles from the others, for Otis had indeed argued brilliantly before the Provincial Court in '61, attacking the Crown's intentions to pry open any ship's hold, or a man's place of business—even his dwelling. Otis lost the case; but ever since, talk had continued of the "rights of Englishmen," and even of a natural law higher than that produced by Parliament.

"But I wonder how intelligible Otis's future argument will be," the captain continued. "For he is clearly not himself these days, as you must have seen. Last month in the Royal Coffee House I heard him insist that young girls who sell fruit in the streets have a right to question how they're governed—" He paused as they all chuckled, but soon continued his warning. "Far worse than that is his bullying and abuse of men on both sides of a question, for he now changes horse in midstream. I believe he may soon become something of a threat to the peace. But I would imagine you've discussed this, Richard, in one of the political clubs you no doubt attend secretly, like everyone else here."

"Hmm—I have seen, Edmund, that he curses friend and enemy alike, and that this madness begins to sound a sad tale, indeed. Though it still comes and goes, almost as if—"

A sharp exhalation from across the table stopped Longfellow's thought, and they paused to see David Pelham dispatch a fly he had trapped upon the tablecloth.

"At any rate, if the next three years go as the last for him," Edmund Montagu concluded, "Otis will soon be far more of a burden to you, than a help."

"To me? Once again, you speak as if we are on opposite sides."

"Yes. Curious, is it not?" Montagu gave him a wicked smile that Longfellow supposed his sister might have envied, had she been there to see it.

Glancing now from one guest to the other, Richard Longfellow asked himself who would be the better match for Diana, Pelham or Montagu—if either could bring himself to ask for her hand. Although descended from the Old World's aristocracy, Edmund currently had little fortune, and his business in the Colony was somewhat suspect, despite the fact that he was a Crown official. Still, the man had a certain charm, and he had frequently glimpsed a promising warmth lurking beneath the captain's chilly exterior. If it were not for his royal and political masters, he might make an interesting and acceptable brother-in-law, after all. Meanwhile, there sat David Pelham in all his finery, his lower lip stiffened by the idea of his new wealth being attacked by those same men. He appeared to ask himself how he might wiggle out from under, if he failed to ingratiate himself deeply enough. Perhaps, Longfellow considered, burrowing might do the trick. Pelham, too, had a certain charm, but it was not far from that of a London fop—and could it be rouge he saw on the fellow's cheeks today? Or had the talk of money simply made the man's blood boil to the surface? Yet if he were to continue to feel persecuted by what was, after all, no more than the wind of Parliament . . .

All in all, Longfellow decided, it looked as if between the two only Montagu would ever be drawn to high thought, or noble action. But to what end? And could the captain be trusted, with a political storm rumbling in on the horizon? Though they were ruled by the same King, he himself would hardly call Montagu a true countryman, at least by any definition the three of them now at table would agree to. Pelham, though he might lack something as a man, did seem to have a way with the ladies. And it would be, of course, Diana's decision. Heaven help them all, her brother thought once more.

Charlotte's return interrupted Longfellow's thoughts, and he found himself wishing she had witnessed the previous performance. He would go over it for her later. Now, he took a moment to admire her familiar figure as she stood at the door, waiting for their attention. "Gentlemen," she began, "if you will come outside, we'll finish with something special."

The west-facing piazza, approached through French doors, was covered with trellises that supported native grape coming into new leaf; as yet, it provided only a taste of the thick shade that would grow there later, when it would be most needed. Beneath the spring-green vines, a table had been set with china and silver, while house finches provided a lively tune for the final course.

"What have we here?" asked Montagu, marveling to

himself once more at the richness and abundance of the colonial diet.

"Lemon cake with beaten cream, and peaches preserved in rum," said Charlotte, while Longfellow helped her to sit.

"The captain has been telling us we will soon be asked by Mr. Grenville to pay him, Carlotta, for a marriage in Massachusetts. What do you say to that?"

"It is extremely kind of Mr. Grenville to offer himself, yet I wonder if any of us could manage to pay what he's worth. Unless, of course, he might consent to a raffle?"

It seemed that a gnat had flown into the captain's mouth, for he suddenly coughed into his sleeve.

"I believe, Mrs. Willett," said Edmund Montagu, once he'd recovered, "that your grasp of finance might well put our Chancellor of the Exchequer to shame. Let me help you to a plate of cake and cream, and we'll try to talk of something more likely to challenge you."

And so the gentlemen spent another pleasant hour amusing Mrs. Willett with lively conversation, while each studied the other, and asked himself why he was the only one able to successfully combine poise, tolerance, and intelligence, all in one go.

Chapter 14

ANNAH SLOAN SET down the basket that held their supper, without so much as lifting the cloth to examine its contents. It was an unusual omission for a woman long devoted to food.

"Have you heard anything at all of the boy?" Mrs. Willett asked, glad to sit for a moment by her own hearth. She was pleased to see that the plump face before her had regained some of its usual color, though its owner still seemed strangely distant.

Hannah looked away, replying with a question of her own. "Do *you* think Will is hiding for the reason the rest believe?"

"I don't know what the rest believe," Charlotte replied, "but I am still sure he will come back when he's ready."

"It's as if he's vanished from the earth," Hannah whispered. She lowered herself onto a three-legged stool, and began to mound the coals under the kettle with a fire shovel. "At least, no one has offered proof against him."

"How could they? We've seen what there was to see. What else could point to him?"

"For one family in Concord, at least, a lack of anyone else to point to," Hannah responded.

It was true. The longer Phoebe's death was left without an official conclusion, the more likely it was that others would seek their own explanations.

Neither spoke for several moments. It occurred to Charlotte that Hannah still could not bring herself to mention Phoebe, though after three days it would have seemed only natural to do so. Finally, a cock crowed in the yard behind the house, breaking the silence.

"I suppose," Hannah said soon after, "Reverend Rowe took a few to task in his sermon this morning."

"At least we were spared hearing it firsthand. You see, there are always some things for which we can be grateful."

"You'd better go and tell Lem his supper's here. His appetite's come back, and I think he slept well. The spots look less angry."

"I'm glad for that."

"With the itch, he's asking for a bath. Do you think it would do any harm?"

"Not as long as he dries gently, so he doesn't dislodge the scabs. You might pull down a little dried lavender from the corner, and add it to the water."

"I'll make sure he doesn't use a flannel. It will be good to fuss over somebody. The Lord knows there's nothing I can do for the lady from Boston, other than stay out of her way."

"Has Diana been unkind?"

"Miss Longfellow is far too busy for that, with all of the comings and goings, and eternally having to change her dress and hair. Too busy to talk with a lowly body in the kitchen, I suppose," Hannah added petulantly, causing Charlotte to suspect the woman's long-held distaste for town ways currently mingled with something more personal.

"It won't be much longer," she said, before thinking of a happy piece of news. "Your young Henry is quite good at milking."

"He's proud of it, too," said Hannah, looking directly at Mrs. Willett for the first time that day. "He told me as much through the window this morning, while I was giving him his tasks. He's a good boy, and no doubt of it," she concluded, adjusting her large bodice to keep her pride in place.

"With the summer's work coming, we might find more for him to do. If you agree?" Charlotte watched the woman lower her head and look into the basket with feigned interest. She knew without having seen them that tears welled in Hannah Sloan's anxious eyes. *When*, she wondered—and just how—would it all finally end?

"IF SHE WANTED to talk, she might have *said* something," said Diana haughtily. "I had no idea the woman might condescend to speak to *me!*"

"She probably thinks you're well beyond her in the art of conversation," Charlotte responded. She glanced around her study with a wave of regret for having given it up, even for a good cause.

"That is obviously quite true—but it doesn't mean I make a practice of neglecting to do a sociable thing, when one is called for," Diana retorted. "I will try to make her more cheerful one way or another, for she has become very sullen lately, for some reason."

"I've just spoken to Lem, and he seems much better. . . ."

"That is what I thought, when I had a peek at him earlier. Though there is really not much to see, which I find a little disappointing. My case, however, is best, for I have no symptoms at all."

"It could be that your time hasn't come," Charlotte suggested, but Miss Longfellow only threw back her head and yawned. "I've brought you some of our lamb, and fritters and peas, for anyone who feels like eating."

"Oh, good! I have a ferocious appetite in the country, though this spring air does seem to be making me feel tired. I only wish I could get some exercise! When I escape this place, I mean to find a ball to attend, if I have to ride as far as Connecticut. By the way, it would seem Mr. Pelham would like to take me off with *him*, on some sort of adventure."

"He told you so?" asked Charlotte, startled by the idea.

"Just this morning. We spoke of traveling, and of spending his money freely and gaily! He has been much maligned, Charlotte, by some in town."

"So I gather."

"But I find him extremely solicitous—especially in contrast with others from whom I expected more sympathy."

"Do you mean your brother, or someone different?"

"Both of them. Lately, Edmund has been the ruder of the two." Playing with a finger ring, Diana suddenly dropped it. She swooped gracefully to reach under the bed. Rising, she considered a second object she had also collected. "Strange," she commented. Then she tossed it playfully to Mrs. Willett. "What do you think?"

"It seems to be a pellet of bread. The remains of a skirmish?" Charlotte asked, imagining Lem and Will Sloan at war.

"Well, it will only bring ants here. You keep it," Diana commanded. Then she lay back, as Charlotte dropped the small, hard object absently into her pocket. "What else did Mr. Pelham say to you?" she asked.

"He told me stories of his travels, which were odd enough to make me laugh a great deal! And we talked of you. Yes, we did! David thinks you are unusual. I imagine he is now also a little afraid of you."

"Why?" Mrs. Willett asked with a sinking feeling.

"You know how gentlemen retreat when they discover any real intelligence in a woman. I told him you are something like the Oracle at Delphi, for suggesting things. He does not quite admit it," Diana went on more slowly, "but I began to believe he suspects Phoebe's death might have been something out of the ordinary."

"Well—" Charlotte began.

"Oh, I know, of course it is. But I think he suspects she could have been *murdered*! Though I have also begun to think Mr. Pelham tends to imagine things. Certain feelings, for instance . . ."

"Murdered—by whom?"

"That is for you to determine, my dear *Sibylla*, if it is true. The less I know of your villagers and their doings, the happier I shall be! But perhaps it was all only a game of make-believe, after all. Heaven knows Mr. Pelham, too, finds the country dismal—except, of course, for me."

"I'm sure," Mrs. Willett answered lightly. But disquiet now lay beneath her ready smile. To be an oracle, she recalled from her reading, required accepting help from the underworld, perhaps in the form of vapors tinged with the smell of brimstone. Was that what her neighbors, some of them highly superstitious, now needed to hear?

But in truth, pondering a murder did take one far from the sunlight, into regions where human pain could challenge even a strong sense of goodness, by putting the inherent worth of mankind into doubt. *Was* she again prepared to investigate such a possibility? Would anyone believe her if she should arrive at an unpleasant answer? Or, in fact, were there others, like Hannah, who felt uneasy as well, but refused to say their fears aloud?

These unsettling thoughts soon sent Charlotte Willett back across her garden, to spend another quiet hour alone.

AFTER THE SUPPER plates were put away, Hannah heated water enough to mix a warm bath by the kitchen hearth. Then she called out to Lem that all was ready.

Obviously mortified, he left his room wearing only a shirt, which scarcely reached his knees. He had given up his hose and pants because of the torment he'd lately had to endure. Now he walked to the bath, and waited for Hannah Sloan to go away.

"Go ahead, climb in," said Hannah, enjoying the sight before her.

The young man had not anticipated this problem. He cursed his luck, and remained where he was.

"I've raised five sons, and I didn't get any of them from a chimney stork! If I haven't seen what you've got, it'll be quite a surprise for us all."

"Turn your back, at least," Lem pleaded, and Hannah, with a mother's sympathy, did as she was asked. She turned again when she heard his body sink as far as his long limbs allowed, while he slopped bathwater onto a square of oilcloth laid over the pine floor.

"Now, mind what I said about scrubbing! Let the water soothe your skin awhile. You won't need soap, since you bathed before this whole thing started. Does it feel better?"

The boy nodded, closing his eyes in blissful relief.

"Not too hot?"

Lem shook his head.

"I'll pour more water from the kettle as you need it."

"It's fine!"

"All right, then. I'll go back to my mending."

On her way to her chair, Hannah looked with amusement at the back of the boy's head, and watched him relax even farther into the herb-scented bath. But Lem's contentment was not to last. In another instant, the door to the room opened and Diana Longfellow walked in, holding a tin in her hand.

"I thought you might each enjoy a shortbread," she said. Her eyes widened when she heard a squeak and a splash. Try as he might, Lem could not manage to submerge much more of himself. He counted on one hand to do whatever duty it could in the bath, while his other frantically caught at the shirt that was scarcely within reach.

"I didn't realize . . . ! But, no matter. I've seen my brother in the bath several times, and he never seemed to mind much, so I don't imagine you should, either. Though washing that shirt while you're in there is probably not a bad idea."

"Miss—" Lem replied in a whisper, wrapping himself into what he'd decided was his best defensive position, given the bleak situation.

"Here, have a cookie. I'll turn my head away while I come over—no, you must have one, at least. If I eat them all, I'll be so plump when I leave I'll rival one of your old hens, and I will have to order wider corsets to hold my stays. I really came in to talk to you, Hannah. Do you think, considering the circumstances, that we might move into the other room, and leave the man of our little household to recover himself?"

"If there's something wrong—" said Hannah.

"No, nothing at all! I only thought that with no one else to speak to—of your own sex, at least—well, I thought you might be willing to chat for a while. If you can find the time."

"I expect I could find some." With a soft grunt, Hannah Sloan rose, and followed Miss Longfellow out.

As the day had been too warm for a fire in the large room, the two pulled chairs up to one of the windows and sat awkwardly in the day's last light, each missing employment for her hands. "Would you like a biscuit?" Diana again asked politely. "They're quite good, I've found, for raising the spirits."

"I might try one," Hannah decided. She leaned forward to take a piece of shortbread from the tin. It proved to be delicious. She had another.

"There. Since we've now shared sweets, perhaps our conversation can proceed along the same lines."

Hannah still seemed unsure.

"What I mean is," Diana persisted, "I would like to say something civil to you, and I hope you will return the favor."

"Go ahead, then," said Hannah, settling herself further.

"Fine. Do you know, I've always admired the . . . the efficient way you run this house. Oh, I know Mrs. Willett tries to be of help, but surely, it's mostly your own efforts that make everything run smoothly. I believe I am right?"

"Well," said Hannah uncertainly.

"There. I thought so. Now, you try."

This took more effort, but soon real curiosity entered Hannah's eyes. "I do admire the way you hold your own, as a woman, and have your way with men. Your brother, even, seems willing to retreat when you order him about."

"Ah, there you have touched on a result not easily achieved. It has taken years of training, but Richard now knows that the satisfaction of having his way is rarely worth what happens when I can't have mine. Once, I told a lady he was fond of that he had taken apart a snake from the cellar with a kitchen knife and a pickle fork. She found the thought upsetting, especially as she was spearing a gherkin at the time, and I'm afraid she has since been rather cool to us both. The amusing thing was that he really *had* done it," Diana finished, laughing at her brother's oddities. "Of course," she added, "that was some time ago."

"My own boys," Hannah replied, "have gotten themselves into their share of mischief. The things I could tell you they've been caught at—" She stopped her tongue suddenly, remembering that her eldest was deep in trouble, and beyond her help.

"Hannah—did you see anything on the night of Phoebe's death to make you think Will had harmed her?" Diana asked abruptly.

"Did you?" Hannah countered, her eyes gleaming with a new fear.

"No. But I know *something* is worrying you, which you might as well let go of. I'll extract it from you sooner or later. You *know* I will."

Anguish too long suppressed came swirling up in a panic. "I only hoped—I just couldn't say what I saw! And I swore I wouldn't tell Mrs. Willett, with her counting on us, and with Phoebe my own responsibility! It tortured me to hide it from her, but since she's always ferreting things out I didn't know what else she might suspect or even say to others—"

"Sometimes," Diana interrupted, "women can do what men cannot, and will go a ways to protect one another. I think we may find a solution to your problem, Hannah. Though by the look of things, the men in this village don't consider Phoebe's death much of a problem at all."

"It would do me good to say it, I know that! For I can hardly stand it anymore—"

"Well, then, go on!"

"I did see something that night, Miss Longfellow. It was before the clock struck three. I woke to hear a noise downstairs; it sounded like someone moving, and I thought—"

"—it was Will, coming in?"

Hannah nodded. "I listened in the hall, but I didn't hear anything further. Then, as the moon was well up, I went down the stairs and out the back door . . ."

"It was a warm night, so rather than use the pot—"

"—I went to the privy. That's when I saw . . . I saw Will climbing out of Phoebe's window. He saw me and stopped, but then he turned and ran away through the garden. I thought, since he'd gone in to her, he'd know he couldn't go home, because he might be carrying the pox. But later, I thought that if he was ashamed to tell me he'd done something worse, then he'd have fled for that reason, as well. And now, after thinking it over and over, I don't know what to think at all! I am sure of one thing—my Will never meant to do Phoebe any harm. But then—" she paused, sucking in a breath, "I went in to see Phoebe, *and found her dead.* She lay all in a tangle with her mouth open—almost like a little bird that's fallen from a tree, and not even cold! I couldn't leave her that way—so I made her ready to be seen in the morning. Then I lay in my bed, and wondered what had happened and how much I should say, until I decided not to say anything at all."

"I see," said Diana. She had been unprepared for the revelations that had come from her attempt at polite conversation.

"What would *you* do?" Hannah asked plaintively.

"Nothing. Nothing at all. I will talk to Mrs. Willett about it, when I see her in the morning. I don't believe there's any need to mention this to anyone else."

"You are very kind," Hannah said with relief.

"Sometimes, I am. It's not often that anyone tells me something so absorbing—something to challenge my mind. Most people I know seem hardly to suspect that

I have one. I'm very glad you are a woman with more sense."

Hannah made no response to this, but wiped her eyes on her apron as she stood to go. Diana thrust the biscuit tin into her hand.

"I meant what I said, Hannah," she said softly.

"What was that, Miss?"

"That these things will make me sorry. Take them away with you—and let me think. . . ."

RICHARD LONGFELLOW SAT watching the last rays of the sun play over Mrs. Willett and Captain Montagu, who had joined him once again beneath his vines. Each hoped, with the beginning of a long twilight, to spend a quiet hour viewing Nature before the candles were lit. As fitted their reflective moods, talk had turned to Character.

"It would seem our physician revealed himself to be a man of explosive passion," Longfellow concluded. "I wonder I didn't see it sooner."

"What one first sees in a fellow is often at odds with what is later discovered," Montagu returned, gazing at the bloodred glimmer hovering on the horizon. "Men, and women, may be easily fooled. Especially very stubborn ones."

"Certainly none of us is infallible. Yet enlightened Reason, based on what we perceive, remains our only basis for civilized behavior—and, for arriving at Truth."

"Richard," Charlotte asked, "can we expect a decision on Phoebe's death soon?"

"Quite soon. In fact, tomorrow, if nothing new comes into our hands. The selectmen will meet again in the morning. The larger issue seems resolved, as I believe you have heard—even if the details remain somewhat confused."

"Do you think there is any hope of learning more?"

"It would surprise me if we do—but just what would you have us discover, Mrs. Willett?"

"I hardly know how to answer. But perhaps I should tell you now of something I thought, at least, that I observed—just before Dr. Tucker seemed to warn us that something was about to happen . . . although I wasn't sure what he meant by it. . . . Oh, how shall I start?"

"At the beginning, Carlotta," Longfellow said kindly. But instead of answering her neighbor, Mrs. Willett addressed a new question to Edmund Montagu, as he dispatched a mosquito attempting to bore through his stocking.

"Did Diana tell you, Captain, that we found a drawing of David Pelham on Friday afternoon, shortly before Dr. Tucker died?"

"No, Mrs. Willett, she did not. But she would hardly seem to need one. Whenever I attempt to speak to her, I find the man himself planted like a rosebush at her side."

"It was in Phoebe's sketchbook."

"Was it?" asked Longfellow, leaning forward intently.

"Near a drawing of an aunt in Boston, a woman named Mary Morris. Do you recall, Richard, Dr. Tucker saying he treated Phoebe for a rash while she was in Boston? He also told us of knowing David Pelham at the same time."

"Yes—but Pelham told us he never met the girl, didn't he?"

"He did. Yesterday when I spoke with him he admitted to the acquaintance; he also claimed Phoebe's aunt warned him to end it, apparently for his own safety. Mr. Pelham believes Phoebe suggested more to him than she should have, and that it was not the first time she had done such a thing. Diana seems to think we may believe what he says."

"Hmmm," was all that Longfellow replied, giving her courage to go farther.

"I doubt Mr. Pelham will tell us much more. He fears upsetting Diana, as well as Phoebe's family. But I think there is something else there. And if someone were to visit Mrs. Morris in Boston, he might look for the journal I assume Dr. Tucker kept, as most physicians do."

"If *someone* were to visit . . . ?"

Mrs. Willett's eyes scanned the clear sky.

"I could take pleasure," said Captain Montagu slowly, "in some mild exercise; I have also thought of putting a few miles between myself and certain parts of Bracebridge for a day or two."

"You may plead special business, I suppose, to travel without risking a Sunday fine. . . ." said Longfellow lightly.

The captain, too, examined a bright Venus for a few moments more, before he decided. "Richard, I'll sleep in Roxbury tonight, if you have no objection to my leaving you for a while. After staying with friends there, I'll look up Mrs. Morris in the tax rolls tomorrow, and pay a call. I will also stop in at the doctor's lodgings. But I would know one thing first, Mrs. Willett. Do you have a specific interest I should know of?"

"I would only like to know the answers to a few small questions, before this is all well and truly settled."

"I see. In that case, take good care of *yourself*, madam," Montagu added pointedly as he stood, giving his companions each something else to think about as he went inside.

A FEW MINUTES later, as the captain threw an assortment of small articles into a saddlebag, Charlotte knocked at his door.

"Captain Montagu," she began, hardly knowing what she wanted to tell him. "Edmund," she ventured.

"Yes?" he asked, as curiosity overcame his surprise, and he moved aside for her to enter.

"I know you haven't declared intentions to Diana, beyond friendship—but I have heard from her that David Pelham has been suggesting things that could indicate much more than friendship—things she couldn't do, in good conscience, without marriage."

"Has he, indeed?" asked Montagu, holding a cambric shirt motionless in his hand.

"Though I doubt marriage has been discussed between them."

"Then what is the object of such talk?"

"On Diana's side, it may only be to test waters that have risen nearly to her feet."

"And on his?"

"On his, I'm not sure. But I think idleness and vanity, when they are mixed with desire, have been known to lead to haste, and even to unintended harm."

Edmund Montagu nodded, examining his visitor closely. He was not about to comment—for Diana's recent accusation of having spoken unfairly of a rival had stung, and continued to do so. However, he told himself, he had a higher duty than to his own comfort.

"So, you distrust the man," he finally answered. "As do I. But I have tried to temper my suspicions. As you might suspect, they may well be influenced . . . by other considerations. You, Charlotte, are in a better position to see him clearly."

She flushed at his first use of her name, and became more aware of the fact that she had invaded a gentleman's bedchamber. But in another moment, she went boldly on.

"I do believe there may be a *great deal* we don't yet see in Mr. Pelham. I am sure he's not been entirely truthful, and I fear he's still hiding something of importance. I cannot know if it is for his own sake he will not speak, or for that of someone else. And then—But I hope to know more, when you return. Edmund, do you think that could be by tomorrow afternoon?"

"Should it be?"

"I very much suspect it should," said Charlotte, her eyes seeming to plead for this favor.

"Depend upon it, then," Captain Montagu replied forcefully as he swung the saddlebag onto his broad shoulders, and went to prepare his mount.

Chapter 15

ACROSS THE STONE bridge, inside the Blue Boar Tavern, the landlord drew enough ale to fill a pewter tankard. He took it to a table, where he set it down in front of a bearded, buckskinned man of the West, who sat on a long bench. The man raised the container and in an instant downed half of its contents.

"Fine stuff," he commented after a belch, watching Phineas Wise with a twinkle in his eye. The tavern keeper smiled to think of the profit he'd make on this traveler, before the evening was out. For Phineas knew the value of each shilling that came his way, which was why he maintained an unadorned but snug room ready for all comers, while upstairs, three dusty rooms with canvas cots (a frugal idea suggested by a gentleman in the Hindu trade) added a crowning bit of glory to the establishment. At least, no one had expired there for several years, Mr. Wise was pleased to say.

"Another?" he asked when the vessel had been drained.

"What else?" the frontiersman asked with a laugh. "For your friends there, too," he cried with good humor, pointing at two old men who sat in the only high-backed chairs in the place, each smoking a long clay pipe. "Your health, sir," called the one known as Flint after they had been served, while his constant companion, Mr. Tyndall (who also answered to Tinder) raised his pipe in a salute.

"The nights are not very cold in this season," Flint went on, "but a measure of ale is always appreciated, for health's sake."

The Westerner, hoping for some amusement, moved closer still, and introduced himself as Jason Clarke, of Pittsfield.

"A Berkshire man?" asked Flint conversationally.

"Indeed, sir. A mountain man, if you will."

"And how do you like coming into civilization?"

"Is that what this place is? It seems rather rough to me, and something of a backwater. Pittsfield, you know, has now over a thousand souls."

"A thousand! Fancy that. What do they all do, to make it so populous?"

"Farm, mostly. And marry to produce offspring."

"Here—have a pipe. I keep a spare or two, in case I break one tapping it on the hearth. And some tobacco."

"Many thanks. I will take back what I said of roughness, for you seem to understand civilized behavior."

Old Tinder polished his nose with a handkerchief before replying. "Civilized, we may be. But you'd be amazed by what else goes on in such a smallish place—involving men and women, both, caught in the throes of will and woe!"

"How is this?" asked the Berkshire man with increased interest.

Then, Tinder began to tell a tragic tale of a deceased maiden of uncommon beauty—her dead physician with a taste for rum and a knowledge of magical potions, whose soul was likely to be anywhere but in Heaven—and a young suitor, barely a man, who had gone to live as a hermit in the forest, where he would surely die all matted and foul, and alone.

Meanwhile, other men walked through the portal into the tavern's musty gloom. One in particular stood at the threshold for a long moment, before his eyes made out Phineas Wise going into the small scullery in back. Leaving as he had entered, the newcomer made his way around the building, then went in again through the scullery door.

At his entrance, Phineas Wise looked up from his simmering stew in surprise, for few ever thought to invade his culinary privacy from that angle. Then his eyes opened even wider, for there stood the lad he had been expecting, yet hardly hoped to find.

"Will Sloan!" he exclaimed.

"Hello, Mr. Wise," said the boy in a weary voice. "I'm glad to see you."

"Will, where in God's name have you been?"

"In the woods."

"For four days?"

"I had to! But then, I got so damned hungry I had to come back in—can I have some of that?"

Constable Phineas Wise studied the boy's flushed face before he picked up a deep plate and filled it. Will sat down onto a bench beside the wall, and the landlord gave him the stew and found a spoon, wiping it first on his apron. The boy then began to eat with the appetite of a wolf.

"About all I could find," he managed to say as he gobbled, "not having my fowler, was mushrooms and pine buds, and a few cattails down by the river. I wondered about the mushrooms, though at first I didn't much care if they killed me or not! But then I decided I'd best save myself, after all."

Wise pondered the boy's high color as he listened to this rambling talk. Clearly, Will was unwell. But was it the result of four days' exposure, with little food? Or could it be the smallpox?

"Will, did you go in to her? Did you touch her, boy?"

"Phoebe?" asked Will Sloan, looking up with another shiver.

"You do know that she's—?"

"I went in, and she was lying there so strange—I *had* to know, didn't I? How did it happen, Mr. Wise? How could it? Was it the smallpox? Have I got it now, too? Am I going to die, d'you think? I don't want to die, but if I do, I suppose I'll see Phoebe, won't I? She'd still be mine, wouldn't she? *Wouldn't* she?" he demanded.

"You're too stubborn to go just yet, Will, I'd guess," Phineas Wise replied brusquely, wondering what to do with this new trouble. Could the boy talk so easily of the afterlife, if he had lately taken a life himself? And yet, he did seem uncertain of his reception there. "Some say you did more than touch her, son."

"How could I? She told me we couldn't do anything—" Suddenly, Will's look of confusion changed to one of anger. "You mean, they think I *killed* her? Is that what they think?" He flushed a bright red, his eyes blazing.

"It seems she died peaceful enough, Will, but with no other sign; after you ran away—"

"Peaceful? But it wasn't like that—it was awful! I had to run—I had to! Only I couldn't go home after I'd touched her, I knew that for certain."

"Then why didn't you go to your mother? She was right there."

"Because I thought—"

Abruptly, Will buried his head into his hands. His shoulders began to heave, as one harsh sob followed another. The earlier fierceness gone, Will Sloan seemed no more than a frightened child.

Phineas Wise's heart softened. "All right, then, go to Mrs. Willett's house, right now. At least you were smart enough to stay away from your brothers and sisters, I'll give you that."

Will looked up. Then, his tearstained face solemn, he nodded. "I didn't want to hurt anybody!"

"Promise me you'll stay there at Mrs. Willett's. I'm telling you officially, now. As village constable. And don't let any of my guests see you go, if you can help it. Did you greet anybody when you came in?"

The boy shook his head.

"Good. It'll be best for you to stay out of everybody's way, at least until we get a few things straight."

"Where is Phoebe?" Will asked suddenly.

"She's in the churchyard, where you can visit her later. Right now, you go to your mother, and stay there."

Will Sloan departed, without a further word.

The boy *was* ill, thought Phineas, and perhaps he should not have sent him to the waiting smallpox in a weakened state—but what else could be done, with no physician anywhere near? And if it *was* the pox, he himself might yet be sorry he had even spoken to Will Sloan! What would Hannah do, though, if the boy should die of it, after all? That was more than Phineas wanted to imagine.

He reentered the main room of his tavern to see his customers still chewing over the week's events, now gone beyond news to become lore. Instead of taking the pair of deaths as a threat, most seemed to talk of the story almost as if it had occurred somewhere else. Perhaps that was not surprising, for few had known much about either of the two unfortunates.

Maybe, thought Phineas Wise, it was all about to blow over, without blowing up. Maybe luck would be with them. Maybe time would put an end to all that had been disrupting the peace in Bracebridge, before anyone else should sicken . . . or die.

ALONE BUT FOR the shadows in the quiet kitchen, Hannah Sloan sat staring at a fading fire, happy to let the light fall so that she might not be drawn from her memories. Yet as the remains of two hearth logs settled with a flurry of sparks, she was startled back to the present by the sound of something new. It seemed like scratching. In a moment, her heart was in her throat, for it was a sign her children had used when they were small, and found themselves on the wrong side of a door.

Hannah looked to the window behind her. This time, her heart nearly stopped, for through the glass she saw a sad, familiar face. A hand to her mouth, Hannah rushed at the door and hauled it open on creaking hinges. Will stood there quietly, his head low. His mother grabbed at a hand and pulled the boy inside, crushing him swiftly to her breast. Then, almost as abruptly, she thrust him out at arm's length to study, before she gave him a clout that sent him sprawling to the floor.

"What was that for?" he shouted, scrambling to his feet in the hope of avoiding another attack.

"Come here," Hannah ordered. This time she reached for both hands and caught them before the young man, whose ears still rang, could run away.

"Sit." She pushed him down, pulling another chair close so that he had little chance to retreat. "Will," his mother said softly. "Whatever have you done?"

Before Will Sloan could answer the door to Lem's

small retreat opened, and the two young friends were noisily reunited.

"Where've you *been*!"

"Me? Where d'you suppose?"

"Was it terrible?"

"Part of it surely was!"

"I was sorry—"

"What about you? Did you get it?"

"Not too bad."

"I see you got some pocks, all right."

"Not many, though they itch like fury—"

"Will," his mother said brusquely, seeing his flush for the first time, "how long have you had this fever?"

"A day or two, I guess," said the boy, brushing off her worried hands.

"Did you go in to Phoebe?" she demanded.

"You saw me, didn't you?" Will returned hotly. "I saw *you*, as well! Did—did you—?"

Now the door to the front room flew open and Diana Longfellow swept in. Recognizing the look of masculine rebellion that turned her way, she placed her hands on her hips and attacked.

"So, it's you! What have you done now?"

"What have I done? What have *I* done?" the boy cried out. "What's been done to *me*, I should be asked! My Phoebe's in her grave, and Mr. Wise says I have to stay here until he tells me different—here in the last house I ever wished to walk into again!"

"Hannah, put more wood on the fire," Miss Longfellow ordered, "so we can see if he is telling the truth. Young man—"

"I'm sorry for his tone, but the boy is ill and tired," said Hannah, protecting her son with her bulk.

"And which of us is not?" Diana responded, standing her ground. "But I have just thought of something else. Hannah, run and fetch Charlotte. Quietly! For Heaven's sake, don't let my brother know what's happening. Richard can ask his questions tomorrow. But I want to hear what's occurred before that, and I'm sure Charlotte does, too."

"He'll need food—"

"I can get him that. Now hurry."

Realizing Diana's orders were for the best, Hannah left her boy behind and hurried out the door.

The next several minutes were spent feeding Will and Lem both from what the pantry held—cold meat and mustard, as well as bread from the Bracebridge Inn, which they washed down with cider. A second meal after Phineas Wise's stew made Will drowsy, but he was not to rest yet, for his mother soon burst through the door with Mrs. Willett behind her.

Charlotte immediately reached out and ran her fingers along the boy's face and hands. "There's nothing under the skin to worry us," she reassured Hannah. "There's hardly been time, but he doesn't have the look to me—although he may still come down with it later, now that he *is* here."

"It would be well deserved," Hannah sighed heavily. "But at least I'll be able to care for him now."

"Will," Charlotte began in earnest, "what happened, when you last saw Phoebe?"

Asked to think again of one he'd lately adored, the boy began to whimper.

"Did you strike her?" Charlotte persisted.

"I wish I hadn't! But I had to do it! She'd just told me—"

"Please, Will, please!" Hannah moaned, fearing now to hear something she'd long dreaded.

At his mother's voice, Will jumped to his feet—for it was as if a voice had come back to haunt him, from beyond the grave. "That's what Phoebe begged me," he cried shrilly. "She told me she was afraid—but I loved her so! I would have forgiven her, too . . . I already had, when I came back—"

"Forgiven her what, Will?" Diana Longfellow demanded. "What had *she* done?"

"I don't know! There was something about her Aunt Mary, and a doctor came for a rash . . . and then I climbed in the window, when she told me she wouldn't say any more! I thought I could make her, when she said she wouldn't wed me—but she wouldn't say why, not even when I shook her!"

"You shook her?" Lem challenged.

Will's anger turned cold, and seemed to renew itself. "She told me I might have known something about her—about us—but since I *didn't*, she thought everything would be fine . . . but it *wasn't*, somehow! After that, she told me again she could never marry me—or anybody else, either. That's when I slapped her, and went back out through the window. I knew if I thought about something else for a while, I'd calm down, and then I'd come back and Phoebe and I . . . we'd straighten everything out."

"When *did* you come back?" Charlotte asked.

"Hours later, I guess. First I lay down, and then I fell asleep."

After weeping away some of his discontent, Charlotte guessed. "And then," she asked, "when you found her . . . ?"

"She was already—gone." The boy stared vacantly as he recalled the scene. "There was nothing I could do. I just left her there, on the floor, and started out."

"On the floor . . . ?"

"And that," Diana interjected triumphantly, "was when Hannah saw him."

"Hannah?" asked Charlotte, startled a second time. Then she understood. Hannah had not wanted to admit she saw Will coming from Phoebe's bedchamber that night. No wonder she had been silent, with such a secret.

"We saw each other," Hannah admitted cautiously.

"After Will ran away, I went in to see Phoebe. I thought to learn from the girl that what I'd feared all along had finally happened. Yet I never imagined—"

"And you, Will, you haven't been home since?"

The boy looked back to Mrs. Willett, and shook his head vigorously. "How could I? Everyone said I might carry the smallpox with me. And I didn't want to give it to Henry, or any of the others, either."

"I see," said Charlotte, looking down at the boy's filthy boots, then up to his stained and torn clothing. "But, Hannah," she continued, "what exactly did you find, when you went in?"

Hannah swallowed hard, thinking back. "I found Phoebe on the floor, like Will said, tangled in her sheets and the quilt. I lifted her, and laid her out as best I could. And then I picked up the book that was under her, and closed it."

"The one on the table?" asked Charlotte. "Was it open?"

"With a page or two wrinkled, which seemed a shame."

"Did you take a bottle from the room? Or anything else?"

"No, I did not." Hannah wiped her eyes with stout fingers, and settled back. "Although—"

"What?"

"I brought a good supply of valerian with me, to help me sleep. I always keep some in my chest of medicines. After that night, it was gone."

"And you think Phoebe may have taken it?"

"Unless Miss Longfellow—?"

Diana looked up, brought back from her own thoughts. "What now?" she asked sharply.

"Have you taken valerian lately, Diana?"

"For sleep? Not I. My conscience, at least, is clear."

She looked pointedly at Will, who had retreated into a corner.

"Do you think," Hannah tried hesitantly, "that it could have killed her? If she took enough?"

"No," Charlotte answered after a moment's thought. "I don't think it will kill anyone, in any amount. I *have* heard of someone sleeping for a day or two after swallowing a large quantity; that's why it's useful after a difficult birth . . . but no, I have never heard that valerian can be deadly."

"So," said Diana, "it looks as if we are back where we started."

"Perhaps not," Charlotte murmured to herself. She rose to her feet, and soon left the others planning what they would say to Richard Longfellow on the morrow. She then made her way to her study, to the table by what had once been Phoebe's bed. The volume of Alexander Pope had been replaced by another. But she found it in the shelf above. Sitting, Charlotte held the volume between her hands, and let the pages fall where they might, discovering that the book opened at the beginning of the well-known poem, "Elegy to the Memory of an Unfortunate Lady." A sad tribute, Charlotte recalled, but could it also be a message? For its subject was a suicide—one who had loved too well. Suddenly remembering something else, she reached through her skirt and drew a small, dry sphere of bread from her pocket. Had it been one of several? Had it been dropped there, and overlooked?

Softly, Charlotte made her way to her desk. She set the ball down, and then, taking a small paper knife, carefully sliced it in two with the point of the blade. After tasting a bit of brown powder, she sat back with a sigh, for what she had found made things a little clearer. And yet, there was still much to be connected. A portion of the story was now before her, though it could not be the whole.

Soon, she thought, there would surely come an accounting. *But what, she then wondered, would be the final cost?*

Chapter 16

—Monday

As spire bells struck the hour of ten, Edmund Montagu knocked on the door of a narrow brick house in Boston's North End. Here in Lime Street, not far from Christ's Church, he hoped to meet Mrs. Mary Morris. As the captain stood on the widow's stoop, steeple bells began to peal, and he noticed a ferry starting out across the river mouth for Charlestown. His eyes and ears might have found the situation more pleasant, had there been less on his mind, or in his heart.

When the door opened, Montagu saw a kindly-faced woman of middle age, modestly dressed in blue linen with a snowy kerchief, wearing a small lace cap. Unpainted and unhooped, she showed no fear of the morning light that illuminated a string of gold beads around her wattled throat. Though she was unsmiling, she regarded Captain Montagu with no apparent concern.

"Sir, may I help you?" Mrs. Morris asked, when she had taken his measure.

"I hope so, madam. My name is Montagu. I had business this morning at Town House, where I found your address. I believe you might help me to learn more about the death of Miss Phoebe Morris—as well as something of a gentleman by the name of Pelham."

Now a frown creased the woman's brow. She examined the captain's features more carefully; then she opened her door wider.

The small but gracious sitting room to which she led him was well supplied with newly polished furniture. After a moment, a young female in a servant's bib and apron was given an order for refreshment. Then they were left alone.

"I was greatly saddened to hear that my niece had passed on," the lady told Montagu, allowing herself a further moment for composure. "And I suspect her mother will struggle a long while to recover from it. Do you know the Morris family of Concord, Captain?"

"Unfortunately, no; nor did I have the honor of meeting your niece. I was called to Bracebridge only after her death. But I've heard enough to suppose she was liked and respected by everyone in that place."

"I can believe it to be so. Phoebe was a child of extraordinary talent, and much goodness, too. When she stayed with me a few years ago, she enjoyed talking to my maid Susanna, as well as with the more privileged young ladies I took her to see about the town."

"That is a wonder, with so many over-proud of their level in society."

Mrs. Morris's eyes studied him shrewdly. "Phoebe did take pride in her abilities, and in her family's circle in Concord, which I know holds many cultivated and serious minds. But my niece was never one to be swayed by fashion, or even position. She did seem to enjoy observing the better folk on our walks, but I believe she had simple tastes, herself. And, of course, she had little experience of Boston."

"Simplicity is a fault belonging to very few young ladies of my acquaintance," Montagu said more comfortably, causing Mrs. Morris to smile at a man's way of complaining about something he must also sometimes admire.

"My niece had a natural charm that might have been hidden, had she possessed a greater sense of style," the lady returned, looking over the captain's uniform.

"Though I believe she was an artist."

"Yes! A very fine one, it seemed to me. I have one of her drawings over the mantel. See the way she caught the trees, and the river. One can almost hear the water sing. . . ."

"Very pretty," was Montagu's vague reply, for his mind had moved on to another subject. "While she was here, I believe Miss Morris sketched one of your friends—David Pelham."

The frown of disquiet reappeared. Mary Morris rose to better study Phoebe's drawing, before she gave her reply.

"I did know Mr. Pelham, who lived not far from me at the time. I often saw him out walking; we were introduced one day by a mutual friend. After that, he came here on several occasions. I believe he found me sympathetic, and enjoyed my home as a sort of refuge. Mr. Pelham told me many of his acquaintance in other parts of the town— some of them quite old friends of his family—had been unwelcoming, after the deaths of his uncle and father. Even suspicious, due to his decline of fortune, he said. It seemed Mr. Pelham had hoped for an inheritance; but there had been little left after the family's debts, and his own, were settled. Nevertheless, I thought him a young man with good prospects—and, as I say, one who valued a quiet, neighborly place to visit. And then, Phoebe came to stay."

"That was in '61?"

"Yes—it must have been, for there'd been the fire in

Faneuil Hall, and Mr. Otis had just argued the Writs case. You're well informed," Mrs. Morris added with an inquiring look, as she sat once more.

"Did you know Pelham as a man of business?"

"I learned that he managed a warehouse for a distant relation, on one of the wharves. But I believe he lacked the money to direct his own affairs. Until his marriage, of course."

"And did you meet Mrs. Pelham?"

"No. After Phoebe left, I did not speak with Mr. Pelham again. And when his marriage was announced, he began a life far grander than our own . . . so it was only natural. . . ."

"I see. Mrs. Morris, I must ask you something else, and I hope you won't think it indelicate to answer, for your response may well affect the safety and happiness of another lady."

"Ask what you will, Captain. I know something about military ways; my brother-in-law is in His Majesty's Indian service. I realize you must sometimes be harsh, in the performance of your duties."

"An uncommon understanding, madam," Montagu replied with genuine gratitude. "What, then, did you think of the seriousness of the relationship that developed between Miss Morris and Mr. Pelham?"

Mary Morris's eyes again grew troubled, but still she refused to look away. "I thought, what a good thing for Phoebe, to have someone of taste and judgment view her drawing. For I was sure that whatever else he might be, David Pelham was a man who understood the finer things in life. For her part, I believe Phoebe brought out a happiness I'd not seen in him before. I had little idea, though, of anything coming of it, other than friendship."

"Because he didn't care enough for her?"

"Oh, I am very sure he *did* care for her! But I also knew

he would never marry without gaining by it. His family had fallen from a very high place, Captain, and I believe David Pelham saw it as his duty to elevate the name once again. Still, I was surprised when Phoebe expressed a fervent desire to quit Boston and return home. She seemed quite unwell. I've often asked myself if I should have warned her. . . ."

"But you did warn *him* . . . ?"

"Warn Mr. Pelham? Of what, Captain?"

"It's of no importance. Did you see your niece again, after that?"

"Oh, yes, when I visited Concord, once or twice. But we were never as intimate as during her stay here. I fear something changed in Phoebe. I don't know if she truly cared for David Pelham, and hated the thought of losing him, or if he perhaps disappointed her in some other way. I did not want to pry. Perhaps he was too blunt, in finally telling her of his intentions."

By now, the servant had brought tea and small cakes on a tray. She set them down next to her mistress and left the room, but Montagu observed a new shadow on the wall of the passage just outside the door. He had little doubt that the girl had not gone back to her duties, but lingered to hear their conversation.

When he had offered his condolences once more, he asked Mrs. Morris if he might interview her maid.

"Susanna? I suppose it would be all right. It did upset her to hear about Phoebe's death, but it might be a good thing for her to talk of it now. I'll send the girl in," she said, rising, "and leave you both alone, for a little while."

Mrs. Morris swept softly across the patterned carpet and into the hall, where she was surprised to see the girl kneeling with a cloth, attacking a crack in the floorboards.

"Go in and talk with Captain Montagu, Susanna. When he's done, come and find me in the kitchen."

Susanna obeyed, going in with her head down, but she soon had it up again to admire the braid on Montagu's coat, and the handsome hat he'd left on a side table.

"Sit down," the captain said, his manner less formal. "I'd like to hear something of Phoebe's visit three years ago. Had you served your mistress long, at the time?"

"Six months, sir. I was yet learning my duties, but I took care of Miss Morris as best I could."

"Did she seem happy when she came here?"

"Yes, sir. Very happy, I'd say."

"Was she as happy when she left?"

Susanna now imagined the captain's eyes resembled chips of river ice, hard and glittering. "I don't think so," she finally replied. "In fact, I'm sure she wasn't."

"Why was that?"

The maid seemed to struggle for an explanation. "I think . . . she had trouble with her heart."

"She had spells, do you mean?"

"Oh, no! Quite another kind, I'm afraid. I think Miss Morris was in love with a certain gentleman. Mr. Pelham, sir."

"And did that gentleman return her feelings?"

Susanna gave him something of a sly smile. "Sometimes, it seemed he did—at least to Phoebe."

"But you doubted it?"

"I can't say for sure, sir. But I saw the way he looked at me, too, when he first visited . . . *and* tried to kiss me. It wasn't entirely unpleasant, but I didn't care to be alone with him! I was raised close to the wharves, you see, with plenty of sailors and soldiers about, so I'd been taught early what such men want."

"Did you suppose David Pelham might use a girl unkindly?"

"I wouldn't say I *supposed* anything like that, sir, at least at first. When he saw Phoebe, I did think he was sweet to her. And then, he stopped bothering me."

"Do you think he tried to kiss Phoebe, as well?"

"More than that, I'd say."

"How do you know?" he asked, suddenly severe. "Your answer will touch the lives of others, so I think you had better tell me *all* you know, and quickly!"

"Yes, sir. I will, then! You see, I was acting as Miss Morris's personal maid. I don't know if you see what I mean, sir, but . . . being a personal maid involves several duties. Especially when there's not a lot of servants, like the rich have, each doing their own little job. The rich may be able to keep their secrets better, but I doubt it. Anyway, I helped Miss Morris dress and undress herself, and I washed all of her personal things, you see. That's how I knew . . ." She faltered, and fell silent.

"Go on," said Montagu, refusing to let the subject ruffle him.

"That's how I knew when her usual time was. And when one day I had extra to do, when it couldn't be that, then I knew she was no longer . . ."

"A maiden?" asked Montagu.

"Yes, sir. There was the garment first, and then her mood, as well. She was upset—didn't feel like eating, or much of anything else. My mistress feared she might be ill . . . but Miss Morris claimed it was often her way, during her times—though I knew it couldn't be, just then."

"Yes," said Montagu curtly, having heard quite enough. Then he had another thought. "What of Mr. Pelham's behavior?"

"He seemed no different. He kept up his visits, and soon Miss Morris seemed quite well again. But after several more weeks, when I saw her time hadn't come, she grew even more upset. This time, Mr. Pelham was, too. At least it seemed that way to me, after I put everything together."

"Was Miss Morris seeing anyone else?"

"I don't see how, sir. The mistress wouldn't let her go out alone with any gentleman, except Mr. Pelham."

"Then what happened?"

"Well, Mr. Pelham kept calling, which I thought was a good sign. One day, Phoebe had a rash, and her aunt called in a doctor for it. I don't know what else happened . . . with the other. She must have lost it. It was all quite sad, really. But I never dared to ask her about it, and I never heard later."

"And Mr. Pelham?"

"He stopped visiting then. We heard he was to marry another lady, a Miss Farnsworth, before long. He certainly advanced himself, from his visits to the docks, to Phoebe, and then to such a fine lady."

"The docks . . ."

"Well, I know a girl from home—Louisa is her name—who swore she saw Mr. Pelham there, from time to time."

"I believe he is involved in shipping."

"Yes, sir," Susanna agreed, but with a knowledgeable smile the captain found disturbing. Yet she was only a servant girl. He himself distrusted Pelham, but it would take more than a mere girl's romantic imagination to convince a British officer of another gentleman's moral failings.

"Tell me, Susanna," said Edmund Montagu, "do you also know a physician named Tucker?"

"Why, yes, sir! It was Dr. Tucker who came to treat Miss Morris. I believe he was first a friend to Mr. Pelham. Or, at least, I believe they knew one another."

"Did you find Dr. Tucker unusual in any way?"

"Unusual, sir? I wouldn't say so. He seemed a nice old gentleman. I remember he told me he had a daughter my age."

"Nothing odd about the way he treated you? Or Miss Morris?"

"Odd? How do you mean?"

"Did he ever bother you, the way Mr. Pelham—"

"Oh, no, sir!" Susanna objected with a firm shake of

her head. "He was quite a sweet old man, I thought. So did Phoebe, I'm sure. Dr. Tucker treated my friend Louisa, too, which was very kind of him," Susanna went on in a confidential tone. "She's a sailor's girl, you see, and not every physician will see such patients."

"A sailor's girl? Do you mean . . . by profession?"

"Yes, sir—though hardly as coarse as some. She's the kind of girl even a gentleman might go and see, every so often."

Edmund Montagu hardly knew what to ask next. "One more thing," he finally said to Susanna, whose eyes sparkled at the thought of telling the captain still more of a wicked nature.

"Yes, sir?"

"Would you say Phoebe was a girl who wanted to climb in social rank?"

"Rank, sir?" Susanna now cocked an eyebrow suspiciously at the Englishman.

"Was there something she would have done much to gain, do you think? Wealth, perhaps?"

"Oh, I see. I have known girls who would marry a purse at the cost of their own hearts, if that's what you mean, sir. The way they do in England, I've heard, where many are even forced! Is that still true?"

"Young ladies often do marry according to their parents' wishes, though these are not always loveless matches."

"I would hope not. Though I'd like to see someone try to marry me off for gold. I think it is a cruel thing, don't you, sir? Though a little gold may be useful, to most of us. As for Miss Morris, I think she was happy to return home to Concord and what she had there, though it wasn't a great deal by the stick of some, I'm sure. And I heard she found a young man to marry her after all. I often thought about her, when Mrs. Morris received letters from her family."

"Did you never tell your mistress what you suspected?"

"I did think of that . . . but no, sir. At the time, I didn't know some of the things I understand now—concerning my responsibilities. I was only fifteen at the time. I've learned a great deal since then," said the girl, looking fearlessly into the captain's eyes. "For instance, I've learned it's sometimes best to keep what I learn to myself. Unless it might have value to others . . ."

"Thank you, Susanna. I think that is all I need ask." He reached into a pocket and pulled out a shilling.

"Sir, may I ask *you* a question?" she asked after she had stood and curtsied.

"What is it?"

"Do you know Mr. Pelham?"

"I do," he replied. Something in his expression made her smile a little.

"You do not like him?"

"Not especially," he confided, feeling that she had earned a small degree of familiarity.

"Has he got his eye on someone you know, sir?"

This, Captain Montagu decided, he must ignore.

"I wish her well, then—and good luck to you and your lady, sir," said Susanna as she gave another swift curtsy and departed—leaving the captain to consider saucy charms that led, all too often, to misfortune.

In a few minutes more, after he had given the proper words of farewell to Mrs. Morris, Edmund Montagu found himself again facing the teeming streets of Boston, with spirits fallen suddenly into confusion.

David Pelham, the captain had now discovered, was what he'd earlier suspected—a man able to ruin and then leave a young girl, even one who loved him. And yet by all appearances Pelham, too, had been in love. Such things happened, even when they were inadvisable. Captain Montagu knew this better than most. The trouble was, such imperfect gentlemen—especially wealthy ones— actually *attracted*, rather than repelled, spirited ladies, whose urge to reform such rakes was well known—and usually led only to more unhappiness. Should he tell Diana of the rascal's reputed affair? What if that course only increased her interest, already piqued by Pelham's passionate attentions? It was also, Montagu decided fairly—though he ground his teeth at the effort—it was also risky business to judge a man's character solely by his sexual appetites. Even among the great, after all, there were peculiarities, and men who satisfied their lusts in ways both common and uncommon. Earlier, in alluding lightly to mistresses among the London aristocracy, Miss Longfellow had not been far wrong—although he had disputed the point for her own good.

Yet would such a man do for Diana? Captain Montagu found the idea too affecting to contemplate for long. Who would choose a better husband for her? Her brother? That hardly seemed likely. Would Richard Longfellow even forbid the match with Pelham, if Diana insisted upon it? And what could he, himself, hope to do about it?

Captain Montagu began to blow on his numbed fingers—and realized that the air had grown cold. He would take a few moments to swallow a glass or two of restoring brandy on his way to his last chore of the morning. Looking forward to little else, he strode downhill through streets and lanes, toward less respectable dwellings and taverns in alleys near the harbor.

An hour later, he was let in to the place Benjamin Tucker had lately called home. A first chamber had several windows, now shuttered, while its furnishings included an examining couch, two chairs and a table, a screen, and a plain chest of drawers, which turned out to hold only objects useful to a physician. The room's one carpet was colorful, but wine-stained and worn. In a corner stood a battered desk.

Clearly, any patients Tucker had seen here tolerated a less than prosperous atmosphere. The place was barely respectable, though it did seem clean. The landlady had been pleased to comment on this herself. She had appreciated her tenant for his habits and his demeanor, she informed Montagu; and, due to the fall in trade and wages, she had few hopes of soon letting the modest apartment to another.

A brief look into a smaller room, once the landlady had left him alone, revealed a bed, a sagging rush-bottomed reading chair, and a number of books on various subjects. Some stood high on rough shelves, while others were lined up on the floor; he found still more in an old barrel. Where most of Dr. Tucker's fees had gone was now obvious. That explained the pathetic state of the man's attire, though it recommended the liveliness of a spirit now extinguished forever.

Going back into the public room, Montagu walked to the desk to glance through a scattering of papers. He soon uncovered a pair of bound, blank-paged books, normally used for record keeping. A cursory examination showed one of the volumes to be, indeed, a history of appointments and charges, while the other contained lists of ingredients for the creation of medical prescriptions; the latter's inside cover also gave the names and addresses of three Boston apothecaries. While some physicians made their own preparations, the captain knew, there were many who felt the practice beneath them. Apparently, Tucker had been one of these—a man who took pride in his position, albeit one that had been considerably reduced. Or had the physician perhaps looked for someone else on whom to cast blame, should his treatments bring poor results?

Reopening the daybook, Montagu leafed through its initial pages, which covered Dr. Tucker's earliest months in Boston. There it was: *David Pelham*, beside a date, *February 11, 1761*. Next to this, in a tiny, nearly indecipherable hand, was a description of a course of treatment. This included Roman numerals, which the captain assumed referred to preparations prescribed. A page farther, there was more of the same, and later, in December, a large increase in the quantity of the numbered stuff, again next to Pelham's name. After that, the patient seemed to have left the book's pages entirely. Flipping back, Captain Montagu looked for another name. He soon found it—*Phoebe Morris, Concord, with Mary Morris, of Boston, first seen September 19, 1761*. There were notations that indicated two further calls to Mrs. Morris's home, as well as the numeral of some substance used in treatment.

Montagu next examined the book of apothecary receipts more closely. There, he found a surprising number of specific clays and metallic salts whose uses were largely unknown to him, at least in the practice of medicine. However, one concoction did jog his memory; oddly, this proved to be the same compound prescribed for David Pelham. And given what Montagu believed to be the chief medical use of its main component—

Again, he felt the air's increasing chill.

If Pelham had purchased *all* of this, and continued to take it . . . then it was lucky the rascal was still alive! It was no wonder that his temper vacillated—but how could it have been wise of Tucker to prescribe such quantities of quicksilver? Or had Benjamin Tucker *intended* to harm his patient? It was indeed a possibility, and a sobering thought—particularly, coming on top of his new knowledge of David Pelham.

Yet one thing more wanted doing, to settle Montagu's immediate curiosity. He continued through the book until he found the notation for the prescription given to Miss Morris. This, he was surprised to see, was only a simple grease salve, enhanced with pitch and camphor.

As he was about to depart, Montagu noticed a letter tucked into a nook of the desk, above the rest of its clutter. It was addressed to Dr. Tucker; however, its waxed seal was unbroken. Surely, it had come here during the man's recent absence, and had been placed there, in all probability, by his landlady. The captain was surprised to see, upon breaking the seal, that the sheet contained no writing, but only a second sheet, folded and sealed as well—this letter addressed to Richard Longfellow, of Bracebridge!

After giving the new matter a bit of thought, Captain Montagu slipped the second letter beneath his coat. Then he took up both of the record books and thrust them under his arm, before gladly leaving Benjamin Tucker's pinched little world behind.

AT THE SAME moment, Diana Longfellow sat in her chamber attempting to soothe her frayed emotions, as a new wail rose in Mrs. Willett's kitchen. She listened to Will Sloan's strident insistence and his mother's flat denial—it mattered little what this new issue was, for they had found several to argue over already that morning. When the commotion settled down, the awful noise overhead could again be heard—for Lem had retreated to Diana's former bedchamber, where he paced heavily over complaining floorboards.

The only pleasure allowed Miss Longfellow this morning was the company of David Pelham, who sat smiling at her despite the intolerable distraction all around them. But even this one pleasure, thought Diana as she frowned ominously, was beginning to pall. And as she had correctly imagined the night before when she'd seen the vile boy again, Will was to be a continuing torment to them all! She was almost sorry that a rest had lowered his fever. This, Diana thought for the twentieth time, was more than one could be expected to stomach! What was worse, her head had begun to ache fiercely, and her skin to prick with irritation. All in all, it was not a day on which she was pleased to suffer fools gladly!

Looking to Mr. Pelham, she saw that he, too, had heard the spat—how could he help it!—although that gentleman seemed more interested in admiring her than in anything else. Which would make what she had decided to tell him all the more difficult. But she *would* do it.

"Mr. Pelham, I have decided—"

"Yes, Miss Longfellow?"

"I will leave here this morning—no matter *what* my brother has said. After all, he can have no idea! I'm sure I will rest far better at his house than in this one. Beyond that, I will then have Mrs. Willett always to talk to. Unhappily, I cannot remember if Cicero has had the smallpox; but if he has not, it is high time that he did. There seems to be nothing to the inoculation I have had, after all. So, if you will escort me, and carry the few things that I will put into this hatbox, someone can come for the rest later. There—I do feel better. But that is usually the case, once I have made up my mind."

"I must say I will enjoy visiting you in your brother's house, Miss Longfellow, even more than I do here," David Pelham replied quite happily.

"Well, that is something else I meant to tell you this morning. At the moment, I think it would be best for me to retire completely from the world, and perhaps for some little time. I believe that family—and Mrs. Willett, of course—shall be my solace during the remainder of my quarantine."

Pelham's smile froze. "Do you really think it wise to leave, Miss Longfellow?" Suddenly remembering something else, he added, "Will you not find Captain Montagu, who is staying there as well, something of a nuisance? Perhaps he can be persuaded to leave—but will you not find you want our cheerful talks again, before long?"

"What I *want* is a little peace and quiet!" said Diana hotly. Then, with a sigh, she relented. "When we are both back in Boston, we will again share an evening. A good game of cards would be amusing, I'm sure—but I am not up to it now."

"It is, of course, your health you must think of first; yet I do hope—"

"It is for the best. I'm certain of it," Miss Longfellow assured him. How weary she was today, and how tired of being pursued. She prayed for an end to all banter, and for a long nap. But first, she moved about the room, tossing several small items into a banded hatbox, which she then covered and delivered into David Pelham's waiting hands.

"There! I know Richard is gone for the morning, so he will be unable to refuse me. Once I am inside, I would like to see him try to throw me out!" Diana then led the way from Charlotte's study. "Hannah, I am *going*!" She flung this over her shoulder in a renewal of her former grand manner, as she passed the suddenly silent pair in the kitchen. She paused to tug open the back door. Then, her cheeks flushed, Miss Longfellow hurried out into the barnyard and down through the garden with Mr. Pelham covering her retreat—on her way, she prayed, to a far better situation.

Chapter 17

SHORTLY BEFORE DIANA and David Pelham entered her brother's house through the back door, Charlotte Willett went out the front. The cool spring air played with her skirts as she walked onto the Boston-Worcester road, headed toward the village. The day appeared fair, with little in it to worry her. But worry she did, as she made her way down the long hill.

Charlotte knew that Richard Longfellow was at the moment meeting with the other selectmen, after an earlier interrogation of Will Sloan. The night before, when she returned and found her neighbor still amusing himself with an old collection of the *Spectator*, she let him know Will had come home on his own, and that he suffered from a fever. She'd also suggested that early morning would be a better time to question the boy, for he had already been put to bed exhausted. Longfellow, though surprised, had agreed.

Diana, too, would now be busy, as she expected a visit from Mr. Pelham after breakfast. Captain Montagu must still be in Boston. And even Cicero had gone out with a pole, hoping to coax a few trout from Pigeon Creek with the aid of minnow or mayfly. It was an occupation she envied.

However, Charlotte had made another plan. She doubted it would have been approved by her friends, had they known of it—nor was she entirely sure her idea was a wise one. Yet she *would* know the truth, even if what she planned to do had already provoked her conscience.

Now, she passed by the Bracebridge Inn, turned off the road, and doubled back through a field that led to a copse of birch; from its shelter she could see the inn's side door and Jonathan Pratt's closet window. Was he there, looking out? Boldly, Mrs. Willett walked into the yard, gained the side door, entered, and stood still. No other door opened; no footsteps approached. Thus far, she was safe.

Softly, she made her way to the back stairs used by the servants, and climbed the narrow steps between white-washed walls. At the top, she turned into the hall and listened once more. No one was about; most guests probably lingered over breakfast, or had ridden out early. The only question was, which door was David Pelham's?

When her knock went unanswered, Charlotte turned the first knob slowly, and peered into the room beyond. Inside, she saw enough baggage to indicate occupancy by two people, and a pair of ladies' shoes by a low chair. Closing the door gently, she moved on.

Her next knock did rouse an inhabitant, who opened the door only a crack as he scowled out. A shaved head without a wig indicated a gentleman, who was obviously not an early riser.

"I'm terribly sorry, sir," said Charlotte, her eyes lowered. "I'm afraid I've been directed to the wrong chamber. I am looking for my cousin, Mr. Pelham. Do you know him?"

"Pelham? No!" cried the man, before he slammed the door in her face.

Charlotte approached the next room with her breath quickened. This time she knocked more gently, hoping to let sleeping lodgers lie if there were any within. Again, there was no sound. She turned the brass knob and slipped the door open an inch or two, cringing as it groaned on its hinges. The chamber was deserted, with no sign of occupancy at all.

Opposite the last door in the row, Mrs. Willett paused to quiet her racing heart. Slowly, she worked the bright knob, then eased the door until she could peep through the long crack to the daylight beyond. At last, she suspected she'd found the right room. Inside, the long curtains had been opened. Hanging on a chair at the side of the ash-filled hearth was a familiar black frock-coat, and an indigo scarf. She was relieved to find the bed already made—the girl who took care of this, and other things, had done her duties, and so would not return soon.

Charlotte entered and shut the door. Swiftly, she made a survey of David Pelham's possessions. A traveling valise, small enough to fit on the back of a horse. There was also a trunk, certainly delivered later by cart.

She knelt beside the valise. Inside, she found only silver bridle ornaments wrapped in brown paper, removed for safekeeping, no doubt, while Pelham's horse boarded in the stable. She suspected the bag's previous contents lay in the highboy that stood against a wall. This, indeed, held various articles of clothing and, in the bottom drawer, more that awaited the wash. She had not yet found what she came for.

The trunk proved more interesting. Here, she discovered a book of plays from London, a collection of ballads—and a magazine sprinkled with lewd and skillful drawings of lusting gentlemen, and ladies in compromised positions. Feeling her face burn, Charlotte soon put all of these items back where she'd found them.

She next lifted out a black lacquered case, and slipped the clasp. Here was a container for medicines divided into several compartments, some containing a box or two, others with a bottle inside. Methodically, she opened or unstoppered each one. She found dried curls of peppermint leaves next to powdered ginger; both were most likely carried to ward off indigestion. The largest bottle was labeled *ipecacuanha in wine*, a stronger remedy to combat poisoning by one's dinner, and sometimes the flux—as its purgative action mimicked and relieved both conditions. These were prudent precautions for the sage traveler. Another bottle, her nose quickly told her, contained a decoction of witch hazel, often used to help heal bruises and scratches, or an injury to the eye. And that was all.

One more package remained inside the valise, this made of silk tied with its own attached ribbon. She loosened the bow, admiring an embroidered peacock on the ivory-colored fabric. Then she unfolded the whole, revealing several sewn pockets of golden satin, two of them full. At last, her efforts were rewarded.

Carefully, Charlotte slipped an object into her pocket, before restoring the parcel. Looking about the room, she checked to be sure that it was the same as when she'd entered. It wouldn't do to have Mr. Pelham know of her visit. At least, not yet. When she was sure nothing was amiss, she walked to the door—and stepped back suddenly as it opened toward her.

"Mrs. Willett?" asked a perplexed voice. David Pelham looked out at the hall again, to be certain he was in the right room. But a quick glance back to his own possessions swiftly changed his demeanor.

"Mrs. Willett," he said in quite another tone. Charlotte continued to back away, as he entered and closed the door behind him. "To what do I owe this honor?"

"Mr. Pelham! I was just—in truth—when I came and saw that you were out . . . I'm afraid I became curious. Which is hardly unusual," she laughed, "as I have always had difficulty keeping my nose, some say, out of other people's affairs! Though I would imagine you find my presence here, in your absence, a little annoying. I do beg your pardon for my weakness."

"I see." David Pelham appeared to resign himself, after sensing the obvious embarrassment of the woman before him. "Your curiosity *is* something you've warned me of, Mrs. Willett. No matter. I'm sure you've found nothing that will long disturb either of us."

"No . . ." she replied, suddenly remembering the magazine, and blushing scarlet. At this, Pelham seemed to weigh the situation anew.

"I don't imagine you are easily surprised, Mrs. Willett," he finally answered. "You have, as they say, seen something of life. Well, you have certainly trespassed against me, but at least I perceive that thievery is not another of your vices, for I don't find anything in your hands . . . and you were clearly ready to depart."

"I can forgive rudeness as a result of outrage, sir," Charlotte returned, hoping to hide her growing fear with a semblance of anger, "but I'm not certain that entering an unlocked room at a country inn is anything very terrible! For surely, there are some who do it daily, to accomplish their duties."

"True. But I have begun to believe you question too much about me, madam. And now, I think, you go out of your way to seek the worst!"

"Is it strange to be interested in a man who seeks the heart of one's dearest friend—a young lady whose qualities, and virtue, I must suppose we both value highly?"

"Miss Longfellow—"

"—who has spoken so warmly of you recently, that I only wished to learn more on my own? Yet I will repeat, sir, that I am truly sorry you've found me here."

"I can well imagine *that*. Might I suppose, Mrs. Willett, you are also envious of my attentions to Diana?" he countered, a slow smile calming his face.

"You might," she replied cautiously, casting her eyes down to his soft boots.

"Tell me," David Pelham said abruptly in a mocking voice, "if there is anything else you'd care to know. Go ahead—do ask me! No—I hardly think you're interested in me for yourself, madam, no more than I believe you are here merely to satisfy the simple curiosity of a country widow. What do you imagine? And what will you do, to spoil my chances with Miss Longfellow?" he demanded, taking a quick step forward.

Near the window, something appeared to move. Charlotte caught a glimpse of what looked for an instant like a figure—then heard Pelham give a cry of alarm. Yet when she looked more carefully, all she could observe was the long curtain of green velvet, bunched against the wall. Whatever had just occurred caused David Pelham to stride ahead and fling the heavy cloth up into the air. Again, nothing; but the moment gave Mrs. Willett an opportunity to turn and hurry for the door.

Before she could open it, Pelham sprang. She winced as his hand gripped her forearm.

"What is it you want?" he cried.

"I want to know the truth!" she threw back. "Why Phoebe Morris is dead—*and* Benjamin Tucker—and why *you*, who knew them both, have kept at least part of the reason from the rest of us!"

"You want to know exactly what I know? All right, then! I only hope the story pleases you!" Letting her arm drop, David Pelham stepped back, and glared at her as he began.

"Three years ago, in Boston, Tucker helped Phoebe Morris rid herself of an unborn child. She wanted it gone, so she'd be free to go home to Concord. The father was apparently some fool who refused to marry her, and insisted Phoebe must not give birth to his heir. As a friend, I was told the sordid story first by Tucker, and then by Phoebe herself, for she had no other she could turn to. The worst of it was, I did truly love her!"

At this, he closed his eyes against the memory. But he soon opened them again, and began to walk about by fits and starts, as if to avoid a ghostly pursuit. "You should have seen her then—for she had a rare, wonderful talent for grasping joy! In a town full of gossiping, scheming, sour young women, Phoebe was so alive! I still see her—"

He wheeled suddenly, going to the window to finger its soft curtain with great deliberation, before continuing.

"It was not only to please her aunt that I spent hours listening to her voice, watching her as she sketched, sharing her dreams. And then, she told me she carried a child for someone else, a man she had discovered was not about to save her!"

He faltered, took a shuddering breath, and forced himself to go on more carefully.

"Perhaps I loved too well—and unwisely. But that all ended three years ago. When I came to this place, I had no idea she was here. I told you later that I feared Phoebe might have renewed her feelings, had I spoken with her again. That was true, for I'm certain she once bore as profound an affection for me as I had for her. But after hearing what she had done, how *could* I wed her? However, I was still determined to protect her name; and then, seeing Dr. Tucker here as well, I realized we were all three on the brink of new lives which might easily be ruined by the past. I knew Tucker had suffered for his foolish deeds. No money, few friends—the man was surely at the end of his rope. As for Phoebe—need I tell you?

"Please, answer me, Mrs. Willett—was it my duty to reveal all that I knew? What would have been my motive? To punish them *further*? And what difference could the revelation of what I knew have made . . . once they were both dead?"

"How was it done?" Charlotte asked softly, while she struggled to imagine Phoebe and her physician sharing such a secret.

"Tucker had experience with these things. In Virginia, knowingly or not, he gave a young woman one of his remedies—mercury, mainly, I believe—which soon killed her child, and then the mother, as well. He told me this had caused him to leave that place, whence he came to Boston."

Again, David Pelham paced, his anger mounting.

"If you had moved in Boston society, Mrs. Willett, you would certainly have heard that Benjamin Tucker was hounded from Williamsburg. There were even whisperings that he murdered my wife, simply because I knew him—though she had her own physician, and distrusted mine! Such ideas can themselves be deadly. In fact, facing enough lies, a man might well lose his senses. I believe that must be what happened to Tucker. His journey to Brace-bridge might have seemed a final opportunity to renew his fortunes—but his conscience must have been a torment to him still. When he recognized Phoebe, I can only guess what feelings and regrets were reborn, in both. The end, of course, was that Phoebe's health broke. Or, perhaps, the poor girl found some poison to end her troubles. Who knows, Tucker may even have helped there, once again! Would that not explain why, in a fit of drunken remorse, Dr. Tucker blew out his own brains?

"Is *that* clear enough for you, Mrs. Willett? Do you now perceive the entire situation? Have the dead been dishonored enough? *Have you any other questions for me?*"

Charlotte shook her head, stunned by the fury and the anguish in Pelham's declaration.

"Go, then, and tell Miss Longfellow what a great sinner I am, for the fault of trying to keep such a tragedy concealed."

"Mr. Pelham, I—"

"Leave me." He uttered the dismissal bitterly, before she could say more. "Go home, madam, and think about all that I have said. Being a vastly clever woman, I know you will understand that what I have told you should go no further."

Chapter 18

STUNG AND SHAKEN by what she had heard, Mrs. Willett eased her spirit (and perhaps, she supposed, her conscience) with a walk that was almost a canter across the fields, in a journey toward the green knoll behind her house. Orpheus came bounding as he abandoned his morning inspection for higher duties. Falling to her knees, Charlotte thrust her face into his familiar fur—and rubbed the old dog's ribs until his tongue lolled with pleasure. A kindness accomplished, she rose and went on with better courage.

The story that David Pelham had revealed to her was not, she had to admit, impossible to believe. She was aware that such things could happen in the world—and she herself had half suspected—

But toss emotion, like a dye, into a pot, and it must surely color any cloth, no matter if it were woven of hearsay or observation. Was it possible to look beyond her own first impressions of Phoebe Morris and Benjamin Tucker? These contained far more of a bright nature than the dark secrets David Pelham had lately revealed. Yet was his reason sufficiently clear of feeling, to focus on the truth?

"A penny, Mrs. Willett!" The voice was startlingly near, but welcome nonetheless. Approaching, Richard Longfellow leaned down to pat Orpheus, who sat and listened keenly.

"I was thinking," she replied, "of the manner of Phoebe Morris's death."

"As was I, earlier this morning. We've now decided, officially, that the death of Miss Morris was misadventure at worst, *perhaps* influenced by Dr. Tucker's care; yet likely nothing more than a tragic quirk of Nature. At any rate, we'll look no further for blame, or for explanation."

"And yet . . ."

"And yet, Carlotta?" Longfellow asked with a qualm.

"Richard, I have just come from David Pelham's room at the inn."

"He invited you there? That hardly seems—"

"I went on my own, and I did see him . . . eventually. I think now you should hear what he told me."

Longfellow sighed, considering the danger of continuing. "What, then, have you heard?" he finally asked her.

Slowly, but with growing excitement, Charlotte relived her painful encounter with David Pelham. First came the story of Phoebe's pregnancy, discovered while she stayed with her aunt in Boston; then, Dr. Tucker's involvement in its end, through a remedy used before in Williamsburg, with similar result; this was followed by Pelham's suspicion of the physician's hand in Phoebe's death—or at least his part in creating the low state of mind that surely helped to kill her; and finally, Mrs. Willett related how Tucker's actions, in a fateful twist, preyed on his mind until he took his own life.

"Can this be true?" Longfellow asked, appalled, when she had finished. "Perhaps Montagu was right, then. '*When lovely woman stoops to folly* . . .' Yet I'm amazed to think Tucker could have gone against his oath as a physician so completely!"

"I confess to going into Mr. Pelham's chamber with another idea, though now, especially after what you've told me, I hardly know what to think! I believe we *can* say one thing with certainty. *Each* of them did lie to us—Phoebe, Pelham, and Dr. Tucker. I wonder if Mr. Pelham is even now telling us all he knows."

"But are his conclusions to be believed? Tucker, as I told you, maintained that Phoebe Morris was, in fact, a virgin upon her death."

"Something difficult for *me* to credit," Charlotte replied gently.

"Why, Mrs. Willett—exactly?"

Charlotte considered carefully before she answered. If she were to divulge her suspicions, and Longfellow were to add his own, they might come to conclusions that would cause even more suffering. Was it right to use one's intelligence, she wondered, to envision what *might have happened*, without good reason? Yet if they did not explore every path, how would they learn what lay beneath this whole matter? She knew her neighbor was not a man likely to seek revenge—but if they found reason to suspect further blame, it would be his duty, as a selectman, to act upon it. That could not be helped, she decided.

"Earlier," she began anew, "I thought more than once that there was something very curious in Phoebe's coming here. She came to marry without her parents arranging it—barely, I suspect, with her father's approval. And yet she often seemed distracted and unhappy . . . until a few weeks ago. *Why* was she not looking forward to her future,

I first found myself wondering, if she loved Will Sloan? Was it because of some cruelty in her past? Or a lingering memory? I guessed she'd once given her heart to someone besides Will, for she was a girl of lively wit and feeling . . . but of all the men in Massachusetts, why would she choose to marry *Will Sloan*? *Why* would Phoebe Morris, who had no reason to lack suitors, but acknowledged to Diana that she had only one—why would she take a boy who is not handsome, witty, or well schooled, and who has little interest in her sketches, or in traveling? Why accept someone with little knowledge of life at all—rather than someone who could open doors into the greater world she longed to see?

"One possible answer occurred to me. If Phoebe did once have a lover, and if she had lost her claim to purity, then she might have feared a new husband would discover the fact, in the obvious way. It would have been grounds for an annulment; it would also be something she would not want her family to hear of, if she was forced to return to them. But—suppose Phoebe were to wed a much older man. Such a man might overlook a past indiscretion, to enjoy a pretty young bride. But then, a *younger* man might be even better, for he might be *unable to tell* that he was not the first! At least, he might be more easily fooled into believing that what he claimed on his wedding night was his alone. Will admitted as much, I think: '*She told me I might have seen something about her—about us.*' "

Longfellow broke in. "And so, Will took the bait. But if he had indeed been fooled, then why . . . ?"

"I suspect that here in Bracebridge, shortly after Phoebe was inoculated, something *else* must have occurred; only then did she seek to escape a future that offered no happiness. For this, at least, I suspect we have some proof."

"Proof?" asked Longfellow, grasping a tangible straw.

"Here," said Charlotte, reaching into her pocket and holding out the two halves of the pellet she had split the night before. Longfellow took them in his palm and studied them.

"Valerian," he concluded while Orpheus inched forward, taking a sniff of his own.

"Yes."

"But . . . what *is* this thing?"

"Bread, I think." Despite the gravity of her explanation, Mrs. Willett smiled. "As children, when we were given distasteful medicine to swallow, Eleanor and I sometimes wrapped it in pieces of soft bread, making something like the rolled pills we'd seen. Like those you probably had from the apothecary, in town."

"You believe Hannah provided a quantity of valerian from her simples chest, to help the girl sleep?"

"No—Hannah was stunned to find her supply gone when she wanted it herself, after we discovered Phoebe's body. I suspect the girl secretly made several of these spheres, Richard, after Will left her. One of them must have rolled under the bed, where it was found. The rest sent Phoebe into a stupor. I presume she believed it would bring on a peaceful death. Young girls often believe what they choose, even against reason, and frequently act against good sense."

"They do," Longfellow had to agree, with a look toward the farmhouse where his sister now resided.

"Then, there is the book."

"The volume of Pope?" Longfellow asked, remembering the scene when they had viewed Phoebe's body.

"Hannah found it creased and on the floor, under the body. Has she said—?"

"The girl was tangled in the bedclothes, yes. But no one mentioned the book, when I spoke with Will and his mother this morning."

"Hannah probably thought it of no importance. Yet

last night, when I let the volume fall open, I saw a poem, 'Elegy to the Memory of an Unfortunate Lady.' "

" 'Is it, in heaven, a crime to love too well?' And there is something about acting a Roman's part—referring to the opening of a vein, I suppose . . ."

Charlotte, who had reread the poem the night before, whispered its eerie beginning:

> "What beckoning ghost, along the moonlight shade,
> Invites my steps, and points to yonder glade?"

"You think she gave us a suicide's message," Longfellow concluded.

"I believe she lay down, stricken, holding the book to her breast—knowing someone would eventually find her. I suppose she hoped we would feel sorry, and forgive her. But when someone did come in while she was in this state, he cared nothing for her pose. Phoebe tried to save herself with the last of her fading strength, and slid from the bed; then, I suspect, he pressed a pillow to her face, after the book had fallen."

"If the girl told Will Sloan more than he now admits, he may have returned in a rage. . . ."

"But I feel we *must* go back and find the answer to one question, Richard. Why *now* did she tell Will she could not marry him, as he does admit—not now, or ever? Phoebe's error occurred long before they made their contract. Could she not have imagined he might forgive her? For I think he would have."

"Perhaps not, if she'd ended a child's life, as well. If she feared Will would be warned by Tucker, or even Pelham—"

"That is possible, I suppose—but what if Phoebe had given herself again—to the same man?" For a moment, Charlotte recalled Dr. Tucker's impassioned face as he held Phoebe's hand, before she left them alone.

"I might almost believe it was *Pelham*, then—except that he would never have dared it, with Diana there. But you can't suppose she and Ben Tucker—!"

For a moment Charlotte reconsidered.

"Will Sloan told us Phoebe would not marry him, but also that she could not marry anyone else, either. Dr. Tucker, of course, *was* married already . . . but why should Phoebe reject the idea of marriage entirely? With anyone?"

"Why, indeed?" asked Longfellow, having no idea.

"I can think of one reason, though it is unusual, and somewhat unrelated. In a few women, the thought of producing children can become a fearful torment . . . and she had lost one, we presume, already, however it happened. As her wedding approached, it's not unlikely that Phoebe sought out Dr. Tucker to talk about the process of giving birth . . . on the very eve of her death." Charlotte continued, losing momentum, "Yet she had at least appeared to be happy before that, when she imagined her life with Will. Why, now, would children . . . ?"

"Who can tell, with women?" Longfellow countered, growing impatient. "All we are doing is guessing, Carlotta, while we have no facts to build upon."

"Yes, but why now, Richard? Does it hinge on something Tucker did . . . or possibly something he told Phoebe? What *could* she have learned from him, to so— Oh!"

Suddenly, she believed she knew. It was little more than an intuition, and yet—! At last, the pieces, like the spokes of a broken wheel, fit together to create a whole. She stood dumb as she tested several connections carefully. Then, Charlotte again put a hand into the pocket beneath her skirt, and brought out the item she'd brazenly taken from David Pelham's room at the inn.

"What is this?" asked Longfellow.

"A buckle."

"I can see it is. But why '*Oh!*' Mrs. Willett?"

Her original, though vague, supposition of that morning now made far more sense, and Charlotte went on rapidly. "I went to Pelham's room looking for this . . . as I believed it possible that he, too, went in to Phoebe, some time between the visits Will Sloan admits to. I blush to tell you, Richard, but I saw new marks on the windowsill the morning we found her. I thought little of them with so much else happening, and when no one else supposed them important. Still, they bothered me. This is a buckle David Pelham wore the afternoon we first met him at the inn—I remembered its unusual silver thistle, with the ruby points. They are quite hard and sharp."

Longfellow took the buckle into his own hands, where its stones shone with the hue of heart's blood. "And you think the spacing of the stones will match the mars in the sill's paint? I did notice them, Carlotta, but I confess I assumed they were made by the claws of our friend Orpheus." At the mention of his name, the dog thumped his tail, rewarded as last for his patient attendance.

"There is a simple test—"

"But why would Pelham climb in to see Phoebe in the middle of the night, when he is clearly interested in Diana's favors?"

"If he had been the father of her child—"

"Even if that were true, I hardly think it would lead the man to murder her! Even if Phoebe *had* told Diana, do you think such an affair three years ago would be enough to utterly deter a woman of Boston, these days?"

"But what if Pelham gave Phoebe something . . . something more than a child?"

"More?" asked Longfellow, waiting for his neighbor to go on, which she suddenly seemed reluctant to do.

"Richard," said Charlotte finally, "imagine, first, that there was an intimacy, and at least the suspicion of a child to come, when Tucker was called in by Phoebe's aunt to treat the girl's rash. Later, Phoebe's child is lost, possibly after she had already gone back to Concord, but before her condition became obvious. But what if that loss was not by plan, as Mr. Pelham suggests? What if it came about only as a result of disease?"

"Disease," Longfellow repeated.

"I think Dr. Tucker suspected Phoebe's situation in Boston, though I doubt he was sure. But then, meeting him again in Bracebridge, she may have spoken of the lost child, as it related to bearing others during her marriage. What if he told her then that she *must not* try for more? Tucker surely saw Pelham's strong reaction to Phoebe's presence here, and that may have made him certain of what he could only have guessed before—that Pelham had been Phoebe's lover. After all, Pelham was one of Dr. Tucker's patients, and so Tucker would also have known *his* medical history—"

She stopped short as Longfellow stiffened.

"And, that he had contracted *syphilis* while he tramped, as Diana tells me, through Europe?" he asked.

"Would Pelham have had to go so far, if he were less than careful on our own shores?"

"Possibly not," Longfellow admitted. "But why, then, would Tucker have allowed Pelham to see Diana? Why would he not have warned us?"

"About another of his patients? Could he, ethically? Although I believe he did try. But he could ill afford to lose a friend. And then, when Phoebe died suddenly, taking with her the knowledge of her disease and her disgrace, might not Tucker have feared for his own life? As the last who knew the secret, save one?"

"Do you now suppose, Carlotta, that David Pelham is a murderer? I can hardly—but if you are right, we must do something, and soon! If he has had the French Disease for this long, it may have come to affect his mind, and make him dangerous."

"It is still no more than a theory," Charlotte returned,

sensing the wisdom of a temporary retreat, as she considered anew her lack of sure evidence.

"Yet one too deadly to dismiss—especially for my sister's sake." Longfellow gave back the buckle and caught hold of Charlotte's other hand. "We will soon test how well facts bear out your conclusions."

Led by Orpheus, they hurried down the side of the knoll, arriving at Mrs. Willett's door a few minutes later.

Chapter 19

A COMMOTION IN the doorway kept them from entering.

"I won't stay here a day longer," Will shouted, "and you can't make me, even if you are my mother!"

"That I am, to my shame and horror!" Hannah exclaimed, holding on to a broom as if ready to swing it. "One whose pains gave birth to a thoughtless, cruel child!"

"Then why should you care, when I'm gone?"

"Because there are others to fear for! If you would *think*, for once—"

"*You're* the witch here—not Mrs. Willett!" the boy accused, pointing a finger at his mother as he glowered.

"What is this row?" Longfellow finally shouted. Hannah put down the broom, and smoothed out her apron.

"I am sorry to tell you, sir, that this willful, selfish thing—"

"—would like to leave," Longfellow supplied impatiently, "though he has been told I won't allow it. Well, with his obvious recovery, it is safe to conclude, Hannah, that your young hothead has not taken the smallpox after all. Perhaps it *would* be wiser to be rid of him, rather than keep him here, for the safety of all concerned! But hear this, boy. You will spend the day, and the night, if you choose, in that lean-to of yours, as long as the weather holds fair— *but you will go no farther*, on pain of a speedy removal to Mrs. Willett's root cellar! You will be as Mr. Crusoe on his island. *This must last* until we have settled the issue of illness. We will see how long you find a solitary life appealing. In the meanwhile, you may speak to no one, and none may speak to you."

"Thank you, sir," Will mumbled, while casting a malignant eye toward his mother. He went out of the kitchen, and they heard him climb the stairs to bid Lem good-bye.

Charlotte, too, quit the kitchen, intent on her own mission. She entered her empty study, looked about for a moment in puzzlement, and proceeded to the garden window. Holding out the buckle she inverted it, lowered it to the sill, and moved it until she saw that the stones did, indeed, exactly match the set of arcs already there. She traced the path once more, barely letting the buckle touch. There could be no doubt. Someone, certainly, had slipped in or out of the window with this buckle on his shoe. That someone, it was only reasonable to conclude, was David Pelham.

She turned as Longfellow entered the room, with Hannah close behind him. His look was answered with a nod. Then, she held out the buckle so that he might make his own trial. "He must have gone out in a state of confusion," she decided.

"Who?" Hannah asked, mystified by the proceedings. Behind her they heard a clomping as Will came back down, and approached them for a final word.

"Mr. Pelham, we suspect," Longfellow told her. It

would, of course, be safer if all of them were to know. "We think he was here on the night of Phoebe's death—and that he may have had a hand in it."

"Mr. Pelham?" Hannah whispered in amazement, while Will, for once, said nothing.

"Where," asked Charlotte, looking about her empty study, "are the others?"

"Lem is in a room above," said Hannah, "but Miss Longfellow has gone."

"Gone!" cried Longfellow. "Will she never listen? She has gone to my house, no doubt."

"Yes, sir," said Hannah, "with Mr. Pelham."

"What!" Charlotte whispered, her eyes widening, but Longfellow's thoughts had raced well ahead of her own. "Cicero is there," he reminded her. "Still, we will go along."

He turned on his heel, forming in his mind what he would say when he confronted Diana. Mrs. Willett, too, hurried forward, and Orpheus soon leaped at her side. Halfway through the rosebushes on the downward track, Charlotte gasped.

"Richard! Cicero is *not* there—he went off to fish as I left, and I doubt he's had time to return!"

Before he could answer, Longfellow's attention was captured by a figure coming through the stable door of the great stone barn behind his house. Edmund Montagu carried his saddlebags over one shoulder, his face grave. Seeing the couple approaching on the garden path, he altered his course and strode rapidly toward them.

"Well met," Longfellow called out. "Come along, Edmund. Diana has left Mrs. Willett's house for mine, accompanied by Mr. Pelham."

"Pelham!"

"We think there may be danger—" Mrs. Willett began, but Montagu had already begun to speak.

"There is a good chance, Richard, that Pelham is not

entirely in his senses. He may suffer from poisoning—from his treatment for the Great Pox."

"We've already guessed as much—at least, of his affliction."

"How could you—?"

"Ask Mrs. Willett—but later, I think. What else have you?"

"Tucker prescribed a compound full of mercury—a very great deal of it—enough to have brought on death eventually, and lesser symptoms long before—"

"He may be again taken by the *syphilis*, as well."

"Quite possibly."

"And yet, the mercury itself might drive him—"

Frustrated by this intrusion of Science, Mrs. Willett made up her mind to run ahead, just as a shriek came from the house.

"Diana!" her brother called out, while Orpheus began to bark. Captain Montagu spared no energy on speech; instead, he dropped the bags and ran into the house, his boots ringing across the floor as he raced from kitchen to front hall with the others close behind. On the stairs, they heard a scream of protest come from the open door of Dr. Tucker's former room. Reaching it first, Edmund Montagu drew his sword halfway out of its scabbard, his pinched face hard as cold steel, his lips white with rage.

"Unhand her, sir!" Longfellow demanded. Even behind Montagu's dangerously poised form, he could see his sister held against her will.

David Pelham did as he was told while he watched the three intruders press in at the door.

"Diana," said Charlotte, making her way to the young woman's side, "are you hurt?"

"I am *furious*," Miss Longfellow retorted breathlessly, *"for this monster has tried to force me—"*

"—only to do what you have long desired, and even

begged for," David Pelham replied quickly, moving toward her again.

While the others remained speechless, Orpheus let out a sharp growl. No one stopped the old dog, whose advance on stiff legs soon made Pelham cower. At that, Orpheus sat with a grumble, awaiting a further move.

"Miss Longfellow *did* invite me here," the chastened man insisted, his complexion reddened with excitement. "She can hardly deny it now!"

"To help by carrying my hatbox—but it was quite against my wishes, after I had retired, that the fiend came back!" Diana declared. "And I hope I never set eyes on him again!"

"That," concluded her brother, "would be an excellent thing, for we have an idea Mr. Pelham might tell us a great deal about himself that will hardly be to his advantage—or to yours, Diana."

David Pelham stood taller as he scanned the company. "I demand to know, sir, what you mean by that," he challenged.

"I refer to your care by Dr. Tucker," Montagu replied, "for the Pox."

"The smallpox?" Diana asked, surprised at an obvious miss. "But we all know of that, Edmund!"

"The Great Pox," the captain replied as he stared into Pelham's face, daring a denial.

"How," Pelham demanded, looking to Miss Longfellow while an aggressive hope lingered in his eyes, "do you come by this affrontery?"

"We have Tucker's journals," Montagu returned. "I have also spoken with Mrs. Mary Morris of Boston, as well as to her young servant, who believes you and Phoebe Morris were lovers—even while Tucker's journal shows he treated you for *syphilis!*"

All eyes turned to Diana, whose face clearly displayed her horror.

"It is a thing," Longfellow interjected, "that would surely have closed my sister's door to you, and which would have lost you the admiration of most of Boston's society, as well—"

"Did Tucker's journal say *exactly* that it was for this I received his assistance?" Pelham asked slowly and distinctly, gazing at Edmund Montagu. The captain's eyes flickered briefly. "I thought not," Pelham said, relaxing. "One, because it is not true; and two, because Tucker hid much about his activities from the world, having been stung for helping others before. It is also something that cannot be proved, you know . . . and I maintain that he treated me only for an eczema of the skin, which has long since disappeared. So you see, even though some may believe your little coterie, others will not—if you should broadcast what you suspect! Of course, there are also legal and moral prohibitions against slander. As for my being in this particular situation, I certainly wonder that you gentlemen are shocked, for anyone who knows of the coquetry of Miss Diana Longfellow—and there are a good many of us!—will no doubt believe I was given at least *some* encouragement!"

"Mr. Pelham," said Charlotte softly, when no one else replied, "I don't believe this is the first time you have invaded a woman's bedchamber. You do know, I'm sure, that Will Sloan has returned?"

"I saw him only this morning, madam. And I can tell you he said nothing to me about any such thing—" David Pelham halted suddenly.

"As your late visit? Or what she said of you, to him? Will told us Phoebe vowed she could never marry . . . just before she attempted to take her life, by swallowing a large quantity of valerian."

"Hah!" Pelham laughed derisively. "I know the herb, and there is no chance—" He paused as he watched her take something from her pocket.

"Did you notice," she continued, "that Phoebe's pillow was wet with her tears?"

"It was—" Pelham glared, on his guard once more. "It was my impression," he began again, "when I spoke with Phoebe, that she had argued with young Sloan, and that he had threatened her. For I did go in to see Miss Morris, at *her* invitation. Why not? We were old friends, and who else here would show her any kindness, once they knew her shameful story? Being unable to sleep, and seeing her candle across the way, I went to have a word; then, she asked me to climb through the window and talk to her more softly, so that we would not wake the others in the house—"

"At what time?" Charlotte asked sharply.

"One o'clock—two—how does it matter? The point is, Mrs. Willett, that the buckle in your hand, which you stole from my chamber this morning, gives you no advantage after all!"

His burst of laughter at their new confusion alerted Orpheus, and the dog growled once more, frustrating Pelham in a further effort to gain the door.

"And yet," said Charlotte, "it might still be possible for some to suspect you of murder, Mr. Pelham."

"Really?" Pelham replied haughtily. "Then sue me, madam! Sue me, and see what happens to your dear Miss Longfellow! As soon as I return to Boston, I shall let them all hear how I was not the first man Miss Longfellow invited into her room, for did you not visit her alone yourself, Captain, on at least one occasion? If you'll recall, her brother invited you to take her upstairs on the afternoon we met! And have you not heard the lady argue that women should be left to follow their own wills, and satisfy their own desires, as men do? We have even discussed running away together, to the Continent! Have we not, dearest?"

Revolted, with her former confidence now destroyed by intense regret, Diana Longfellow looked helplessly to

Edmund Montagu, who could see a kernel of truth in what his rival had to say. But the look he returned expressed only his sympathy, and indeed his love.

Seeing Diana's relief, David Pelham lost his composure entirely.

"*Now,* I know how it is!" he exclaimed in a strangled voice. "She bids one approach, only to refuse him when she has lured in yet another! You must imagine the two of you will laugh at me, Captain, while you take what I have long desired! But will you have it, in the end? No—not while I can stop you! Your name, and the lady's, will soon be dragged through the gutter, and for good cause!"

"I would suggest, sir," Captain Montagu replied coldly, "that we leave this lady in peace, and settle our affair as gentlemen."

"What! A duel, Captain?" Pelham appeared to take delight in the idea. "I had not thought of that; but yes, indeed! I would be glad to oblige you, if you care to die for such a poor thing as a whore's honor—and a Boston one at that! But not," he added slyly, "with swords. Oh, no. As long as you have asked, I will exercise *my* right, and I choose pistols. Do you know, there is a lovely brace kept by Diana's brother just below. I don't imagine he will mind lending them, only for a little while."

"Richard, no!" Charlotte cried. But Diana's hand caught at her wrist and held it.

"How many more will this beast torture, Charlotte, before someone puts an end to it?"

"But Diana, only think—!"

"I realize," Edmund Montagu interrupted, "that you mean to help, Mrs. Willett. But it is a thing beyond stopping."

"Beyond reason, Edmund?" she threw back.

It occurred to the captain that he'd not seen Mrs. Willett as adamant, or as frightened, before. The observation was a painful one, but it did not deter him.

"Perhaps," he answered her, "even beyond that. But I agree with Miss Longfellow that this is the only way to achieve a desirable end."

"Unless it achieves your own!"

"A challenge has been made and accepted," Montagu replied as he looked away from her entreating eyes. "It is up to each man to appoint a second; they will decide the rest. Richard, will you stand for me?"

Longfellow slowly nodded.

"And who for me?" Pelham wondered aloud. "I will ask my landlord, for Pratt looks honorable enough. I'll go back to my room and send him to you. Tomorrow, at dawn? I believe that is the usual thing. In secrecy, of course, or we will have the law down on our heads. Now, I must take my leave. I have letters to write, and a terrible thirst."

The uninvited guest advanced suddenly, elbowing his way through the others. Then, with a laugh of defiance he bounded down the stairs, leaving a jumble of emotions behind.

THAT EVENING, CHARLOTTE sat alone on the stone bench inside the entry to Richard Longfellow's glass house. She hardly noticed the scents of growth and good earth coming from beyond, which she had earlier hoped would give her comfort.

Jonathan Pratt had earlier come to Longfellow's door to declare himself David Pelham's second, a thing he seemed unable to avoid. But, as he rightly reasoned, if a duel had been agreed upon, someone had to support the other man. Over port, Pratt, Longfellow, and Captain Montagu had discussed the details.

Later, the rest of the household learned that the site chosen was a sandy flat parallel to the Musketaquid, a mile north of the village and away from any road. Its lush grass made it a popular picnic destination, protected on both sides by hummocks overgrown with trees. It would also serve well, they had decided, as a place to quietly court Death, at dawn.

Charlotte looked up through the overhead glass at a sprinkle of rain that had begun to make a small, appealing sound. Then she was startled by another, as she heard someone approach. To her relief, his own lantern soon revealed Captain Montagu, who opened the glass door and came to sit beside her.

"I could not go, Mrs. Willett," he began, "without offering my apologies for what passed between us this afternoon. I wish it could have been otherwise."

"So do I," she assured him, examining his face in the faint light.

"Yet it is, I think, my duty."

"And if you are killed?" asked Charlotte softly.

"A soldier's fate is to be shot eventually, Mrs. Willett. As the third son of an earl, I will hardly be missed at home—which is why many in my position take on the honor of protecting the King's possessions."

"But, Edmund, if you fight this man for your honor, you must appeal to his own—and of what value is that? David Pelham seems to be a man to whom the idea means little—and it is even unclear if *sense* can now be said to dictate his actions."

"I understand you, but I am afraid that is not enough to save him. I know I am right—yet I deeply regret exposing you to the worry you obviously feel—for which I sincerely thank you, Charlotte. You may take some comfort in knowing that I have stood the test before, and do not suppose I will suffer overmuch."

"How?" she asked, curious despite the revulsion she felt.

"Sabers. The man had disparaged my cousin's honor."

"Was he killed?"

"No . . . only wounded. It was enough."

"Then, perhaps . . . ?"

"That would hardly meet our purpose, would it? No, this time I will hope to bring about my opponent's end—as I expect he will attempt my own."

"Edmund, have you taken your leave of Diana?"

"I have, for she cannot be a witness to this. I wonder if she yet realizes the depth of my feelings—but perhaps it is best she does not, in the event that I do not survive. May I ask if *you* will consent to go with us tomorrow?"

"I?" Charlotte returned abruptly.

"Our friend Mr. Longfellow tells me your skills in medicine are unmatched in the village . . . and he assures me you may want to witness such a thing for yourself."

At that, she slowly nodded, and the captain moved as if to go; yet he remained, looking out across the darkness. For several minutes, neither spoke.

Gradually, it occurred to Edmund Montagu that it was a very unusual thing to be alone with a young woman who offered no words. Tonight, they seemed to share something rare—companionship that asked for nothing, while giving solace to both. The captain found his heart had warmed, and asked himself why the situation worked so strongly upon his soul.

But before he could find an answer Charlotte rose to her feet, and turned to face him. She offered her hand, which he took and held, sensing a further bond in the making, a further message imparted. Then she was gone, leaving Edmund Montagu to ponder alone the dark abyss that seemed to stretch before him.

Chapter 20

⟶ Tuesday

WITH TWENTY MINUTES to spare for a walk along the Musketaquid's edge, Charlotte rose fully clothed from her bed. She had managed to accept the morning's events as inevitable. Now, as she took up a canvas bag full of wool lint and strips of linen, she felt her heart leap again with foreboding.

In one brief hour, Edmund Montagu might lie dead near the cold bank of the river. And for what? The chance to make David Pelham pay for sins the law might be blind to? Blind Justice: could it not, perhaps, be *made* to see? And what of Divine Justice? Montagu was prepared to let his own life hang in a deadly balance, for the chance, at least in his own mind, to be an instrument of retribution. Would she have done the same?

Yesterday, when they were alone, she might have told David Pelham exactly what she suspected, hoping to shock him with her knowledge, and to keep him from harming another. Yet his behavior on being found later in Diana's bedchamber had been enough to assure her he would always risk much, to get what he desired. Diana might have been saved—but what would any of them have felt, on hearing of Pelham's next conquest?

Burdened with these thoughts, Charlotte again envisioned the morning's possible outcomes. She believed that of the two adversaries, the most skilled—or the luckiest—would remain alive in an hour's time . . . rather than the one most valued by Heaven. Many believed in God's favor, but she could not. For when had Heaven shown a strong desire to leave the best on earth, while dispatching the wicked?

But she could speculate no longer, for the time for questioning had come to an end.

"IF WE MUST go," said Richard Longfellow, "then I might as well make sure it's all here." He examined the rosewood case to see that it held sufficient powder and flints, six acceptably round balls, and a ramrod. When all were accounted for, he closed the box and looked up.

"Shall we start?"

Meeting Charlotte in the kitchen, he and Edmund Montagu put on outer garments and walked past Cicero, who shook his head with disapproval while he held the door. Charlotte shivered at the air's bite, noting that the new grass under her feet had so far refused to hold the frost. Strange weather, bringing another highly uncertain day.

They saw the light of a second lantern far ahead of them as they walked through a long meadow, past unmoving fountains of lone elms, lacelike against a suggestion of dawn. Somewhere above, as the sun approached, a waning moon sailed serenely. But close to the earth, almost unbelievably, the sky began to drop flakes as fat and soft as down.

Charlotte experienced a moment or two of queer pleasure.

"An interesting spring," remarked Longfellow to Montagu.

His companion remained silent, grimly holding his jaws together.

They followed the river's bubbling, then climbed to the edge of a natural levee left by some ancient flood, and crossed over to the broad depression they sought. In the middle of the flat, they could see that two figures waited. Longfellow raised his lantern; Jonathan Pratt lifted his own. In another two minutes, they stood together: four men moved by the excitement of the proposed action— and one woman who faced it with resignation, while she held on to a supply of bandages.

"I see that you have not succumbed to flight, Captain, as I had expected," said David Pelham. Montagu returned the other's forced smile, feeling some small pity for the man at the very bottom of his soul.

"We might as well begin," Jonathan decided. "Richard, will you load the pistols?"

From under the folds of his greatcoat, Longfellow removed the rosewood box. This morning, its reddish veins glowed with life in the soft light—until large splotches of white extinguished them. Slowly, the faces of the assembly looked to the sky.

"Do it under this," instructed Jonathan Pratt, producing a length of canvas brought for another purpose.

Silently, Longfellow made his way to a glacial boulder, and sat with the box upon his knees. The others held the sheet over him, while they watched his careful motions. First, he tried an action, to see if flint produced a spark against steel. Seeing that it did, he poured a small amount of powder from a brass container into a spoon, and let it sift down the mouth of the barrel. A spherical lead ball wrapped in a small circle of deerskin followed, and was gently tamped into its seat.

Longfellow looked up to be certain all were satisfied. He gave the first pistol to Jonathan to hold under his coat. The second pistol was then treated in the same manner, until it nestled temporarily under the innkeeper's other arm.

"Is there no chance," Jonathan then asked solemnly, "that this matter can be settled without resorting to weapons?" The three witnesses watched as the antagonists eyed each other closely. Neither made a sign.

Charlotte drew a heavy breath. The underlying absurdity forced her lips to produce a small, incredulous smile quite against her will.

Observing it, David Pelham concluded that she mocked his situation with veiled mirth, something he had observed too often, which made him hate this woman even more. How he wished he could end that smile! Perhaps, it was not yet too late . . . ?

"Let us begin," said Jonathan Pratt. The air had become brighter, while visibility had improved with a thinning of the wet snow. "I believe," he continued, "that we're agreed on twenty paces? You will stay here, Mr. Pelham, while I walk off the distance. As there is no sun to give any directional advantage, I will go with the course of the land."

When Longfellow got up to follow Jonathan Pratt and Captain Montagu, Charlotte sank down onto the granite boulder.

It took only a moment to situate Pelham's opponent, after which the landlord and Longfellow moved out of the line of fire. Then, Jonathan called out to both of the duelists.

"We are agreed that the parties will stand full face, rather than in profile? Fine. A coin toss will decide who chooses and fires first." He felt in his waistcoat for a shilling, coming up empty. Longfellow reached into his own and handed over a guinea.

"I don't know why they can't fire together, but I imagine *that* would not be elegant enough," Jonathan muttered. Then he tossed the coin and caught it, and slapped it onto the back of his hand. Before raising his fingers, he looked to each of the two men facing each other on the field. Pelham called out his choice.

"Tails!"

His second raised his fingers slowly, showing the results to Longfellow.

"Tails," Jonathan Pratt called out clearly.

The seconds took both pistols to David Pelham, who chose his weapon. They then delivered the second pistol to Edmund Montagu, and moved away.

The moment had come. After once more checking the position of everyone in the clearing, Pratt glanced about to be sure they were still alone.

"You may fire, Mr. Pelham, when you are ready."

Pelham cocked his weapon. He raised his arm, and calmly peered down the pistol's barrel. For a second, then two, then three, the clearing seemed to hold its breath. Did Pelham wait only to relish the fate of his victim? It seemed so to Charlotte, who looked away as a wave of indignation rose within her. Then she heard the shot, which resounded from the trunks of the trees on either side, and sent a pair of mourning doves whistling up and across the field.

Edmund Montagu spun a quarter turn and fell to his knees, having taken the ball in his left shoulder. Charlotte gasped, and David Pelham looked in triumph from Montagu's kneeling form back to the others.

But in a moment, they saw the captain lift first one

knee, and then the second, until he stood, his right hand still clutching his pistol.

Now, Montagu took time to aim carefully. And yet, it seemed that the strength of his will would not be enough to hold his arm true. For a moment it swayed, and the weapon fell. But with a terrible effort the arm rose once again, and the act of precise calculation was repeated.

When the next report came, it took them by surprise. All eyes flew to David Pelham, who seemed to be lifted up, before he fell prone into the thick grass.

Charlotte turned back to the captain, and saw that he appeared to be puzzled as he stared down at his weapon. She could not now recall seeing it recoil. Suddenly, she knew the reason for Montagu's apparent confusion. For in fact, the second shot had come from the belt of trees behind them. As the echoing crack subsided, it was not an easy thing to decide which way to go, but her heart made the choice for her. Mrs. Willett ran to Edmund Montagu, who sat down awkwardly as he fumbled inside his coat for a handkerchief.

"Is it a serious wound?" she inquired, reaching to help him slide the linen between his shoulder and his bloodied hand. She was relieved to see a ragged grin cross the captain's face.

"I am alive," he said. "Though I'm not certain the same can be said of Mr. Pelham." Even at that distance, they could both see a glistening patch on the back of his black frock-coat, as Pelham lay quite still.

"Perhaps you should go and see," Montagu suggested, touching her bag of bandages.

Mrs. Willett stood and made her way across the grass as in a dream, although she was able to note that Longfellow had gone to stand at the edge of the trees. Then, abruptly, he turned away.

Richard Longfellow had seen enough, for he had

whipped around as soon as the unexpected report of a rifle had come from behind and above his head. In that frightening moment, he caught a glimpse of a glinting barrel between the dark trunks. He ran closer to the wood's edge, seeking its protection while he peered through the trees to see who had fired. Recognition kept him from pursuit, as he perceived a figure walking slowly away. After a moment's thought, he turned his attention back to the field of honor, and saw Montagu sitting alone.

"You're wounded, Edmund," he said when he arrived at the captain's side.

"True. Now, you might go and see what you can make of my adversary."

"We will both go. I assume you can walk? I hope so, for I have no desire to carry you home."

"I can stand, at least," said Montagu, rising to his feet with help. "However, I'm not yet sure what has happened. Do you know?"

"I believe so."

Montagu soon had little attention to spare, as he attempted to walk while supported by Longfellow's impatient arm.

When they reached the others, they saw that David Pelham's wound was, indeed, serious, and that it might prove in time to be fatal. Jonathan Pratt retrieved his piece of canvas. Then he and Longfellow slid Pelham onto the cloth, and lifted the two ends between them. Meanwhile, Charlotte bent to hook her shoulder under the captain's good arm, while he objected to her assistance.

"Your clothing may be stained," he protested, with a consideration Charlotte thought idiotic, and so she ignored it.

"Richard," Jonathan asked in due course, "did you see who it was, up there in the trees?"

Longfellow's response was limited to an observation

that the snow had stopped, and that the returning sun would warm them on their way.

"As I feared," Charlotte murmured, earning a new look of interest from Captain Montagu.

The little party then moved off deliberately, climbing the hill and keeping the river on their right, while the sun beamed out from between retreating clouds.

"YOU'RE QUITE FORTUNATE, you know, that the ball went through cleanly," said Charlotte as she tended the captain by Longfellow's kitchen fire, which Cicero had built up once again. "We will keep warm poultices of herbs over both sides of the wound, until it begins to heal. Richard, can you find trillium leaves? I should go home and bring back thyme and lavender oil. And Tucker's bag upstairs contains poppy gum—in case the pain becomes too severe for sleep."

"I will escort you," Longfellow insisted, fixing her with sharp eyes.

Charlotte rose to leave immediately, though she was concerned for Diana—for the young woman sat staring oddly at Edmund Montagu, occasionally reaching out a hand absently, then letting it fall back.

"We should return within the hour, Edmund," Longfellow added.

Captain Montagu was about to reply when a look to Diana stopped him. He saw again that a long night and an uncertain morning had left her tired and withdrawn. After the door closed, he settled back with a groan and shut his eyes, as she had, to rest for a moment. He listened to what he recognized as one of Luther's old hymns, hummed softly by a dry old voice, accompanied only by an occasional quiet prodding at the fire. In a few moments more, he slept.

• • •

THEY FOUND THE trilliums easily, nestled where many came up each year, under the oaks and maples on a north-facing slope not far from the inn. In less than a quarter of an hour, Longfellow, Charlotte, and Orpheus (who had been overjoyed to be finally let out of the house) approached Mrs. Willett's kitchen door.

Upon entering, Charlotte first looked to see that Aaron's rifle was over the fire; then, she noticed that Will Sloan sat between his mother and Lem, looking down into the hearth's bright dance.

"Is all well here?" asked Longfellow.

"Will woke us both this morning, creeping in to sit next to the fire." Hannah spoke with concern apparent on her broad, ruddy face. "Since he seems sorry for the loss of our company, even for a night, I thought it was all right to let him stay and sit. Though you did say . . ."

"Never mind that," Longfellow told her, while Charlotte approached to study the boy more closely. He appeared to have been weeping, though not, she was sure, due to the loneliness his mother imagined.

"Mr. Pelham," she said to Hannah, "has been shot."

"Shot!" the woman cried. "How?"

"As usual—in the woods. Someone must have been out hunting . . . while Mr. Pelham took an early turn. He is seriously wounded, but still lives."

Lem, who knew Charlotte's moods well, pricked his ears at her tone, but Hannah seemed to notice nothing out of the ordinary. "And a poor time for hunting deer, too," the older woman returned with a shake of her head. "You'd think they'd know better! Will, you've gone white as a ghost! I'm not at all sure you're over your illness, and to stay out in the frost all last night, as well! You go upstairs and get into bed. I'll bring you a hot jug and some broth. You always were more trouble than any three of my others," she concluded, pulling him up by the arm and urging him out toward the stairs.

"And probably always will be," said Longfellow with a worried frown of his own, as he watched the young man go.

AS HE AND Charlotte walked back to his house, Longfellow realized that several roads lay open to them. But he now knew he had the approval of Mrs. Willett in saying nothing. After all, what would be accomplished, if everyone were to know? Such a secret would be enough of a penance for the boy to live with. And yet, would he feel remorse, after the shock left him? It *had* been revenge—for Will had heard what the buckle told them, and knew Pelham had invaded the bedchamber of his bride soon before he himself had found her dead. Longfellow supposed that in this case, it was best to let hot blood take care of itself. Although if Pelham were to live, and were to demand an explanation, what then would they do?

He continued to wonder until they reached the kitchen and found Montagu still asleep, though Diana opened her eyes and looked at them with confusion. As Charlotte went to comfort her, Diana moved a hand across her forehead, shifting a ringlet of hair.

"Perhaps," Charlotte advised, "you would be more comfortable in your room for a few hours?"

"I would like to move away from the fire, and the light, for it seems to hurt my eyes this morning," Diana answered slowly.

It was then that Mrs. Willett felt the young woman's forehead, and found it fevered. But there was also something else—something like rice, under the silken skin. Her eyes met Diana's, and in that instant they exchanged a frightening knowledge.

Longfellow looked up to see them clasping each

other's hands tightly. It was a pretty picture of friendship, even of devotion, he thought with pleasure.

"Richard . . ." he heard his sister say softly. Something in her voice made his smile fade away.

"Richard, I believe I am unwell. . . ."

Chapter 21

IT TOOK MORE than a week for the worst of the disease to run its course. Even then, Diana remained in a greatly weakened state. She showed far less resilience than Lem, who had already resumed his duties about the farm.

The smallpox "flowers" multiplied on her face and hands, filling with fluid like painful burns. Mercifully, all were not deep enough to scar. But a few reached well below the surface, promising a lasting reminder of the serious affair Miss Longfellow had so recently presumed to be only a flirtation.

During the crisis, Edmund Montagu stayed by the young woman's side, even though his own wound should have kept him resting in bed. For two days, the captain sat and accepted no more than light meals and poultices, while he waited for a sign of recovery. He relented only when her fever fell, and she slept deeply.

When Diana finally awoke, she quickly demanded a

looking-glass. Once she had seen for herself, she tried to send the captain away. But instead of leaving, Montagu insisted she muster her courage, while he continued to watch as Charlotte applied cooling cloths.

Meanwhile, a physician from Worcester had come and gone. The man had advised heavy blankets, a high fire, and tightly closed windows. Longfellow, after consulting with Mrs. Willett, decided on a modest flow of air, often-changed sheets that would not further irritate his sister's blistered skin, and a constant watch to learn what Diana herself desired. In the end, he had been able to congratulate himself on the patient's improvement.

One morning, a week into her recuperation, Diana was well enough to be carried out onto the leafy piazza, where the company began to talk of subjects beyond her own state. Surprisingly, she found this to be a great relief.

"And yet," her brother now continued, "when we did read Tucker's letter, Diana, it appeared he was not without his strengths. It could be argued he might simply have disappeared into the night—but he did expose Pelham after all, if somewhat belatedly. His death could even be taken for a selfless act, intended to save you."

"Where is he now?" asked Diana.

"In a corner of my pasture near some trees, where Cicero and I buried him. I wrote a letter to a friend in Williamsburg, who will tell the family. After I sell his books and instruments, many of them to myself, probably, I'll send them the proceeds. With a bit more," he sighed, causing Charlotte to smile.

"And what happened . . . to the other?" Diana asked obliquely. Her brother decided she was now well enough to hear the story's end.

"Pelham's wound was not immediately mortal, as we had supposed it might be. But, he insisted he required a Boston physician, so we sent him jostling off in a carriage, which was unwise. He died a few days later of fever. If

Tucker had been with us, perhaps Mr. Pelham might have survived. Divine Justice, I suppose. . . ."

"And a fitting end," said Captain Montagu. He anxiously searched Diana's face for her reaction, but could find nothing more than relief.

"Did he finally confess to murdering Phoebe Morris, to save his soul?" she asked.

"He—did not," her brother answered slowly.

"Oh," Diana replied, disappointed. One by one, the others moved uneasily in their chairs, during a silence that followed.

"I still believe," Montagu finally went on, to clear the air, "that you should have seized Will Sloan, Richard, and sent him to Cambridge for trial. I doubt many who think the thing over will believe Pelham's death an accident—especially when the true story is whispered about your village. And while you may think this balances the scales of justice, I suspect it is a dangerous thing when common men take the law into their own hands—especially when an execution is the result!"

"Was it so different when *you* faced Pelham?" Longfellow returned calmly.

"That was an act between gentlemen, involving mutual consent, and honor. Surely you can see the difference?"

"I see that in either case, the intended outcome was to fill a coffin."

"But what do you suppose will happen if you continue to allow your children to murder, and to do so while hiding behind trees?"

"The outcome was far better, to my mind, than what you yourself were able to arrange, Edmund. If you had missed—as was very likely, given your condition—and if Pelham had taken a second shot . . ."

Montagu saw that Diana was in agreement, for once, with her brother. "Well," he declared, "it must cheapen any nobility that ordinary men may be said to possess, when they're allowed to snipe at one another from cover, as if their targets were nothing but quail! Not only is a man who does so spiritually lessened, but so are his fellows . . . and soon, society as a whole. Who *then* will keep the peace? Let Will Sloan go free, and you damage your entire legal and moral structure. Without that, what can be expected to bind your people together?"

"An interesting question," Longfellow admitted. "But I doubt if my sister would have enjoyed the boy's trial, if the reasons for your duel became a part of it—unless you feel that particular illegality might be overlooked? As I am a representative of the law here, I must say you have already presumed a great deal."

"Then let the boy go," said Montagu. "I've done my share of shielding the rashness of youth, I suppose. If the village is willing to say Pelham was killed while out walking simply for the sake of his health, so be it. But remember my warning. Times are not what they once were."

"And never will be," Longfellow replied, shifting his long legs as they cried out for some sort of activity. "So, it is all over. Now that Will Sloan is back home, I'm certain he has been given more than an earful by his father, which I hope he'll remember."

"All the same," said Charlotte, "I suspect he's found a new interest to help him forget his woes."

"Who is that?" Diana's voice, though still little more than a whisper, betrayed her pleasure in a fresh piece of news.

"Phoebe's younger sister, a girl named Betsy. During Reverend Rowe's moving funeral service for Phoebe, she seemed as affected by Will's tears as he was by hers. I'm not sure how much she understands of what happened in Boston, or what took place here. But I wouldn't be surprised if Will were to follow Betsy Morris back to Concord, and marry her one day."

"Perhaps she will be able to tame some of his wickedness," Diana said presently.

"Perhaps . . . " Charlotte replied with less conviction.

"A fine solution," Longfellow concluded. "Marriage is, after all, a very good thing for *most* young women."

ON THE ARM of Captain Montagu, Diana walked first about the house and piazza, and finally out into the sunshine, where the pair quietly enjoyed the splendor of early summer together.

Diana's first walk away from her brother's house marked her return to society. It also allowed her to watch Hannah's three daughters as they gave Mrs. Willett's home a top-to-bottom scrubbing, and to see Lem admiring those cheerfully efficient young women in their jaunty caps and raised skirts. He was eager to help whenever they called, and several times a day, a whistle or a wink summoned or dismissed him. The entire experience, Diana supposed, was a useful addition to Lem's limited education.

One day, while visiting Mrs. Willett, she looked again upon the face of David Pelham, which stared up at her from the sketchbook Phoebe Morris had kept. It gave Miss Longfellow great satisfaction to tear it out and light it at the kitchen hearth, where she held the flaming page until much of it had turned to ash. Later, she gave the book to Hannah, who marveled at the renewed serenity and beauty of the lady who presented it, despite several new dimples she knew would remain covered with powder until they were sufficiently faded.

Later that same afternoon, Charlotte happened to see Diana and Edmund Montagu from a distance, as they stood speaking earnestly among her brother's roses. The captain held Diana's hand. Having abandoned his wig, he looked far more like a country beau than ever before, thought Charlotte. Then, quite suddenly, Diana lifted her face and he kissed her, enfolding her in a passionate embrace. Lowering her own head, Mrs. Willett went back to clipping sprigs of herbs.

From that day, it became clear to everyone that something of consequence had occurred between Miss Longfellow and Captain Montagu. Just what that was, or how far it had gone, was a frequent topic of village conversation. But Diana soon gave Charlotte the happy news of their proposed nuptials, warmed again by the glow that comes from the confession of new love.

soon after diana's revelation, the two women drank tea in Longfellow's study, while its usual inhabitant was out. On a table between them were Dr. Benjamin Tucker's medical diaries and his last letter.

Diana picked up the letter, and began to read it once more.

"I can hardly believe," she said eventually, "that Pelham stole Dr. Tucker's investment money, as he supposes, in order to court and marry Alicia Farnsworth. And then, to poison her slowly with his own prescription, on their wedding trip—!"

"I have written to Dr. Warren, who tells me that she did, indeed, have a stomach ailment of long standing. . . ."

"It seems," said Diana, reading further, "Tucker could scarcely believe Pelham to be the father of Phoebe's child—though he did suspect her condition long ago in Boston."

"Dr. Tucker," Charlotte responded thoughtfully, "seems to have leaped from great trust to an equally strong abhorrence—both of which make reasoning difficult. And extreme views often give only part of a true picture . . ."

"Yet I should say he was justified, in his latter opinion of Mr. Pelham, at least!" Diana looked down at the page once more, and read its final lines to herself.

> Thus, on the eve of her marriage, I was forced to explain to Miss Morris why it would be very unwise of her ever to attempt Childbirth again. Now it is only another step to believe that Pelham saw he could no longer trust the girl to keep her Past to herself—and from Miss Longfellow. For this reason, I believe he may have found means to effect the Poor Girl's death. I also fear that he may next look for a way to cause my own! God forgive me! Although I am a Physician, I truly long to end the life of this man, to repay the harm he has so cruelly done to me, to my family, and to others. But what would be my Reward from a Boston court, or even a higher one? David Pelham is more Beast than man—but how can I alone stop him, with a body that is growing old, and a heart saddened near to Death? I do not wish to harm my family further, by sealing my own fate. Yet what of Miss Longfellow? I have attempted to warn her, but what proof can I offer? I do not know. *I do not know!*

Here, the letter stopped in a blot of ink that told how the pen had rested, and bled its burden onto the page.

It was, Miss Longfellow decided, as a tear traversed her newly marked cheek, a pitiful good-bye given to her by a man of education and privilege—one who had never been brave, perhaps, but who had been hounded by a tenacious cur without a soul, into a pauper's grave.

For Charlotte, the situation was somewhat less clear. *In defense of my treasure, I'd bleed at each vein . . .*

Had she been right in her final guess? Or, perhaps, in her first?

Had Benjamin Tucker truly found the Great Pox in his patients? For if not. . . .

Could it be that David Pelham was only terribly eager to gain respect, and love?

And did Will Sloan have reason to take a life, assuming, as she had? . . .

Still, it was over, if she could not quite feel it to be so. Will, at least, had been given another chance. But she wondered with a sudden chill if they would all, one day, be made to meet again.

IN ANOTHER WEEK, Diana and Edmund Montagu were gone, leaving two country households to restore themselves to their normal states. On the morning of their departure, Mrs. Willett went walking, while she mulled over some of the recent changes in Bracebridge.

After accompanying Betsy Morris home to Concord, Will Sloan had written back that he would stay for a time, if that met with the approval of his parents, which it did. Lem was again well and strong, although possibly less interested in his studies. Cicero and Longfellow had returned to battling over philosophies, and reading aloud bits from newspapers and pamphlets, especially those relating to the proposed Stamp tax—an amusement shared by a great number of men in the countryside, as well as in Boston.

Charlotte now found that she had wandered into a far meadow, as a hot wind rushed over the drying grass and into the forest beyond. Suddenly, she squinted, trying to make out something in the green haze at the edge of the trees. Was someone there, waving to her? She was too far away to be sure. Walking forward, she watched the fluttering of a handkerchief, or a sleeve, perhaps? Until suddenly, the waving figure whirled and was swept up into the dark shadows beyond.

She supposed her eyes might have been affected by the sun and the wind, and that Richard Longfellow would have called her vision nothing more than a mirage. But she had seen enough—felt enough—to believe that a young girl had stood there, beneath the full-throated rushing of the forest. She was still not positive—but that no longer mattered. It was enough to welcome the calm of peace, and a growing sense of grace. Then, a couplet from Pope's elegy came back to her.

> Yet shall thy grave with rising flow'rs be drest,
> And the green turf lie lightly on thy breast.

Until that time, thought Mrs. Willett, she herself could do something more. She leaned down to pick a small bunch of wildflowers, thinking of a corner of the churchyard where she would go to whisper a final farewell.

About the Author

Margaret Miles is the author of A WICKED
WAY TO BURN, the first Bracebridge mystery.
She lives in Washington, D.C., where she is
at work on her next mystery, NO REST FOR
THE DOVE.

If you enjoyed the second book in the Bracebridge
mystery series, *Too Soon for Flowers,* you won't want to
miss Margaret Miles's third mystery, *No Rest for the Dove.*

Look for *No Rest for the Dove* at
your favorite bookstore in spring 2000.

NO REST FOR THE DOVE

A Bracebridge mystery by Margaret Miles

Coming in spring 2000 from Bantam Books

BARELY AN HOUR earlier Caleb Knox had driven along through the heat on the nearly deserted Boston-Worcester road, longing to be home. The farmer had given the reins he held a mild shake, causing them to ripple. But in the end this was not enough to alter the pace of the plow horse who pulled his wagon. Judy kept plodding, and the rude conveyance rolled on, slow to suit the weather, its sleepy driver again drowsing to the creak and rumble of heavy wheels.

While a field aflame with tall goldenrod went slowly by, Knox saw himself seated behind his own horse. The smell of hot sun on his linen shirt reminded him of his old dame's ironing, which she did in summer beneath the kitchen overhang. If only, he thought, he could get up and walk down to the spring for a drink of cold water! The ale he'd consumed at the Blue Boar, once he'd left the mill where he'd exchanged sacks of grain for flour, had not really helped to quench his thirst at all. Neither the first pint, nor the second . . . nor the third.

The horse neighed unexpectedly, almost as if she followed his idea of a drink, Caleb imagined with a wobbling grin. But then he saw that something else concerned her. Beside the road, next to a long hedge of hawthorn, stood another horse, this one wearing bridle and saddle while it grazed peacefully. A curious thing? On such a warm afternoon, perhaps not.

The farmer pulled himself erect and looked out attentively from beneath his rime-encrusted hat. The rider was no doubt asleep near his horse; as far as Knox could tell, it looked as if a nest of sorts had been made there. But why would he be *there*, when he could have chosen the hedge's shade? Why would anybody lie out full in the afternoon sun? And what were all those flies doing? Despite the heat, he felt a chill pass through him. Though he did not relish the exercise, it did seem the situation might be worth a closer look.

When his wagon came even with the saddled horse, Knox gave a pull that made Judy shake her head and stop. He climbed down, giving further instruction for the animal to stay where she was. Precariously, he leaped over the ditch at the side of the road, landing on both feet. Then he wound his way through the weeds until he reached the silent rider.

The man was not resting. It looked as if he would have no need for rest ever again. Noah Knox knelt down to make sure. After that, he spent a few more minutes in quiet speculation.

Surely the poor devil had been drunk—he could smell that, and it appeared the sot had even lost some of his liquor down the front of his old black coat. A sad thing, very sad. One hated to see a man enjoy himself and then choke for it! Unless, now, unless he'd been thrown? That might account for the liquor coming up again, for a knock on the head sometimes did affect the stomach, he recalled. Maybe the poor fellow had directed his horse down from the road, intending to give them both a rest, and maybe it shied at a viper—that was quite possible! He only hoped the snake, if there was one, had taken itself away. Or it could be the horse had stumbled into a hole, for there were always plenty about. Though the animal hardly looked injured. But if the man had some form of drink with him, where was it now? Not by the body, that was sure. But might there be something else of interest nearby?

Caleb Knox soon came upon a few pieces of Spanish silver in a pocket, along with some coppers and even some brass, all of which he returned. Better to leave them for burial, he thought. For he sensed that the curious man who lay there was far from home and might never be missed at all. Besides, it wouldn't do to rob the dead—although right there, next to him, was something that had a pretty shine to it and even a small gem or two! Did it belong to the stranger? Though it lay close, the answer might be . . . maybe, and maybe not. Wouldn't it be something sweet to give to the old dame, as long as he never told her where he'd got it? She'd long forgiven him a great deal—and would forget even more, he imagined, if he were to offer her such a gift one day soon, telling her he'd bought and paid for it on market day.

At last decided, Caleb Knox put the small, glittering object into his pocket. After that, he walked around a clump of yellow stalks full of bees. As he approached the riderless horse, it raised its head with a whinny. Clucking to keep it calm, the farmer crept the last few feet, then grasped at its bridle. Before long he had the mount tied to the back of his wagon, to the intense interest of Judy. Then, leaving the two to become acquainted, he returned for the corpse.

He felt a little foolish picking up the man's dark hat

and setting it on top of his own. He lifted the pair of legs and hauled as he walked backward, causing the other's coat to drag over a new furrow left in the vegetation. At the ditch Knox lifted up the dead weight, grunting fiercely as he carried it down and back up, and at last rolled it into his wagon. He took another few moments to arrange the man decently before climbing forward to his seat. Finally he turned Judy around on the road, heading the wagon back to Bracebridge.

Looking both ways, he still saw no one ahead or behind him. But soon there would be many clamoring to hear his story, for a reward of a tankard or two. The farmer felt for the object in the pocket of his coat on the wagon's seat, to make sure his secreted prize was still there. At least he would amuse them by telling most of what he'd discovered, if not exactly all.

But first he would do his duty and go and unburden himself to someone who held a position of authority, who would surely know what else needed to be done.

"NOT A PLEASANT picture you paint for us," said Richard Longfellow, smoothing his gathered hair further with a callused hand. They had all, he suspected, become increasingly aware of the heat and stillness of the afternoon since Caleb Knox had brought Death to intrude upon them. "And you believe he met his end only an hour or two ago?"

"Aye," the farmer replied, his eyes drifting to reexamine a man unknown to him standing at the edge of the arbor.

Longfellow turned abruptly to Gian Carlo Lahte, who adjusted his coat sleeves over lace cuffs. "You saw nothing, I would imagine, on your way here?"

"Nothing of that sort."

"Where again was he, Caleb?"

"Some two miles east of here, by a hedge of hawthorn."

"You recovered his horse, as well. A good animal, is he?"

"Not for working fields. For walking, maybe—though he may well have bloat by now."

"Spirited?"

The farmer considered, rubbing at the stubble on his neck where sweat continued to trickle down. "Not as I could tell," he decided.

"Hired in Boston, probably. They often have their own tricks to get rid of a rider." Caleb Knox snorted his agreement, though he had never hired a stable horse in his life. "So," Longfellow continued, "he went off the road, was thrown and landed hard on his head, and stayed where he was until you picked him up and brought him in to us. You're sure you haven't seen him here before?"

"Nor anywhere else, I'd say. Though at first I thought I recognized him for a drummer. His clothes are like that of a gentleman, but too old for one, you see. Castoffs, maybe, but still queer somehow. And he had no tin box of goods, nor even saddlebags."

"No wallet, I presume?"

"A little silver was nearly the sum of his pockets." Caleb Knox shifted uneasily before he went on. "When I looked into them, it was to see if he might have a letter on him or a note of credit—so we might learn where to send him. Then when I found little, and knowing he shouldn't be left to lie there, I hauled him into my wagon, tied his horse on behind, and turned round to bring both to the meetinghouse. He's in the village cellar now."

"A tragic tale, but one hardly surprising among riders both poor or proud who find it advisable to race from here to there."

"Amen to that," exclaimed the farmer, whose plodding Judy had feet the size of firkins.

"You found Reverend Rowe?" Longfellow asked after a sigh.

"Heard he went over to Brewster's, so I sent a boy running for him."

"I will guess, then, that our unknown man came out to visit someone and planned to return to his lodgings by nightfall. A small mystery, but one we'll understand shortly, I'm sure. My thanks to you, Caleb."

The man nodded as he put his hat back on, then lifted it again briefly to Mrs. Willett. But still he did not go. Instead he gave a shy bow to the man he did not know, hoping to have one stranger's presence, at least, explained that day.

"Oh, I see," said Longfellow. "Well, since we may all soon be neighbors—Mr. Caleb Knox, farmer and native son of Bracebridge, I would like to present Signore Gian Carlo Lahte, a gentleman of Milan."

Though it seemed Lahte jumped, he graciously offered a salute that was returned with pleasure. At that, anxious to tell a yeasty story that had now risen into a nice, substantial loaf, Caleb Knox disappeared around the corner of the large house.

"Will you come with me, Lahte, and offer your opinion?" asked his host. "This thing will be likely to have one or two scientific points of interest, I am sure. Cicero? I thought not, on those feet. Mrs. Willett? Will you wait here, or will you return to your own duties?"

"Richard, if we are to suppose this unfortunate man traveled to meet someone, as you say, then might it not be wise for me to go with you, as well? For what if he came to see me?"

"To buy a pound of butter? Unlikely, but as good a reason as any, I suppose, to view a corpse. Come along, then, Mrs. Willett. But wait a moment . . ." Longfellow strode past Cicero into the kitchen and came back carrying a small box of coals. "Now I believe we are ready," he said, and with that the small party walked off on a path across the dry fields, leaving Cicero sitting silhouetted under the cool green vines, finishing a plate of pears.

"IT IS A thing we made this spring," Longfellow explained as they approached the cellar behind the meetinghouse, walking along a mossy path between the headstones in a shaded burial ground.

An underground chamber had seemed a useful idea when suggested by a pair of men in need of work, and so the selectmen gladly approved the digging of a temporary site in which to deposit the dead, when weather or other circumstances kept them from being immediately put into the churchyard above. Everyone knew it was no easy thing to take a pick to frozen ground, nor did anyone want to worry about the possible spread of putrid fever in warmer weather.

"Just down these steps. Leave the door open, while I touch a scrap of paper to these coals and light the pair of candles down here. No, I don't know this man. Mrs. Willett?"

Charlotte, too, climbed down into the close, timbered space, where the good smell of damp earth was a background for an odor of mold. She looked instinctively to the closed eyelids, then at the waxy face. The state of its features suggested a man of perhaps forty years and certainly something other than a farmer who spent his days toiling in the open. His oily hair had a reddish hue, as did the short curls on the knuckles of relatively smooth, un-bruised, and unadorned hands, whose nails were clean as a benefit of being long gnawed and sucked at by their owner. She quickly speculated this had been a person whose fortunes had moved up and down, for though his apparel was quite worn, it appeared to be made of thin-stranded and tightly woven fabric, surely not home loomed. It also looked to her as if the cut of the coat was original and the stitchwork good; there was also something unfamiliar about the proportions of the garments, as well as their finishing details. And over much of them there was a dark stain, which accounted for the smell.

Looking up, she shook her head to Longfellow's question and noted that Signore Lahte, too, must have been staring hard and long into the stranger's face. She saw him pull himself together with a shudder.

"Can it be," Longfellow asked in surprise, "that *you* know this gentleman, Gian Carlo?" A wave of the other's hand dismissed the idea, but Longfellow persisted in his concern.

"You appear unwell. The stagnation of the air seems to have made it lose its potency—er—so perhaps we should move on."

Lahte then attempted an explanation. "A man of art, of strong feeling, is sometimes overcome . . ." His handkerchief appeared, and he wiped it over features that had begun to quiver, though he still tried to contain his distress.

"Something of a shock, I agree. I, too, have little stomach for viewing death—though I would guess that Mrs. Willett might like to linger awhile longer."

Charlotte looked up from examining a hat, largely intact, which she had found on the floor. "I think a brief prayer would do no harm."

"Hmmm," Longfellow responded, as he led Signore Lahte up the wooden steps set into the soil, rising toward warmth and light.

When she was alone, Charlotte closed her eyes, while the two tallow candles continued to smoke and sputter. A few seconds later she slid behind the trestle table that supported the body, and carefully lifted up the head with her hands. His neck was undamaged, she thought, yet the top of the skull was obviously indented. That was odd. And the affected area was not swollen. This told her he must have died suddenly, very soon after the injury had occurred. Though he may, of course, have died of inhaling what he could not swallow. Nearly overcome by the horrible thought, and the odor, she looked away, then forced herself to examine a patch of the matter on the coat more closely. It was unusually dark . . . but it most probably had little to do with whatever final misfortune had overcome this man out on the road. Why, then, did she have a nagging suspicion?

Charlotte seemed suddenly to hear the echo of a familiar voice in the close chamber. Again she heard the angelic song of Gian Carlo Lahte, and felt a sudden rush of warmth as she realized that this death affected her somewhat less than had the recent discomforts of *Il Colombo*. But could *he* know this stranger? Or had her imagination, too, become feverish? Longfellow had asked the same question—but if it was true, why would Lahte not say so? Well, if he would not or could not enlighten them, the dead man might yet tell them something, after a bit of wheedling and teasing—perhaps even enough to satisfy her own suspicious spirit.

Blowing out both candles, Mrs. Willett hurriedly pulled the door closed behind her, to join the two men waiting above. At her appearance Longfellow walked forward. His guest continued to pace slowly among the village stones, some distance away.

"Mrs. Willett! Are you satisfied? He *was* thrown, it would seem to me."

"Well . . ."

"Of course you question, too, where he has come from. But we may know more when I have made a sketch of him and sent it off to Montagu in Boston. Though I believe all signs point to a trader from abroad. I might even guess, from his physiognomy, that he is of a European race which I have observed near the eastern Mediterranean and up toward the Slavic lands. The reddish hair and pale skin are similar to those of many Scots and Irishmen, yet there is something else about the face which reminds me of the residents of Prague. The clothing seems inconclusive. His Spanish silver, of course, could have come from anywhere. Have you an idea of your own?"

"He seems to have lost some of the wine I presume he drank while on the road earlier today—"

"No doubt of that, by the aroma."

"But when?"

"When?"

"He could hardly have vomited the wine up, I think, after his fall—if death was due to the injury to his head. For that must have come only moments before his heart ceased to beat . . ."

"You refer to the lack of swelling in the depression over the brain. Not unlike the difference between a deer killed outright and one whose wounds fill with blood when he must be chased down. Well, perhaps the man's stomach rebelled first, then. He may have gotten off his horse, had another drink, vomited it up, then stumbled. And having fallen back upon a rock—"

"But then how do we explain the great force of the blow? For I can hardly believe—"

"All right, then—he was thrown *after* he regurgitated, which he did while still *on* his horse. In either case his death would have been an accident and thus should cause us no further concern."

"Yet if he died because he choked on what he tried to expel, one could not blame the horse, which might otherwise be destroyed for killing a man. And would the village not rest more easily if he were examined by a physician, so that we might learn exactly how he came to his end?"

"I suppose it might. But nothing points to anything more worrisome, you will agree?"

"Except for his face. It did occur to me that he might

have suffered a recent illness. Perhaps even a very serious one. Richard, the dark vomit—"

"Yet he appears to be unaffected by jaundice, if you are trying to tell me it might be the yellow fever. And he would have been ill indeed, in the last stages. I doubt he could have sat on a horse all the way from Boston. Still, it may be wise to post a sign warning others not to enter, since it can be highly contagious . . . especially, now that I come to think of it, in August and September. I believe I will make my sketch quickly and close the place up. When I send off my handiwork, I will enclose a request for Warren to come to us. It will give him a healthy ride. Now, where has Lahte got to? There he is, over by the Proctors. Shall we go and take him home? I suspect he, too, is not entirely well, though melancholy may be his own particular ill today."

As they walked to join Signore Lahte, they saw that his good humor had evidently returned. This was fortunate, thought Longfellow, who also saw that the Reverend Rowe approached them on the main road. "Gian Carlo," he called over the quiet stones. "Are you sufficiently recovered to meet what passes in Massachusetts for a holy man?"

"I will be delighted," the *musico* answered, coming forward with a confident stride.

"I doubt that!" said Longfellow with some certainty. "But we shall see."

"YOU ARE A Roman Catholic, *signore?*" asked the thin man, clothed in his usual ill-fitting suit of black broadcloth. Christian Rowe said the foreign word with distaste, after receiving what he suspected was a sinfully excessive bow.

"I was raised in the Church, certainly, good Father. But I dispute the laws of Rome, and I repent of my part in its superstitious ceremonies."

"Oh?" answered Rowe, brightening a little as he readjusted his stiff hat over a halo of golden hair. "Then am I to presume you are now a Protestant?"

"I protest much in this life, Father, and pray that you will take me into your flock. Like a poor sheep, I look for guidance. And you see I have heard of your wisdom even in Boston before coming here."

"Really!" the reverend responded, rising on his toes. He gave a fond thought to several slim copies of his sermons, printed the previous winter and left in a King Street shop. Perhaps not all of them had languished, after all. "That is gratifying," Reverend Rowe allowed, giving the gentleman before him a faint smile. "Although as I am a minister, rather than a popish priest, I should be addressed as 'Reverend.' Or simply 'sir.' And we do not think of men here as sheep—nor do we see their spiritual leaders as all-powerful. Yet ministers *are* well respected for their wisdom and learning in this place. You do realize," Rowe went on with sudden suspicion, "there is no question of a Roman mass ever being said here in Massachusetts?"

"But of course, reverend sir! Who would dare to pollute such . . . such a grave and pure place?"

This time Rowe answered with a look of beatific mildness. But as another slight movement drew his attention, his expression changed once more.

"Madam, *have you, too,* examined this man's body?"

"I have looked at his face, Reverend. Since no one yet knows him, I thought it my duty."

"Duty! Something one hardly expects to hear from you, Mrs. Willett!"

Longfellow caught the preacher's eye, then gazed pointedly at the new slate roof of the stone manse behind them, which was a recent and expensive gift.

"But you are correct," Christian Rowe continued more cautiously, "in suggesting it is the duty of all to help our fellow creatures. Quite correct. Someone, somewhere, must be searching for this unfortunate, whose death, I am told, was an accident?" His challenging stare relaxed only when the preacher was sure he would receive no more unpleasant news from those who stood before him.

"Then I believe we are all agreed," Longfellow concluded, rubbing his hands. "It will be quite unnecessary for you to take more than the briefest look at the body, Reverend. I have some fear of possible contagion, as it is the height of summer, so rather than ask you to prepare him for burial I shall call for a physician, at the town's expense, who may do so. I plan to take the likeness of the corpse myself, so that they might ask in town who he was, for it seems he came here by way of the Boston road. Town House might hear a complaint that the man is missing, as you say. If not, there will be plenty of lodging houses to examine."

"Your friend Captain Montagu might be of some use in that."

"So he might! What a good idea, Reverend. I'll be sure to let him know you thought of it. Now we must be off, but I will return shortly with paper and pencil."

As the minister walked back to his parsonage, Richard Longfellow and his friends began to climb the long hill that rose to the east of the village. "A nice piece of flattery," he soon commented to Signore Lahte, who replied with a dubious smile.

"I have had much practice, in the service of others."

"You did warn us of your dramatic accomplishments. Here, however, they may be viewed as the mark of a wastrel and a truth-slayer if you are found out."

"Ah, yes. If . . ." Lahte returned.

"I will be busy for a while. Settle yourself in my house with Cicero's help, and enjoy a siesta. I hope tonight you will delight us with more of your voice and show us your skill at the pianoforte. After that, perhaps we might take a closer look at the sky."

"The sky?"

"The telescope," Charlotte informed him, "is one of Mr. Longfellow's favorite hobbyhorses."

"And a far-reaching breed, capable of allowing us to fly into the astral realms—much like your splendid arias."

"Oh, yes," *Il Colombo* replied with a weariness that Mrs. Willett noted with increased sympathy. She had already wondered at Lahte's apparent desire to ingratiate himself with the Reverend Rowe. Now she asked herself if he felt he must pay for his supper and for the company of others. And might the man not tire of being eternally reminded of the singular difference that set him apart from the rest of his gender? These questions were soon joined in her mind by several others, as the trio moved quietly through the afternoon heat. Like small feathers, such unanswered questions had a way of tickling one that did not always turn out to be entirely pleasant.